Something deeply wrong...

At the side of the road, a woman in a blue sarong stood with a small girl protectively in her arms. With the fierceness of the woman's look, it would have made a good illustration shot if Kaitlin was doing a story on the feel of Cambodia. The people were fiercely protective of what they had.

At least Champei had been. The woman at Sovanna Phum had been, as well.

But when you have nothing, you tend to protect what you have. Like your child.

The woman stared in the direction they were going, but when she saw the moto-taxi she fled into the shadows underneath her stilted, thatched house. As if she didn't want to be seen.

Something not right there. A tower of smoke rose from somewhere beyond the trees up the road.

"Just how much farther is Jorani's? We've been traveling at least an hour."

"We're almost there." But B.J. craned around in his seat and caught sight of the smoke. "Bloody hell, no!"

He yelled at the driver in Cambodian and pointed at the column.

No way someone would light a fire like that. Not on a hot day. At least not for any reason she could think of.

B.J.'s tanned face had gone almost white. His rigid jaw showed striated muscles as the motorcycle revved and leapt forward over the broken pavement.

"What is it?" she yelled over the wind in her ears.

When he turned, fear filled B.J.'s gaze.

"The orphanage."

Books By the Author

Romance
Ashes and Light
Shades of Moonlight
Judas Kiss
Second Spring
Mutable Things
A Different Nightmusic
Shadow Play
Coming Down Christmas
Surviving Safe Harbor

Fantasy
***The Cartographer Universe* series:**
The Cartographer's Daughter

Afterburn
Aftershock
Aftermath
Afterimage

Terra Incognita
Terra Infirma
Terra Nueva

SHADOW PLAY

KAREN L. ABRAHAMSON

Dedicated to Selma who fell off the Cambodian map with me,
and the Cambodian people.

SHADOW PLAY

Prologue

March, Phnom Penh, Cambodia

Jeremy Blackwood shook his head, ran his hands through his thinning hair, and tried to look calm and collected in the cushioned wicker chair at the bar's glass-covered wicker table. He sat just off the main street of Sisowath Quay, watching the night mists off the Tonle Sap River turn yellow in the long line of haloed and pulsing streetlights along the road. They could lead you on like a young man's hopes. Or an old man's.

Beneath the lights, in the sweltering heat and next to the French colonial buildings, ran the seething mass of taxis, moto-taxis, motorcycles, and cars that belched out carbon monoxide and noise. It was the perfect bedlam for this grimy strip of real estate that housed the tourist bars and guest houses, and the dissolute expat community of Phnom Penh.

Which meant it wasn't so much mist around the streetlights as air pollution.

Time to stop looking at the world through shit-tinted glasses, old boy. After all these years, things were going to change—had changed—or would once the paperwork got signed at the Ministry of Lands.

He pulled his precious canvas satchel close beside him on the table, checking the flow of people along the boulevard. Nothing to worry about. Once the paperwork was signed, he'd be gone—at least long enough to prove to Kaitlin she'd never have to work again.

In this part of the street, upriver from the crenellated golden walls of the Royal Palace and the faded glory of the Foreign Correspondents' Club, he'd left behind the well-heeled tour groups. Here, the cheapo independent tourists filled the run-down, open-air restaurants with the rowdy sounds of drinking, surrounded by shifting halos of begging orphans, working girls, touts, and taxi drivers waiting for the tourists the drinks knocked down. It made him feel old. He'd given up drinking-for-the-sake-of-drinking a while ago. All it did was keep him from focusing on what he had to do.

But he was enjoying a drink here in the hole-in-the-wall restaurant just far enough off Sisowath that the crowds looking for entertainment rarely showed.

It was what Jeremy needed, after his years up-country. He'd spent enough time in the mountains to get used to the quiet, and Phnom Penh was anything but quiet. The city rumbled like an earthquake about to happen. It was almost too much—people—noise—entertainment.

He sipped his celebratory wine and frowned at the acrid taste—Cambodia was no place for wine. Not that Kaitlin would approve of him drinking anything. Again.

But the wine was red, rich with tannins. Not bad, given Pol Pot and his gang had destroyed pretty much everything French during their reign of terror. So civilization—if you could call it that—was just coming back to the city.

And soon he would enjoy the good life. He closed his eyes and let himself sink into the wicker chair's cushion, thinking about the new life he could finance for himself, his wife, and his daughter.

And bolted upright when the hand grasped his shoulder.

"Jerry? Jerry Blackwood? That you, mate?" Spoken with a thick Aussie accent and a little too much strength in the grip of the fingers.

It took a moment, but the lined, blue-eyed face pasted on the bald, bullet-shaped head gradually formed into someone he recognized, but bigger than he remembered. Older, too. But the years hadn't shrunken this guy's muscles any. It looked like he'd gone on steroids—or maybe it was his own paranoia talking. He swallowed.

Don't want to be tossing those shit-colored glasses just yet, big guy.

"Brian Jones. Now aren't you a sight for sore eyes. Or one to cause them."

Brian grinned, but the smile didn't reach his cold blue eyes. Without invitation, he pulled out the empty chair at Jeremy's table and sat down. His black t-shirt was pulled tight over his broad chest, and his light linen jacket wasn't loose enough to hide the bulging muscles—or the gun he wore. The waitress, a petite young thing with the usual short-shorts, midriff-baring top, and head of long black hair, hurried to the table.

"Singha, sweetie." He named an Indian beer and leaned back in his chair like a crocodile eyeing its prey.

Just how did a guy close to Jeremy's fifty-two years come off looking like he was barely forty?

Jones shook his head and studied Jeremy with those flat, reptile eyes. "How long's it been, mate?"

Jeremy shrugged. The man Jeremy had first met ten years ago when he had arrived in Phnom Penh had been one of those seemingly jobless men who knew everyone. In their brief association, Jeremy had come to think of Brian Jones as a 'fixer.'

You need drugs? He could get them.

You get arrested for drugs? He could help with that, too.

You need a new backpack? A gun? A girl? Insert here what it was you wanted—and Brian Jones was the man for you. Back then, Brian had been a hard-bitten man of indeterminate age, who'd traded on his physique and square jaw to impress the ladies. He'd also been a drinking buddy.

He definitely wasn't the person Jeremy wanted to meet tonight.

"Eight, nine years."

"Nah. Longer, I think, mate. At least ten."

Jeremy nodded. The conversation lagged, and Jeremy wished he was back on Sisowath instead of this backwater eddy of a place, because the stream of tourists would at least give him something to talk about.

And witnesses.

Brian jerked his chin at the canvas satchel. The neon reflected off his shaved head.

"You been busy, I hear," he said, the neon catching the skin around his eyes and revealing deeper lines that made him look older than the almost fifty years Jeremy had given him.

The waitress brought his beer and he met Jeremy's gaze and leaned across the table. "So you want to tell me about it? Enquiring minds and all that shit…?"

The wine soured in Jeremy's stomach, and he pulled his satchel onto the floor beside him, because no one should be hearing anything about what he'd been doing. Unless he'd seriously miscalculated.

"Who're you working for, Brian?"

Brian smiled his broad, predatory smile, exposing the gap between his teeth that, at the moment, looked like a deep cave. "Let's just say a businessman, and like any businessman, he knows a good investment when he sees it."

Brian's smile faded, and behind it lurked the ruthlessness that had helped him assume a role in Phnom Penh that had existed since the Portuguese and Dutch set up shop in the city in the 1600s. The role had reached its heyday during the Vietnam War, and had resurrected itself after Pol Pot's reign came to an end. Then, as now, men sold influence through violence, and Brian was their tool.

"No one's seen anything, Brian." Except the staff at the Ministry of Lands had seen his geological survey. His stomach sank and a bead of sweat ran out of his hair and down his temple. He swiped it away, but not before Brian saw.

Jeremy didn't want to talk about it. He didn't want to talk about it here—out in the open with the two older tourist women eating at the next table and congratulating themselves about how brave they were, eating off the main tourist strip.

He shoved his wine glass away, the tannins too sour on his tongue.

But then, maybe talking here with the women around was the safe way to go. Safety in numbers and all that.

He hauled his canvas bag onto his lap. Opened it and pulled out the least of the samples he'd taken and shoved it across the table at Brian. Brian covered it with his broad palm and then lifted his hand like he was uncovering cards.

Brown rock was what it looked like—until Brian turned it over. His eyes widened a little and he casually turned it over again, hiding the small, rough, red gems poking out of the grey-brown corundum.

He nodded. "Nice looking, mate. More where that came from?"

Jeremy gave a single shrug and hated that he did. If he were a stronger man, he'd just tell Brian Jones to get lost. Hell, if he were a stronger man, he'd never be here at all. But not being stronger, he'd find a way around Brian. He'd always found the words to talk his way through problems.

Well… most of the time.

Brian slipped the sample into his pocket without asking permission, and a chill ran down Jeremy's back, even in the sweltering heat. Brian smiled that crocodile smile again: *gonna eat you, mate.*

"Then it seems we got cause for celebration, don't we? Our new partnership."

He reached over and emptied the wine bottle into Jeremy's glass.

"Drink up, mate. We got places to go, people to see. Then we're going t'get rich. *Together*."

No choice. *But you always have a choice, Dad*, Kaitlin would say. A choice and a plan.

He picked up the glass, knowing this time his daughter was wrong.

Chapter 1

June 1st, Phnom Penh, Cambodia

Typical. Dad *would* drag her into miserable weather. Of course, he'd dragged her into so many other dodgy situations that monsoons were probably the least of her problems.

Probably. Knowing Dad.

Kaitlin Blackwood hunched down Sisowath Boulevard. The monsoon deluge flooded the streets, pounded the sidewalk, and sent two-inch rivers running down the pavement and over her newly-purchased street hikers. It beat on the roofs and storefront awnings—and her head—like a drum. It pummeled the broad, silver river beyond the road so that the air filled with the cacophony of water on water that made her ears ring.

More filthy water poured in gushing torrents off rooftops and filled the air with the stench of wet dog and garbage. Come to earth it split into tributaries as she stubbornly dragged her overnight suitcase down the sidewalk-turned-river.

Another wave of street-water sprayed her. The damned taxis, motorcycles, and odd-shaped moto-taxis—motorcycles with small, covered four-seater trailers—belched exhaust as they plied their way up the river-nee-street. Their drivers' calls beat at her, as incessant as the pounding rain, "Taxi, miss? Taxi. It rain hard."

It was hard not to scream at them, but then she'd never been a screamer.

She straightened, determined to look like she knew where she was going. Yeah, it rained hard here. It rained hard in Seattle, too. Maybe not like this, but she was used to getting wet.

Of course, she had a Gore-Tex jacket there.

She tossed her head, but her mass of rain-blackened blond hair just slapped her in the face and plastered there. *Perfect. Perfect in every friggin' way, Dad. You are sooo going to hear about this. It's a good thing I love you.*

Her clothes—light t-shirt and denim capris—plastered to her, too, so the passport carry bag she wore under her clothes from a cord hung around her neck stood out like a third breast on her chest. But she was *not* taking a taxi.

It was one of the damned taxis that had deposited her at the dive of a hotel she'd spent last night at not-sleeping. They could just take her out and shoot her before she'd trust another one. In fact, she'd break her own rule—buy a gun and do it herself—before she'd trust anyone in this stupid country again.

Locals and tourists wore cheap, see-through rain slickers and dodged around her like the rain didn't matter. She'd buy one, but she was so soaked now, what difference would it make? Besides, buying one would require energy to communicate across the language barrier. Energy she didn't have.

She waded northward on Sisowath—at least she thought it was northward. As jet-lagged as she was, she wasn't sure of much except that the darned taxi driver had pointed this way along the street last night when she'd asked him about the address.

She looked down at the soggy note in her hand. Ink pooled on the paper and ran onto her fingers. By the numbers on the restaurants and bars and tourist shops, the place she was looking for should be right around here. At least she thought so. She paused for a moment, studying the numbers and wiping rain out of her eyes.

Yes, it should be.

A petite female shopkeeper wielded a broom to keep the water out of her trinket shop and a tidal wave rolled across Kaitlin's feet right up to her ankles.

Perfect. Just perfect. Kaitlin sighed.

The shopkeeper said something that might have been an apology, but then again it probably was more like get out of the rain you stupid woman, and while you're at it, get out of my country.

More than happy to. In fact, she'd be downright ecstatic.

If she could just find the darned address. And her father. Then she'd give him a piece of her mind and be on the next plane out of this stupid country. Cambodia. *Now I ask you?*

A tug on her suitcase turned her around and she found herself facing a man. Cambodian — she thought. Oriental at least. Five foot eight?

Shorter than her five foot ten, at least, and dressed in a khaki-colored shirt and trousers that even in this deluge looked pressed.

But his hand was holding the handle of her suitcase and all her internal alarms went off. Another taxi tout?

His black gaze met hers. And then he smiled, exposing a mouth of blackened teeth that made her skin crawl, but in a country like this, dental hygiene couldn't be what it was in America.

"You are lost, Miss? Perhaps I can help. Perhaps you need a hotel. Or a taxi."

Kaitlin jerked her suitcase a little closer, but the darned guy didn't release it. "I'm fine. Thanks. I'm just looking for an address, but it has to be near here."

"What is the name and I will help you?"

She rolled her eyes. Couldn't these guys figure out she wanted to be left alone?

"All right. I'm looking for the Mayview Hotel."

"Ahh, yes. That one. Is good, but not as good as my place. You have a look, okay?"

That blackened smile again, and it frankly turned her stomach, but she supposed the poor guy couldn't help it.

"It is on the way to Mayfair. Come."

She hesitated—but it would be good to get there and out of the rain. Finally she nodded. "The Mayview," she corrected.

"This way, please." He caught her wrist with strong fingers and started to lead her back the way she'd come.

"I've been that way," she said.

"Mayfair sit on different road and my place this way. We go my car."

She stopped. The internal alarms jangled again. Something wasn't right. "The address I have is for Sisowath Quay. And it's the Mayview."

"No. No. No. Mayfair — it move."

The blackened smile again, but his eyes didn't match.

"No. It move."

The lack of expression reminded her of a young Disciple gangbanger she'd interviewed for a story back home. The guy had come across as a psychopath in her estimation. And the story she'd written for the *Post Intelligencer* had earned her a credible enough death threat she'd had police checking on her for six months. The gang member had turned up dead in a prison hit not long after.

And this guy's eyes were just as dead to emotion. And now that she listened to her instincts, the cut of his clothing just didn't fit a tout. Or a taxi driver. It had a military cut to it.

She tried to ease her hand free. "I don't think I need any help, thanks."

He didn't release her.

Internal air-raid sirens klaxoned through her head. She tried to twist loose, but he didn't release her.

"Dammit, let go!"

He half-dragged her toward the street corner. If he got her off the Sisowath Quay, who knew what would happen. The question was what to do? All the self-defense training seemed to disappear.

So she kicked him.

His grip only tightened.

She could stomp on his foot if she could find it under all this water. She could slam the heel of her hand into his nose. She could....

"Bloody hell, mate. The lady doesn't look like she wants to go with ya."

A booming voice that was weirdly familiar, but then she was rattled. And the voice spoke English like a native speaker, even if it held a thick Aussie accent.

She ripped loose, grabbed her suitcase, and ran.

"Hey!" The Aussie voice she hadn't even thanked, but she needed to get out of here. Some place where she understood what was going on. A place where she could figure things out.

She splashed back the way she'd come. Past the hotels. Past the bars. Past the trinket shop where the woman had drenched her shoes. A set of clean stairs in a yellow-and-white painted building came up on her left. A brass sign read *Foreign Correspondents' Club*.

Well she sure was foreign. And a journalist.

She almost ran up the two flights of stairs, her suitcase bang-bang-banging behind her, and she hated the panic pounding in her chest. Not like her. Not like her at all, dammit.

She was cool. She was Kaitlin Blackwood, crime reporter, friend of district attorneys, lawyers, gang-bangers, and mob bosses alike.

It had to be the jet lag that left her feeling as fractured as some gothic romance heroine. And the fact that she hadn't planned for things like what had happened in the street. If you could plan things, you could be prepared.

At the top of the stairs waited a large open-air space with broad ceiling fans futilely turning the rain-soggy air that came in through the room's two open sides that overlooked the streets and the Tonle Sap River. A high counter ran the perimeter of the room to allow patrons to partake of the view, and the open space was filled with low tables and well-worn, low-slung chairs. An actual bar sat against the wall next to the top of the stairs, and a door to the rear gave a view of the rain-darkened tiered roofs of a magnificent building of ancient Cambodian structure.

She sank down into an ancient leather chair that smelled of years of cigarette smoke and spilled beer and dug her fingers into the scarred armrest. She closed her eyes and regretted the people moving around her. The darned migraine that had been coming on since just before her plane landed sat like a sniper just back of her eyes. If she didn't get some rest soon, it was going to catch her right in the forehead and then she'd be down for a day at least.

Another gift from her father dragging her half way around the world. She fumbled her note pad and a pencil out of her purse to make a new list.

"May I help you?"

She looked up to a slim young Cambodian man in a pale yellow uniform standing above her. Beyond him the huge ceiling fans churned the humid air, and outside the open-sided room, the sheets of rain still fell.

"Tonic water and lemon, please." The sun wasn't over the yardarm yet, so no booze, though, frankly, a little alcohol would probably go down good now. In the face of the neatly clad waiter, she tried smoothing her sodden shirt and capris, but only succeeded in sending a new runnel of water onto the leather chair and the floor. Drowned rat wasn't the half of it. Her hands were frigging shaking! But the voices of the people behind her were like hammers on pipes in her head, and booze was never good with a headache like this coming on.

"Very good." The server wandered away and she took a deep breath.

The restaurant/bar had none of the feel of her favorite haunts back home. No photojournalist's shots on the walls. No framed newspaper tear sheets. None of the feel of dust and dirt and old smoke and crime that went with most reporters' haunts. Instead, pale yellow walls held a few photos of Angkor, and to either side of her along the rail to the street, a few young tourists and a couple of older expats sat, singly and in small groups, getting quietly drunk.

But the low tables and leather chairs must have been a pretty nice spot to wait out the Vietnam War. For some. A view of the river and none of the bombs that fell on Saigon.

She shook her head. She never had understood the call of the wild that made people become foreign correspondents when there was so much to report back home. She looked back at her note pad, trying to decide where to start.

Find hotel. And find her father. Go home. Pretty basic. What else did she need?

The young server returned and smoothly plunked the drink amid the water marks on the low wooden table, then left without even a smile. Not exactly the kind of service she was used to, but at least a twist of lemon floated amongst the ice.

She sipped, and it was a godsend of cool in the overwhelming heat and humidity. She sweated, even though her clothes still stuck to her from the rain. And her hands had barely stopped shaking.

Darn it, what was going on with her? She'd had close calls before.

But none so far from house and home.

And home was what she was going to lose if she didn't find her dad and get home. Mac could only keep the publisher happy with guest columnists for so long, before they started thinking about giving someone else her column space.

And if that happened, her dad would have put her in a worse position than he had so many times before. She'd just dug herself out of the debt he'd put her in when, unbeknownst to her, he used *her* condo as collateral for a loan on a boat he'd decided he was going to sail to South America.

Of course, he'd sunk the damn thing somewhere off the tip of Baja and she was left paying. And paying. She picked up the bill for the tonic water. Three-fifty. Three-fifty flippin' U.S. dollars for a drink in this flippin' country with none of the comforts of home.

"And I'm still flipping paying."

"Well, if that's a problem, I s'pose I could help ya out. Can't have a pretty lady drinking with the flies, now can we? Course maybe she could buy me a drink fer helpin' her out.…"

The suggestion came in thick rolling round vowels that were a tad thickened with liquor, but she was pretty sure it was the same voice she'd heard in the street. The voice of her savior and she shouldn't be ungrateful, but the slow Aussie drawl sent a jab of migraine pain right into her left eyeball. She refused to turn around, because making eye contact was where the trouble always began. Strangers could move right in on you and she really just needed to recover right now.

Out of the corner of her eye, a strong arm rested on the wooden arm of another of the worn leather chairs. Sun-bleached, blond hairs curled on its tanned and freckled back. Strong fingers curled around a sweating glass of beer. They were long. Almost artistic.

The kind of hand she always found attractive.

She looked away. Mac might not be her 'type,' but they were an item. He was a great guy. Stable. Just what she needed, not that she'd let it advance beyond dating. But she might.

Besides, Aussies were trouble.

"Thanks, but no thanks. But I'll buy you that drink for the help in the street. It was appreciated." She waved at the waiter and pointed at the Aussie's table without even glancing at it. There. Duty done. He should get the message.

Another sip of the tonic and the tension started to dissolve out of her shoulders. Too bad her clothes wouldn't dry just as fast.

"Yer lookin' a mite put out. Guy scared you, did he?"

Dammit, he wasn't going to let go and it wasn't true. She was capable. She didn't need saving. But he did deserve a thank you.

"Thanks, but I don't need any company. I'd prefer to be alone." She sipped her drink—well, maybe more of a gulp. Just finish and get out of here and find the Mayview.

"Now that's a sad tale, ain't it, lovely lady wants to be alone."

That was it. Enough, even if he'd helped her out. She turned her cold-blooded glare on him for an instant, then turned away.

"I *said*, no thank you." A slick of ice had crept into her voice.

"B.J., I think the lady wants to be left alone." A clipped British accent that seemed harsh after the lazy, rolling Aussie.

Thank you, lord. She almost looked at her defender, but something stopped her. Something he'd said. And her brief glance registered.

Oh-friggin-no....

She looked over again, into a boozy set of mocking blue eyes she had thought—no, make that hoped—never, ever, to see again.

Chapter 2

In the rain-faded natural light of the bar, the intelligent, if slightly inebriated, bright-blue eyes of B.J. McCallum were set under a thatch of blond hair that she knew would be thick and wiry in her hands. Right now the hair fell into his eyes, like a boy's, but his strong-boned face carried just a bit too much macho confidence for her taste.

Make that Aussie macho confidence. The worst kind. The kind that could get away with wearing the puke-green shirt with the so-nicely rolled up sleeves that exposed strong arms.

She needed to vacate the premises A.S.A.P.

The boozy blue eyes blinked and crinkled at the edges, reminding her of the bonhomie of a surfer-boy-gone-a-little-to-seed. But this was a surfer-dude who was frantically trying to match the woman in front of him to a face in his memory and the pictures hadn't quite matched up yet.

"Do I know you?" he asked. "Beyond helping you with that bloke, I mean? What was all that about, anyway?"

It was a little wounding that she recognized and remembered B.J. McCallum so well and he hadn't recognized her. But after seven years and a bit of a makeover, what did she expect? She'd had pixy-short hair way back then and had never worn makeup, when she'd believed that not looking feminine helped in the male-dominated newspaper business. Now, beside the long hair, eyeliner, and mascara, a few extra pounds had eased the stark angles of her face—or so her friends had told her. The streaking in her hair hadn't hurt, either.

Besides, B.J. McCallum had probably fried every brain cell with booze. Frankly, she was surprised he hadn't blown his brains out after the debacle at the paper that had led to his quick departure.

Which should put him on the defensive, not her.

"Kaitlin Blackwood. And I believe you're still B.J. McCallum." She didn't bother to stick out her hand.

The way his gaze suddenly cleared and his Adam's apple bobbed, she'd shocked him sober enough that the face cards he'd been shuffling all fell into place and he was remembering more than he was letting on.

"Well, I'll be gobsmacked. Kaitlin. Bloody hell. Look at you!"

He was out of his chair and, before she could react, hauled her up into a surprising bear hug she couldn't escape, and spilled her notepad into a pool of water from her suitcase. The scent of him—man-sweat and a pleasant hint of oriental spice that no aftershave could copy—reignited an unfortunate, old, toe-curling feeling right down where it shouldn't have.

She elbowed herself out his embrace and rescued her notepad, but B.J.'s immense paw still claimed her hand, and he turned to the other man settled in one of the leather chairs. Tall, with the stick-thin build and the pale, shiny skin and reddened nose of the well-practiced drinker who didn't get much sun.

"Nick, this's Kaitlin—er—Seattle. She's the author of *The Blackwood Report* and one of the youngest reporters ever to have her own nationally-syndicated newspaper column. Bloody hell, luv. How long's it been?"

Seven years, four months, fifteen days since the fight she had walked out on. Why that exact figure came into her head, she didn't know, but she'd lay money on it being true. And she still hated it when he called her 'Seattle' and 'luv'.

"A while." Dammit, an old zing still came through his hand, and that, she definitely didn't need.

Nick stuck out his hand and she managed to get B.J. to relinquish hers. Nick's was cool from the G and T he nursed.

"Nick Mayerthorpe. He's mentioned you."

But the way he considered her suggested he'd heard more than a mention. B.J. probably railed against her as the bitch that ruined his life. She glanced back at him and felt a little guilty, but darn it, it was his fault.

"What brings you to Cambodia?" she asked B.J.

"Me? Hell, I been here—what?—it's got to be six years now. Live up-country in Siem Reap. Got things good. Mostly. Just down here on official business." He glanced at Nick and shook his shaggy head as if he were trying to get rid of the booze. He pushed away his half-finished pint of beer. "Nothing works like it should in this country."

Aside from the bleariness of his gaze and his rain-sodden attire, he actually looked good in his ridiculously colored shirt—where did men get their fashion sense, anyway?—and a pair of worn, Dockers-style trousers. He never did take care of anything except his camera equipment.

"How 'bout you?" he continued. "This's about the last place I'd expect to run into Seattle Blackwood. Thought you were on the fast track for the *New York Times* or something. Or are you here on a story? And what was the deal outside?" He nodded towards the street, where the rain continued to pummel the pavement and vehicles and any fool brave enough to be out in that weather.

Was that a jibe buried in there somewhere, even though he'd kept track of her enough to know she had her own column now? Her drive to make it in the cutthroat world of journalism had always made him laugh at her.

It was one of the reasons things hadn't worked between them: she was a serious journalist and he—though gifted—couldn't be bothered to work his way into a permanent photojournalist position at the Seattle *P.I.* He preferred the uncertainty—what he called the 'freedom'—of freelance work.

And then there'd been his trouble.

She should just get up and leave. Just talking with him was bad for her reputation.

"I'm not here on a story. And the guy outside was just an overeager tout."

"Then it's gotta be yer dad, right?"

Flipping hell. How had he known? He made every muscle tense in her too-tired body, just like he always did when he made some leap instead of carefully considering the facts. She shouldn't let him get to her like this.

"Why I'm in Cambodia is my business." Another gulp of the bitter-cool tonic, and the darned glass was empty. She set it down in a jangle of ice cubes and a flush of cold that made her shiver even as she wished there was more. But she had things to do, and no time to reminisce or cry in what B.J. McCallum would call her 'be-air.'

She stood and grabbed her suitcase handle and her bill. "I'm off to find a room. Nice seeing you again. And thanks for the help outside. I could have handled it, but I know you were trying to help."

She nodded at both men and strode for the cashier, hoping that ridding herself of B.J. McCallum would also ease the pounding in her head. Then a flipping paw of a hand with a light scattering of curled blonde hairs fell on her shoulder as B.J. caught up to her again.

She glared at him.

And he released her instantly in an annoying, too-well-remembered, little-boy-innocent, hands-off motion.

"Whoa, there, luv. I didn't mean anything."

"What do you want, then?" And she hated herself for the acid in her voice. Knew she was acting like a bitch, while he was Old Home Week, but her headache was sucking out the back of her eyes.

"I thought—if you don't have a room—I could recommend one. Clean and safe…" He said it like a peace offering—like he'd offered things before to mend their many fights.

"I can take care of myself, thanks. I have the name of a place." She tossed her head and her damned hair slapped her in response. Not exactly the cool look she was going for.

But the last thing she wanted was a debt to one B.J. McCallum. Her association with him had almost ruined her reputation as well as his own. It had been the proverbial straw when B.J. had faked photos to 'prove' a certain Lee Chang was smuggling little girls from Asia to America for the child prostitution industry. It had led to a too-successful libel suit against him and the paper. She'd barely held onto her job, which had led to the last fight they ever had.

She left money on the counter and abandoned him for the stairs to the street and the monsoon rain. Paused at the bottom of the stairs to check the street for the black-toothed man before she stepped into the deluge. She ducked her head against the rain and turned upstream, seeking the address. She was pretty sure B.J. McCallum was watching her from the club until she shoved through a stand of potted palms that some idiot had set out to block the sidewalk.

She paused to check behind her. No B.J. on the street and no black toothed guy, either. She exhaled in relief.

Maybe it had all been a mistake. Maybe Black-tooth really had been trying to help and had just misunderstood the name of the hotel. Or maybe the problem was her jet lag and the fact she'd been forced to come here when she'd sworn, after her father's last debacle, that she would *never, ever* step foot out of the States again. Of course, when it came to her father,

her resolve rarely held. Even though as a child she'd rarely seen him, for some reason he'd always fascinated her. Maybe it was the mystery of the relationship she always wished they'd had.

The flipping headache was starting a low jackhammer, like hearing the infernal rattle a city block over.

If she could just get some sleep, with her Percocet she might still get past it, but if she didn't get the rest, this was going to be a doozy.

A white awning spread a patch of alluring dry across the pavement. A narrow, white façade beside a white foyer held gold lettering on white marble: THE MAYVIEW.

So she *had* been right.

Had the man purposely been trying to lead her astray? Now she was turning paranoid. Not a good sign.

Suitcase trundling behind her, she entered the foyer, her soaked shoes schlepping across the white marble floor. The pounding rain was replaced by the steady thud-thud-thud of her headache and the whir of an oscillating fan blowing fast enough to chill her. She stopped at the counter.

The place looked—if not nice, at least better than the place she'd stayed last night. It was antiseptically clean—with a single wicker chair, a few art-photos on the bone-white, marble walls, and a chugging soft drink machine that sold Coke and florid orange and pink liquids in brands she didn't know.

Tension ran out of her shoulders. Dad would be here and she would bail him out of whatever trouble he was in and then go home.

But there was no concierge, though a neat set of ledgers sat on the counter, and beyond it a single incense stick trailed a thin line of smoke up from a small floral and rice offering set on a white dish. The sweet scent on top of her headache sent her stomach flip-flopping.

"Hello?" she asked and her voice echoed hollowly back at her.

She glanced back at the street. No black-toothed man and no B.J. McCallum. She wasn't sure which she dreaded seeing more. But the rain no longer bounced a foot off the ground. The monsoon storm was passing.

Typical.

"May I help you?"

A young Cambodian woman with long dark hair coiled up on her head had materialized behind the counter. She wore a simple, pale green sheath dress that set off her golden skin. Her serene face could have been a model for one of the Apsara dancers on the cover of Kaitlin's *Fodor's* guidebook.

"Thank God. You speak English." Kaitlin shoved back her sodden hair and the sense of being a lumbering moose around a woman this petite. "I'm looking for someone. He was staying here—at least this was the address on his last letter."

Good. She sounded like herself: a professional.

The young woman's perfectly composed face showed a hint of caution as she looked Kaitlin up and down.

Then the woman's eyes widened and all the blood seemed to run out of her face.

Then she turned and ran.

Chapter 3

B.J. sauntered back to his chair, shaking his head and trying to figure out how he felt about this sudden sighting. He settled in his usual chair and snagged his beer towards him. Moisture still beaded the tallie—the tall one—as he knocked back the amber nectar and then ran the bottle over his brow.

"Shit." He felt stonkered—knocked on his arse—just as he'd felt the last time he saw Kaitlin Blackwood, and he didn't like the feeling.

"She got you all hot and bothered, brother?" Nick asked. The Englishman was doing what he did best, nursing a drink and having fun at his friend's expense.

B.J. sent a glare his way and shook his head. "More like kicked in the gut. What kind 'a friend are you? Kick a man when he's down?"

"Just taking the piss outta you—isn't that the expression? But then, maybe that little woman is what you need. You've been spending an awful lot of time alone."

B.J. waved him off. "Not alone. And what I don't need is Kaitlin Blackwood."

"And why would that be, old man? She's pretty enough. You could do a lot worse."

"Her looks aren't the issue, mate. We're oil and water. No good at all."

Another long pull of the yeasty beer, and the boozy glow he'd lost when he realized it was Seattle he'd helped, started to return to his brain.

"Like I need the trouble that girl brings." Shook his head. "I think I got enough going on with my visa renewal and the permits for Maly's medical trip and the orphanage. The visa shoulda come through two weeks ago and the bloody clerk just looked at me like he expected a bribe or somethin'. Yeah, that'd be right. Too much trouble."

"You could leave and renew the visa in Thailand. Take a break and see some civilization?"

"And just what do I do if they don't renew it? I can't get into the country then." He checked his watch and heaved himself upright again, already missing the friendly chair where he'd spent most of his first year in-country. "We gotta be going if we wanna catch our flight."

Nick swallowed back his drink. "You didn't give her enough credit when you described her, Beej," Nick said around ice.

Wouldn't the bloody man just leave it alone?

"She looked different back then. Hair was shorter. She was skinnier, too." Not that the extra flesh hadn't seemed to accumulate in all the right places. And she hadn't worn makeup that made her brown eyes huge pools. Ripper eyes, those. Brown eyes that'd just about reach in and tear out a man's heart.

"Those bones of hers looked pretty nicely covered now."

And B.J. didn't like that Nick had noticed. Bloody hell. Seeing her had dislodged one of the pieces of flotsam he'd sunk into a carefully-dug, fathom-deep hole in his brain.

"A whole whack of good times and a whole lot of bad—that was Seattle Blackwood," he murmured, knocked back the last of his beer and wiped his lips.

"Funny. I always hear ya talk about the good."

B.J. gave him the one-finger salute and threw his dollars on the table.

Then he headed for the airport, hoping that putting half of Cambodia between them would keep Kaitlin Blackwood's memory at bay.

CHAPTER 4

Kaitlin spun to see who was behind her, but the lobby and the sidewalk beyond were empty. Stay or go? Too quick a decision. "Stop!" Kaitlin yelled and wished she hadn't.

Too much re-charged adrenaline sent her chasing after the woman. Down the dark corridor that led back into the hotel. Past a column of light that lit a steep set of stairs, past bicycles leaning against the walls, though a darkened room with a hotplate on the floor and the smell of cooked rice, where she almost plowed into the woman and felt like a flipping keystone cop.

In the darkness, the concierge spoke rapid-fire Cambodian to a jeans-and-red-t-shirt-clad young man with a round face and hair moussed in a free-form Mohawk cut. Both turned to Kaitlin, the woman's face a mask again.

Kaitlin drew herself up to her full height. *Think, woman. Think before you act.* That was her mantra in life. She reclaimed the composure she'd cultivated for dealing with hostile informants.

"Is there a problem?"

Even though her heart hammered in her chest, the words came out ice-calm—the tone that had earned her the bitch-goddess nickname around the news desk.

The young woman glanced at her companion. "No. No problem. You—surprise me. That is all."

But her gaze kept moving over Kaitlin's face as if she were trying to work something out, and the young man clutched the woman's arm as, together, they eased Kaitlin back towards the foyer.

Kaitlin stopped when she stood next to her suitcase. Something was going on and she wasn't going anywhere until she found out what. She started again, slowly and calmly, her words marching thump-thump-thump in her brain.

"I'm looking for a man. His name is Jeremy Blackwood. Is he here?" She used simple sentences to make sure she was clear and because the headache made it hard to think.

The woman shifted uneasily. "There is no Jer-e-my Blackwood here."

But she wouldn't meet Kaitlin's gaze, instead casually sliding the hotel ledger into a drawer. Kaitlin reached over the counter and stopped her.

"Jeremy Blackwood is my father. He sent me a letter from this address. He said he was coming home to see me. He never showed up. That was a month ago. So I came here to find him."

The woman's gaze turned assessing and Kaitlin wondered how much the information was going to cost her. But finally, the woman nodded. "He was here. He gone now."

Kaitlin closed her eyes. "Damn. I should have come sooner."

It was the truth, but it had taken a few weeks to put her affairs in order after her dad hadn't shown. And frankly, she'd been pissed off enough she had actually thought about just leaving him to deal with his own problems. For once. Besides, he'd never been there for her.

The jet lag settled like a million pounds on her shoulders. The jackhammer in her head increased its decibel. She blinked back pain. "When did he leave? Where did he go?"

"I don't know," the woman said.

The woman glanced at the young man, who looked enough like her to be her brother. He shook his head—and what the hell was going on here? Even through her headache, she could tell something wasn't quite right.

"Well, you've got to know when he left, right?"

The woman stared at her blankly.

"The ledger? It will show when he checked out, won't it?" When the woman still hesitated, Kaitlin plucked it out of the drawer, just like she'd eased stories out of reluctant informants. "I need to find my father."

It was as if the young concierge's resolve broke. She looked at her brother and said something. He argued, but she shook her head. She opened the ledger and flipped the pages to a date about two months previous, then she turned the ledger around so Kaitlin could read it.

Neat English listed names of guests and their nationality and passport numbers along with dates of arrival and departure. Kaitlin's eyes trailed down the list. She flipped the page and checked there. Turned back and checked the names there, too.

No Jeremy Blackwood. But something was off. The dates in the book didn't work. One page ended on the twenty-seventh of March, but the next page started with April ninth. Her father's letter had been dated March thirtieth.

"Is this some kind of joke?"

Then she saw it. The torn bit of paper sticking up from the binding between the two pages.

Chapter 5

Kaitlin went cold and the pounding in her head broke through to her eyes. The migraine's first bright flash of light almost blinded her and her stomach heaved.

"Why has my father's name been torn out?" she demanded and swallowed back bile.

She'd been wrong to be angry at him. Sure, her dad was a rounder and a nomad, but he was hers. Something *was* wrong. A hotel didn't tear a page out of a ledger.

She touched the torn edge, and the pain behind her eyes shifted to a vise that ratcheted tighter and tighter, and for a moment she went blind. Her knees went weak and she thought she might fall from the thickening pain and the fear.

The young woman must have thought so, too, for she said something to her brother and he suddenly had the lone, wicker chair behind her and eased her down.

More than the foyer fan radiated cold, even though the hot monsoon rains still patted the street. The traffic still hissed just beyond the white awning. The color photos on the walls—studies of architecture and of impoverished people of Phnom Penh's streets—did nothing to relieve the bone-colored walls. In fact, they just reinforced the darkness closing in.

The incense, the car exhaust, and the mud-scent of the river all turned her stomach. She thought of the black-toothed man. It couldn't be a coincidence, could it?

She needed to think. She needed to assess what her next step was—but just trying to think hurt her head, and she was sure she was leaping to conclusions.

She didn't know for certain that anything had happened to her father. He was, after all, an impetuous man who wouldn't be beyond tearing a page out of a ledger himself if he were trying to conceal that he'd been here.

He was also the kind of man who made enemies easier than he made friends, and most of his friends became enemies at one point or another.

Get a grip, Blackwood. You're acting like one of those hysterical women you hate.

She struggled up and stood, swaying.

"Why tear out the page with my father's name?"

She blinked at the young clerk. The woman really showed no emotion in that face. Not friendship, not interest, not dislike—just—nothing.

"We did not tear out the page," the woman said.

"Did he?"

The woman shook her head.

For some reason that was almost a relief. He wasn't hiding from her. So something *had* happened. She would deal with it, just like all the other times. She was in control. She was Kaitlin Blackwood, author of *The Blackwood Report*, the award-winning crime column.

"So who did? How did it happen?"

The woman looked at the Iroquois-haired young man, who shook his head and muttered again in what must be rapid Cambodian.

"His friend. They come here together—Jer-e-my Blackwood and his friend—and they pack up Jer-e-my's room and leave. Then the friend come back and take the page."

"Where were they going? Who was his friend?" Kaitlin asked.

The young woman conferred with her brother again. Finally they both shook their heads. "Don't know."

But their faces didn't agree. There was something more here, but the pain and nausea overwhelmed Kaitlin's frustration. She closed her eyes.

At least she knew when. But eight weeks gave them a hell of a lead time. They could be back in Seattle, or anywhere else in the world, by now.

Not that she believed that. She needed a clue.

"Please. Think hard. There must be something they said or did. Something to suggest who his friend was. What did he look like?"

They young woman's face softened—the emotionless mask slipping a little as if she could empathize with what Kaitlin felt. This time she didn't check with her brother.

"The man big. Tall. Strong like a soldier. He had light hair. And an accent. Australia, I think."

That was something—a start. She thought of B.J. He fit the description, and he and her father had met. He could be the friend. Which meant that B.J. McCallum had known that she was looking for her father as soon as he'd seen her, and he'd been making a fool of her the whole time they'd talked.

Bile soured her throat. "Please, where did they go?"

"Some place important, I think. Some place that made Jer-e-my afraid."

"Afraid?" Kaitlin echoed. Not a usual emotion for her father. Nope. He usually blithely went into places no right-minded person would go.

The light had coalesced into a shimmer that surrounded everything in the foyer. The migraine coming on was worse than she'd thought. The kind she couldn't put off or shove away. But for now she did. She'd pay the price later.

"What made you think that?"

"Your father—Jer-e-my. He moved slowly, as if he did not wish to go. He did not smile with his eyes when he said goodbye. And he did not carry his bag—his friend did."

"What bag?" But she knew. Listened absently as she thought of the canvas bag she'd sewn as a high-school project when she was fifteen and into cameras and couldn't afford the kind of bag she wanted. When she'd given the pictures up in favor of words two years later, her dad had asked for the bag. He'd been carrying it ever since, and that was what? Thirteen years?

Every time she'd had to deal with one of his harebrained, get-rich-quick schemes, he'd still had the damned bag over his shoulder. Like the damned shoulder strap was the only thing that still held them together as a family.

Maybe it was. She looked back at the clerk and her brother. "If you had to tell someone where they were going, where would you say?"

But the woman shook her head. "I told you. We do not know."

"I know. But sometimes people say or do something that you don't even remember, but your brain does. Just answer the question. Just guess."

The young woman's mask was back. She said something to her brother and the two conferred again. Finally they turned back to Kaitlin. "Not in Phnom Penh. My brother thinks they went north."

That was something, but she needed more. North was a lot of country, from what she'd seen of the map. A sense of urgency filled her. In the past, he'd usually been waiting right where he called her from—either in debt and needing her money to "help him get on his feet," or else in jail because someone had realized he was running some scam.

This time, just like all the other times, his letter had said things were different.

Right, Dad. This time you got yourself disappeared—which pretty much wasn't a surprise, because she'd always known that someday he was going to get himself into something he couldn't get out of. And this was Cambodia, capital of the disappeared. The Khmer Rouge had executed at least 200,000 people, and estimates put the number of those who had died of starvation or been worked to death during their regime as high as seven million.

Pretty good company, Dad. But her skin was ice cold. Her mind, her body, felt frozen solid.

"Can I see his room?" she managed.

The woman frowned. "The room was rented many times since he leave."

Kaitlin shook her head.

"Is it rented now?" she asked through gritted teeth.

A shake of the head.

"Then I'll take it. I need a room anyhow. It might as well be his." She pulled her passport wallet out and fished out the document, and the explosion in her head almost sent her to her knees. Her time putting the headache off had just run out.

Chapter 6

June 2nd, Angkor, Siem Reap Province

The angle of the morning sun placed perfect light and shadows across the renowned faces of the fifty-four towers of Angkor's Bayon Temple. B.J. had known the light would be good at this time of day, but the perfect scene couldn't get another face out of his head.

Bloody hell, Seattle Blackwood. The perfect bloody ending to a perfect bloody trip to Phnom Penh. After checking with the visa clerk one more time, *she'd* had to be the bloody damsel in distress that he was stupid enough to help, and then he'd been idiot enough to try to pick her up. Until he realized who it was.

Kaitlin 'Seattle' Blackwood in the bloody Foreign Correspondents' Club. About as likely as rocking horse shit, that was.

She had looked good, too. Good enough that old memories had kept him awake last night. A bit of macadam less traveled and all that. *Get over it, mate.*

He focused on the scene through the viewfinder again and his 35 mm back-up Nikon banged against his chest.

The pool of monsoon rainwater reflected the fading apricot in the pale blue sky and the towering clouds that trundled overhead. The air was cool and moist and lightly scented with wild jasmine and mud. A light mist hazed the undergrowth of the tattered jungle that surrounded the temple, but already the grinding gears of the whale-like tourist busses echoed along the road. It was like the beach early in the morning before the white-back tourists got up.

They'd be here soon enough.

He adjusted the height of the tripod for his medium-format camera and readjusted the aperture for a wide depth of field.

Perfect. Just bloody perfect. Or it would have been bloody perfect *if* sneaking in past the tourist gates hadn't taken longer that he thought and *if* the visiting monk he'd met in Siem Reap had actually shown up for the shoot like he'd promised he would.

He'd planned this shoot. The morning mist. The watered sky. The monk was supposed to be sitting in the pool of light between the temple columns, his bright saffron robes reflected in the pool of water so that the viewer's eye bounced back and forth between the monk and his reflection.

But that isn't what the shot is going to be, ya wanker, so get over it and get as best you can. He ran his fingers through his thatch of hair. *It was you who chose to lug in all your equipment. Besides, there's a chance you can Photoshop the monk in later.*

He aimed his camera and shot. Changed exposure to better catch the light changes in the sky and shot again. Changed exposure again to capture the inscrutable faces on the Bayon's many towers. Shifted position and changed exposure to catch the details in the faces and took advantage of a flock of mottled geese in the pool to add movement to the photo. Solid enough shots, he knew, but simply stock. Not quite the art pieces he'd planned, and without the art pieces there was little chance he'd earn a livable income, let alone earn money for Maly's medical trip abroad.

He swore again as the sound of diesel and motorcycles came closer. The hordes were about to descend.

Another shift of position, careful of the huge spider webs in the trees—coming from Australia, he loathed the horrible, deadly things, even though most Cambodian spiders were apparently not *too* deadly. He lowered the tripod to frame the temple and pool in trailing branches. A postcard shot, but it would at least earn him something. He positioned the gold-wrapped Buddha figure at the entry to the temple where it would catch the viewer's eye, but something wasn't right.

Something red caught the light and refracted burgundy highlights into the shadows from the rubble stacked outside the temple. It threw the entire composition off.

"Bloody hell!" He stood up and remembered to duck the web at the last minute. Give up the whole shoot as a bad business, or run over, hide what was undoubtedly tourist garbage, and then race back and take his picture?

B.J. scrubbed his rumpled hair. In the parking lot, two buses had disgorged their loads and the milling tourists had their eyes on the temple like crocs teased by a cow. If their guide didn't get them into the temple soon, he'd have an uprising on his hands. But he was giving instructions in three different languages so that might leave enough time.

If B.J. moved fast.

He abandoned his heavy equipment bags and camera-laden tripod and ran, his 35 mm banging against his chest. He loped around the pool, batting brush out of his way and scaring one of the feral cats that seemed to live amidst the temples—probably because the tourists fed them.

International archeologists aligned with the APSARA Authority and its predecessors had stacked unused stones from the ruins into long rows for future restoration efforts. Now they provided a place for tourists to stand to take pictures of the Bayon. But not today, not yet.

B.J. hurdled the first row of stones and swore when he almost twisted his ankle. Even though he'd always held onto his swimmer's physique, he was getting too old for this.

He dodged through a break in another row of stone. There. Another glint of red, and beyond it bright saffron.

And the crimson gleam of new-spilled blood.

He screeched to a halt, the copper-bright scent filling his nose. He'd seen this kind of thing before—when he was still shooting for the news desk at the *Sydney Herald* and at his ill-fated job at the *Seattle P.I.*, but usually from beyond a line of crime scene tape.

Now he stood right above the monk he'd arranged to meet. The man lay twisted between two rows of rubble, his robe—pulled loose and over his head—flowing out beyond the row as if he'd been trying to escape his killer, but whoever had done the deed had held him by his robe. But it wasn't the robe that had caught B.J.'s attention.

What had, wasn't clear.

The sound of tourist voices came behind B.J. He went down on one knee and flipped the blood-stained robe off the monk's face and almost fell on his ass.

Dead-dead-dead.

A single bullet—execution-style—to the back of the head had blown off most of the monk's face. Horribly dead.

Awfully dead. Executed, Khmer Rouge fashion.

B.J. leapt up and tried to unstick his brain. *Get the mind working, mate. Decide what to do. Report it, certainly.*

But you were inside Angkor Park illegally, ya wanker. That alone means a fine or jail. And you were the one who arranged to meet him here.

"Bloody hell."

A scrape of stone behind him. He turned to face a tiny Hello-Kitty-clad Japanese woman, mini-digital camera in hand, balancing on the rubble for her shot of the temple.

She caught his glance and did a double take, her eyes widening like a kangaroo in headlights as she took in B.J and what lay at his feet.

B.J. Looked down at himself. Blood on his hands and the knee of his trousers. *Fuck.*

"It's not what it looks like, luv," he said, stepping towards her.

The woman screamed and dropped her camera.

Chapter 7

June 2 — Phnom Penh

The room at the Mayview was better than Kaitlin had hoped. Clean—in fact, pristine—after the dive she'd stayed in the night before. The place smelled of fresh paint and cleaning fluid, and the floor had squeaked under her bare feet when she'd first settled in and showered.

White walls except for the outside wall, which contained a tall door and iron-grilled and louvered-wood-shuttered windows that gave onto a balcony that looked over Sisowath Quay and the Tonle Sap River. Inside there was a small wardrobe that doubled as a television stand, a single chair, and between two white-covered beds, a bedside table that held a kettle and tea packets, her passport wallet, and her pack.

She still lay in one of the beds, because after a few hours of exhausted sleep, traffic noise and the nascent and then not-so-nascent pounding of a nightclub next door had kept her awake. So now the glimmer at the edge of her vision said the jackhammer operator had traded places with a Taiko drummer and the noise had subsided for the moment, but the migraine could still lay her out for days.

She glanced at her watch. Nine a.m. At home she never stayed in bed this long, but since she'd woken at one thirty, she'd been lying here and had done nothing but file a torn nail that kept catching on the bedding. The semidarkness that the louvered shutters and door allowed once dawn came hadn't shut off her brain, even though exhaustion had sapped her will to move.

Her light undershirt and panties stuck uncomfortably to her skin in the humid air. Cambodia was definitely not her favorite place. In fact, the sodden country was fast rising up her list of places she most definitely did not want to be in.

The faint drip-drip from the shower had escalated into a booming drum. The sound of traffic from the wet streets was a roar she couldn't get rid of, and the lemon scent of the cleaning fluid had her stomach churning. Or maybe that was hunger.

It was a long time since her last meal.

Get over it. You could lose a few pounds anyway. Damned B.J. McCallum didn't even recognize you.

She should be thankful for it. If only finding her dad would prove as easy as walking away from B.J. McCallum had been.

You talking about the first time, or this time?

She shook her head and the darned drummer sent a staccato pounding through her brain. *That* was almost as big mistake as coming to Cambodia had been.

See what you've gotten me into, Dad? See?

But that was being petty. In the emotional rock-paper-scissors that was dealing with her father, worry trumped anger every time.

What had he gotten himself into? How bad was the situation this time? He might have lived on the edge all his life, but that didn't mean he could take care of himself.

She hauled her pen and notebook to her and flipped it open to an empty page. A list of possibilities would at least give her some place to start her enquiries.

It could be as simple as him falling in with other big-time schemers and shifting hotels. Or it could be bad—he'd fallen in with people who used him often enough. Not that he'd admit it. He was always good-natured about his losses: easy come, easy go.

Not that he'd ever really had much to lose. Except a family.

She pressed her lips together and uncrumpled the thing that had lured her to this god-forsaken country, to read it once more. This time was different, the letter said. Sure.

> **"I've done it, girlie!"** The usual swirl and flourish on his capital letters that had always made her feel important when she was little. **"This time I really have hit the big one. The big time. This time you can believe it. The money is going to come in like mad and you can quit**

that darned job and live in the style I should have provided for you and your mother all those years."

Too late for Mom, Dad. Too late by six months.

But then you *wouldn't know she was gone, because nobody knew where the heck* you *were and* you *never check your damned Hotmail account. Or maybe you had and it just wasn't important enough to you.*

She slowed her rough breathing.

Face it, Blackwood. You've got two options. Cut him out of your life or forgive him. That's who he is: an example of a dying breed—the hard-drinking grifters and adventurers of the 1950s and '60s.

She squeezed her eyes shut. It wasn't fair that she loved him this much when he'd always failed her. The trouble was, he was all she had.

"This time things are going to be different, girlie. This time I'm doing things right—all the paperwork and all the legalities observed—just like you always said, because I can't afford to let this one get away. I even sat down and wrote a list like you're always telling me to do. Proud of me? I hope so. I'm looking forward to spending lots of time together, and maybe you can introduce me to all those smart friends of yours this time."

Almost convincing that he'd listened to her all the times she'd railed against his drink-fueled 'get rich quick' schemes that far too frequently skirted the law of whatever country he happened to be in. Almost, but not quite.

Jeremy Blackwood was a schemer and a manipulator of the first order. He had to be, given he'd managed to keep her loving him even though he was never there, was always breaking promises, and had left her mother to work at two jobs to make ends meet and cover the costs of Kaitlin's university beyond her scholarships. Even the flipping letter hinted at the relationship that the little-girl part of her had always yearned for.

"Useless as a father, but a charming man." At least that was what her mother had always said. He had to have been, to not only get mom to marry him, but to stay married to him right to the end.

A soft knock at the door brought her upright on the bed, and the whole room swung around her. Sweat ran down into her eyes and was sticky on her skin.

Another soft knock.

"Just a moment."

"I can come back, Madam." The young clerk's voice, but less certain.

"No, I'll be right there."

She staggered up and the room spun so she thought she was going to be sick. She leaned her head against the wall, *cool, thank God*, and pulled on a shirt. Looked down at herself. Pale bare legs and feet, but it was going to have to do.

She wobbled to the door and pulled it open a crack. A flood of rice and curry scent, overlaid with a faint scent of the woman's frangipani, emanated from the darkened hallway. Kaitlin's stomach did another flip-flop.

Maybe it was better she *hadn't* eaten.

The clerk stood there, looking pristine and perfect in the same green, Chinese-cut dress. Her black gaze ran up Kaitlin to her face and Kaitlin shoved her sweat-damp hair back.

"Yes?"

The way the woman's eyes widened, Kaitlin knew she had to look a wreck. She was probably the color of the foyer walls.

"Sorry. Migraine."

As if the woman would even know what that meant.

"You are sick. Perhaps I should come back? Or call a doc-tor?"

"I'm up." Kaitlin hauled the door open farther. "Come in." If you dare. "A doctor isn't necessary. I just need to sit down."

She stumbled back to the bed and collapsed on the edge as the woman followed cautiously inside and stood above her, holding a large, bubble-wrap envelope.

But the clerk's careful composure seemed to shred. She licked her lips. Her hand fumbled at her perfect hair and then at her dress, and she wouldn't meet Kaitlin's eyes.

If she'd been an interviewee, this was when Kaitlin would have had to decide whether to tread delicately or go in for the kill. The migraine sorta took the kill out of her.

"Yes? What did you want?" Just asking the question seemed to sap her strength. She really just wanted to close her eyes in darkness and silence—an apparently impossible luxury in this city.

Finally the woman held out the envelope.

"Your father. He gave me this to hold, but he did not ask for it back when he left."

She handed it to Kaitlin, who turned it over.

"It has your name and address, but he never ask to post it. My brother did not think I should give it to you, but it is your name. And your father—I did not like the man he was with."

The words tumbled out of the woman and the headache haze almost made it hard to follow. Little red flashes had joined the glow at the edge of her vision as she turned the envelope over and assessed what she had.

Large. Ten by thirteen—no—even bigger, of the usual gold-brown envelope paper. It felt light, like there was not much more than a few pages of paper inside, but why have bubble-wrap unless you were trying to protect what it carried? She sniffed the package, but there was only paper and incense and perhaps a whiff of plastic and something else—sour?— she wasn't sure of.

"I guess I should open it," she said looking up at the waiting woman. "I feel at a little disadvantage. You know my name, but I don't know yours."

A small smile crept into the corners of the woman's perfect, bowed mouth and seemed, for the first time, to unfreeze her inscrutable eyes. Attractive. Someone who might be a friend under other circumstances

"I am Champei."

Kaitlin slid her finger under the envelope flap.

"Well, Champei, why don't you have a seat?"

Chapter 8

In the half-light through the closed louvered windows, Champei gracefully perched on the edge of the straight-backed white chair beside the TV wardrobe. Kaitlin tore open the envelope and winced at the rip of the paper tore through her head. Just the rustle of Champei's dress and the traffic noise were—well—the kiss of death to any clear thinking she should have done.

Like she should never have invited Champei to stay, because clearly the young woman was curious to know what was in the envelope, and this was something Kaitlin should have done alone. You don't go around showing strangers what you have—especially not in a foreign country.

But she was committed now. She glanced at Champei and then two-fingered the envelope open to peer inside.

Not much there. A single sheet of clear, plastic-covered cardboard. She frowned and pulled it out. Well, maybe more than cardboard.

What looked like a dark, red-brown cutout figure of a tree lay flat on a sheet of plain white cardboard.

She flipped it over.

Nothing. Just bare cardboard.

Flipped it over again and checked inside the envelope. Empty. She glanced a question at Champei.

"It is a shadow puppet," Champei said, leaning forward to see. "The tree of life, it looks like." She frowned. "But the shape wrong."

"Shadow puppet?" Kaitlin remembered skimming over a sidebar of her *Fodor's* that set out Cambodian culture. She hadn't figured she'd need to know much about art forms when she was coming to find her father. *He* was more likely to be in a bar.

"One of the *sbeik touch*—the small skins. They have been used in performances in Cambodia for a thousand years." Champei reached for the cardboard.

"See, it is made of carved leather." She ran her manicured finger along the edge of the plastic-protected leather that was no thicker than a very fine watchband. "The talent was almost lost in the bad times, but the art is coming back."

"But what's it for?" Kaitlin asked.

"To tell stories. To teach the ways of life. I hear that students use them to teach about AIDS and clean water in the countryside." Her face brightened. "There is a place in Phnom Penh where they teach how to make them. They will even teach tourists. Perhaps your father made this?"

Kaitlin accepted it back and considered the puppet. Not exactly a normal thing for her father to do. "But why send it to me?"

She turned the puppet package over in her hands, then looked at the envelope again. Her father's flourish of lettering spelled out her name and address in bold blue ink. She could practically hear his voice calling her 'girlie'. He'd definitely planned on this getting to her.

"He didn't ask you to mail it?"

Champei shook her head, sending a whiff of her faint perfume into Kaitlin's tender nose.

"Where's this school?"

"Across the city. A place called Sovanna Phum. It does nighttime shows." Champei paused, her face once more a mask of non-emotion as if she wanted to hide uncertainly about what she was about to say.

"What is it?" Kaitlin asked.

Champei met Kaitlin's gaze and held it, and the smaller woman gave a little nod as if Kaitlin had passed some test.

"When your father leave here, he come to the front desk and say he to pay for his room. Strange this, because he pay for two weeks when he arrive and had not stay full time. I try say no when he give me the money, but he look so hard at me I stop." She pulled a slim roll of bills out of a hidden pocket. "Sorry I did not tell you. It yours and I refund what you pay for this room, too."

Kaitlin accepted the money, surprised at the woman's honesty, but also surprised at her father. He could be generous, but to simply give away—she opened the roll and counted—three hundred dollars in fives, tens and twenties, was beyond even his generosity.

"Thank you, for your honesty. Not many people would have given it back."

Stranger and stranger. She rubbed her head, the churning worry cut through the migraine and left her feeling hollow as the Seattle viaduct.

But things were not normal, and when things weren't normal, she needed to expose why—and fix it. That was what had driven her to expose a fencing ring within a suburban police department and the Seattle end of a tentacle of an international human smuggling ring.

She flipped through the bills again. Too much money and a shadow puppet. *What the heck are you trying to tell me, Dad?*

"Can you get me a ticket for a Sovanna Phum show? For tonight, preferably."

Champei nodded, but looked concerned. "Are you sure you ok?"

Kaitlin stood up, ignoring the pain. The little tingle in the back of her neck said that her investigative radar had locked on something.

A sound in the hallway, followed by another knock on the door, brought Champei to her feet. A voice came through the door.

"Pich. My brother."

Kaitlin nodded and Champei opened the door. Pich shoved inside, his Mohawk disheveled. The metallic tang of his fear undercut the hallway scent of rice and curry. He didn't even look at Kaitlin's bare legs.

He grabbed Champei's hands and words rushed out of him.

"What's happened?"

"Men came. They ask for the Blackwood woman," Champei said, her face tight with fear. "It happen again."

The frangipani-scent swirled and Kaitlin swallowed back bile and the memory of her confrontation in the street.

"What men? What did they look like?"

Champei spoke rapidly and then translated her brother's answer.

"One was small, thin but strong, with a terrible scar down the side of his neck. He wear simple pants and a shirt, but he did not look comfortable in them. The other taller. He wear brown shirt and trousers—like uniform."

"Let me guess—he had black teeth."

"How did you know?"

The same way she had known there was a story inside the anonymous phone call she'd received about the Everett police department. Or the way she'd known something wasn't right about the woman who claimed she had adopted five foreign orphan girls, all between the ages of five and eight.

The same way she knew she was going to follow her nose and find out just what mess her father had landed her in.

Chapter 9

Sweat ran a river down B.J.'s back and chest, plastering his shirt to his skin. The sun beat down like a forge hammer on his head and placed stark shadows on the Bayon Temple's many faces. Towering thunder clouds, blown northwestward up the length of the Tonle Sap River and Lake, promised more monsoon rains. The rain had already shifted the direction of the river into the northward inundation that annually flooded the huge inland lake and surrounding countryside.

But right now, the bloody heated moisture in the air meant nothing, because all the heat was coming from the man in front of him.

"I didn't have a damn thing to do with it," B.J. said. "I had arranged to meet him here to take photographs, but when I got here, I didn't see him."

The small man in his khaki uniform just puffed on the ubiquitous acrid cigarette, adding his nicotine stench to the tang of bus diesel as the tour-bus groups were waved off by the hordes of police guarding the crime scene.

Not good for business, that. The Vietnamese owners of the Archeological Park were going to be right pissed off.

The officer's eyes were masked by a pair of well-cared-for Vietnam War era aviator sunglasses, but he seemed to study the body before them. The police hadn't even covered the dead monk's face, and now a seething pall of flies battled over the blood and gore like something out of a horror movie. B.J. wanted to look away but knew he'd lose face, and this was one of those match-ups where the small guy was trying to prove whose pair was bigger.

"You ask him here. This suggest you have something to do with death, Mr. McCallum."

"I told you. He agreed to meet me to do some early morning shots. I wanted to compete with John McDermott—if that's possible."

The cop barely shrugged under the weight of the attitude he carried. As if he didn't know or care that John McDermott was the artist who had taken some of the seminal shots of Angkor. "And so you were successful in getting him alone. A good time to kill him."

"In a pig's arse. I wasn't successful. He never showed up."

The cop glanced down at the body as if that were proof enough.

"Okay. He was here, but I didn't know it. This must have happened before I arrived."

But the bloody cop just wasn't getting it. He didn't want to get it when he had a perfectly good foreign fall guy standing in front of him.

Or else the cop was purposely being thick—which he could be, if he were expecting some kickback to make this go away.

"I think you will come with me, Mr. McCallum. We will talk more fully at the station." He motioned towards the paved walkway that led between the temple and the parking lot. A busload of tourists were corralled at the parking lot edge, where the young woman who had found B.J. was the center of attention as she sobbed and retold her story again and again.

"Maybe you should take care of that, mate. Yer witness is being contaminated."

A slight flush rose above the smaller man's collar. "I know my business, Mr. McCallum. Now you will come with me."

"But I've told you everything." B.J. wanted to grab the cop and shake him like one of those cheap little plastic ball games, where you tried to get all the metal balls into multiple slots.

"You were witnessed over the body. You have blood on your hands. That is a good enough reason?" The cop tipped his head to peer over his glasses.

The man had to have kangaroos loose in his top paddock, or bats in his belfry as the Americans said. B.J. took a deep breath and let it out, tasting the cop's lovely secondhand smoke. He could use one of the bloody tubes o' death himself right now.

"Why would I pack in all my equipment, if I wasn't here to do photography? Stuff weighs a ton."

"And where is that so-heavy equipment, Mr. McCallum?"

B.J. blew out a long, overtaxed breath. "I told you. I left my camera bags and tripod over by the trees."

"And there is the problem." He tugged off his glasses to expose eyes so black and opaque, B.J. almost took a step back. Crazy-man eyes. Then the cop smiled, and that didn't help matters, either. Worse, in fact, when the lips smiled, but the eyes did not.

He waved at the pond and a cop stepped out from under the trees and shook his head.

"We know there is no equipment, Mr. McCallum. Foolish to use a story so easy to check."

Everything inside B.J. went cold even as sweat stung his eyes.

"But I carried the stuff in…."

The cop caught his arm.

"Enough lies, Mr. McCallum. What I want is the gun."

Chapter 10

How much farther is it?"

Kaitlin leaned forward out of the four-seat passenger compartment to tap the helmeted moto-taxi driver on the shoulder. He barely glanced back at her as he dodged through the huge melee these people called a traffic circle, and then turned down a side street lined with walled compounds.

Seven twenty p.m. after a day of nursing the migraine and eating the rice and fish curry Champei brought her that, thankfully, wasn't too fiery. She'd called Mac to tell him she was going to be a few more days and he'd understood. At least he said he did, but she knew he didn't like her 'just running off.'

Dusk over Phnom Penh had turned the sky a bruised purple-blue, filled with clouds of huge bats that Kaitlin's *Fodor's* said lived in trees and in the tiered temple-like roof of the National Museum—the place she'd spotted behind the Foreign Correspondents' Club. The scent of charcoal braziers and roasting fish filled the air—along with the constant whine of the bone-jarring, migraine-bursting, moto-taxi. Each bump brought a renewed burst of jackhammer pain, but she could do this.

Except the damned ride was taking long enough that maybe she wasn't being taken to Sovanna Phum. Maybe the good-looking young taxi driver was working for Black-tooth. Except Champei and Pich had vouched for the driver.

She was being stupid. Everything was fine.

The machine bounced over the pitted pavement, and a rising, rain-scented wind played in her hair and tossed in the trees that still lined some of the stately old streets of the city. Surprising that the buildings were still there. According to her *Fodor's*, Pol Pot and the Khmer Rouge had razed many of the old French buildings as he emptied the city.

The moto-taxi shook-rattle-rolled around a corner onto what looked like a residential street, and pulled a U-turn to stop in front of a dilapidated, metal-sided building that wouldn't have claimed the dignity of 'warehouse' back home.

A painted sign with pictures of shadow puppets proclaimed it to be Sovanna Phum. Not exactly what she expected, but what had been, so far?

She paid the driver and he revved his engine and rattled off down the street, and for a moment she felt cut loose and alone and floundering in the shadows that spread in the street. So she had better do this. She'd made up her mind when she added talking to the puppet makers to her list of things to do.

A front gate guarded a small, paved courtyard lit by a single, swaying electric bulb. A crowd of local people and a few ragged backpackers filled the space and she hugged her day-pack closer to her side. The backpackers eyed her tidy shirt and trousers with a road-weary superiority. A cacophony of Asian musical instruments wafted from deeper in the building and set her vision trembling.

"For show?" A short, round Cambodian man smiled and pushed a ticket at her as a local family with three neatly dressed young children eased past into what had to be the performance area. At least, that was where the annoying—well, maybe not annoying, but certainly weird—music came from.

She shook her head at the ticket seller.

The eldest child—a boy—smiled back at her. "Hello," he said. "Pen?" Hopefully.

His mother shushed him and dragged him inside before Kaitlin could react. She turned back to the ticket seller.

"I need to talk to someone about shadow puppets."

He grinned and nodded. "For show?"

Clearly, her English was beyond him.

She scanned the people for someone who might speak English. One of the backpackers shook his head, whether in answer to her seeking, or in dismissal that she even wanted someone who spoke her language.

She sighed and turned back to the ticket seller. In for a penny, in for a pound. If she wanted to speak to anyone in authority, she obviously needed to get inside.

She held out the ticket Champei had got her, and the little man studied it for a moment and then stepped aside.

She followed the crowd inside to a small, better-lit area that included a gift shop.

Hung among Sovanna Phum t-shirts and brightly painted demon-like masks, four-foot tall shadow puppets hung from the ceiling like pterodactyl wings. The huge, intricately carved, red-brown leather forms made her puppet look like a child's work for its simplicity. The light through the puppet's elaborate cutwork reminded her of the paper snowflakes she and her mother had made and hung on their tree when they were too broke for real Christmas ornaments.

But these were far from geometric cut-outs. They were intricate renditions of men or women or monsters walking or riding chariots. Animals were carved at their feet, and foliage or towers surrounded them.

"What can you tell me about them?" Kaitlin asked the young shopkeeper wearing a Sovanna Phum t-shirt.

The girl considered the huge shadow puppet of a man driving a chariot with palm trees and flowers behind him. The girl only produced a book and flipped the pages until she found the puppet Kaitlin had admired. She slid her finger down to the price.

"Three hundred fifty dollars," she said in a lilting voice.

Clearly she wasn't going to get questions answered here, either.

Frustrated, she followed the crowd into a long, narrow room that filled the front of the building with a three-foot high stage set before a set of rickety bleacher-style seating that backed onto the building's metal siding. Basic, but functional.

Dim lights illuminated an empty stage, backed by a plain white sheet that shifted as the air moved. To one side, a group of musicians tuned their godawful instruments. At least she hoped they were tuning them, because right now, the sound caused little shooting stars behind her eyes.

Dammit, where were the managers? Where were the ushers who answered questions? Where was anyone who could look at her puppet and tell her something about it?

Because there had to be something unique about it, some clue that would help her find her misbegotten father.

"Good evening, everyone." A slim man, with a thick head of black hair slicked smoothly back, suddenly appeared out of the crowd wearing another of the theater t-shirts over a dark sarong. Then he launched into Cambodian and people hurried to take their seats.

Kaitlin, more interested in questioning him, perched on the bleacher closest to him and let him talk. But he said very little in English. Just that the performances were the result of performers who had survived the Khmer Rouge's terrors. That the few survivors had created a cooperative that brought them together to present new forms of entertainment that included many of the ancient art forms.

He stepped back into the shadows and the lighting darkened over the bleachers. Spotlights flared on stage and the music began.

And drilled Kaitlin right between the eyes. She winced and dug her fingers into the tops of her thighs. Fought pain with pain, and tears started down her cheeks.

On stage danced a phalanx of ornately dressed female dancers, golden headdresses and gold-flecked, slim-fitting dresses of green and blue and saffron flashing in the spot lights.

Interesting, but not what Kaitlin had come for. She eased towards the shadows where the announcer had been, but he had folded himself to sitting cross-legged amongst the band and narrated in Cambodian.

Damn.

"Would you sit down, already?" An impatient American Southwest accent.

She returned to her seat.

The dancers *were* beautiful. Graceful beyond anything she ever hoped to be, with her big feet and her writer's long, bony fingers. These women looked like their delicate hands were lotus blossoms that could be bruised by a breeze.

When they shuffled delicately off-stage, a bright light shone behind the sheet at the back of the stage. It illuminated huge, fan-like shadows that depicted a princely entourage. This puppet that had to be four feet in diameter danced across the sheet until a male warrior-prince dancer and another dressed as an ogre leapt onto the stage.

The audience leaned forward. There was no hope of talking to anyone at the moment. They were all involved in the performance.

Ornate fabric flashed as warring kings and demons, an ancient wizard, a lovely maiden, and Hanuman, the green-faced monkey-king, all cavorted across the stage.

Behind them, black and white battled as huge, intricate shadow figures interacted and interlaced with small, amazing, jointed puppets, frisking across the sheet at the rear of the stage. Of course, the shadows of the puppeteers also shone through the sheet, but they danced in unison with their puppets so their grace came through. Even though she didn't know the language, she could follow the story well enough: the abducted princess, the handsome prince, and Hanuman, the monkey-king, who helped defeat the demon and rescue the princess.

The audience was rapt. Even the toddlers. Only the backpackers squirmed a little on the hard seats at the low-tech performance.

And her. But heck, after sixteen hours in an economy seat from Sea-Tac Airport, how bad could this be?

Flutes wailed, cymbals crashed, and sparks shot through her vision, but when the show ended, it left her feeling empty again—like she'd peered through a screen at something rare and lovely and almost lost. Which was a whole lot of hooey, and probably just the result of the jet lag.

Then the narrator spoke in English again, offering the chance to try working the shadow puppets.

Kaitlin was on her feet and first in line, ignoring the dancers who posed for photos.

The narrator led her and two others around the stage to where white light glared against the fabric, and tried to hand them off to the puppeteers and a carved leather puppet the size and shape of an elephant's ear that was held up by a rickety bamboo support system.

"Please." She stopped him before he could leave. "The puppets are wonderful, but I need to talk to someone."

He looked back the way he'd come.

"We are busy. You see?" He waved an arm towards the front of the house. He was a small man. Neat. About forty, if she could read Asian faces. The glaring light placing skeletal shadows on his face.

"Please?" Kaitlin turned her best smile on him. "I'd be happy to wait. I need someone to look at a puppet and tell me what they can about it."

The man frowned. "Take it to puppet maker."

"That's the problem. I don't know who made it. I was hoping it was made here."

"You come back tomorrow." But by the dismissive way he said it, she was certain that tomorrow the place would be closed or there'd be no one who spoke English.

"I can't," she insisted and felt the glances of the tourists learning about the puppets and knew her insistence was everything people hated in American travelers. "I was given the puppet as a gift by my father. It's important I learn where it came from."

She didn't want to give away her situation, but perhaps trading on his sympathies would help. She leaned towards him, aware of the strong curry scent off his clothes, and lowered her voice. "Please. He's disappeared."

His gaze skittered away like he wanted to bolt. Or send her away. He *was* the right age to have lived through the mass disappearances of the Khmer Rouge, where knowing someone who had disappeared was a good way to disappear yourself. Had she made a mistake?

He ran his hands through his slicked-back hair, leaving it harried and jagged and looked at the puppeteers, who had both stopped their demonstrations. Past them were shadows beyond the light, where his gaze locked as if he were afraid of something.

Or someone.

All the little hairs rose on the back of Kaitlin's neck.

The man grabbed her wrist. "You come with me."

The gesture was so reminiscent of Black-tooth's actions that she almost resisted. But she needed his information. She followed, out from behind the stage to the musician's area and across it.

He pushed open the door to a room with a small, night-darkened window, a cluttered desk, and a single glaring electric bulb. "Wait here."

He almost shoved her inside.

Then the door slammed shut behind her.

Chapter 11

Edith Marie McCallum hadn't raised stupid sons—or at least B.J. kept telling himself that as he shoved the damned bike with the deflated tire through the night-masked jungle of Angkor Archeological Park. Spectral ground mists threaded through the huge fromage trees, hiding the trees' trailing roots so they blocked the limping roll of the bike and he stubbed his toes. The mosquitoes buzzing his face and arms demanded a continuous Aussie salute, and frogs and night insects cheeped all around.

It wasn't stupid that he was headed back to the "scene of the crime" and sneaking into the park with only the moon behind the clouds to light his way. Well, not shit-house crazy, anyway. And he did have the torch and jackknife stuffed into his back pocket, but he was saving the battery for when he reached the Bayon. And the jackknife—well, that he hopefully wouldn't need.

Nope. Not stupid. At least not stupid enough, but then, what is after about six—or was it twelve?—tallies of amber fluid and a conversation with Nick in the Traveler's Bar. Nope. Not much was going to dissuade him from returning to find his camera equipment.

The stuff couldn't just bloody up and walk away on its own. Nope. Someone had relieved him of his equipment and he wasn't having none of that.

Nick always was one for the good idea—this time with his hilarious tales of the Cambodian police's incompetence.

If he really thought about it, it was actually the police who left him with no choice but to do this. Forced him, really.

First not believing him, then the arrest, and then the hours of farcical interrogation at the police station, because they had no gun and nothing but circumstantial evidence. When the police captain had still wanted to hold him apparently because he *was* a foreigner, only the surreptitious transfer of an American hundred dollar bill and the confiscation of his passport had helped oil the police doors open. How many ways could he be accused in pigeon-English of something he hadn't done before it became as absurd as a Monty Python skit?

Well, he was going to prove them wrong—or liars. Twenty grand worth of professional photography equipment did not just go walkabout. Not when there had been exactly no one at the site except him yesterday morning.

And a dead monk.

Seeing Maly this morning had just reinforced that he had to take action. It had been right after the police released him and after the motorcycle ride out to the orphanage. The wood-sided, stilted building had gleamed in the late morning sunlight, mist rising off of the ground around the buildings and from the water in the greening rice paddies beyond in the blazing sun. He'd slung his leg off of the motorcycle and arranged for the driver to pick him up a little past three that afternoon. He carried with him his usual small bag of gifts—pens and crayons for the children, new chalk for the school blackboards, a new storybook written in Khmer that he'd spotted in Phnom Penh.

He hadn't even been there a minute before there came a shout and a flood of kids came shoving out of the school building. The older kids, all of eleven or twelve; the youngest only five. They came laughing and yelling out to him, plucking at his hands, shouting greetings, the littlest ones hanging off his legs as he held the bag above them.

"You are not teaching them anything of manners," said Jorani, proprietress of the orphanage, with mock sternness as she exited the school, wiping her hands on an apron. She was a slim woman, as all Cambodian women were slim. Of middle age, her face was still relatively unlined and her dark hair was still black except for the slightest grey strands around her face. All of this belied the extraordinarily difficult life she had lived. She moved with a smooth grace and calm and gentleness that was what these children needed after what they had been through.

She ran her hands over small dark heads as she came up to him and, feigning indignation, held out her hands. "So. Give it to me. I won't have you teasing them."

B.J, made a show of being a bad boy caught in misbehavior and relinquished the bag.

"Thank you," she said sweetly in Khmer. "It is very kind of you to bring us gifts." She gave the evil eye to the children around her.

"It is very kind of you to bring us gifts," the children chorused on cue.

"Very nice. Now head back to the school and keep working on your numbers. I will be back in a moment and will decide who deserves these fine gifts."

Suddenly the flock of twenty-five children dispersed and were gone. B.J. almost felt lonely after the crush of childish warmth. "Sorry," he mumbled. "They saw me before I had a chance to get the stuff to the office."

"And you are not sorry at all, you bad influence. You have got to think twice before bringing new gifts like clockwork every time you go to the city. The children are going to start thinking about you like they do the tourists."

He turned to face her and caught her arms, then shook his head. "I will never be just passing through, Jorani. I'm not one of those people who comes for the short haul. I'm staying." He nodded at the bag. "There's school supplies and so on, a couple of bottles of aspirin and antibiotic ointment, along with more water purification tablets—hopefully enough to last until we get the well situation sorted out." He'd paid for a well to be drilled, but the water flow seemed sporadic, so he'd arranged for the driller to return—something that was eating into the little operating reserves they had.

"It is not all on you, B.J. I have plans to bring money into the orphanage."

"So how's Maly?" He changed the subject and held his breath, just like he always did when he'd been away for awhile. She hadn't been amongst the other children, and that never boded well.

Jorani dropped the mock scolding and shook her head. "In her dorm, being quiet. I did not want to stress her. She had another spell this morning."

Another spell. His stomach clenched and his shoulders with it. "Damn it. And it isn't looking like I'm going to get that visa any sooner." He held back on telling her anything about his adventure at the temples earlier this morning. It would just worry her and running an orphanage was surely enough worry.

Maly had begun having these *spells* not long after she'd joined them three years before. In addition to the sexual abuse she'd endured at the hands of a child prostitution ring in Phnom Penh, she'd also been beaten. She'd started having what they'd first thought of as fainting spells, but now they looked to B.J.'s untrained eye as something akin to epilepsy.

"Guess I'll visit her, then." He expertly relieved Jorani of the bag and fished in its contents for a single wrapped candy and held it up in triumph when Jorani grabbed the bag from him. "A single sweet isn't going to turn her into a beggar. Now leave me be."

He grinned and headed across to the dorms, leaving Jorani shaking her head behind him.

The girl's dorm was identical to the boys, a single-story stilted, rectangular building built over a shaded open area, with hammocks hung between the stilts and children's toys scattered about. Child-sized shirts and skirts and trousers were hung on a clothesline to dry around the base of the house.

"B.J.!" came a little-girl squeal, and then a dark-haired missile launched itself at him from the ladder up into the dorm. It forced him back into the shadows of the area under the building. Maly's arms were around his neck in the nicest welcome he'd had in years. He held her away from him. She had waist length black hair, dark brown eyes, and a crooked smile that could melt your heart. She also had a horrible white scar along the hairline on her left temple that ran back into her hair, the gift from some none-to-kindly patron.

"I thought you were supposed to be resting?" he said with a mock scold in his voice.

"How could I rest when I saw my old friend B.J. was here? Besides, it's boring." She spoke in careful English, partially learned from the foreign men who had abused her.

It broke his heart, and yet it seemed to have made her even more determined.

She bounced on her toes with all the energy of a child cooped up for too long, but it was for her own good. He produced the candy. "For my best girl."

A quick grab that he didn't try too hard to avoid. "Thank you!" she said from around the sweet.

"And then there's this." He magically produced a book from under his shirt—it was in English—and held it out to her.

Maly's eyes grew huge. "For me?"

"Of course for you. Who else is learning English so well? Who else has plans to be an interpreter and someday work for the United Nations?"

She accepted the book and clutched it to her chest like she was afraid he might take it back.

"I just saw it in Phnom Penh and thought you might like it."

She held the book away from her chest and then looked up at him and shook her head. "This is different book. Good book, good cover, and it smell different, too. Not like Cambodian."

Gods, she was sharp. He couldn't even put that over on her. Actually, he'd ordered the book online months ago, *A Child's Treasury of Fairy Stories from Around the World*. He'd thought she'd enjoy reading it because it would give her an insight into the beliefs of other cultures.

"So should we read one of those stories, then?" Time to change the subject. The way she was looking at him with those huge luminous eyes, it was like he was her savior or something—and he didn't fancy being anyone's savior. Far too much pressure.

So they'd sat in the shade below the dorm, Maly rocking in a hammock and exclaiming over the stories and the pictures, and him seated on the ground beside her, helping her with the words that were new and explaining some of the concepts to her. She was always a delight to teach.

But the whole time, all he could think of was how his passport had been confiscated and just how was he going to help Maly if he couldn't take her out of Cambodia for medical attention—or worse, if his visa application was denied because of the murder accusation—and he couldn't help Jorani with the orphanage.

And so, twelve hours later, he was here in the Archaeological Park, because under Nick's tutelage it had seemed like such a good idea to try to prove someone else had been at the Bayon and taken his equipment. Someone else who could have killed the monk, which might help to clear his name.

Of course, once he rented the bicycle and started the over-seven-and-a-half-mile ride out here, things started to go wrong. First the problem with his ass on the worn seat, and then the way his little Nikon 300 banged against the handle bars, and now the bloody flat tire.

Things were definitely mounting up in the 'you might want to rethink this' category.

"Bollocks. 'Am not tha' drunk," he said, and tripped again on one of the bloody tree roots.

Ahead, moonlight filled the wide, gravel parking lot and the road that led from the Bayon back towards the overgrown walls of Angkor Thom, the largest of the temple complexes. The same road continued through the park and on to more of the ruins. He paused in the shadows of the trees, inhaling the night moisture and the scent of monsoon mud and green growth.

A hint of something burning made him scan the area. Huge, harmless fruit bats skimmed the surface of the trees, their wings making ghostly whooshing sounds. The constant cheep-groan-hum of insects and frogs was enough to make his head ache and the bloody mozzies—mosquitos—feasting off him would have made a tourist run screaming.

He futilely waved them off.

In front of him, the Bayon hunkered, its fifty-four moonlit, four-faced towers gazing at him as if they could barely believe he was back.

"Yeah, I'm here, ya wankers. Ya saw something today and I'm gonna find out what."

The faces remained annoyingly impassive, until they disappeared in darkness as a rain-heavy wind blew towering cumulonimbus clouds across the moon. Darkness flooded everything, erasing the reflections from the pools near the temple, and with them some of B.J.'s boozy good vibes.

Something wasn't right.

The burning scent wasn't a cook fire from one of the vendor kiosks farther down the road. Besides, any of those should be closed at two in the morning. If someone lived there, the scent should be lost before it reached him in the misty miasma of heated jungle and cooling night air.

He inhaled deeply. *Clear the haze from the ol' noggin, mate.* But the cast to the air smelled like—tobacco. Something any ex-smoker would recognize.

Which meant perhaps the Bayon ruins weren't as abandoned as they seemed.

He carefully leaned the useless bike up against a tree, grabbed the camera around his neck to stop it from banging into anything, and ultra-silently—he hoped—began to circumnavigate the parking lot to the road. It made the most sense that any police guard for the crime scene would probably be there. He'd learned that much, trying to beat such cordons in search of the perfect front page photo.

Course, that was a long time ago, but he still had the chops.

Lamb chops, ya bloody wanker. That's gonna help ya a lot.

He pushed through tree branches, eased along small paths worn down by the kids who touted post cards and t-shirts, hoping no one noted the occasional snap of a twig or the low oath as he stumbled.

No one camped out along the edge of the parking lot.

Which left the road, which was sheltered by another screen of trees.

He slid through the shadows, waved off the mozzies, and stepped cautiously.

The road came in from the entrance to the park, past famous Angkor Wat, then through the gates of Angkor Thom. When it reached the Bayon, it turned ninety degrees and, still within the Angkor Thom complex, headed towards the crumbling Baphuon and the Leper King Terrace, with its fake of the original statue. A guard could be placed anywhere along the road, but he'd bet on them being at the corner.

When he was almost there, the alluring, bitter scent of burning tobacco found his nose. He stopped.

Somewhere near. The mozzies took his stillness as the opportunity to swarm his nose and eyes, but finally he was rewarded by a small red flame flaring in the darkness, revealing two men side by side, facing down the road towards the park gates and Siem Reap.

B.J. grinned. Score one for the good guys. Situated to guard against anyone approaching, they'd left the Bayon wide open to anyone who was inside, because they weren't looking in that direction. Plus the screen of trees would block him.

He shivered in the cool night air and realized the lovely alcohol glow was passing. Nothing another beer wouldn't fix, but that would have to wait for the stools at the Traveler's Bar.

Back to the parking lot and its moonlit expanse to where the Bayon's many faces reflected in the stillness of the monsoon-created pool. Along the shore huddled the small forms of the geese that paddled there during the day. He skirted them carefully, because the last thing he needed was raucous geese tearing into him.

The tree where he'd left his camera gear sat with long branches almost trailing in the water. He ducked, careful of the spider webs. Bloody poisonous bastards gave him the willies, with their four-inch-long legs and their bloated red-brown bodies, even though they weren't as deadly as the bird spiders he'd run into in China. He took out his torch, narrowed the beam as much as it would go, and checked over his shoulder for the guards, but there was no way a casual glance from their position could see him. He flicked it on.

Yeah. There.

Right near the water for a view through the tree branches, and just as he'd said during the interrogation. Three distinct round impressions from his lightweight, carbon-fiber tripod. Of course, overlaid on them were lug-soled boot imprints. The idiot police hadn't even looked for the marks—or if they had, they'd done their bloody damndest to muck them up. They'd already made up their minds that B.J. had a nice easy target on his back.

Bastards.

He bent down and photographed the scene, making sure both the tripod impressions and the lug sole footprints were clear, and checking over his shoulder each time for the guards.

Completely oblivious.

He shifted angle and was about to snap another shot, when something stopped him. The prints weren't all the same.

Yeah, there were the police prints, but a single large boot print with an odd wave pattern sole stood out like a ram's pecker in a herd o' sheep. Bigger than the Cambodian police prints. He placed his booted foot beside it.

Almost as big as his.

The bastard who had stolen his equipment?

He snapped a couple more photos, his jackknife laid beside the print to provide scale, and stood up.

Right into one of the bloody spider webs.

Fuck.

Chapter 12

Kaitlin spun around as the office door slammed shut.

Flipping hell, what was going on?

The room's single bare bulb swayed back and forth, sending wild shadows over the room's corrugated metal-and-wood walls and battered desk and chairs. Her heart raced and her headache surged. He'd locked her in. He'd damned-well locked her in.

The room stank of cigarette smoke and something sour. Like the bile in her throat—or her fear.

One stride had her to the door, but it swung open and a young woman stood there. Not the woman from the gift shop, but she could be her sister.

Were all these people related?

Long dark hair coiled up in a neat twist at the back of her head. A sarong skirt and the ubiquitous theater t-shirt covered her from head to foot. She had direct, luminous eyes, much like Champei's, but her nose was narrower, with a higher bridge, as if perhaps she had European blood somewhere back in her family tree. Harmless enough looking, but that didn't mean she was.

Her gaze matched Kaitlin's, as if daring Kaitlin to explain what was going on. But that was the woman's task.

"Why was I locked in this room?" Kaitlin demanded.

"Locked? The room was not locked," the woman said coolly and stepped inside.

"Interesting, given I distinctly heard the lock snap shut."

The woman gave her a pitying look. "Now that *is* interesting. Perhaps your imagination runs wild? This door has no lock."

She swung the door towards them. There was no latch at all.

Embarrassment flooded Kaitlin, but she forced herself to meet the woman's gaze. "I'm sorry. I don't know what to say. Except I've had a difficult day, and I think I'm starting to get a little paranoid with all the people pushing me around."

"Paranoid." The young woman mouthed the word as if she tasted it, assessed it.

"It means I'm starting to think everyone is out to get me."

"Ah." A slight bow of head. "Thank you. A new word is a precious thing."

"Your English is very good already." Kaitlin decided to try this again. She held out her hand. "My name is Kaitlin Blackwood. I'm here because I'm trying to find my father and I'm hoping you can help me."

"Now it is my turn to be—paranoid. Do you believe I had something to do with your father?"

"Perhaps. I understand that Sovanna Phum teaches people how to make shadow puppets. I think maybe my father took a lesson."

The woman thought a moment and nodded.

"I am Veata." She pronounced it vee-eh-ta. "I am responsible for the shadow puppets here." She waved her hand in the direction of the stage. "The puppeteers. Ensuring the correct puppets are used and that the lighting is correct for our work."

Kaitlin nodded. "Then you're the person I want to talk to." She swayed. Jet lag, adrenalin overload, and relief all conspired against her. "May we sit down?"

Veata motioned to the chair in front of the desk and swept behind it to take a seat. Kaitlin sank down in relief. The chair was uncomfortably hard and narrow, between arms that seemed placed too high, but she wasn't going to fall down, at least.

She hauled the foot-tall puppet out of her day pack and handed it to Veata. "What can you tell me about it? Did my father make it here?"

Veata hesitated, but then began a critical appraisal of the shadow puppet through the clear plastic.

"May I open it?"

"I suppose…."

"If you are worried about protection, I can have our gift shop rewrap it for you afterwards."

"That would be appreciated. Now what can you tell me?" She leaned forward, elbows on Veata's desk.

Veata scanned the puppet again, turned the package over, and scanned the back of the cardboard once more before meeting Kaitlin's gaze. "First I would understand what this is about." She shook her head. "I am sorry, but I will not make trouble for people. My country has had too much as it is."

That set Kaitlin back in her chair, a small, sick laugh escaping her. Caution said she shouldn't share her whole sad story, but what did she have to share except that her father wasn't where he said he'd be and that she had the puppet?

"That's half the problem. I don't really know what's going on—except that I received a letter from my dad saying he was coming home from Cambodia. But he didn't show up, so I came here and tracked back to his hotel. They had this in an envelope with my name on it. I'm trying to find him."

The expression on Veata's face was unreadable. Her gaze hung on Kaitlin as if assessing, but finally the Cambodian woman shook her head and smiled.

"I'm sorry. It is the nature of Cambodia now to hold suspicions. Our country was betrayed from within and even now our countrymen betray us." She stopped. "But I speak of things that should not be spoken of. To lose someone—to have them disappeared—that is a thing that steals a soul. You spend your life seeking them, always catching glimpses of them where they do not exist. Always hoping." She nodded too knowingly and looked back at the puppet.

"This is similar to a tree of life puppet. They are commonly sold as tourist puppets."

Kaitlin closed her eyes. She'd been afraid of this. Her father had simply left her a trinket like the ubiquitous t-shirt: *my parents went to* place name of foreign country here *and all they brought me was this t-shirt.*

The crackle of the plastic being removed brought her eyes open. Veata had the fine piece of leather out and had turned it over. "As I thought. This is a student's puppet." She must have caught Kaitlin's puzzled glance for she continued. "Across Cambodia, those who have the old skills are trying to save our ancient arts after the Khmer Rouge almost wiped them out. They have started weaving schools and dance studios and schools in the making and performance with the *sbeik touch.* This puppet comes from such a school."

"How can you tell?"

Veata smiled. "That is easy. You see here?" She pointed to a small indentation of the leather. "The maker began to punch a hole and then stopped himself."

She frowned and turned the puppet right side up again on the white cardboard, then turned it over again, before settling it on the cardboard.

"What is it?"

A shake of her head and another frown, and Veata motioned Kaitlin to be quiet as she bent to study the puppet more closely. Finally she exhaled in seeming frustration and raised her gaze to Kaitlin.

"This puppet is a puzzle. Its shape is not right for a true tree of life, though generally it is like a tree. It shows uncharacteristic marks—like the mistakes of a student, and yet the chisel and hammer marks of the cutouts show the clean edges of a master puppet maker."

As she spoke she showed how the tree should be fuller at the top, and not so spread out. This tree of life puppet had drooping foliage, more like a weeping willow that had had its long tendrils cut off like bangs, exposing the broad, twisted trunk.

"See how the trunk twists into the branches? That is not right, either. It should flow straight up and disappear immediately into the leaves."

Veata shook her head and placed her hands on either side of the puppet. She stood. "I'm sorry. That is all I can say. Your puppet is an... enigma. At least I think that is the right word. Often, if the puppet is made by a master, I can tell who the maker is, but this is unclear—almost as if the maker wished to hide himself or herself and so he makes mistakes on purpose." She slid the puppet across at Kaitlin, who had no choice but to stand as well.

Frustrated, she picked the puppet up. A lot of technical puppet-making stuff that really didn't make sense and a whole lot of nothing else helpful. "So the puppet might have been made by a student, or by a master trying to hide that he made it."

"Yes."

"Why would a master puppeteer do that?"

Veata shrugged, but then met Kaitlin's eye. "Sometimes being known for your work is not a good thing. The Cambodian people learned that under the Khmer Rouge. Those who were known for the excellence of their work were the first to be taken away. Or perhaps there is something more to this puppet and they do not want their identity known for other reasons."

Dammit, wasn't anything in this going to be easy?

She wanted to swear at the puppet, at her father—at anyone involved in this fool's errand she'd been sent on—but most of all at her dad.

She should have gone straight to the airport when she'd found out her father wasn't at the Mayview. She shouldn't have let herself be sucked into his ridiculous ventures, but now—now she had to admit she was getting intrigued. Not only had her father disappeared, but there was a puzzle in this puppet, and puzzles—real-life puzzles, not some silly paper-and-pencil crossword or Sudoku—were things she liked to solve.

"All right. So the puppet maker doesn't want to be known. Where might such a puppet maker be?"

"You would try to find him—or her?" Veata's expression had turned to one of concern, perhaps more for the puppet-maker than for Kaitlin.

"Please. I have to find my father."

Veata thought a moment, as if carefully choosing her words. "There are makers of tourist puppets all over Cambodia now, but traditionally the puppets were made near Siem Reap, near Angkor, where legend says they first came into being when a housekeeper in the King's household saw the shadow patterns that could be made with a piece of cow hide. That is where the oldest masters teach. That is where I would go."

The way she phrased it, it was almost like Veata was reluctant to make the recommendation. Was she protecting Kaitlin, or was she protecting someone else? Either way, Kaitlin felt like a vortex was sucking her in—to her father's stupidity if nothing else.

But Veata edged towards the door, clearly wanting free of Kaitlin.

Smart girl.

Kaitlin sighed and slid the puppet back onto the cardboard and wrapped the tatters of plastic around it. "You said you could rewrap this for me."

Veata nodded and led her from the room. The performance area had emptied out, leaving only the musicians in the shadows, putting their instruments away, and a lone man with a broom, sweeping away the audience debris. The curtain billowed at the back of the stage, but without the light and shadow of the performance, the stage seemed lifeless.

At the gift shop Veata flicked on the light and went to a small machine in the rear of the store. "It will take a moment to heat up."

Silence filled the room and Kaitlin shuffled around, examining the puppets. Huge elephant-ear panels and smaller figures with moveable parts manipulated by sticks attached to the limbs of the figures. "There seem to be two types."

"Yes. The *sbeik thom*, or big skin, can be as big as two meters and tells the traditional story of the Ramayana. The small skins, or *sbeik touch*, like yours, are more common. They are used for tales of everyday life and of battles and heroes and villains." She smiled and touched a lovely little puppet of a monkey with moveable legs. "They allow the puppeteer to get involved with the performance more. And children love them. Ah, it is hot enough."

She turned to the machine, wrapped fresh plastic around the tree puppet, and set the plastic against the heat to seal it. "There you go."

She handed the puppet back to Kaitlin and then ushered her out of the store to the street entrance. "I hope you enjoyed the performance."

"I did. Very much. Thank you for your help."

Veata nodded and then Kaitlin stepped outside and the door clicked shut behind her.

Around her the street was in darkness, save for a distant streetlight. A few passersby glanced at her, and a cool, moist wind carried the scent of mud and fried fish, and heavy clouds promised more rain on the way.

But no moto-taxi plied the streets and she had no idea which way was home.

Chapter 13

The cool night air suddenly went frigid around B.J. Sticky webs surrounded his head and a tree branch almost stuck him in the eye. He could feel the bloody spider's weight shifting the silken lines—or at least he thought so.

A yell bubbled up low in his chest and he didn't dare let it go or he'd be running like a friggin' girl across the parking lot and into the jungle.

Calm, ya wanker. This's what you get for knocking back a few too many tallies.

He sucked it up and slowly, ever so slowly, tore loose of the web and then dove through the trees, whacking his shoulders and head and stomping his feet in a wild dance in case any of the bloody eight-legged freaks had come with him.

When he'd finished and only the occasional tremor ran up his spine, he remembered the police cordon and looked towards the road. Nothing. Thank the gods of drinkers and fools. Or the god of both. Behind him the many famous faces of the Bayon temple stared out at him.

He should just leave. Get out while the getting was good and all that, but he wanted to see the crime scene again. All day he'd been thinking about the bright red gleam he'd seen. As far as he knew, the police hadn't found anything.

Besides, if he was going to be accused of killing the monk, then he wanted a better sense of where it had happened. Better to build a defense that way.

Around the pool, he picked his way through the lines of stones. His nice glow was wearing thin enough that caution began to set in. He was an idiot for doing this, but he needed to know, and the only way that was going to happen was if he saw the scene again. That was what a photographer did, didn't he? He helped clear everyone else's vision with his photographs.

At least that was how it'd been when he worked as a photojournalist. Before all the shit came down.

Well, you're making your own shit up now, boyo. Yer dad would be so proud.

Hell, his father would disown him if he saw what B.J. was doing with his life. Thank God the old man was dead.

When he got to the roped off area, he hurdle-stepped over and hauled out his flashlight, made sure it was on the finest pencil beam and, after checking over his shoulder once more, clicked it on and kept the light close to the ground.

The scene was the same as he remembered, except instead of sunlight, there were only the stars and the moon and the monsoon clouds over the many-faced spires of the Bayon. He shot it a couple of times using infrared film so a flash wasn't necessary, using the police procedure of setting the scene with an establishing shot, and then moving in for the midrange and close-ups.

There were the two lines of stone—some stained black with the monk's blood. He'd been stretched out here, almost like he'd been running, or had fallen as he reached for something.

Something that gleamed red.

B.J. ran his narrow light along the trench between the stones. More dark stain. It looked sticky where pools of it had dried. What would bring the monk out here—other than the photo shoot? Was the photo shoot just a convenient cover for some other meeting the monk had?

But what for? He was a monk, fer God's sake. How many clandestine meetings would a monk have?

He slid the light along the trench, but anything that might have been there had been scooped by the police. Which was a good thing, if he thought they'd do something with it.

He moved down the trench to where the monk had been reaching. If he'd been running to get away and been killed as he ran, then he might have let something fall down here.

The trench was barren except for the straggling grass that grew up between the stones.

Something red flashed as he passed his light over the stacked stone and he brought his flashlight back. Another flash and he went down on one knee. A crack in one of the lines of stone was directly in line of sight with where he'd been shooting from this morning. He held the flash in his teeth and parted the grass, and something bright tumbled back into the crack.

Bloody hell, what was that?

He tried to wedge his fingers into the crack, but succeeded only in tearing a nail to the quick and sat back on his haunches. Then he hauled out the jackknife and poked it into the crack.

A small click of metal on something harder than stone. Hard, and slick enough the point of the blade just slid right off.

He eased the knife blade a little higher and farther back and gently flipped whatever it was forward. Again. Again.

Something almost round tumbled out of the crack and into the grass. B.J. scooped it up and played the light over it.

Large, covered in rough stone and earth, but the stone beneath it glowed red at its heart.

The last of B.J.'s alcohol haze disappeared.

Big red. Just what the hell had he gotten himself involved in? A low whistle escaped him and he shook his head.

Which sent the blow, aimed for the back of his head, glancing sideways off his left shoulder.

He toppled sideways, fighting the fireworks in his brain and the crippling numbness in his left arm that made him drop his flash.

Darkness—and he could barely see except for the larger darkness coming at him.

B.J. threw himself sideways again, then saw the dull gleam of gunmetal in the moonlight. Shit.

His knife was a piece o' shit against that, but for some reason the guy hadn't shot him already, and that was bloody good news.

He got his feet under him and lunged at his attacker, keeping the red stone in his fist like a roll of quarters. *Blam.* His right fist found the other man's face.

The gun came up and B.J. fought for his life, wrestling the gunman with his bad arm to deflect the aim outward.

Shitshitshit.

The stink of mud and rice-breath filled B.J.'s nose. Not clean as most Cambodian's were, and the man was Cambodian. At least he was small, quick, light, and wiry. Too strong for his size as he wrestled the gun free. Turned it towards B.J.

"Stop right there!" in quavering Cambodian.

The yell from the parking lot froze both B.J. and his attacker. Count on the police to come now. Good thing, right, mate?

Like he could afford another trip to the station.

His attacker was already fading back and away. Not a bad idea.

B.J. grabbed his flash and ran.

Chapter 14

The sweeping, white façade of the Grand Hôtel d'Angkor and the lush lawns before it seemed surreal after the too long, too crowded, too bumpy bus ride from Phnom Penh to Siem Reap. Brilliant calla lilies bloomed amidst the pink and purple bougainvillea. Palms placed long, evening shadows across the white façade. Jasmine even scented the air that was heavy with exhaust fumes from the nearby highway that Kaitlin's rear end knew far too well.

Eleven. Frigging. Hours. Eleven hours of her life she'd never get back, following a last hellish night in Phnom Penh after being locked out of Sovanna Phum and having to find her own way back to the Mayview Hotel.

She'd started walking in the direction she thought she should go, feeling conspicuous and vulnerable but determined not to show it. Just be her reporter-self and she was good to go—wasn't she? It had done her well back home and had taken her into some of the worst gang and crack houses in the Seattle area. Of course, then she'd had time to plan out her approach.

But in Phnom Penh there'd been no plan and no time to create one, complete with all the requisite lists. It had just seemed that the stupidest thing she'd done in her life had been coming here. The trouble was, she'd been picking up the pieces for her father for too many years, and this was typical. He always dragged her in and left her spinning like some leaf in a vortex.

It was a long walk to the next main street, and the darkness of the road seemed like her life. She always looked for the darkness, didn't she?

Her father had said that to her once. "You gotta look at the upside of things, kiddo. You can cut through a heap of crap that way."

"Well, it feels like I'm smack dab in the midst of the crap, Dad," she grumbled through gritted teeth.

Thank God she'd reached the next main road without being attacked. And when she got there, she'd managed to hail a moto-taxi and show him the card for the Mayview and safety.

Where she'd made her lists and finally decided to come here—swallowed farther into this godforsaken country.

So when she'd stumbled off the bus in Siem Reap at six o'clock, she'd asked the moto-taxi driver to take her to the best hotel in town. She deserved that, at least.

She climbed the broad stairs and went through the double doors into—cool.

Slow-moving fans stirred the air in the cream-colored foyer. Small, ornately-carved tables carried towering, riotous flower arrangements that perfumed the air. Iron-railed broad stairs led up to the next floors. Music reminiscent of that played at Sovanna Phum tinkled through the air, reminding her she wasn't in Seattle anymore. As if she needed that reminder, hot and sweaty and as desperately in need of a shower as she was. But she was tired and she deserved to stay in a nice place tonight.

Squaring her shoulders, she crossed to the broad, floral-carved teak front desk and set down her one small bag. At least she was secure. There was even a security camera high up on the wall.

The male clerk in the pristine white jacket smiled at her. "May I help you, madam?"

At least he was gracious enough to look past her grime and fatigue. "I'd like a room, please. With its own bath." She fished her passport out from under her clothes in readiness for registration.

A slight smile as if to appease someone ridiculous. "All our rooms have full ensuites, madam. And your name is?"

"Kaitlin. Kaitlin Blackwood." To one side of the front desk, a door gave onto a dimly lit room that could only be a bar. The sound of laughter and modern music wafted out like a breath of fresh air.

"Madam, I am sorry. I have not got you listed. Have you a reservation?"

"A reservation? Do I need one?" She turned back to him. "Surely to goodness—you've got a room, right?"

The young man shook his head, his face turned to that neutral Cambodian mask she was beginning to hate. At least back home you knew what people were thinking, because it was written all over them. Here, though, she was beginning to think nothing and no one was what it seemed.

The clerk's fingers flew over his computer console, then he looked at her again. "I am most sorry, madam, but we are fully booked. Perhaps you could try the Angkor Century. It is just down the block. I could call them for you, if you like."

For some reason the announcement that there wasn't a room was the last straw. The migraine she'd babied along sent a jab of pain into her head and she almost staggered before she caught herself. "Please."

She stood there, tapping the counter with her passport as he made the phone call. He spoke rapidly and then covered the receiver. "They are also almost booked, but have a few suites. Would you prefer the Deluxe or the Executive Suite?"

A little alarm went off at the mention of 'suite' because it had taken a good chunk of her savings just to get to Cambodia. While she wasn't averse to spoiling herself, there was no reason to be stupid about it. "Can you ask them how much they are?"

His face twisted a moment as if people didn't speak of cost much here. But he asked.

"Three hundred and eighty for the Deluxe. Four hundred and eighty for the Executive."

Way too rich for her blood. She shook her head. "I—I think I'll think on it for a moment. Thanks very much."

She turned away and the door to the bar bloomed in front of her again. She felt parched and exhausted and way too filthy for these environs, but dammit, she deserved this. At least a drink.

While she decided if she wanted to put her Visa through its paces with an over-the-top luxury room?

The answer was simple. She was thirsty, after all. She stuffed her passport back under her clothes.

The bar still had the cream walls of the rest of the hotel, but the open spaciousness had been replaced by potted palms and glass-topped wicker tables set discretely amidst the plants. The smell of moist earth cut through the international yeast-scent of beer that reminded her of the Raintree Pub she frequented with her best friend Chloe.

Along the wall, a broad bar had mostly male-occupied stools fronting it, while the tables were filled with khaki-clad tourists nursing gin and tonics after a day spent at the temples of Angkor.

She wound her way through the tables up to a vacant stool beside a man who was drinking alone, because she felt more akin to the men than to the yapping, well-heeled tourists. She sank down, her daypack and rolling suitcase beside her, and a gentle breeze of air-conditioned air blew across her skin. She closed her eyes at the small mercy as the migraine fluttered behind her eyes, like an insistent moth.

"What may I get you?" The bartender, a handsome, white-jacketed Cambodian made her open her eyes.

"A G and T, please. Gin and Tonic." She pulled her pad and pen out of her daypack, intent on planning her next step.

"Well, hello, luv. Fancy meeting you here."

The not-quite-familiar voice turned her in her seat, so she found herself facing the thin form of the man B.J. had been drinking with in Phnom Penh. Her stomach sank. After the arduous trip from the city, the last thing she wanted to do was make conversation.

"Why, hello." She tried to be pleasant. "It's Nick, isn't it?" Meyer or something, and darn it, she should remember. Names were her life.

He stuck out his narrow hand. "Nick Mayerthorpe. I must say, I didn't expect to see you here."

"Why's that?"

"Well, from what B.J. said, you don't enjoy travel. I thought you'd be staying in Phnom Penh, not traveling into the hinterlands, so to speak. It's Seattle, isn't it?"

So B.J.'d talked about her after they'd met in the city. *That* didn't exactly make her happy. She shook her head.

"It's Kaitlin, and I have business here."

The bartender brought the drink and Nick showed a drinker's courtesy and let her sip in silence. "Mmm. Good."

"Best in Siem Reap and why I keep coming back. Inflated prices, though, the buggers."

Nick raised a glass and clinked her rim. "To chance meetings."

She hesitated, but didn't want to appear rude, so she sipped the drink again and faced forward in the international symbol for "I want to be alone."

"Beej, old man, look what the cat dragged in." Nick's voice boomed out across the bar towards the door, and Kaitlin stiffened.

Not that. Please God, not that. Not right now.

But the gods never listened to her, did they? Leastways the tall, male presence that soon loomed up behind her said they certainly weren't listening this time. She should have known. That wasn't an empty seat on the other side of Nick.

The trouble was, she actually felt the heat of the damned man, and, disgustingly, her toes curled with the awareness. The chemical reaction B.J. evoked had always been the problem. *Time to take the offensive, woman.*

She turned on the chair and looked up into his too-bright eyes. Laughing again. Probably at her. They always had.

"You again. I thought we'd agreed you'd stay out of my life," she said. He looked good, even in the gawd-awful chartreuse-colored shirt and tan pants, even if they were grimy at the knee, and looked well-lived in.

"Hard to do, luv, when ya waltz right into *my* bar." He motioned to their environs.

"Well, there should have been a warning label on the bar, then, shouldn't there?" She tossed her sweaty head of hair and turned back to the bar, too aware of his gaze on her back.

"Pardon her, Nick. She never did have a lick o' humor unless someone teased her into it."

"I *have* a sense of humor, thank-you-very-much. It just disappears with liars and cheats."

"Well, old man, I'd say she just took a shot."

She caught a glimpse of Nick's look of admiration. At least she hoped it was admiration. Might have been surprise, too.

"She's good at that. And walking away."

By his tone, he'd be happy if she walked away right now, but she wasn't going to give him the satisfaction. She'd paid for her drink and she was going to enjoy it.

But the bloom had faded off the rose, so to speak. The cool liquid seemed to catch in her throat as B.J. slid onto his stool and turned to Nick. His gaze too often found her as well, and it was like a pressure on her to speak. To be civil.

For Nick, at least, who must hate finding himself in the middle. She took a deep breath.

"So I didn't ask: Just what is it you do in Cambodia?"

Nick and B.J.'s low-voiced conversation ended and they both turned to her. Nick looked surprised, but B.J.'s eyes held that infuriating twinkle.

"I'll be blown, Nick, Seattle can be civil. I'd forgotten that."

She felt the heat creep up her neck. Dammit, how did this man always seem to turn her offensives into defenses in the space of one sentence?

"I'm sorry, okay. I've just traveled up from Phnom Penh. It was a long trip."

"Let me guess: by the dust, I'd say by bus. Should've taken the boat. Or the plane, if you can afford it." B.J. picked up his sweating pint of beer and took a long gulp that worked the tendons in his throat, and for a moment she remembered how those tendons flowed into the muscles down his chest.

Stupid, stupid, stupid, and she wasn't a stupid woman, except she hadn't thought to check for flights to Siem Reap.

And except where B.J. McCallum was concerned. That had been the biggest mistake of her life.

She gripped her drink and turned back to the bar. "I didn't know there were so many options."

"It's a nice bit of scenery up the Tonle Sap River. Gives a sense of the real life," B.J. said.

She didn't answer even though it was impolite.

"She asked what you were doing up here, I think," Nick Mayerthorpe reminded.

But she hadn't asked B.J., she'd asked Nick. Now she just wished they'd just let the conversation die a natural death.

"Been taking photos, if you must know. Tourist shots. Tryin' my hand with a little art stuff now and then."

"And there's Maly, don't forget her," Nick chimed in and she caught B.J. throwing a resentful glance his friend's way.

A girl. Typical. She'd read about western men who felt compelled towards the 'grateful' women of foreign countries.

"How nice for you," she managed and drained her glass and stood. "Nice to see you again," she said—to Nick—and nodded to B.J.

"You don't have to rush off because of us, now do ya, Seattle?"

Damn it, he still could see through her defenses.

"I'm not 'running off.'" She hooked her fingers in air quotes. "I've got a hotel to check into."

Not that she was going to the Angkor Century. There had to be something more reasonably priced in town, and she didn't need B.J.'s recommendation.

She skirted the potted palms and the laughing tourists, striding more confidently than she felt. His gaze was on her. She could feel it. Across the cool breezes of the foyer and out into the heat, where she stopped. The long shadows of the late afternoon lay across the verdant lawn and the circular driveway. She'd wasted enough time traveling today. Find a hotel room and then start her investigation.

She went down to the driveway and two men stepped out of the shadows of the bougainvillea. Both were neatly dressed in simple black tunic jackets and trousers that said hotel staff.

"May we help you, Madam? A car, perhaps?"

A line of taxis stood off to her left, but one of the men had already raised his arm and a small black car with a dented left fender came cruising from the street into the horseshoe-shaped hotel drive.

Something didn't feel right. This was too much like the meeting with black-tooth in Phnom Penh.

But she wasn't in the city anymore. She was in Siem Reap. In Angkor. But something about these men was familiar. They made her think of when she'd climbed off the bus here. Had she seen them there?

Then the black car pulled up in front of her and one of the men grabbed her wrist. The other opened the car door and both pushed.

Chapter 15

The glare of the late afternoon sun outside the hotel half-blinded Kaitlin. The inside of the car yawned dark. The stink of curry-rich sweat off the smaller of the two men was almost as much of an assault as his grip on her wrist.

She tried to twist loose, but the hold on her wrist was too tight. She dropped her bag, prepared to fight, but one of the men scooped the bag up and the other shoved her towards the seat again. As if they knew she'd try this.

If all else fails, scream: the old lesson from self-defense class.

"No!"

"Kaitlin!"

The two men released her—thank God—as B.J. leapt down the stairs far more spryly than she'd have thought his alcohol levels allowed. The sunlight made his evil-colored shirt even more evil—if that was possible—as he caught her hand.

"Glad I caught you. I thought maybe you might want a contact in town. Nick suggested I give ya my card." He held out a business card.

Kaitlin grabbed her bag and stepped away from the car.

"Thanks. I've changed my mind," she said to the two men, not wanting B.J. to know how afraid she'd been. She shifted away from them and accepted B.J.'s card, and waited as the men climbed into the car and sped away. And all the while B.J.'s presence was a palpable heat beside her. Not what she needed. Not what she needed at all, though she was tempted to follow him into the bar again. Another G and T was surely called for after this little episode.

But the last thing she needed was B.J. McCallum knowing something was going on. The darn guy was always acting like a damned knight in shining armor and charging in—except his armor was a tad tarnished these days. Nope. No help from B.J.

She looked down at the card. "Thanks. If I need something I'll call." Like she ever would.

"Is everything all right? Who were those guys?"

She shrugged. She didn't need an idiot Aussie getting involved in her search for her father, even if he did know the country. If B.J. could find his way around, so could she. "Drivers. Just a little more insistent than most." She picked up her bag. "Thanks again."

She motioned for one of the taxis, but B.J. didn't leave. He waited as she climbed in and he passed her bag in after her, then leaned in, those baby-blues intensely on her, another card in his hand.

"If ya haven't got a hotel picked out, for what it's worth, I recommend this one. The Jade Violin. Safe. Clean. Friendly. A couple of gals I know operate it."

She looked at him, but finally accepted the card. He probably knew the 'gals' in the biblical sense, knowing him.

But he smiled, nodded. "Check it out. If that doesn't work, call me. I can suggest something else."

She was just considering a smart retort when he hauled his lean torso out of the taxi, but then bent to the open door one more time.

"Ya can call if ya just want a drink or something, too."

"Sure. I will." Like hell.

He probably saw it in her eyes because he simply closed the cab door and didn't look back as he returned to the hotel.

Kaitlin sank back in the seat, and that was when the shaking hit. Her hands. Her knees. Shit. If B.J. hadn't come out right then, what would have happened to her?

She closed her eyes and fought to keep her breathing steady.

"Where you go, Madam?"

Where, indeed. She sighed. "The Jade Violin."

She wanted to find her father, but safety was suddenly at a premium.

§

Shaking his head, B.J. climbed back on his bar stool next to Nick, letting the breeze from the ceiling fan play over his skin. Even that brief step outside had set the sweat pouring again. Or maybe it was the infuriating 'Seattle'

Blackwood. Damned woman and her pride. Damned woman and her stiff neck, because something had sure looked like it was going on with those men.

But she hadn't said a word. Which was so like Kaitlin.

And so he'd let her go. *Getting' to be a habit, old man.*

He snagged his beer. Moisture still beaded the bottle as he knocked back a long swig of the amber fluid and then ran the bottle over his brow.

"You gave her your card?"

"Yeah. I did. She's probably dropped it already. Stupid thing t'do. No reason in the world for 'Seattle' Blackwood to have anything to do with me. You saw. She couldn't get outta here fast enough when she saw it was me." He shook his head. "Besides, about the last thing she needs is my kind of trouble."

He went for another swig of beer, but the bloody bottle was empty. He raised two fingers at the bartender, who nodded and slid a new G and T and a bottle smoothly in front of them. "Ya gotta give these blokes credit. They know how to run a bar."

He tried the new bottle and declared it good. "So where were we before we were so rudely interrupted by my past?"

"Getting drunk trying to figure out what shit you've fallen into, Beej." Nick clinked his fresh G and T against the neck of B.J.'s bottle.

The nice glow he had been feeling didn't quite cut it now. "Another reason Kaitlin wouldn't want to be around me."

"I thought you called her Seattle? And I'd have thought she could help you. You said she was an investigative reporter."

"Is. She is an investigative reporter." B.J. rolled his eyes and downed another pull of beer. It was slidin' down too sweet and fast right now— probably because of one Kaitlin Blackwood. She still looked good. Still felt good under his hands, too. He shook his head.

"I don't need a journalist t' help me, ya Limey bastard. I've had enough of that kind to do me for five lifetimes. What I *need* is ta figure out how ta deal with this thing—and if worse comes to worst, how to get the hell outta the country without my bloody passport."

Nick was silent a moment, considering the ice clinking in his glass. Then he met B.J.'s gaze.

"Maybe you should be thinking about getting out of Cambodia first and foremost, old friend. I don't know what you've stepped into, but the fact that someone attacked you last night at the scene—that suggests you've gotten involved in something a hell of a lot bigger than a murder."

"Yeah? And what's bigger than a dead monk?"

"You tell me."

The stone suddenly weighed in his pocket. He'd held onto it like his life depended on it when he'd run through the woods from the Bayon. He'd stuffed it in his pocket and kept running, abandoning the borrowed bicycle and knowing he was totally screwed if the police were advanced enough to track down the owner. He'd chanced hauling the stone out of his pocket only when he got here and used the privacy of a cubicle in the men's washroom. Going home hadn't seemed an option.

Which meant he might have recommended a hotel to Kaitlin Blackwood that was anything but safe when he'd suggested the place he lived. But then, what were the chances she'd follow any of his advice?

Nick still awaited his answer. He sat on his stool in his pale blue shirt and navy trousers, his thin brown hair shoved behind his ears and curling around his collar like a much older, dissolute version of The Blue Boy painting. But the expression on his face said "So?"

After all their years of drinking together, the man deserved an answer. B.J. leaned in close enough to smell the other man's unwashed clothes. 'Limey bastard' was right. Man barely bathed.

"All right. What I didn't tell you about last night was that just before I was attacked, I found something." He hauled the stone out of his pocket and placed it on the counter between their drinks.

In the bar's dim light the stone still managed to collect enough light to glow red like an angry eye. The layers of common dirt were like cataracts over clear sight.

"Christ. Is that what I think it is?" Nick didn't touch, but he leaned down to inspect the stone.

"You tell me. You spent some time prospecting, didn't you?"

"Yeah. In Northwest Thailand. I was hoping for a strike like the Burmese mines at Mogok, but no dice." He glanced up at B.J. "You mind?"

When B.J. shook his head, Nick picked the stone up and turned it over. "Christ, it looks like a ruby, but I don't recall one this size ever being found. Not locally."

He picked at the soil around the rough stone. "Looks like alluvial clay."

He tapped his fingers on the bar for a moment, his face screwed up in concentration more than B.J. had ever seen it. Then he shook his head.

"Can't be. Just can't be."

"What can't be, mate?"

Nick met his gaze. "Old man, this ruby bears all the signs of being a Thai or Cambodian stone. Same sort of alluvial soil. I know. I've seen the operations in Trat province of Thailand. Open pit things. Filthy, muddy operations. Here in Cambodia there were mines across the border from Thailand."

"That's where this's from then?"

Nick shrugged. "Don't know, but I'd say 'no'." He must have caught B.J.'s impatience because he went on. "You see, the area was pretty much mined out by the Khmer Rouge. While they were enslaving their country, they were digging out the rubies and sapphires to finance their government. Between the mining and the land mines that they put in to try to stop the Vietnamese advance during the liberation from the Khmer Rouge, the area is pretty much used up or too dangerous to exploit."

"Then where the hell did this come from?"

Nick hefted the stone in his hand and shook his head.

"The stone's got to be a clue to what the blinking hell this's all about." B.J. caught himself and lowered his voice. "Come on, mate. Give me something to work with here."

Nick set the stone down on the bar, his hands still cupping it to hide the red glow. "I can't be sure. Not without looking at it more closely, but I'd say it's from Cambodia—maybe around Pailin—though that doesn't make sense given all I've just told you.

"A thing like this in Thailand would be rushed to production. It'd be a national treasure, one this big would probably be presented to, or purchased for, the King. But the way you found this, the fact a monk had it and died, well, I'd say you've stumbled into something big that someone is trying to keep a secret. Like a new gem field." He nudged the stone toward B.J. "And that, my friend, means that—to quote our American friends— you are in a shit-load of trouble."

Chapter 16

Safe. Kaitlin looked past the dark head of the young woman showing her the hotel room. The wrought iron bars on the room's windows promised that to Kaitlin, and for a moment she resented that damned B.J. McCallum for being right. So maybe he didn't always lie. Once she'd thought he was truthful, but that was before he faked evidence to try to put the leader of a human smuggling ring away. He'd actually lied on the witness stand until the evidence proved that his photos were faked and the kingpin walked.

Kaitlin looked around the bright, third floor room with its pristine floors and the twin beds made with military precision. Not as swanky as what she would have had in a suite at the Century Angkor, but definitely clean and serviceable. And safe. Safe was good.

Safe and secure and—dammit—she was an investigator. Safe wasn't worth a hill of beans if she was going to lock herself in a room and not find the answers she was looking for.

"I'll take it."

The smiling young woman who had brought her upstairs looked her up and down. "You make yourself comfortable then come down and register, okay?"

So she looked as done in as she felt.

Kaitlin nodded, the exhaustion battling with the nervous energy so that her hands trembled a little as she dug some money out of her purse.

The woman waved her money away. "You pay when you come down."

"It might be a bit. I might have a nap."

"Okee-dokey."

The young woman grinned and Kaitlin almost cringed at the Americanism. But then what did she expect in a country that had figured so prominently in the Vietnam War and that now made its living through tourism?

Go globalization. It meant she didn't even have to speak the language.

She let the woman out, accepted the key, and collapsed on the bed. She didn't even have the energy to shower. But she needed to, didn't she?

Safe, secure, and in the dark like a mushroom.

She couldn't waste time napping when her father was missing.

And someone had tried to abduct her again.

She stopped herself. That conclusion was the product of a too weary mind running on instinct. She had no proof there was something nefarious behind those men, and yet, her instinct was usually good—it had kept her alive in the past. These guys had *pushed* her, but given her experience in Phnom Penh, perhaps it wasn't unusual for drivers to be insistent.

But not all the drivers had been like that.

She closed her eyes. Imagination? The product of jet lag? *Reserve judgment, Blackwood. Maintain your objectivity. If you really think something happened, then why aren't you going to the police?*

She sat up. Maybe she should.

The thought of getting tied up with petty, local officials wasn't exactly appetizing. The US embassy?

They'd probably just tell her to go stateside and wait it out, when every one of her journalist spidey senses were telling her something was here to be investigated. When the jackhammer wasn't pounding.

"Sorry headache, I'm taking you for another walk."

She rolled off the bed, showered, and pulled on clean clothes. Amazing what clean hair—pulled back in a fresh ponytail—and clean clothes could do for a woman's self-concept. She hauled out her mascara.

Why bother? There was no one around here she was trying to impress.

She shoved the tube back in her bag, grabbed her daypack with the shadow puppet, and jogged down the stairs. There she took care of registering, tucked her passport back under her clothes, and hauled out the name the woman at Sovanna Phum had given her.

"I'm looking for this person. Can you tell me where I can find him?"

The young hotel clerk examined the paper. "This is far out of Siem Reap. A school for orphans."

"I'm looking for a puppet-maker's school."

The woman shrugged. "Same same. You go tomorrow. Too late today. You rest. Have food. Ready to go tomorrow."

Kaitlin didn't need, or want, a mother.

"But if I wanted to go tonight? It's very urgent. This man has information I need."

"Not man. Woman. Jorani."

As if that told Kaitlin anything.

"Jorani very busy. She need her sleep. You leave Jorani to tomorrow."

Kaitlin fought down her frustration. Experience told her arriving at a place when people were abed was no way to enlist their assistance in an investigation. Sure, she'd done it a time or two to people who were avoiding her, but this situation didn't call for a stalker.

So she'd wait.

She sighed. It was like the whole darned country was putting up roadblocks. But then, from the few things she'd read in the newspapers back home and in her *Fodor's,* there wasn't a lot of infrastructure here and things you thought were arranged could go sideways anytime.

"Thanks. Could you arrange a taxi for me for tomorrow? Bright and early? Say seven o'clock?"

When the woman nodded, Kaitlin considered just giving in to her body and going back to her room, but she'd be damned if she was going to let a couple of little incidents make her afraid. She could still be wrong, and the whole thing could just be a misunderstanding.

Sure. You go right on believing that.

But she'd seen signs for international phone calls and internet cafés just down the block. She'd call the office, get them doing some research, and check in with Mac. Make sure he missed her and all that.

The open front of the Jade Violin gave onto a partially paved street that collected mud and half-filled puddles. Across from her guesthouse stood a small snack shop and another guesthouse, this one with white marble columns that made it look like it had pretentions of grandeur. The Jade Violin was definitely homier.

She checked both ways out of habit and headed down the rough pavement and gravel toward what looked like a main street at the end of the block. Tourist-laden motorcycles and moto-taxis buzzed past, sending up sprays of dirty water that she leapt to avoid. Her stomach growled at the yummy scent of grilled fish coming from a small thatch-roofed restaurant. Traditional music trailed out of homes that advertised themselves as money exchanges. All to be expected, she supposed. Siem Reap was a backpacker's destination.

Overhead, the sky's blue had deepened as the sun fell. A corona of gold seemed to rime the tops of the buildings and place a dishonest beauty on the huge thunderclouds that threatened from the south. There was a reason there was water in the streets, and more was apparently on the way. She really should have bought one of those rain slickers.

She was just deciding to venture into the town to find one, when a vehicle turning onto the street caught her attention.

Car. Black. Dented fender.

Crap.

She ducked through a glass door into the icy air of an internet café and crouched down behind a computer. Heart racing, she peered around the monitor and out the window hoping she hadn't been seen.

The car cruised past slowly. It wasn't her imagination, and how many small black cars with a dented left fender could there be in this hick town?

Probably more than you know.

"Excuse? You must pay first."

She turned around to the youth at the desk that sat by the door. He must be all of sixteen, by the look of him. And bored silly, while her heart was still racing

With another glance out the window at the rear of the car as it glided down towards the Jade Violin, Kaitlin went to the kid to pay. The place wasn't exactly an internet café. Or at least they'd forgotten the café part of the shop. But it had a bank of computers and a desk with two phones and it smelled of heated electric wires above the air conditioning.

Kinda bleak, but serviceable.

She checked her watch. Seven p.m., and Cambodia was fifteen hours ahead of Seattle time. Which meant it was around five a.m. back at the paper. Mac would have just arrived at work. Or he could have been there earlier, now that she was wasn't there to distract him in the mornings.

It had been a convenient little affair over the past eighteen months. Mac—James MacKillup—the news editor of the *Post Intelligencer*, had been widowed three years ago. Before breast cancer had taken Beth MacKillup, the three of them had been good friends, attending plays and movies together, and playing on the paper's softball team. Beth had taken it as a personal mission to set Kaitlin up on a few blind dates in hopes Kaitlin could be as happy as Beth and Mac, but nothing had taken.

After Beth's death, Mac had become a recluse, only going out when Kaitlin dragged him. Then he'd met someone and dated for six months before breaking it off and falling into the casual little fling with Kaitlin.

It worked for both of them.

"I'd like to place an international call," she told the young proprietor.

"Three dollars a minute," he said handing her the phone. "Cheaper if you Skype."

Yeah, she could Skype, but she wasn't sure about the computers here. They looked old, and frankly, an old-fashioned phone call would be nice.

She shrugged and dialed, suddenly wanting to hear Mac's voice. At least *he* wasn't a liar or a fraud, like someone else who should remain nameless.

The ringing, through a cracked, buzzing line, sounded like it was a million miles away. But Mac's voice would reinforce normal, and after the last few days, she could use a dose of that.

"MacKillup." Mac's voice sounded thin and thready over the distance.

"Mac? It's me. I thought I'd phone."

"Miss me, do you, Katy? 'Bout time you called. I thought maybe you'd run off with someone exciting you met over there." His broad smile came over the miles and she could picture him stretching to push his door closed, then leaning back in his chair with his long, lanky frame stretched out.

But missed him? She'd hardly thought of him until this afternoon. Too many things going on.

"Sorry about the delay. I've been busy."

"Have you given that wandering father of yours a piece of your mind?"

"That's the trouble. He's disappeared. Or it seems like it."

"What'd'you mean?" She could hear the newspaperman's alertness for a story in his voice, could picture him sitting up, his brown gaze intense.

"I got to Phnom Penh and he wasn't there. The staff at the hotel where he stayed said he checked out with another man, but he left stuff there—an envelope for me with a shadow puppet inside that no one can make sense of."

It wasn't initially why she'd called, and she was quite capable of using the internet herself, but it made sense now that she thought about it. Keep

Mac involved and don't use local computers where her research could be noted.

"Have you gone to the police or to the embassy to report the situation?"

"No. I don't know if I trust the local police. I've had to deal with enough corrupt officials getting Dad out of jams before. And as for the embassy, they'd just tell me to leave it to them."

"Well, maybe you should. They've got the connections. Safer, too."

Which was why she hadn't told him about the black car and the incidents with the men. Mac was always worrying, and she didn't want that. He was a good friend and a thoughtful lover lover, but she was responsible for herself.

"I'll think about it. Right now I think I'm going to get dinner and head to bed."

"Alone, right?" Joking.

"What else?" What was this? Had Mac crossed the line beyond casual sex?

"Then you take care of yourself, Katy. I mean it. Be careful."

"And when am I not?"

"Oh, God, are we in trouble." He was laughing and shaking his head, she was sure. It had been a point of contention even before they became involved. She might be good at lists and planning, but her adventures into investigative reporting were still more than he apparently felt comfortable with. "Now you listen, Katy. No unnecessary risks, you hear?"

"No problem. Talk to you tomorrow."

She hung up, hating the way she felt like a child when he talked to her like that. When had she ever taken risks? She always thought things through. *Katy*, indeed. In that he was as bad as B.J.

And that was the stupidest thought she'd had all day.

She paid and left, aiming for the thatch-roofed restaurant, a meal, and bed; but the sight of a lone black car parked down the street changed her mind.

Maybe the Jade Violin could bring food in.

Chapter 17

If the hangover didn't kill him, the look on Seattle Blackwood's face certainly would. She faced him in the early-morning-sun-filled open-air lobby of the Jade Violin, looking hauntingly like he remembered, with her hair pulled into a ponytail and sans makeup. She was dressed in khaki trousers and a figure-hugging khaki blouse that looked hotter'n hell in all the very best ways, but he was not going to tell her that.

All the chords in her neck already stood out and little spots of color sat high on her cheeks. The last time he'd seen her like this was when she'd found out about his doctored photos. If he was out to poke her in the eye, this was how to do it.

"What do you mean, you're my driver?"

B.J. tried to remember why, when Kunthea, the hotel clerk, had told him Kaitlin planned to visit Jorani today, it had seemed like such a good idea to go with her. Hadn't he spent last evening telling Nick that he wanted Kaitlin around about as much as he wanted a case of the runs? Besides, did he really want to take a chance of dragging her into the trouble that seemed to be following him?

All good reasons *not* to do what he was doing. But there was something about the chance to spend time with 'Seattle' Blackwood...

B.J. shrugged. "I know the area. I know Jorani. I was planning on heading out there today anyway on some business of my own. Seemed to make sense and saves us both some money. Isn't that what the paper always tells their people—save money?" He grinned and watched the anger flare and fade, flare and fade in her eyes as she thought of all the things she was too polite to say. It took a good man a while to get far enough under

Kaitlin's skin that she'd cut loose. Him, it would only take half as long. At least it had in the past.

Something to look forward to. And maybe that was why he was doing it. A diversion. Poking Kaitlin was like the local kids tormenting a rat. Wasn't that why he was calling her Seattle, a name she hated almost as much as she hated being called luv? She'd turfed him out, after all. So this was payback.

He grinned at the way she ground her teeth, and only felt a little like a heel. The way she looked around as if seeking a way out exposed the length of her neck and a knotted cord that must attach to one of those personal safes where tourists carried their passport. The cord looked too pristinely white against her golden skin.

"I'll find my own taxi, thank you very much."

"Will ya? Go ahead." And maybe that *was* the wiser alternative. He shrugged one more time. "Hopefully the driver speaks English well enough. Jorani's is a bit back o' Bourke. Not many folk take a taxi there. Wouldn't want you to get stranded or anything."

A shadow of concern crossed her face, and that was strange. Kaitlin had never been afraid of anything—and her fearlessness had left him always feeling he needed to be afraid for both of them, even though her fearlessness usually came out of a considered decision and careful planning.

It was also what made it so easy for her to walk out on him when he betrayed what she held most dear—her professional ethics and reputation.

Which meant something had her spooked.

Maybe his memory of the day before hadn't been fueled by too much amber fluid. Maybe those blokes at the Grand Hotel had been doing more than helpin' a lady into that car. And maybe the incident in Phnom Penh had been more than she said it was, too. That would explain why she'd been spooked enough she'd actually looked relieved when he showed up with his card. And used it, apparently.

So maybe pushing her to bail out on her own wasn't the thing to do. He sighed.

"Listen, I'm not some mongrel. I didn't steer you wrong with this guest house. So I won't steer you wrong today, either." He almost added that his presence might add some security, but knowing her, that would only make her more insistent on going alone. Something he didn't want to do after what he'd seen.

He could practically see the damned wheels of consideration turn in her head, but finally she met his gaze. "I don't want you involved in my affairs."

"I hear ya. Consider me your walkabout guide. That's all." And that *was* all. He'd spent three years dealing with this woman and six years getting over her. He didn't need her anymore.

"Good." She hefted her shoulder bag and tucked an envelope under her arm. "Let's go, then."

His turn to smile. "Could have left a half hour ago."

Her reaction was predictable: crossed arms, a roll of eyes, a sigh that brought back a rush of memories. How he'd loved to tease that mad out of her, because it had usually led to something much more incredible.

She climbed in the moto-taxi, allowing him a chance to remember all the things he admired about her ass. Then he climbed in beside her and enjoyed the way her face changed. American pissed-offedness definitely in high gear.

"I thought you were driving."

"Nope. Give the business to the locals is my motto. How else do they build an economy?"

"So, what? You're a philanthropist now?"

Always have been, luv. But you just couldn't see it that way. He shrugged. "I do what I can."

She snorted and B.J. leaned forward and told the driver where they wanted to go in his almost-passable Cambodian. As much as Aussie-accented Khmer could be.

They shook-rattle-rolled down the pitted street and onto pavement. This early in the morning, the tourist part of town near the river was still pretty quiet, but as they rolled up through the commercial areas, traffic picked up and B.J. sat back on the bench across from Kaitlin watching her take in the view. She was like a sponge, this woman, and rarely forgot anything.

Like you, ya wanker. And what ya did.

"Ya know, I was gobsmacked when ya walked into the Club in Phnom Penh. Coulda knocked me over with a feather."

"Bull. You didn't even recognize me."

"I didn't. But, godstrewth, it was because you've changed."

"More likely it was because you were drunk." She glanced at him, but one of the many markets that sprang up along Siem Reap's streets caught her attention with its bright parasols and heaps of red tomatoes and glistening green limes.

Kaitlin Blackwood had never been easy to deal with. But the thought of spending the hour ride to Jorani's sniping at each other didn't do anything to help his hangover. He'd sort of hoped they might be able to get past the bad times and talk about the good, like old friends did.

So much for hope.

"So I drank a little. Maybe I had a reason, just like you've got a reason for being in Siem Reap and not wanting to talk about it. Just like maybe you've got a reason to be a little concerned about security right now."

There. He'd said it, and the way her shoulders stiffened and she sank back onto her seat said he was right on the mark. He grinned at her.

"Knew I shoulda been a reporter."

"Fuck off." But it wasn't forceful enough for Kaitlin Blackwood.

"So those guys at the Grand weren't exactly your friends."

"I don't know who they were." She wouldn't meet his gaze, but her tone said she didn't want to talk about it.

But this was Kaitlin, and even if she'd walked out and left him to deal with his scandal alone, he didn't want to see anything happen to her. Hell, the reason he'd *let* her leave had been to protect her. Her entire career as a reporter would have come to an end just through their association.

He gave her a few minutes to calm down. That was what had always worked before. Gentle nudges until she could let go of her information.

"So what's happened with your dad?"

Her gaze slowly came back to him. "I never said anything had."

"Never denied it either, didja? An' your old man's the only reason I ever saw ya set foot outta the States."

"I might love traveling now."

"And I might be a king kangaroo—in some other bloody life. Come on Kaitlin, I was part of yer life. I know you like travel about as much as a dog bite. And I know about the trouble you've had with yer old man, pulling him outta the frying pan all the time."

Her gaze held on his and then she looked away. She shook her head in that helpless way she had that always had made him want to run in and rescue her, but really just expressed her inability to fathom why people did what they did. She'd shaken her head the same way when she'd learned about his failure.

"He's disappeared. He sent me a letter from Phnom Penh saying the usual—big plans and things were going to be different this time. He said he was coming home and gave me a flight number. I went to pick him up, but he wasn't on the flight. I gave him a couple of weeks to get back in touch, but he never did. That's when I knew something was wrong."

Her worry overrode her anger as she spoke. She was one hell of a woman to keep coming back for more from her father. She was always stubbornly there for him—a strange bond it was indeed, between Kaitlin and her father—and it left her with no capacity to 'be there' for anyone else, not even herself.

"So you flew to Phnom Penh. What got you to Siem Reap and Jorani?"

Her gaze flashed up to him. "Maybe you *should* be a reporter. Get me to relax. Show empathy. Get me to talk. Good work, McCallum, but this is my business, not yours."

"Hey, I got to watch one of the best in action. I learned something." Another beat as he considered. "So the way I figure it, and knowing Jorani, I figure it's either got to do with orphans, the sex trade, or shadow puppets."

"That's quite the triumvirate. What the hell makes you come up with that combination?"

He could have laughed at her surprise. "Not that good a guess, really. Or didn't you know Jorani runs an orphanage and rehabilitation center for children rescued from the sex trade?"

"I *thought* she was an expert in shadow puppets."

"So it's the puppets, is it?" Not what he'd expected. What the hell kind of get rich quick scheme—and that was the only kind of story her dad would be involved in—involved shadow puppets?

"Yes, the damn puppets. My dad left one for me at the hotel in Phnom Penh and I'm trying to figure out where he got it and what it might mean. An expert in the city said Jorani was my best hope."

Her slender hand stroked the brown envelope on her lap.

"May I see it?"

"No." She turned back to the landscape. They'd left the town center and were traveling around the fringe of Angkor Archeological Park where the jungle grew lower because of deforestation of large trees like the huge fromages that overgrew some of the famous temples. Meandering rivers wound through rice fields that cut broad swathes of brilliant green through the brush. In some fields, people planted. Water buffalo lumbered plows through the mud and the rich scent of wet earth filled the morning air.

A thin line of sweat ran down the side of Kaitlin's neck and he had the urge to brush it away. Idiot thought. She'd knock him into next week.

"It's going to get hotter. And humid."

"Great. Something else to be thankful for." She tossed her head.

"You know, I was just going to let you walk outta that bar. It was old Nick who said I should give it a fair go and be friendly. Only reason I listened is I *thought* that all yer journo training said you should be unbiased. At least that's what you always used to say."

Not exactly true, but close enough. Not that 'unbiased' ever applied to their personal life.

"What I said, Mr. Helpful, is that journalists have to be objective. Or the best ones are. Of course, a story or an issue can make you mad, but you never let that come through in the work."

"Is that right?"

She met his gaze and a small, grim smile grazed her lips. "As if you didn't remember. I believe those were about the last words I said to you."

At least it was a smile.

"They do have a certain ring of familiarity. Sort of like my Mum's harping to comb my hair when I was a kid."

She snorted. "Like that'd help."

And for a moment the chill in the taxi eased and she was almost the Kaitlin he'd met way back then, before the loving and before the end.

"So you live at the Jade Violin?"

"You could say that." He shrugged. "It's comfortable. I don't have to cook."

"I'd want my own space." She shook her head.

She always had, and the space always took on a special feel when she was in it. Warm and intimate, like those Barbara Walters specials had always never quite been able to imitate.

He shrugged again. "I don't need much. Stuff just ties ya down."

"But you said you'd been here six years?"

"Sure. But what do I need? Clothes, my camera gear." He shook his head.

"What?"

She was still bloody quick in picking up body language.

"Nothing."

"What?"

"Some wanker ripped off my camera gear, except for this." He patted his trusty old Nikon.

"That's the same one you used in Seattle, isn't it? It's got that scratch."

The scratch he'd been horrified at when a gangbanger swung at him and knocked his camera out of his hand.

Make that bloody quick *and* observant, but she was softening, engaging in conversation she wouldn't have an hour ago. So he still had the touch where Kaitlin was concerned.

And why the hell did he even care? This was supposed to be about pissing in her ear, wasn't it? But...

"So maybe we could try this again? Name's B.J. McCallum. Pleasure to make your re-acquaintance." He stuck out his hand and—wonder of wonders—after a moment's hesitation she accepted it.

Then she slipped a pair of sunnies over her eyes and turned back to the fields again. It shut him out, but he liked the small smile that played on her lips; and maybe she needed a moment of remembering things that made her smile.

Because if her old man had disappeared in Cambodia, it couldn't be good. People who disappeared here had a habit of not being found.

Not alive, anyway.

Chapter 18

They passed a row of thatched kiosks filled with amber and russet-colored baskets and elongated, woven reed tubes that could only be fish traps, and Kaitlin finally started to relax—as much as she could with B.J. beside her.

The whole trip out she'd been keeping an eye out for the black car. It had been gone from the road outside the Jade Violin this morning. But nowhere through the winding streets of Siem Reap, or out in the postcard-green countryside, had she seen it. Mac would say it had to be a figment of her overactive imagination. He'd always said she had one, and that it was what had led to her ability to see where a story *might* be, instead of just those that were right in her face. But that wasn't the case this time.

Right now there were no people in the kiosks they passed. Maybe it was too early. Or maybe the people were staying safely in the shadows of their shops. Already the sun felt like an assault, and it was barely ten o'clock.

The moto-taxi's whine and jouncing ride had rattled the headache forward in her head like a marble that kept hitting her behind the eyes. She winced and shook her head to roll it away again, but the heat over the steaming landscape only made it more difficult. So did B.J.'s overwhelming presence, and his soap-and-water scent just made it worse, because it seemed to crawl right up into her head so she was too aware of it.

Only the blessed wind through the open front and sides of the vehicle made it livable. Her clothes stuck to her—her trousers too long and bulky, her short-sleeved blouse too heavy. Sweat made a river down her back, and she was pretty sure the waist of her slacks was soaked as well as her underarms—not to mention her passport.

Attractive, Blackwood. Very.

Not that it mattered. There wasn't a damn person in this godforsaken country she had to be attractive for. Just talk to Jorani and find her dad. And get the heck home. That was the order of business on her latest list.

At least B.J. had quit trying to engage her in conversation. So he'd gotten her message that she didn't want anything to do with him—but then he'd have to be deaf, dumb, blind, and a fool *not* to get her message.

Of course, he *was* Australian—and about the most pig-headed excuse of a man she'd ever known. Mac was soooo different.

He knew Kaitlin would handle things herself in Cambodia, whereas B.J. would have come running after her to help. And annoy her.

But B.J. seemed different. A little more subdued, maybe. And less of a tease. Hangover, probably.

At the side of the road, a woman in a blue sarong stood with a small girl protectively in her arms. With the fierceness of the woman's look, it would have made a good illustration shot if she was doing a story on the feel of this place. The people were fiercely protective of what they had.

At least Champei had been. The woman at Sovanna Phum had been, as well.

But when you have nothing, you tend to protect what you have. Like your child.

The woman stared in the direction they were going, but when she saw the moto-taxi she fled into the shadows underneath her stilted, thatched house. As if she didn't want to be seen.

Something not right there. A tower of smoke rose from somewhere beyond the trees up the road.

"Just how much farther is Jorani's? We've been traveling at least an hour."

"We're almost there." But he craned around in his seat and caught sight of the smoke. "Bloody hell, no!"

He yelled at the driver in Cambodian and pointed at the column.

No way someone would light a fire like that. Not on a hot day. At least not for any reason she could think of.

B.J.'s tanned face had gone almost white. His rigid jaw showed striated muscles as the motorcycle revved and leapt forward over the broken pavement.

"What is it?" she yelled over the wind in her ears.

When he turned, fear filled B.J.'s gaze.

"The orphanage."

Chapter 19

The bloody moto didn't go fast enough. The engine whined and roared, but the taxi still moved slowly enough B.J. swore he could run faster past the tall stilted thatch houses and the palm trees. Not true, but he could have sworn.

They swung off the main road and jounced down between the stilted huts along the road, between the pens where water buffalo lounged and the life-giving green of the rice fields. Black smoke billowed ominously up over the trees and ash rained down in wispy grey into his face.

Not this. Not—bloody—this.

These children had been through enough. Jorani had been through enough. And Maly as well.

If anything had happened to her... He tried to breathe calmly, but his lungs wouldn't fill. Like a croc had pulled him under water and he couldn't breathe.

Let Maly be safe. Let Jorani and the older children have got the younger ones to safety.

The road swept around a copse of trees in time to see an explosion of sparks and flame as the roof of the three-year-old orphanage collapsed. Sparks caught in a nearby palm and the tree burst into fire like a hideous, too-bright candle. The stench of boiling sap joined the horrible reek of burning.

Villagers crowded the road, useless buckets still in their hands as the taxi sent them scattering.

It screeched to a halt and B.J. leapt out. He ran for the dormitory, but the heat blistered his skin. Smoke blinded him and sent him coughing before he could get close.

"B.J.! No!" A hand on his arm again, hauling him back. He stood there uselessly.

"Don't you dare try that again, you hear?" Kaitlin's voice. As if he needed to listen to her.

Gone. The whole damned thing—and five thousand Aussie dollars—was gone. The concrete foundations he and the villagers had poured themselves. The school. The dormitory. Even the small thatched house they'd built for Jorani.

How the hell had it happened? How the hell had they all burned so fast?

He swung around and found himself facing a bewildered Kaitlin. He shoved her out of the way and went to Samnang, the elderly, village headman.

"How…?" he demanded in Cambodian.

Samnang shrugged in that way that too many Cambodians had—an apology and yet not.

"We were too late. We could not stop it."

B.J. scanned the crowd, the fear crowding in. "Where are the children?"

Samnang just shook his head in that Cambodian way that couldn't quite mask that something horrible had happened.

B.J. grabbed Samnang's scrawny shoulders. "Where are they?"

Samnang wrenched free.

B.J. took a deep breath and forced his fists to uncurl. He'd worked with this man to build this place. Be calm. Surely they could have got the children out if the fire had started in the school. Or Jorani's.

But if it started in the dormitory….

He was going to be sick if he didn't so something. He grabbed Samnang's bucket and ran to the pump, filled the bucket.

"Come on, ya bastards. We've to stop this. We have to save what's left."

A gentle hand relieved him of the bucket.

"It's over, B.J." Kaitlin said and placed her hand on his arm.

He pulled loose and pinched the bridge of his nose.

"It's not over. It's fucking all gone." His voice sounded hoarse. He turned and walked back to Samnang. "What happened? Where's Jorani? The children?"

The man nodded at a small cluster of people in a copse of trees at the edge of the orphanage property. It was the place they had built the spirit house, and each day, even though there was never enough food to fill everyone's stomach, Jorani and the children placed offerings of rice and bananas at the entrance to the small, ornately carved building for the ancestors and land spirits who could keep the orphanage safe.

And that had worked so bloody well.

Shut up. Shut up. Just find Jorani and the kids. Just make sure everyone got out. Maly.

The little girl's huge brown eyes and too-grave expression filled his head. And her laughter, on those few occasions when he could get her to laugh.

Thankfully, playing the big, white, Aussie buffoon who'd come with food and clothing donations had seemed to charm her. Once she'd gotten over her initial fear.

As he approached, the gold-painted spirit house stood ignored amid the trees. Instead, the group of people—women mostly—crowded around two figures on the ground. The village healer—basically a wise woman with knowledge of local herbal remedies and the first aid kit B.J. had donated to the village—knelt beside a prone figure collapsed amid the offerings.

Jorani. No kids. Panic started to set in.

Jorani had once been a lovely woman. A beauty really, but when B.J. met her in Phnom Penh's huge Central Market, she had just been a bent, haggard woman selling wilted lotus offerings. She had survived the Khmer Rouge and then supported three orphans who had escaped from the child sex trade. After he'd learned her story, he'd helped her build the orphanage, and she, the last surviving child of a master puppeteer slaughtered by the Khmer Rouge, had built a school that taught the ancient skills she knew.

Over the years, pride had straightened her back and laughter had smoothed the lines from her face, but now her limbs were tangled in her sarong like an Irrawaddy porpoise caught in a fisherman's net. Her long black hair had come loose from her usual neat bun to cascade around her shoulders and half cover her breast.

The ends of her long hair were sodden red. So was her white blouse, where a ragged wound pulsed blood.

B.J. went to his knees beside her, across from the healer. He caught her hand—almost frozen, it was so cold.

Shock. He knew at least that much. When you head into the outback, you better damn well have an understanding of first aid if you want a hope of coming back.

"What happened?" he repeated his question.

The healer shook her head, but Jorani's eyes flashed open, locked on him.

"B.J." barely a whisper.

"Shh." He shook his head. "Save your strength."

He smoothed her hair off her face, but she shook her head. Her bloodied fingers squeezed his and he held on tight.

"I tried…," she gasped in Cambodian.

"Don't talk. We need to get you to a doctor."

"No. Listen. You must stop them."

Jorani shook her head, showing the dogged determination he'd always admired, but he had to do something.

Ignoring her protests, he tore a strip off her sarong and plastered it onto the wound on her chest. Applied pressure. *Make it work. Make it work.*

The fabric turned sodden immediately. Too much blood. Too much blood. It welled through his fingers, too warm. Too full of life, and hers was leaking away right in front of him. His hands were soaked in it. The ground was soaked with it and a weird sense of déjà vu washed over him.

Jorani's fingers scrabbled at his hands like small helpless animals. "B.J. They came. They took the children."

His gaze locked on hers, the panic turning to terror. "What? Who?"

Her fierce gaze demanded his attention more than her wound. With his help, Jorani had built this place, but it was her determination and love that had poured into the children and created a safe refuge.

What it had been.

She closed her eyes and her hands clenched and strained as if she fought for strength.

"Jorani? Who took them? Where have they gone?"

A slight shake of her head and then she met his gaze as if she tried to pass information telepathically. Blood stained her lips red as a betel chewer. Her mouth moved, but her wounds denied her breath.

"Men." It finally came out in a bloody burble. "I tried…stop them."

"Bloody hell." And they'd done this. "What men, Jorani? Who were they? Where did they go?"

With this much blood it was hopeless, but he willed her strength. Willed her to live. He had to know more if he was going to find the children. Save them.

But the fierceness faded from her eyes. Panic filled them as her lips worked. She grabbed his arm and dragged him closer so bloody breath sprayed his cheek. "Police… with them…."

Her voice faded to nothing and her grip released, and he couldn't be sure what he'd heard. A sigh escaped her, sending a thin stream of blood out from between her slack lips.

He sat up. What had she said? Had he really heard what he thought he had?

Jorani's empty eyes stared up at the sky and he wanted to cry for the loss of such a lovely-hearted woman, and wanted to punch something. He wanted to howl at the moon.

"Who did this?" He demanded of the healer.

The woman shook her head and began to minister to Jorani's body.

B.J. grabbed her arm and yanked her forward. "I bloody well asked you a question! Who did this?"

Fear filled the woman's gaze. Of him? He released her.

"Please? I have to find the children."

Bloody hell, he was begging. He scrambled up and scanned the crowd. "Please? We have to find the children. Who took them? Where did they go?"

His voice rang over the crack and roar of the fire. It was dying now, most of the wood consumed. A shifting wind sent the heat and smoke billowing over him and smothered the palm fronds overhead in ash. It was—surreal—like he was dead and this was hell.

People moved away from him like a flood water receding. Or zombies. He was in a bloody B-grade movie.

No. He shook himself. He had to find Maly and the other kids.

And this bloody mob was going to help him.

He strode across the ash-covered grass and grabbed Samnang's arm. The man had been an ally, once. He had provided the land because Jorani had convinced him that helping the orphans would bring money to the village. This village and those of the surrounding commune had helped to supply food to the orphans, and the orphanage's shadow puppet work had brought income into the area.

But the man looked at B.J. now, like he knew nothing about the place.

"She's dead. Are you happy? Jorani's dead and the kids are gone. Now you're bloody well going to tell me who's got them, or…."

Or what, McCallum? You going to beat him up? Fuck. He was acting like a fucking mobster with all his threats—or the fuckers of Pol Pot's regime.

He exhaled and released the village headman, swallowing back the panic. *Think man, think. Don't just react.*

"Please. I can't let those kids be taken. They've been through too much. You know that. What they'll do to them…."

He closed his eyes, but the images he'd seen stateside would forever be burned in his brain. First there had been Cora. His sister, so fair and lovely and, after the drugs got hold of her, so strung out she'd sold herself onto the street. And died there, because he hadn't been strong enough to help her. That was the shame he'd carried all his life. Then, years later, he'd found that group of kids destined to be auctioned off to wealthy deviants across the U.S. The sight of it, and the chance to redeem himself, had sent him on a mission to catch and convict the bastards. Unfortunately, he'd failed when he stepped over the line.

The villagers had gone quiet. He opened his eyes and half-expected to be alone, but Samnang still faced him. The old man shook his head sadly.

"A man come. Secret, he say. The men—they warn us: Do nothing or they will come back and take everyone."

The scorching heat off the fire suddenly went cold. "They didn't threaten me. I can find them. Stop them. Who were they?"

Samnang's wife, Chhean, caught the old man's hand and shook her head. "We have our grandchildren. We must protect them."

"Please. They're children, too. Help me find them." Couldn't they see he was begging?

"Jorani—she helped." The old couple shook their heads, and dingo-howling was looking better and better.

"B.J.?"

The cool voice was almost a shock. He turned to find Kaitlin, her face, hands, and clothing covered in soot.

"There wasn't much to save, but I got a couple of villagers and we wrapped wet cloths around our faces and managed to save a few things that were close to the buildings. Some clothes. A couple of bikes."

He just stood there. Why was Kaitlin Blackwood here?

He'd left her behind in the States when everything went bad. He hadn't wanted to get her involved.

"B.J., are you all right?"

A warm, sooty hand on his forearm shook off the shock. Meeting her in Phnom Penh. The journey out here.

"They've taken the children and Maly," he managed to choke out. It had to be the smoke, for the words ripped up his throat. "And this mob won't tell me where they've been taken."

She looked away and smile-nodded at Samnang and Chhean. That was Kaitlin, always trying to keep people happy, though she didn't even realize it. "They look afraid, to me."

"Bastards who took the kids threatened them. They said men came."

"There's tire tracks heading back towards town."

That got his attention. So whoever it was thought they could just drive kidnapped children around with impunity. Jorani's words about police sent a new chill down his back.

"B.J., I think we should go. The fire's contained and these people don't need more trouble."

She was right, of course. Kaitlin-bloody-Blackwood was always right about when to leave. Except when she'd left him. He'd needed her then, just like the kids needed him now.

He shook his head. "I need information."

"We both do. One of the villagers who helped me said the men talked about Pailin. He said it's in the west, near Thailand."

The sudden information stopped him. More than he could have hoped for. "Bloody hell."

He yanked her into a bear hug and planted a big one on her lips.

Chapter 20

B.J.'s unexpected assault enveloped Kaitlin in wood smoke and coppery blood at the same time as the fire's smoke stung her eyes. Then his lips found hers and, for a moment, she responded.

This was a man she might have been happy with, and it made her feel like crying.

Except he was too much like her father.

And he had betrayed everything they were.

And chose to do something that would have destroyed her.

This was a man she had loved.

And he had let her walk away.

No way was she letting the old feeling back in.

She elbowed her way free, stumbling back when he released her.

The fire-heated surroundings had nothing on the old flames flickering inside. No way. No frigging way was she letting him get inside her heart again.

"What the hell was that?" she demanded. Smoke-blackened people ringed them, and beyond were singed palm trees.

"What the bloody hell was that for?" he protested, rubbing his side.

"You grabbed me. I don't like to be grabbed." She swiped at her lips and felt grit smear on her face. Lovely.

"Well, I wasn't grabbing you for a pash, if that's what you thought. I've got better things to do. Now come on."

He grabbed her hand and—hadn't he been listening? She didn't want to be grabbed.

She clawed at his hand.

"The puppet. I need to talk to Jorani about the puppet."

He wouldn't let go and dragged her across the ash-covered yard. "Your little puppet's about the least of our problems, luv. Jorani's dead, and the bastards who did this have got twenty-five kids that were rescued from the sex trade. I'm betting they're all in the truck the villagers saw and headed back into that hell if I don't stop it."

"You don't know that!" Why she questioned him, she didn't know.

He stopped, turned back to her, his face grimmer than she'd ever seen. "I do know that. It's happened before. Back in 2004, ninety-one women and girls were kidnapped from a women's shelter in Phnom Penh and never seen again. They'd previously been rescued from the trade."

"But the police must have investigated."

He snorted—actually snorted—at her. "The police, my dear Kaitlin, were apparently part of the group that kidnapped the women."

"But the government…."

"Let me guess. The government must have done something. Sure. They did. They fired the head of the unit that had rescued the women in the first place and they appointed a woman to head the Ministry of Women's Affairs. Nice, except the bloody new gal happened to have a record for human trafficking in Thailand. Now, you got any other good ideas? Because I really feel the need to get going."

That stopped her argument. They ran to the moto-taxi.

"By the way, it was a thank you, nothing more," B.J. said from behind her as she scrambled aboard.

He must have seen the confusion on her face as he settled across from her and instructed the driver. "The kiss. It was thanks for the information, that's all. Sorry I got your knickers in a twist."

Then he was craning forward like a dog in a car, as if he could will the taxi faster. His whole being looked on the edge of panic. His knuckles stood out white as he clutched the edge of his seat. The veins in his jaw looked like they might pop.

She'd seen this before—once. Then he'd gone far beyond what she thought was safe investigative work.

He'd fashioned himself a child porn photographer and worked to get inside the organization and hopefully find the latest group of children. It hadn't worked, and when one of the children had turned up dead in a snuff film, he'd faked the evidence.

So he was still ruled by his passions and just as obsessed. If she wasn't careful, he'd sweep her up again into his quest—hell, she was already swept up in it, if what he said was true.

Because she wasn't going to stand by and let children be dragged into what she'd seen in her investigation stateside, but she wasn't going to give into B.J. McCallum's all-consuming madness, either.

She still had a missing father to find.

"I'll call Mac when we get into town. Get him to light a fire from the diplomatic end."

"Won't help. It's been tried before."

"B.J., I can't just run off and forget my father."

He glanced back at her, and she didn't like to see anyone in so much pain.

"I didn't ask you to, now did I?"

"He needs me."

"*He's* a grown man."

And by extrapolation, that meant he could get himself out of whatever frying pan he'd gotten himself into.

"I've always been there for him."

"And I've been there for these kids."

That stopped her as the moto turned a corner and sunlight found B.J.'s face.

"You've been helping to finance this orphanage all along, haven't you?"

"I helped Jorani start it. For all the good it's done." He turned his haggard face back to the road, yelling instructions to the driver.

No wonder he was in a panic. It shed a new light on him, too. The B.J. McCallum she'd known had never set down roots, nor done anything like this. It didn't jive with the man she knew, though it was consistent with his passion to help kids in the sex trade. She'd never understood where the passion had come from, but it sure as hell had been there.

"You're not going to get there any quicker hanging over him like that." She said it gently, trying to ease him back.

"Back off, would ya? I need to think. Plan."

Like he'd given her that courtesy when she'd asked him to leave her alone. Frustrated, she stayed silent, then pulled out her notepad, but was forced to give up her list due to the moto-taxi's bouncing.

The taxi careened down the road from pot hole to pot hole and then swept onto a wider road where the little engine wheezed louder and higher. Green fields, green trees, stands of pink dragon fruit, and an old, wooden-wheeled ox cart pulled by two white bullocks—all whipped past and disappeared behind them. She let B.J. think—and planned herself.

She couldn't walk away from the search for her father, no matter what B.J. said, but she couldn't let children get abducted, either. In the U.S. she'd go to the police. That was the right thing to do. B.J. couldn't be right, could he? When they got to town they could go their separate ways. B.J. could run off on his mad pursuit and she'd take the more thoughtful route: call the police and send them after the truck to backup B.J. Then she could get on with finding her father.

"What are you going to do?" she asked.

"Get home. Grab some cash and a car and head to Pailin."

Like she'd thought. Run off without thinking. But B.J. was a man you didn't convince otherwise once he made up his mind. "All right. I want to help, but… my dad."

He turned around to her then. "Listen, I don't need your help. I know you're worried, so go find your old man."

The trouble was, she didn't know where to go next. Jorani had been her only lead. Ask B.J. for help? The alternative was to return to Phnom Penh and visit Sovanna Phum again.

"The problem is, without Jorani I don't know where to go." She drew the puppet envelope out from where she'd stuffed it in her shirt while she helped with the fire. "The woman at Sovanna Phum said that it looked like an expert had made it, but they'd disguised it to look like a tourist puppet made by a student. I think she thought Jorani and her students had made it, but she didn't want to say it outright."

"Really? Let's have it then." He snatched the puppet from her and she nearly protested. This was her only connection to her father.

She watched anxiously as he slid the leather puppet out of the envelope and scanned it through the plastic.

He frowned. "Means nothing ta me. Odd lookin' tree, though." He shrugged and was about to slide it back into the envelope when he stopped, tilted the puppet, and his eyes widened. "Well I'll be gobsmacked."

Kaitlin craned to see what he was looking at, but it was still just a piece of carved leather laid across strong knees that knocked against hers too frequently as they bounced along the road.

"What is it?"

"Look. What'd'ya see?" he swiveled the puppet towards her, but it was the same puppet she'd studied too many hours already. She frowned up at him.

"A leather puppet," she said dubiously. "A tree. With flowers and birds in it."

"Look at it again. The shape."

She did. "It looks like one of those cliff-side trees contorted by ocean winds. You remember. Along Long Beach. How all the branches were twisted eastward."

But he was shaking his head. "Try again, woman."

She stiffened. He was friggin' enjoying himself, because he knew something she didn't.

"Why don't *you* tell *me*. I don't do guessing games."

It came out cool, reserved, and he must have heard it because he rolled his eyes.

"Don't throw a wobbly on me, Seattle. I'm checking whether I've gone bonkers. You've got one of those guidebooks in that pack o' yours, don't you? Haul it out."

She dug for her *Fodor's* and handed it to him. He paged through, shaking his head like a flipping disapproving teacher.

"What is it now?" She crossed her arms, but a massive pothole sent her head slamming into the metal crossbeam of the canvas roof. She scrambled to regain a handhold to hold herself in place. B.J. barely caught the puppet before it careened into space.

"Not much of a guidebook, luv. Just a lot of pretty pictures. Nice pictures, though." He flipped the book around to her at a map of Cambodia. "Here. Instead of yabbering, I thought I'd let you take a look."

He held the book, opened to a Cambodian map, beside the puppet, and at once she could see what he had. The puppet had been carved in the shape of the country, with the trunk flowing down into—Vietnam. She craned forward to see the caption on the map. A river. The Mekong.

The trunk swept up into the tree and divided into two major branches. One swept almost due north toward Laos and China. The other headed northwestward, if the tree was turned to match the map.

She ran her finger up its length.

"Ya got it. The Tonle Sap River. And if ya look, there's buds in the tree for Phnom Penh and Siem Reap and Battambang and the other cities. But look in the west."

She knew about the flowers, had run her fingers over them enough time, but—still feeling resentful—followed his finger as it swept over the puppet to a point near what was Thailand. There the leaves and blossoms had thickly woven together to frame a single open blossom.

"Why is that flower larger than the others?"

"Too right. A very good question."

He humped himself around so he sat crowded beside her on the bench seat and placed the puppet across her knees, while he held the book. He scanned the map as he ran his finger down the puppet leather and she could feel the heat of his finger through the leather and cardboard, and the excitement vibrating off his skin.

His other finger tapped the map where the overlarge blossom would lie, and when he turned the book to her, his expression had gone hard.

"Pailin. It seems both our roads lead that way."

Chapter 21

It didn't make a bloody bit of sense that Kaitlin Blackwood's puppet was a map that emphasized the same border town that one of the villagers had told Kaitlin the kids might be headed for, and yet, weirdly, it did. Pailin had a reputation. It was a Wild West town. It was a smuggler's den. It was the kind of place Kaitlin's father might end up.

B.J.'s gut told him that was the case, and he always followed his gut. Kaitlin, however—seated beside him on the taxi bench, she didn't look quite so convinced.

"You look." He shoved her guidebook back at her and closed his eyes, inhaling the increased exhaust stench as they neared Siem Reap. Even after six years in a country whose people he had fallen in love with, the roar of the moto-engines, the car horns, and the voices could still exhaust him. To say nothing of the oppressive heat and humidity at this time of year.

He opened his eyes and Kaitlin was pouring over the map. Beyond her, the sky showed a heavy convoy of thunder bumpers heading towards them. A bloody righteous storm coming their way.

Kaitlin ran her finger over the shadow puppet in that precise way that had always driven him crazy for the time it seemed to waste, and yet had always brought brilliant results. Precision, even in the bedroom.

He jerked at the sudden flush of heat the memories evoked. Kaitlin leaning over him, refusing to let him move until she had completed her careful ministrations. Back then he'd thought he was going to go mad with lust. *Damn it, man. You're over her.*

Kaitlin looked up at just that moment, and whatever she saw in him deepened her frown. *Good job, mate. Make her think yer a perv, along with a cheat and a liar.*

But she just closed the book and slipped it back into her pack, then looked down at her puppet. "You know, I still don't get why they call this a puppet."

He caught it from her and tapped his finger on the holes in the leather. "Well, it's not like the tree would dance, or anything. And it's not like we think of puppets, with jointed legs and everything, but these puppets were used to tell stories with light and shadows on walls. I guess that makes it a puppet, doesn't it?"

Her lips screwed up as she considered. "I guess. And dad used that to leave me a map."

"Too right."

"I guess I'm going to Pailin."

"Nice ta have ya aboard, mate." He stuck out his hand. *Keep it simple. Keep it friends.*

She hesitated, but then accepted his offering.

Her slow smile and the warmth of her hand almost broke him.

§

The moto skidded to a stop in front of the Jade Violin, raising a nice little dust cloud that set Kaitlin to coughing. B.J. leapt out of the carriage and turned back to her.

"Pay him. I'll be in my unit makin' some calls."

He left her swearing at him for dumping her with the bill. He'd make it right with her later. He ran through the lobby, but ignored the girl on the desk when she called to him. Too much to do. Too little time. And Maly's injured brown gaze kept staring at him every time he closed his eyes.

He was not seeing his little girl returned to that hellish life.

Up the four flights of stairs to the flat he rented on the third floor by the month. He'd had one bed removed and had furnished the room with a better desk and chair. On the side nearest the tiny bathroom, he'd installed a darkroom work table and drying racks for his old-fashioned film work, and across the windows he'd put solid shutters that kept out the light. All of his digital work he kept on his computer.

The caustic stench of photographic chemicals met him halfway up the last flight of stairs.

He slowed. He'd always managed to contain the chemical smell in his room by opening the windows after each bout of developing and printing. He climbed another two steps until he could see the door to his room.

Open.

Fuck.

The door yawned open onto darkness, so someone had drawn his dark room shutters. Even more trouble. And anyone in the room could see him in the stairs if they were looking.

He crept the rest of the way up the stairs, wishing for a weapon and hoping like hell Kaitlin took her time paying the moto driver. He didn't need her walking into trouble, too.

No sound came from beyond the open door, but that didn't mean someone wasn't waiting. Silently, he crept along the wall to his door. Listened.

A small sound. Something dripping? A scratching sound? He couldn't decide which. *So get off it. Ya goin' in, or what? No time like the present.*

He leapt through the door and stabbed his hand at the light switch. The room burst into view.

Bloody hell, the place had exploded.

Chemicals—everywhere. They stained the white walls, soaked his bedding, clothes, and books, and dripped-dripped-dripped from broken bottles on the work table onto the floor to pool. Furniture was tossed over. The desk had been emptied in a hailstorm of paper that stuck to the chemicals like confetti.

His computer had been smashed on the floor, the external back-up drive beside it. He stood rooted, taking in the destruction. Everything. Absolutely everything he owned destroyed, including his precious photos. Sure, a lot of them were stored by the stock photo companies he dealt with and others were backed up through the wonders of the on-line community. But everything recent was gone, except for the photos he'd taken at the Bayon two nights ago. Those were still in his camera.

His hand went to the Nikon protectively, but a scrabbling sound beyond his bed, whirled him around. The sound a small animal's claws might make. Had one of those damn cats gotten in with the door left open?

Cautiously, he rounded the bed.

Nick Mayerthorpe stared up at him, covered in blood, one hand scrabbling at the floor.

"Fuck me. Bloody hell."

He shoved the bed out of the way and went to his knees beside his friend. Nick had been trapped between the bed and the wall. A huge hole had been blown in his chest—a wound B.J. knew far too well.

He scrambled for his medical kit, but the bastards who had done the destruction had found it, as well. The kit was smashed and filled with chemical. He threw it down, disgusted.

He grabbed a shirt that hadn't been too damaged and ran to the door. "Call an ambulance," he roared down the stairs in Cambodian.

Then he was back at Nick's side, pressing the next-to-useless cotton shirt against the sucking chest wound.

Nick shook his head. "I thought I'd wait for you, tell you what I found." A spasm of pain crossed his face and he gasped for breath.

"Just shut up, ya Limey bastard. Just let me help ya."

There was so much blood. More than with Jorani, but then she'd been on soil that could absorb it.

Nick shook his head and swallowed, sweat beading on his forehead. "A couple of men seemed to have the same idea. Bastards caught me here. Not locals, but Cambodian. They took the stone from me."

The stone. The ruby he'd found at the Bayon. He'd left it with Nick for safekeeping.

Nick started to cough and tried to sit. B.J. helped him up, but the blood just kept coming up in thick gobs, spewing over the wall, the bed, B.J. He tried to push Nick down again. Where the fuck was that ambulance?

Nick slid down, but the coughing continued. His watery blue eyes caught on B.J.'s in panic. He couldn't breathe. Dammit, he couldn't breathe, and B.J. couldn't help him.

In what must have been a tremendous effort, Nick swallowed back blood. "They're looking for you, Beej, old man. You gotta go. They're coming back."

His words were followed by a huge spume of blood and a paroxysm that curled his body in on itself. Then the coughing stopped and the faded blue eyes of Nick Mayerthorpe, friend, went flat.

Chapter 22

The dust and grit from the fire and the wild ride grated in Kaitlin's eyes as she dug in her bag for her wallet to pay the motorcycle taxi driver. Around her, the normal lives of the Cambodian shopkeepers continued. Young men lounged in shop doorways, small children played in the shadows just outside, motorcycles and taxis cruised past to deposit or pick up tourists for the temples. A pair of slump-shouldered older women trudged down the street towards the restaurants. No black cars with dented fenders, thank God.

Normal. So normal.

And she—was not.

She fished out the right bills and enough for a tip.

"Thank you. You drove very well." *Aside from the potholes almost taking off the top of my head.*

He grinned and stuffed the money in his pocket and then swung his leg over his motorcycle like an old-fashioned gallant, revved the engine, and putted down the street in a cloud of exhaust fumes. Well, maybe not so gallant. She headed inside.

"May I use your phone?" she asked the girl at the desk. "It's a local call."

The girl nodded and turned the phone in her direction.

"I want to call the police. Can you dial them for me?"

The girl gave her a look akin to eye-rolling, but dialed and waited for someone to answer. Then she handed the phone back to Kaitlin. "English."

Kaitlin accepted the phone. "Hello?"

"This is Detective Lon Nol. How may I help you, please," said a male voice.

The English sounded totally rehearsed, but then they must love dealing with tourists. She thought of B.J.'s reluctance to go to the authorities. Was she doing the right thing? B.J.'s hesitation had to have something to do with all the trouble he'd gotten into back home, and things were serious now. Deadly serious. A woman had died out at the orphanage and her father might be in similar danger. That decided her.

"My name is Kaitlin Blackwood. There has been a problem at the Jorani Orphanage." If that was what it was called. "A fire has burned the place down, Jorani has been killed, and the children taken. We believe they're being taken to Pailin. Please, we need your help to stop them."

Stick to the facts. Make them understand, and bring assistance as fast as they could.

A pause at the other end of the phone. "Your name again, please?"

"Kaitlin Blackwood. I'm a reporter. From the States. With me is B.J. McCallum, the Australian photographer."

The sound of rapid Cambodian over the phone, then another voice came over the phone, cold and clear. "Where are you, Ms. Blackwood?"

She looked at the phone, suddenly uncertain she should be doing this.

A crash and frantic shout came from upstairs in incomprehensible Cambodian, but she knew the voice. B.J.

She dropped the phone and ran for the stairs, taking the risers three at a time. One flight. Two. Three—this European floor numbering system where the ground floor didn't count still confused her.

She came up the fourth flight and the stink of chemicals sent her coughing. A single door yawned open.

Go in? She stopped at the door and peered cautiously in.

A devastated room, although she recognized the puke-green shirt B.J. had worn yesterday amid the tangle of clothes on the floor. What had happened? B.J. was a lot of things, but he wasn't an untidy man, especially where his camera equipment was concerned.

She hesitated, then stepped inside, and found herself facing B.J.'s back as he bent over Nick Mayerthorpe, who was surely dead, judging by the amount of blood.

Call an ambulance. Call the police. Administer first aid. Preserve evidence, and above all, get the story. At least that was what Mac and the other editors expected, but there were people here who needed her.

She'd dealt with blood before. Maybe not this much, but she could do this even if she didn't like it—had to steel herself when going into crime scenes.

"B.J.?"

He was on his feet and to her in what seemed like one movement. "You shouldn't see this."

But she was staring at *him*. Fresh blood covered his camera and shirt and trousers. It spattered his face and hair.

That was the difference between them, wasn't it? B.J. McCallum was a runner-inner—the kind of person who ran into danger to help in an emergency. The kind of person you wanted around when things got bad, like on 9/11. The trouble was, that kind of person didn't live that long.

She, on the other hand, took the more thoughtful approach. Yes, she'd be there, but she'd consider the options before she ran in.

"My God, are you all right?" She backed up a step. All of her careful considerations whispering up into smoke.

"I'm fine. Thanks fer asking. We gotta leave."

He shoved her back and she dug in her heels, her gaze drifting from the shock of his face and clothing to the person on the floor. "We should call an ambulance."

"Too late, I'm afraid."

"Then the police." Of course, she'd left them on the line downstairs.

"Weren't you listening? They're likely involved."

He was serious. Really serious, and a sick feeling formed in the pit of her stomach. She needed to think this through.

"Then… then… What do we do?" Flipping hell, she hated it when she felt so uncertain. That wasn't how Kaitlin Blackwood was.

"We're getting outta here, just like Nick said. That's going to be us if we don't rack off now!"

He shoved her towards the stairs, his grip on her arm so tight her hand started to go numb.

Down one flight before she got her brain going again. She grabbed the banister to stop him and held on. "Stop. Would you just stop and think about this a moment."

He turned on her, a snarl on his face, and too much grief in his eyes. "You think I can't get Nick outta my brain? He was my friend, goddammit. So was Jorani. What the fuckin' hell is goin' on?"

"I don't know. But we can't just go running out into the streets. Look at you. Just the sight of you'd send most people running. Maybe we should stay and talk to the police."

"Are you nuts?" Then he looked down at himself. "Shi-it. Can't go out like this."

"Come on." She dragged him onto the second floor landing and to her room. Inside and to the bathroom. "Strip."

"Be still my beating heart. If I'd known ya wanted me…."

She shoved him towards the small bathroom. "Just do it. I'll wash out your shirt while you shower."

He still hesitated.

"I've already seen your equipment, if that's what you're worried about."

He obeyed, the two of them uncomfortably close in the tiny, white-tiled bathroom. The shower didn't have an enclosure, which meant B.J.'s shower sent liberal amounts of water over Kaitlin. By the time he was done, at least the worst of her grime was washed off, but she also needed a dry change of clothes.

She changed and started to pack her bag while B.J. toweled off and put on his sodden clothes.

"No time for that, luv," he said when he saw what she was doing. "Grab yer money, yer passport and anything you can't bear to leave behind, then we're gone."

Distant sirens screamed closer.

"Dammit," he swore. "Come on."

"We need to call the U.S. embassy. And Mac."

"A waste of time." He herded her towards the door.

He was pushing her too fast. She needed time to think.

"Would you just hold on?"

The sound of the siren coming around the corner of the street took her choice away.

"Fuck me!" he grabbed her and half led, half dragged her down the hall to a narrow set of stairs at the rear of the building. "Fire escape—and the way those bastards got in, I'll bet."

Heavily booted feet were pounding up the stairs.

"Come on!" He hauled at her.

Stay or go? He knew the country better than she did, that was true, but it went against everything she'd been trained to believe. And if what he said was true, then what she'd done by phoning the police was the worst thing possible.

She had to decide. Two bodies in one day, and somehow they were linked to her father and his clever, ridiculous, shadow-puppet map.

She went.

Chapter 23

Dragging Kaitlin Blackwood into this mess was a bad idea.

He knew the country. He knew the language. And it was him that somehow found himself connected to three bodies and a ruby the size of his palm.

Kaitlin, on the other hand, knew almost nothing of Cambodia, and her only connection to this mess was a carved leather map. A connection no one knew, except the two of them.

Given that the murders were clearly linked to him, he really needed to revise his plan and just get Kaitlin to safety and leave her behind. Best he could do for her. Things weren't going to get any prettier any time soon.

A pair of dusty windows at the top of the stairs provided the only light for the stairwell, so he plunged down into darkness, dragging Kaitlin after him. The scent of rice water and Cambodian curry rose to meet them from the restaurant next door and reminded him it was a long time since dinner yesterday. He'd planned to eat at Jorani's.

From above came a yell and the sound of more voices.

"Sounds like they found Nick." He rounded on her. "Listen. They don't know we're connected, but me—the police are already watching. Once we get out of here, I say we split up. I drop you at the Grand Hotel Angkor and get you out of the line of fire while I head after the kids."

He didn't wait for her agreement and dragged her down another flight before she put on the brakes.

"Not going to happen," was all she said. "We stay together. There's no evidence to show we killed anyone. The villagers know that. The desk clerk might, too. They can testify on our behalf."

"Until they're told what they're supposed to say." He held up his hand to stop her argument and they both hurried down to the rear door of the guesthouse. A long hallway led toward the lobby, but was tastefully concealed from the front by a bamboo room divider. Through it came loud, authoritative voices and shadowed figures.

A too-familiar voice was peppering Sam, the desk clerk, with questions. The same police investigator he'd run afoul of at the Bayon. That'd be right, given how his luck was running. But how the hell had the man known to come here?

He held his finger to his lips and eased the rear door slightly open onto a narrow yard filled with clotheslines. No one here—yet.

He shoved Kaitlin in front of him and tried to block the light streaming through the door with his larger body. She slipped through, her neat rear end tucked quite comfortably against his belly as he pressed behind her.

When they were outside, he led her silently through the lines of damp sheets to the concrete rear wall.

"We go over and then get to the next street. If anyone sees us, we split up. Grab a moto back to the Grand Hotel. We'll meet up in the bar." Or not. Mostly 'or not,' if he was going to keep Kaitlin out of whatever this was.

She looked at him dubiously, but finally nodded and turned to the barrier between them and freedom.

"Hold a minute, luv. I'll give ya a boost. Be careful, there's glass at the top."

He caught her trim waist and felt her stiffen, but too bad for her. She'd get over it once she was safely at the hotel and he was on his way. She might even forgive him for not turning up. Hell, let her have a little of her own back, given she's the one who'd walked away in the past.

He hiked her up—not much heavier than he remembered—and she grabbed the top and hauled herself up. When she was up and balanced she reached down for him.

"Come on, B.J. Tit for tat. There's a lot of glass up here. You don't want to come up blind."

"A little cut could be part of my disguise, luv." He motioned at his sodden shirt, the cream now stained a bloody brown that he doubted would ever come out. "Cut myself shaving, now didn't I?"

"Just give me your friggin' hand."

He did and leapt, trying to keep his weight off her, but in the end he couldn't because the bloody glass was more wicked than he'd expected. He still cut his hand and it bled like a bitch as he scrambled up and over. She was stronger than she looked.

They thumped down in the adjoining enclosure and sent a flock of chickens squawking and fluttering around a dusty yard, but it couldn't be helped. They dodged around piled-up car parts and into the back door of a building that he knew was a mechanic's shop in the bottom and a house of ill repute in the upper floors. Handy, he supposed, to the rousing night club down the block.

Oil-soaked air slicked his nose and killed all other scents. Exclamations of surprise came from mechanics as he dragged Kaitlin around motorcycles and a taxi in for repair and out into the street.

A group of men looked up from a late lunch of rice and fish and B.J. yanked Kaitlin towards him. "Keep your face averted, luv. Don't want to make it any easier to identify you than it already is." Shook his head. "We stand out like a shag on a rock, as it is."

But they were free for the moment. He headed them down the street toward the main street. There would be taxis there aplenty. One of them could take Kaitlin to the hotel. Another could hopefully get him to the Tonle Sap harbor before the police could put men at all points of egress from Siem Reap.

A boat to Battambang was his best hope to beat a truck load of children on their way to Pailin. The roads went in a huge loop up towards Sisophon, and then back to Battambang before turning towards Pailin—a three-to-four-hour trip at least in a trundling truck, whereas the boat could be there in less than three hours if he could get one of the speed-boat operators to cooperate.

Not if. He would.

Chapter 24

It was all happening too fast. Kaitlin jogged up the street behind B.J., trying to sort everything through. Ahead lay the main street with taxis galore. That and so many tourists were a good thing. Whoever had done these things couldn't very well shoot her and B.J. on the street.

At least she hoped not.

But then the fire at the orphanage and Jorani's and Nick's murders were just the latest in too many things that shouldn't be happening.

All since she'd arrived in Cambodia.

B.J. pulled her around the corner and up to two moto-taxis pulled up to the curb. He spoke in rapid-fire Khmer, gave some money to the drivers, and pushed her towards one of the contraptions.

"Like I said, luv. We split up and meet again at the Grand Hotel Angkor. Make finding us a little harder for the police or whoever."

She started to climb aboard her taxi, but something about B.J. wasn't right.

The way he wouldn't quite meet her gaze, before he turned to scramble into the other taxi. Almost like he couldn't get away from her fast enough, which was kind of strange given she'd caught him looking at her ass a couple of times with a certain lasciviousness she remembered too well.

Flipping hell, he was trying to dump her, and head off on his own wild chase, just like he'd done with the case back in Seattle.

And that had worked out *so* well for everyone.

She wasn't going to let him do it again. Not when the shadow puppet clearly indicated a connection between Jorani and her father. She stopped. Something more was obviously going on than the abduction of the children. Heck, her father might be the one snuffed out next time.

She yelled at her driver and dove out of the taxi so fast she barely grabbed her pack free, tripped, and twisted her ankle. Pain shot through her, but dammit, she wasn't going to let him do this to her. She *would* go to Pailin to find her father, and better to do that with B.J, who at least knew the country and the language.

B.J.'s taxi had left the curb and entered traffic as she limped after him. It started to pick up speed and she had two choices: protect her ankle or catch the bastard.

She ran, ignoring the sharp pains that jolted her leg. Dodged through traffic and—thank the powers that be—a traffic light changed and stopped the flow of traffic. Caught up to him and swung herself into the moto-taxi. Glared up at him and then smiled sweetly.

"You Aussie bastard. Don't think you can lose me so easily."

§

Forty-five minutes later, they were still arguing, and the rice fields and forest were giving way to flooded fields and stilted houses marooned in the midst of water. Kaitlin braced herself against the sway and stagger of the bouncing moto-taxi and shook her head.

"I don't care what you say. You can't make me stay behind. I'll pay for my own boat to Battambang." So there. She felt like a school kid about to stick out her tongue, but that would be pushing B.J. too far. He was frazzled enough as it was.

"Quit bein' an idiot, Kaitlin. You've got no idea what you're in for."

"You said that already. He's my dad. They're your kids. It means we're in this whether we like it or not."

"That still doesn't make you any more suited for a walkabout to back o' Bourke."

She rolled her eyes. "You know, one of these days I'm going to go to Bourke and see all the people that made it there just to prove you're wrong. I can do whatever I turn my mind to."

It was his turn to roll his eyes. "You don't know anything about anything in this country."

"So teach me what I need to know, instead of arguing with me. You know I won't change my mind."

B.J. looked skyward. "Lord save me from fools and idiot American journos." He did another of his checks behind them as if they weren't quite as safe as he'd have her think.

"And Lord save me from impossible misogynist Aussie males."

"My God, the woman has a sense of humor." He grinned.

She just snarled because she wasn't going to let him flippin' charm her again. And B.J. McCallum *was* a charmer.

She crossed her arms and leaned back to stare out at the passing landscape.

The road now traveled along a long isthmus in a surreal landscape. Low-slung, canvas-roofed, wooden boats hung between the deep blue sky and cloud-reflecting water over what must be drowned fields. Houseboats reflected blue-painted walls in blue water amidst treetops, and what looked like stilted restaurants lined the sides of the road—except they were filled with lines of empty hammocks, not tables and chairs.

So foreign it left her feeling kind of numb. Or maybe it was everything that had happened. A shiver ran up her back whenever she thought of the fire, Jorani, and Nick Mayerthorpe. She had *known* him. Someone she *knew* had been murdered!

Just what were she and B.J. in for?

She looked at her hands, still clenched in her lap. One was covered with road rash from her stumble out of her moto.

The other she clenched extra hard, but red still oozed around her fingertips. She'd cut it badly on glass on the top of the concrete wall, but she'd rather take the pain than show B.J. any weakness.

She clenched it tighter, and something sharp grated in her flesh. Pain, ripe and acidic as an orange, cut through her. She inhaled deeply. Fresh mud and cooking fires. A village ahead. Maybe she could find a first aid attendant, because her hand had been bleeding far too long. The moto-taxi slowed.

"How much farther?"

"To Battambang? About two hours. To the harbor, a minute or so."

"What's Battambang like?"

He shrugged. By the set of his jaw, he was still angry he hadn't convinced her to give up on the journey. "Second largest city in Cambodia. A dive."

He checked behind them again, but all that followed were the occasional moto and a distant car.

Around them a string of stilted houses stood along the road with boats tied to their rear, and more houses sticking up out of that surreal surface of water like out of a fairy tale or a *National Geographic* special. Small boats slid over the shallow water like so many dragonflies. Hell, she was *in* a fucking *National Geographic* special.

Laughter burbled unhealthily in her chest. "And I'll just bet Battambang's better than this, right?"

"Too right. This's just a village harbor. Battambang's the jumping off place for Pailin. The city's across the lake, and I'm betting we can make it there before the truck with the kids can." He ducked forward to yell something to the driver, who sped up. The vehicle jounced out of town on to a jumbled, man-made spit of land covered in the deep ruts of heavy equipment.

On one side of the spit, a cavalcade of shallow boats painted red and blue and green over white hulls were hauled up on shore. Beyond them, more water and treetops stretched as far away as she could see, but out beyond an open channel of water lay what looked like a veritable floating city.

The taxi roared to a halt and the world went wondrously silent. She paid the driver and climbed out, but when she looked up they were surrounded. Men. Slim. Dark.

Too similar to the men who'd tried to abduct her—yes, she had to admit it—abduct her.

And more were coming from the lined-up boats, as if the boats somehow spawned them. All of them were talking—make that yelling—at once.

She backed up a step and B.J. caught her shoulders. "It's all right, luv. If yer comin', that is. Unless you'd like to reconsider, they just want us to hire their boat. Take us for a right nice cruise, if that's what we were lookin' for."

She jerked loose of his too-hot hands. "Don't call me 'luv'." She stepped forward, determined to be in control. "We need to rent a boat. A fast one."

"These folk don't understand much English." He launched into amazingly fluid Khmer. She was reasonable at Spanish, but he was speaking like a native.

A bit of conversation and then: "Come on."

He led her at a jog after one of the men. Flippin' hell, she was following along like a puppy, and that wasn't her modus operandi. She lengthened her stride to catch up to B.J.

"So what's going on?"

"He's got a boat, but he keeps it for the locals."

"How much?" She thought of her rapidly diminishing bank roll and wondered if he accepted credit cards. Stupid thought.

He looked away for a moment. "Pretty dear. Hundred U.S. dollars. You got the money?"

"What!" She screeched to a halt.

He stopped to face her. "A hundred is what it takes to shake a man loose from making his living for a day. Now are ya in or out, Kaitlin? If you say no, that's fine, and I'll be thankful."

"Dammit, B.J., if you think paying the damn bill is going to stop me, you have another think coming. You're not getting rid of me. I'll pay the damn bill and take it out of your hide, later."

The light that lit his eyes was almost hopeful. "Well, won't that be bonzer."

She rolled her eyes, disgusted at herself for giving him that opening.

She hid her injured hand behind her back and walked past him. "I'd smack you if I thought it'd do any good."

He only worked his eyebrows like a cad and passed her so she had to speed up.

The owner yelled at them from down the ranks of boats. When she stumbled across the last rough ridges of ground and around the worn prow of a boat that held what looked like an entire store on its deck, the craft they'd hired came into view.

She didn't know much about boats, but she'd seen enough of them from her apartment above Lake Union.

"Are you joking? A hundred bucks for this?"

Shallow drafted. Three aluminum hoops held up a faded canvas roof above a narrow hull that held three hard benches. A long, pointed prow held a loop of plastic flowers. As she watched, the owner loaded a few bottles of water and tossed them under the canvass cover.

"It's this or nothing, luv. They use this kinda boat when someone needs to get somewhere fast. See the engine?"

She followed his gaze. A huge, gleaming motor sat tipped up off the back of the boat. It did look like it meant business.

"It's not going to just break down somewhere?"

"Trust me."

Like that was going to happen. She'd trusted him once before, and that had turned out so well. But his eyes said that lives depended on this, and one of those lives might be her father's. Besides, it was this or nothing.

She climbed aboard and settled on the first of the narrow benches, her hurt hand cradled against her. B.J. and the owner shoved the boat out into the narrow strip of blue water between the other boats. Both men leapt lightly aboard. B.J. set about rolling up the canvas sides as the engine roared comfortingly into gear and they started out into the open channel.

"Hitch over will ya?" She did and B.J. settled beside her, too close because of the narrowness of the seat. Wind whipped into her face as the boat picked up speed and headed north and west out into a great sea of green.

Not treetops, she realized. Or there were some, because the lake was flooded, but most of the water surface was covered by floating green islands of tangled vines, like a regular Sargasso Sea. Only narrow channels were written through the islands in a calligraphy of blue.

"Water hyacinth," B.J. yelled above the engine roar.

The needle-shaped boat rose up on its wake, sending long undulations behind them through the thick mass of green. "It's killed a lot of the lake, just as bad as the over-fishing. Between the fishing concessions to wealthy friends of the government, the Vietnamese fishermen, and the locals, they don't seem to understand about sustainability. They will when the fish disappear. I hear they already are."

He shook his head, always a man of strong opinions, and looked out over the plants. The wind smoothed his hair off his strong, handsome face as he squinted against the glare. Then he checked behind them again as if he expected something to be there.

Behind there were other small boats in the lake. A few followed in their direction. But surely they couldn't catch them, because for all its looks, this boat *was* fast.

She looked back at B.J. but he hadn't relaxed now that they'd put some distance between them and the shore.

There were more lines around his eyes than she remembered. But then she had a few more of those, too. The way he strained forward on the unforgivingly hard bench, he looked like a sleek dog on scent. Or, she had to allow, maybe a little like she did when she was on a story. Or like he had, just before everything went horribly bad in Seattle.

She was going to have to be very, very careful she didn't let him drag her into some wild scheme. If she was going to do this with him, she'd have to be the careful one for both of them.

And leave him behind if things got too wild.

She glanced at him. She could do that.

She would.

Chapter 25

The open water of the lake was behind them and so was their speed. The bloody driver had decided to take a short cut, and now the boat had cut speed to crawl along a narrow channel between the tops of trees as it cut across one of the Sangker River's oxbows. Bright blue and yellow butterflies rose up at their passing, and the bloody bugs could have beaten the boat in a race, they were going that slowly. He cranked around to the boatman, but the man was concerned for his engine—rightly.

B.J. forced himself back down on the bench and fought down his frustration. There had been other boats following them out of the harbor, but he had to believe that the police, or whoever was involved, wouldn't be able to follow their trail from the Jade Violin.

At least not quickly.

Still, they needed to go faster to stand a chance of finding the children in Battambang. Faster, when the world was forcing him to go slow. He felt like he was running in a dream and would never get there.

The tops of the dead canopies of drowned trees held huge, ungainly cranes and silhouetted cormorants with wings spread like puppets. They reminded him of all the diplomats and foreign governments who didn't really want to do what it would take to stop the trafficking of children.

The air smelled of murky water and green and sweat.

His sweat was tinged with the iron of his anger, but there was also something lighter and sweeter that brought back old memories of lying-in together on a Sunday morning and pouring through the newspaper to find their articles and photos over the morning's first cup of coffee.

There had only ever been one woman who evoked such strong memories, and she was sitting beside him and, as usual, asking the hard questions. And he didn't want her here, dammit.

"So what's the plan? We go head-to-head with armed men? 'Cause I don't feel ready to do that with only my day pack for a weapon."

The engine noise helped erase the annoyance of Kaitlin's words as swiftly as they were spoken. B.J. looked out over the sun-heated water and considered his answer.

"I haven't quite noodled a plan out yet, luv." He shook his head. "Maybe we go to the authorities in Battambang. Maybe there's someone there who's not on the take. But then, maybe not. Too much chance of word getting out about where we're headed, ya know? I'm thinking we find a way to stop the truck and free the kids. If we do it in public and there're enough blokes around, the bastards might be less inclined to use their weapons."

He felt her looking at him and met her gaze. She shook her head and then looked away, as if she had something to say she wasn't sure she wanted to share. She clearly thought he was crazy.

"Cooie. You got a betta idea, luv?" he let his accent come on thick, because the Crocodile Dundee affectation had always bugged her and, predictably, she stiffened.

Good.

"Better than you, apparently. You don't know the police in Siem Reap were involved and you haven't said word one about how we find my father."

The ice in her voice was enough to freeze tits off a witch. *Good on ya, B.J., you've got her mad now. Like that's always worked so well for you.*

"Actually, I do know—about the police, at least. Jorani said there were police there when the kids were nabbed. We had to get outta Siem Reap. The best we could've hoped for was to end up in jail, and I couldn't take that chance. Not with the kids… Besides I don't think Jorani's the first they've killed."

She didn't say anything, which had always been one of the things he liked about her: she was capable of silence. Contemplative *and* angry.

"A couple of days ago I was out at the temples. A monk was to meet me, but he turned up dead." He shook his head.

She still looked at him, with that utter stillness. Even with her hair whipping her cheeks and catching the light in silver-gold glints, and with the boat vibrating beneath them, nothing else moved. That was how she went when she was considering things.

"So you were drowning your sorrows when I saw you at the hotel." So she thought he was a loser.

"You might say that." He'd actually rung up Nick to pick the man's brains about the stone. Along with needing a tallie to quench a hellish thirst. "There's something else, too. I found a stone with the monk—a ruby. Largest bloody thing I ever saw."

"A ruby. That's the kind of thing that would attract my father."

Too true. He hadn't thought of that connection. He glanced out at the water. They were coming back into the Sangker River's main channel again, and a large floating town lay ahead. Green- and blue-sided boats, barge-houses, and trees reflected in the rippled water with Dutch Master colors. He really should spend some time out here with the village people and photograph their way of life.

He turned around to yell for more speed when the boat's gunnel exploded beside his hand, sending a shower of sharp wooden shards into him.

Bullet.

He shouted at the boatman and dragged Kaitlin down.

Damn and damn and damn and damn.

"What?" Kaitlin struggled under him, her scent of roses and pine filling his senses.

"Stop yer struggling, woman. Someone's shooting at us."

She went still. The boat's engine roared. The craft hesitated, then picked up speed, the prow rising above the water.

The boatman was yelling as another shot ripped through the canvas.

Damn it, where was the shooter?

B.J. chanced a heads up and scanned the town. There. In the center of the town, a barge-like vessel held a white-painted store with a viewing platform on the roof. A man in fatigues stood there and a boat roared out from behind the building and headed towards them.

How? How had they known to be here?

"Faster!" he yelled to the driver, but the man shook his head.

"Those are police," the boatman protested. He cut the engine.

"Bloody hell! You'll do as I ask!"

B.J. stood, and the narrow boat shifted precariously under him. Another shot, and the report thundered across the water, but the bullet just sliced the water. Thank God, they were out of range. For the moment.

But the boat from the store came on, the sunlight glistening on too many weapons.

B.J. shouted at the driver, but the man shook his head. B.J. lunged over the awning and slammed his fist into the man's face. The boatman tumbled into the water and B.J. turned to the engine.

Honking big and nothing he was familiar with. He slammed open the lever the boatman had used to slow the boat, and the vessel bucked under him, then lunged forward.

The force threw him backwards. There was nothing to stop him. He staggered back, and the bloody boat seemed to run from under him. Bullets slammed into the stern.

He grabbed the engine's lever and held on. Regained his balance, but the boat slammed to dead stop.

Bullets whizzed too close to his head. Wood exploded around him, something pinged off the engine cladding. The bastards were in range; now they just needed to improve their aim. He threw himself down.

"Hold on!" he yelled to Kaitlin.

"Are you nuts? What'd'you think I'm doing?"

He slammed the lever forward again and the little boat leapt in the water. It picked up speed. Their pursuers came after, narrowly missing the boatman, paddling in the water.

He aimed the craft at the center of the river as it streamed through flooded open fields. No way in hell he was losing them here. Either the men pursuing had already been in the town and someone had radioed ahead, or the boatman's time in the oxbow had slowed them more than B.J. had realized.

Either way, they'd known where he and Kaitlin were headed.

More shots, but nothing came close to the boat. He glanced back and the pursuers seemed farther behind.

He might do this. He might. A giddy sort of thrill filled his chest and escaped as a laugh.

"What the hell's so funny? They're shooting at us."

Kaitlin climbed out the back of the awning to join him in the exhaust fumes at the stern of the boat.

"We're outrunning them."

She glanced over his shoulder. "For the moment."

"Always the optimist."

"Realist, more like. How the hell are we going to get out of this?"

The lovely bubble of euphoria burst in his gut and left it sour. He glanced behind them again.

"How the hell did they know we were here? It's too fast for them to have put the pieces together and tracked us from the Violin."

Kaitlin looked at her hands. All the blood seemed to leave her face and he glanced behind. Not the pursuers causing the reaction. He looked back at her face. No question.

"What the hell didja do?"

She chewed her lip before answering—a sure sign that whatever she was going to say was bad.

"Back at the Jade Violin. I thought you were wrong, so I called the police. I think that's why they got there so fast. I—I gave them our names and said we thought the kids were going to Pailin—and that we were after them. I—I'm sorry." She hung her head.

B.J. just went cold. The engine vibrations rammed right up his arm to rattle him as badly as Kaitlin's news. It felt like his whole life was going under, just like the landscape. "You fucked up good, Kaitlin. Real good. The bastards'll be waiting for us."

He could barely hear himself over the engine roar, but she heard. She knew.

"I'm sorry. I'm so sorry. I've made things worse."

He closed his eyes, surprised he was this calm. That he hadn't chucked a wobbly and yelled was a bloody miracle. "Yeah. Sure. Battambang is about the last place we should be headed."

He glanced back. The other boat was still there, but it had turned into a ribbon of shore in the midst of the inundation. It slowed and a couple of men leapt off. The boat headed back into the river and picked up speed.

This time faster.

"Fuck." He pushed at the lever but it was all the way out. The other boat started to eat up the distance. "This is why I didn't want ya t' come. I didn't want ya involved."

"You should have thought of that before you invited yourself on my trip to Jorani's."

"That was different. I was trying to protect you." Dammit, that wasn't supposed to come out.

"Protect me?" She reared back like she'd been struck. "I don't need anyone's protection. Never have, never will."

"Like hell. I saw those guys at the hotel, Kaitlin. Didn't exactly look like a welcome party."

She thankfully went silent—for a moment.

"Well that should tell you I *am* involved. My father's involved."

The boat jetted around a curve in the channel, the river banks were rising. If he stayed in the river they'd be committed to that direction only.

He needed to decide what to do. He glanced behind. Yes, the distance had lessened between them, and soon the bloody weapons would be in range. He needed to take away the police's advantage.

"In case you haven't noticed, *this* is dangerous. More dangerous than anything you've experienced in the States. You've got no police to ride to your rescue here. Instead you've got corrupt officials. Hold on!"

He threw the long tailed propeller to one side and the boat swerved sharply. He aimed for a break between two stilted houses and a stand of bamboo. If he could get them into a channel like the oxbow, he might stand a chance of losing their pursuers.

"Duck!" They slid between the two houses and the stand of bamboo loomed up ahead. The stalks might look slender, but B.J. knew just how strong they were. They'd shatter the hull if he rammed them.

He glanced over his shoulder again. The other boat came on. He slewed their boat around the rear of one of the houses and skirted the bamboo, looking for a break.

There.

Kaitlin chose that moment to protest. "You're wrong, just like always. I'm just as suited as you are to deal with this. Hell we don't even know what this is!"

He'd had enough. He sat up. "You want control? Fine. You take the lever. You get us out of this."

He took his hand off and the boat's speed died. The roar of their pursuer's engine echoed around them. If they didn't get through that bamboo and gone, they were caught.

"You decide where we should go, Kaitlin. Given we can't go to Battambang because some idiot mug told the police where we're going. Or better still, why don't you just turn the boat around? You trust them. Probably greet us with a hug or something."

If looks could kill, hers would have. She grabbed the lever and looked back at the police boat, nearing the front of the houses.

Then she let go and it was like she deflated on her seat, the canvas awning shadowing her face.

"Get us out of here, B.J. Just get us out."

He could almost feel sorry for her. It was never easy to admit your failings. But B.J. just grabbed the lever and used the long shaft with the prop to skew the boat around and amidst the bamboo.

Green pillars surrounded them, knocking hard against the gunnels. They placed barred shadows across Kaitlin's face and hair. The air was cooler here—until he drove them past the bamboo and out into the open water.

Sun blazed into his eyes like a searchlight. He couldn't see, with the burning reflection off the wide sheet of water.

An open rice field. Across it waited a dense mat of treetops. If they could make it, they might stand of chance of evading their pursuers. If they could make it.

He aimed the boat straight across, but something wasn't right. The boat lugged in the water.

The engine coughed.

Chapter 26

Kaitlin hated helplessness. She had no respect for people who feigned helplessness or for those who collapsed in the face of bad odds. If life was a card game, when you were dealt a bad hand, you considered your options and bluffed. You never let someone know what you were feeling.

Except now. Now the damned fear and guilt almost strangled her into immobility as she looked back at the wall of shifting bamboo. The tall stand shifted like a curtain, showing hints of the houses beyond.

And the pursuing boat.

They needed to get out of here. She'd sort things out with B.J. later. And in the meantime she had to control her mouth.

The engine coughed.

Coughed again.

"Bloody hell!" B.J. swore and shoved at the lever.

The engine caught and they skipped forward, the front lifting as they picked up speed. The reflected blue sky and clouds made it seem like they were caught in some surreal place between sky and water. She craned out to look around B.J. The pursuers' boat nosed through the bamboo.

"They're coming."

B.J. glanced behind.

"Where are we going?"

"The trees. We might be able to lose them there."

Not what she would have thought of doing, but then she wasn't sure what she would have done. That fact left her uncomfortable. In this situation, B.J.'s ability to react *without* thinking seemed to work better.

The engine coughed again.

"Dammit to hell!"

B.J. slammed his fist against the engine, and yipped and yanked his hand away again. "Bloody hell." He stuck his burned knuckle in his mouth.

Kaitlin couldn't help but smile, until a rifle report cut through the engine sounds.

Something slammed into her. Shock ran up her arm.

The force hurled her off her seat and back under the awning. She lay there, stunned, on a bed of old rags, breathing in the wet wood and creosote scent. Above her the tattered canvas placed weird designs across the blue sky.

Maybe she should just stay here. She was out of B.J.'s way. Couldn't cause any more trouble.

She'd made the wrong call when she'd contacted the police. She understood that, now. And he hated her for it.

Rightly so, when she thought about it. There was no way in hell they were going to make it to Battambang on time at this rate.

More gunfire from outside sent her scrambling up. B.J. Was B.J. all right?

She scrambled out from the awning shelter. B.J. was craned backwards, keeping an eye on their pursuers as he hunched over the engine. The engine coughed again and he twisted around and swore—until he caught sight of her.

"You're alive!"

"Feels like." She nodded.

"I thought you were shot."

"Not quite." Or at least she didn't think so. Her arm had a number of long wooden splinters, but nothing else she could see, even though it hurt like heck. She yanked one loose and winced, but held it up. "Just wood."

Visible relief crossed B.J.'s face.

"What? You worried about me or something."

Another volley of bullets cut off any response.

B.J. ducked down. Kaitlin dove for cover.

They were almost to the trees, the long wake fanning out behind them as they arrowed for cover. They were going to make it. They had to make it. For B.J. For the kids. For her father.

B.J. yanked the lever back and the engine slowed, momentum carrying them under the treetops.

Twisted trunks surrounded them, broad leaves placed them in shadow.

"Make yourself useful and get forward. I need you to take the oar and fend us off from the trees."

She scrambled under the awning. Paddle. Where? She fumbled in the boat and the hull slammed into a tree. She almost went over. Grabbed a tree branch for balance and almost got pulled out of the boat again. *Klutz. Idiot. Fool.* Maybe B.J. was right in more ways than he knew.

But her stumbling unearthed the oar and she fumbled it up and tried to do what B.J. asked. The darn thing kept slipping in her sweaty palms. Make that bloody. And her hands were shaking. Actually, her whole body was shaking.

Stupid, stupid, stupid. She wasn't afraid. She wasn't.

The boat crept forward.

The police came behind them, their engine rumbling under the trees. She dug the oar into a crook in a tree and shoved, almost upending herself into the water again.

A hail of bullets slammed into the trees around her. She threw herself down, but the prow neared another tree. If they didn't turn, they'd plow into a tangle of dead branches and get hung up there.

She climbed to her knees and brought the oar up, balanced it with a sense of a bull's eye on her back.

A shove off the tree trunk and a bullet found the oar blade. The paddle disintegrated, leaving her with a tattered pole to work with.

More bullets pinged off tree trunks, but all she could do was pray they'd miss their mark, given the twisted route B.J. had them on.

She looked back. Surely the police boat fell behind. She doggedly kept easing them away from snags, then checked behind them again.

The police lagged farther back. They looked like they were conferring.

"I think they might be giving up."

"Just up and keep at it."

The engine coughed again and a flood of blue-black smoke belched from the exhaust.

B.J. swore again and checked behind him before yanking off the engine cladding. A cloud of smoke and the stench of burning filled the humid air.

He waved the smoke away and bent over the engine.

"What's the matter?"

"Nothing a complete engine overhaul wouldn't fix, I'm guessing."

"You never were an engine kinda guy."

He glanced up at her. "Cameras were my thing. But necessity is, they say. I've picked some smarts up, living here."

He fiddled with the exposed engine, a flood of murmured 'bloody hells', and 'bastards' floating forward.

"I'm not sure how long I can hold this thing together."

"Then we better hope that they really are deciding not to come after us."

They putted forward, the engine's stutters more frequent. Behind them, the pursuers' boat disappeared in a maze of never-ending tree trucks and acres of light-infused murky water.

Then the engine coughed once, twice, three times in a row and went silent.

Heat and the sound of lapping water coalesced around them and Kaitlin's legs gave, so she slumped down at the prow. Too much heat, so her shirt stuck to her. Blood on her arm and the leg of her trousers, but she didn't feel anything. Just sat there, watching the leaves place patterns over the blue sky.

The boat shifted under her and B.J. blocked her view.

"I think we're off their radar for the moment. How bad are you hurt?"

"Not at all." She smiled up at him, feeling almost drunk with the fact that she was still alive.

"Let me be the judge of that, luv."

"Will you cut it with the luv? I'm not your luv. I'm not anybody's luv."

Flipping, hell, even her words were slurred.

Then he was crouched in front of her, grabbing her arm to examine it. His too-critical gaze assessed her flesh, and she didn't want that. She had more years on her now. She could take care of herself.

She pulled loose. "See. A flesh wound."

"It's a little more than that, luv. See?"

His grave expression made her look. Something, wood possibly, but it may have been the bullet, had gouged a deep furrow through the flesh at the base of her elbow.

He shook his head. "Any closer and it would have shattered the joint."

The pain cut in then, as if his words released a dam, and she thought she was going to be sick. Tasted bile in her throat. Dammit. On the back of her tongue.

She lunged for the side of the boat and lost what little was left of what she'd eaten that morning. But her stomach kept spasming, dry heaves wracking her body.

B.J. gently held her shoulders and held back her hair. She twisted away.

"Dammit, I don't need your help."

"I'm all you've got, luv."

She palmed water over her face before pulling back into the boat, but wouldn't meet his eyes. Being sick, like this. Being injured. She didn't like the vulnerability. Especially with B.J. McCallum.

He offered her a bottle of the boatman's water. "Wash your mouth. Ye'll feel better."

"Spoken like a man who's had a bout of the 'chunders' during one of his numerous hangovers."

"You knocking on me, then? I thought I was doing you a favor." He caught her chin. "Kaitlin. You need a doctor."

"So? You're all I've got, remember? I believe those were your words."

He nodded, but he still kept his too-assertive hold on her chin. Damn him for being gentle. Damn him for being more gentle as he smoothed the tangle of her hair away from her face. The way he was looking at her, he might try to kiss her—not a good thing.

She grabbed his hand and winced.

"What is it?"

When she shook her head he grabbed her wrist and forced her hand open. She bit back a small cry of pain as he exposed the deep bloody score that oozed fresh blood across her palm.

"Jeezus, Kaitlin. How the hell'd you do this?" He uncurled her fingers and examined the wound. "There's something in there."

Kaitlin felt faint. She swallowed back the desire to vomit again. "Glass, I think. I cut it going over the wall behind the Jade Violin."

His gaze jerked back to hers, concern and anger on his face. "And you leave it to now to tell me?"

"No. I wouldn't have told you."

"Don't be a mug."

She just wanted it all to go away, B.J. included—even if his touch was gentle. "I seem to recall being a tad too busy running after motor-taxis and for boats to tell anyone anything. There wasn't exactly a lot of time."

"There was on the boat."

"Fine. I fucked up again, all right?"

She glared at him.

She pulled her hand back, wishing he'd just leave her alone, because every time he touched her it just made her vulnerability worse and she *hated* feeling like that. Hated feeling like she had felt as a child when her mother took her to food banks for food.

"I've dealt with it this long. I can a little longer. Besides, it's not that serious. Neither is the elbow. A couple of bandages and I'll be good as new."

"You don't deal with this properly and infection could set in. You want to lose that hand? That arm?"

She rolled her eyes. "You can't be serious."

He swore and grabbed her chin again and turned her head to look over the side of the boat. "Look around, Kaitlin. There's nothing sterile for miles. Cleaning your wounds and keeping them clean has got to be a priority."

"Let's not cloud the issue, here. The kids are the priority and so is my father."

He stiffened and looked at his watch, a bleak look crossing his features. "We've missed them. A truck on the highway would have made the turn to Pailin by three at the outside."

"Then you better fix that engine, hadn't you? Leave me the water and I'll take care of myself."

The damned man shook his head. Nope, B.J. McCallum was never any good at listening. "Fraid not, luv. When you took me into your moto to go to Jorani's, you took me on as a partner. I'm not losing a partner to infection. Or pain. First we get you taken care of, then we head after the kids."

So she was forced to accept him holding her hand as he poured bottled water over her wound, then used the tweezers of his pocket knife to extract a wicked shard of glass. The piercing pain in her hand reduced to a manageable throb.

"Damn." He looked at her with what might have been admiration. "And you poled all this way, with that in your hand."

She didn't say anything. Didn't move, because the look in his eyes was trying to tell her something. It might have been affection. It might have been that she went up in his estimation, but more likely it was that he felt a failure for not noticing and not protecting her. Well, he needed to learn something.

Kaitlin Blackwood didn't need anything or anyone, and she certainly didn't need a macho Aussie making her feel like the little woman in need of protection.

She held out her uninjured hand. "Fine. I'll keep it as a souvenir of our *last* meeting."

Not exactly a good put down, but it was the best she could come up with at the moment.

Chapter 27

Getting rid of Kaitlin was going to be a lot tougher than he had thought. B.J. bent over the oil-soaked boat engine and glanced her way. The liquid light of the drowned forest shimmered around her like light through a cool pint of amber beer—and he could use one of those right about now. She sat in the prow of the boat, her spine still stiff, even though, by the slump of her head, she'd finally fallen asleep in the heat.

Good. He swiped a greasy fist across his brow.

She needed the rest after all she'd been through. Hand deeply wounded, the gouge on her arm, and the various other wood slivers he'd forced her to allow him to take care of. The way she'd clenched her jaw and wouldn't watch as he worked, he wasn't sure whether it was the pain or his touch that bothered her the most. But he'd at least managed to bandage her wounds with what appeared to be clean cloths stacked inside the awning.

He turned on the gas and ignition and pulled the engine cord. In response, the engine rumbled to life and sent up a new blue cloud. Good enough for the girls he'd go with.

At least it wasn't black like before, but the hull shook roughly. So it wasn't quite in good running order, but he'd nurse it to shore some place they could get to the road and on to Pailin.

And Maly. He shook his head and set the engine cowling in place.

When he looked forward, Kaitlin was watching him. Her face was pale and her grey eyes looked huge and dark in skin that the watery light painted green. Not an attractive light, and yet Kaitlin was still one of the most attractive women he'd ever known.

And infuriating. Don't forget infuriating.

She staggered up, the broken oar in hand. "Where to?"

"How about you come back here and work the rudder. Save your hand." He wouldn't be that far from the engine if the darn thing broke down.

Kaitlin looked dubiously from him to the engine. Then she shook her head. "Not a good idea. If the police turn up, there's no way I can work that thing like you did."

Well, halleluiah. The woman *could* admit limitations. She was probably right, but…. He finally nodded.

"Have a care with that hand then, luv. It took a while to get it to stop bleeding."

"Do I have a choice?" she asked, cocking her brow as she stood and ducked a tree branch.

The truth was, he'd put her in position after position where she hadn't had a choice, and he was beginning to regret it. Had he done something similar in their relationship before, until he finally pushed her too far?

And you're doing it again, mate.

"Have a care with the spiders. Bloody things like to put honking big webs in the trees. They're poisonous."

She paled—a little—but then rolled her eyes. "Terrific. Something else to look forward to."

Sarcasm became her.

He shook his head and eased out the throttle.

The engine grumbled and belched, but the rhythm caught and they slowly got under way. Kaitlin finessed them through the narrow, liquid channels under the trees. At times it was like they glided through caves, all sound erased by the white noise of the belching engine—a problem, because their pursuers could hear them, too, but there really wasn't much choice. He had to hope the mass of trees would make it hard to tell exactly where they were. The waterlogged air was overwhelmed by the carbon monoxide.

The trouble was, he didn't know how far this forest stretched, or if there was land on the far side. The annual flooding of the Tonle Sap Lake, when the river reversed its course, sent hundreds of millions of gallons of water out over the landscape. It could still be miles to shore. Except the Sangker River banks had been rising. Battambang and solid ground couldn't be that far away. But the police could be waiting on the other side of this forest, too.

Too right.

Kaitlin probably realized exactly that, but she still gamely used the pole to ease them on their way. It had to hurt like hell. The woman had a pair, he'd give her that.

They bumped their way through the flooded forest, leaves raining down on them. An occasional egret or cormorant would take flight and he regretted that the birds might give away their position. Gradually, the sun overhead passed away westward.

He checked his watch. Maly and the kids would be trundling northwestward to slavery, and nothing and no one was there to stop it. The sick frustration twisted in his gut. He just prayed Maly didn't have one of her spells. There was no telling what her captors would do with a kid with a flaw like that. Each easy moment, each slow glide and bump against tree trunks only reminded him that somewhere twenty-five children were caught in terror.

And he couldn't stop it, where he was.

"Bloody hell," he swore.

Kaitlin glanced back, but said nothing, as if she knew exactly what he was thinking. Perhaps she did.

§

The gleam of sunlight ahead became a beacon. Not the leaf-and-water colored light that came from all directions. This was the gold of real sunlight, the brilliance of it caught on waves. Kaitlin prayed it was really the end of the forest. She'd been fooled a few times already when they came on open areas surrounded by trees.

Truth be told, she was beginning to wonder if they had simply been going in circles, lost in a maze of trees. And she didn't know how much farther she could go on.

The palm of her injured hand burned like a blistering fire. She was having a hard time hiding how her injured arm shook so badly. She could barely hold the oar.

She bit back another epithet as she wrestled the broken paddle into position and pushed the boat away from a jagged branch and towards the light.

"Head into the light." She snickered and knew the giddiness was just the latest sign that her body had had about enough.

But this whole venture wasn't over and she'd be damned if she was backing down at this point. Not when the children were getting farther and farther away, and not when she still didn't have her father. The one good thing was that the damned migraine seemed to have passed in all the excitement.

Make that two good things. She could positively see that realization that they were in this together for the long haul settling on B.J., the way he craned forward. The poorly masked devastation whenever they'd come out into one of the false openings.

The boat slid closer to the sunlight and B.J. throttled back and cut the engine. She slowed the boat until it came to a stop in the shadow of the trees, and the hull wobbled a little as B.J. came forward.

He gently eased her down and back as he slid forward to peer out over the water. He went so still the only things moving were the wind in his hair and the slight rise and fall of his chest.

They really had reached the end of the trees. A narrow sheet of barely rippled water stretched before them, reflecting towering clouds and a sky deepening towards evening with striations of gold from the falling sun.

Across the water lay another line of trees, but this wasn't a flooded forest. This was what looked like a spit of land interspersed with stilted houses and small runnels of smoke rising from cooking fires. And beyond the houses—was that a moto-taxi? A road?

"Look!" She slid forward, beside B.J., and pointed.

He followed her finger and nodded, but held a finger to his lips, then pointed along the edge of the trees.

She craned to see past him, and was suddenly aware of the heat of his body and the way his thigh pressed against hers.

A few hundred yards down the line of trees, a boat slid along their edge, men in uniform scanning the trees.

She might have frozen, but B.J. grabbed her shoulders and eased her back. He caught the oar and poled them back into the trees. Then he scrambled back to the stern in case he needed to start the engine, while Kaitlin hurried to pole them back even farther. After all this, they couldn't be seen. Everything was silent except for the rumble of the other boat's engine.

Kaitlin sank down on the floor of the boat, then scrambled back under the awning. The last thing they needed was for the sun to catch on her pale face and hair.

But the light was dimming moment to moment, and beyond the trees, the sheet of water turned golden. The sun must be setting. Insects and frogs began to sing and rumble

From out on the water came the sound of voices made incomprehensible by engine rumble. Then the boat's silhouette blocked the gleam of the water. Five men in a boat that was at least twice as long as theirs.

Kaitlin huddled lower and prayed they couldn't see her eyes, or B.J. where he hunkered down beside the engine.

Let them look like a log, a twist of root, a shadow on the water. Let them look like anything except what they were.

The boat seemed to slow and the conversation increased. Something plopped in the water and something gleamed in one of the men's hands.

Kaitlin froze. She closed her eyes.

A shot rang out, and she jerked, expecting the bullet's impact or the shatter of wood.

But instead there was laughter.

She opened her eyes.

The boat had stopped and shifted direction amid excited voices and laughter. The prow eased in amid the tree trunks and Kaitlin almost sat up. Almost yelled.

The police were coming directly towards her and she caught a whiff of—was that beer?—undercutting the diesel.

She shifted back farther under the awning and the boat swayed in the water. Small wavelets thunked and hummed against the hull. A hiss came from behind her.

She turned and caught a glimpse of B.J.'s silhouette in the failing light. He shook his head and held his finger to his lips. Stay silent.

Well, he wasn't sitting out here like a flipping figurehead near the front of the boat.

She forced herself down. Gritted her teeth to watch as the police boat slid further into the trees.

Surely to goodness they must see the boat. It was right there, for God's sake. She could spit in their faces, if she ever spit.

But they were intent on something else. Something in the water.

Kaitlin pressed her eye against a tear on the awning in time to see one of the men reach into the water and come up with something long and struggling in his fist.

Snake. At least six feet long, by the look of it.

They must have spotted it, and the chance to amuse themselves through the boredom of a long afternoon stakeout had been overwhelming.

When they'd shot it, they hadn't killed it and it dropped into the water. Until they shot it again. Well, better they kill it than the creature drop in on her.

They hauled their catch into their boat and then backed their boat out into the open water. Kaitlin held her breath as they turned to continue following the edge of the trees.

Gradually the voices faded.

A hand on her back made her jump and she knocked her head on one of the bentwood supports that held up the awning.

"Don't do that." She rubbed her head as B.J. slid in beside her.

"And how was I supposed to announce myself?"

She shook her head. "Just not that way. Whistle or something, would you?"

"A jaunty tune, perhaps?"

"Shut up." She wasn't going to put up with his annoying behavior. "Just where did you learn that stuff—moving so silent. All those hand signals."

"Gulf war, remember. Nasho—National Service—saw me there. But you knew that."

And she did. He'd served in the Australian military. "I just never saw you act like it before."

"Lots you don't know about me, luv. But right now I think we should take a chance at some shut-eye and let those blokes tire themselves out, before we try to cross."

She looked towards the edge of the trees and the hope of dry land beyond. "I s'ppose you're right."

"What? No argument?"

She rolled her eyes and made a show of spreading some of the cloths in the boat to make a makeshift bed. Then she stretched out on it to stare up at the awning and the trees and sky beyond. The sky backlit the leaves with honey amber. The water gurgled and hummed and the first mosquito buzzed around her face. Great.

Even better given she could feel B.J.'s gaze on her as he sat at the rear of the awning, still apparently keeping watch.

All the aches in her body seemed to coalesce into exhaustion and she closed her eyes. Dozed, only to become aware of the boat shifting under her. A long, warm shape stretched beside her and an arm settled over her side.

She stiffened, but fatigue stole her strength.

Sleep took her again and the warmth—was almost nice.

Chapter 28

It was dark when B.J.'s internal alarms woke him. He lay still, for a moment disoriented. Water gurgled around him. Something unyielding dug into his back, but something soft and warm and scented of roses and rainwater was in his arms. A soft breath blew across his face.

He opened his eyes to stars through rents in the heavens and a set of luminous eyes from Kaitlin above and to one side of him. That was what woke him—the sense of someone watching.

Everything flooded back. Kaitlin. The kids. The pursuit.

He knew where he was. And his own stupidity dragging Kaitlin into this. Now he had to find a way to get her out of it.

"You were sleeping so soundly."

He could hear her smile in the darkness.

"So were you." The scent of her, salty sweat sweetened by roses and rainwater, was almost intoxicating. He inhaled it at his peril, because a moment like this evoked so many memories it was almost painful to think they were over forever. She shifted her position, her breasts soft against his arm, and the boat quivered just like his pulse.

Strewth, if he didn't move, something was going to happen here.

But he didn't move. Kaitlin sat up above him, her long hair stained darker by the darkness and the rent-revealed stars surrounding her head like a crown.

"Thank you. For getting us away, and for taking care of my wounds."

She leaned down and placed a soft kiss on his lips that lingered a moment too long for his resolve. Too soft, too sweet, too Kaitlin.

His arms came around her and pulled her down.

Her lips parted against his and he drank her in. Felt her yield and—holy mother of God—what was he doing? He wanted Kaitlin, but he wanted her far away and safe even more.

He turned his face away from the kiss and held her away.

"Don't think this is really a good idea, luv."

Her whole body stiffened and she scrambled back—out from under the awning to the front of the boat, bitterly back-handing the kiss from her mouth.

"Bastard," she swore and turned away to the water, but carefully contained Kaitlin leaked emotion all over.

Crap.

He heaved himself up and slid forward towards her, the boat shifting under them. Outside of the confines of the awning, the night was cooler and silent except for the wind in the leaves and the song of the water around the tree trunks. And the damned insects that demanded an Aussie salute to keep them out of his nose and eyes and mouth.

"Kaitlin. I'm sorry." He almost touched her, but knew that would only make things worse.

"I'm sorry, too. It was a stupid thing to do on my part. I just got thinking about our situation and I thought—I thought—oh, God, I don't know what I thought."

Her voice was still thick with emotion. Hell, he could feel it himself, like something sticky and cloying in his mouth.

"We both know it was just the situation," he said.

"It was. And I was tired. That's all."

"Strewth." He swallowed, feeling helpless and angry with himself because that wasn't it, at all.

"And stupid." She still didn't look at him.

"We both were."

A silent, strained moment, where B.J. could have kicked himself right out of the boat and right down the Tonle Sap for being six kinds of a fool. She was tired and afraid and dragged into something she wasn't prepared for, and he did what? Almost took advantage of her when she kissed him, and then, idiot that he was, he offended her.

God's truth, it was a no-win situation, but when had he ever won where Kaitlin was involved?

There were a lot of good times, a small part of him said. *Think.*

Like he needed those memories and the pain they brought.

"I can't hear the other boat. Maybe they gave up."

He looked up at her shift of conversation. Her voice was clear of all emotion.

Beyond the tangle of trees around them, the watery fields glimmered in the starlight. Far away to the east, the over-bright star of a streetlight said they were nearer to civilization than B.J. had thought.

"I don't think we should start the engine. The sound would carry for miles."

She finally turned back to him, her face devoid of emotion. "Then what do we do?"

"Row."

"With one oar?"

"One and a half. And I suspect we'll be able to pole ourselves part of the way, judging by where the water is on the trees." He nodded towards the forest around them. "See? More trunk than where we first entered the forest. The ground must be rising."

He hauled out the oar that had dug into his back while he slept and worked his shoulders. Kaitlin picked up the broken oar and couldn't hide her wince.

"Your hand. It's bad, isn't it?"

"It hurts, but that's to be expected."

"If it hurts too bad, it's liable to be infected. I should have grabbed a torch before heading out on this bloody little adventure. That and a medical kit."

"Hindsight's always twenty-twenty," she said coolly, but she snagged her pack and dug inside, came out with a handy little metal maglight torch. Snapped it on, making sure the light was lost in the boat's awning. She handed it to him. "Your wish, and all that."

She turned away as if to ignore him.

"Your hand?"

She stuck out her bandaged hand, but kept looking at the water. He stuck the torch in his teeth and worked quickly, unwinding the blood-clotted cloth. Finally her palm came up, flesh pruned and pale, but the edges of the glass cut an angry red.

"Bloody hell. That's got to hurt."

She said nothing, but he imagined just the air on it would hurt like hell, and there was nothing he could do for it.

"You don't happen to have any antiseptic or sterile bandages in that pack of yours, do ya?"

"Yes. And a doctor on call." She turned to him. "Of course I don't have anything. If I had something I'd have given it to you when you were bandaging it the first time, now wouldn't I?"

Misdirected anger radiated off of her. Dammit all, didn't she see he was trying to help her?

"Let me check your arm?" He motioned to it, but she pulled away.

"My arm is fine."

He bit back a comment about stiff-necked idiots. "All right. Let me just rewrap your hand and we'll get going. But when we land in Battambang, we're finding you a doctor." And a ride out of here.

He re-wrapped her hand and grabbed the broken oar from her.

"Just get out of my way, luv." He knew the luv would push her away, just as well as the oar would.

The boat wobbled under them as he poled them off the tree trunks to the edge of the trees. Kaitlin sat in the prow like a brooding figurehead.

Well, let her. He'd kissed her, for God's sake, not raped her. And she'd started it.

Chapter 29

Stupid. Stupid. Stupid.

She'd actually kissed him. And given B.J. all kinds of wrong ideas. But surely to goodness he could figure out it was only a kiss.

Kaitlin stared out over the open stretch of black water towards the shore that was only a darker line in the darkness. Not even the stars reflected except far to the west a single streetlight sent a long spear of light down the lake. Or maybe it was a lifeline, but it didn't reach her.

Here, everything was black and she was surrounded by the sigh of wind over water and trees, the plop of things in the lake—snakes?—and the sting of swarming insects. It was like she was *in* the flipping water instead of floating on it. She was struggling against the murk while something pulled her under.

She shivered and the boat wobbled under her. The soft strokes of B.J.'s uneven paddling had stopped and he shipped oars and made his way forward.

She sidled away to avoid him, but she couldn't in the confines of the boat. He brushed past her to kneel in the prow and study the water and the edge of the forest. His scent of sweat and her soap overlaid the muddy scent of water and rotting wood and was unconscionably familiar.

Way too familiar, the way it drew her.

Flipping hell, this was B.J. she was talking about. B.J., the man who, next to her father, was the *most* infuriating man in the world.

"Looks clear," he grunted.

"I can't see anything."

"Too right. That's about what I meant, luv. As good as we're going to get."

He turned back to her and eased past, brushing against her bad arm. She hid a wince. The darned arm hurt worse than her hand, and she knew it was pure cussedness and a smidge of one of her father's emotional reactions that had stopped her from letting him check it. And it was all because B.J. evoked those unthinking emotional reactions.

Like the darned kiss.

"Keep an eye out, would you?"

His voice came from behind as he took the broken oar and tested the depth of the water. It reached bottom about three quarters of the way up the oar.

"Damn. Still too deep," he mumbled and shook his head.

He set the other oar in position and began rowing, and the boat's immediate reaction was to turn toward the side with the broken oar.

"Shit." He adjusted his paddling and Kaitlin left him to it and turned forward. It hurt to lean forward. It hurt to sit. Actually, it pretty much hurt to move at all. Yeah, her hand hurt, but her arm was a bright flame. Maybe it was only muscle soreness from all the poling.

She hoped. But hell would freeze over before she'd let B.J. play doctor again.

The water slopped, plopped, and gurgled along the sides of the boat as they took a drunken man's route across the water. B.J. swore with each correction he had to do due to the broken oar. Paddling apparently wouldn't work because of the width of the craft. Finally he gave up on rowing altogether. The water had grown shallow and he was able to pole them through the water in a series of slow-mo heaves.

A stilted house materialized against the night sky and grew larger as they neared the shore. Then a tan-colored dog ran down to the water's edge and started barking. B.J. swore.

"Go on. Get out of here," Kaitlin stage-whispered and tried to wave the dog away. It was futile. The dog only growled and its yips and yaps were picked up by other dogs along the water's edge until the night seemed filled with their chorus.

No way were they getting away unnoticed.

B.J. drove the boat for the shore, and the prow ground over soil. Then he scrambled forward, shouldered her out of the way, and leapt onto the shore, shooing the dog away. He turned back to haul the boat up behind him.

He grabbed her hand. "Got your pack?"

She nodded.

"Come on."

He grabbed her injured arm and she half-fell, half staggered onto solid ground. Her knees almost gave as the pain shot through her in waves.

"Christ. Your arm's worse, isn't it?" he hissed.

She wouldn't meet his gaze. She shook her head and, cradling her arm against her, started up the steep bank to towards the house. They'd find help in Battambang. She had to keep telling herself that.

A sarong-clad man materialized out of the darkness, wielding a shovel like a weapon, and Kaitlin staggered back to avoid the blade.

Dammit, she hadn't done anything.

The man demanded something in Khmer and she had to look to B.J. to answer.

He swiftly explained—something—and the man argued a moment and then escorted them past his house to the road. The door to his house was lined with faces of his children and wife, who quickly disappeared back into the house when Kaitlin looked at them. So much for help here.

And no help farther along, either. She stumbled through a hedge of papaya trees and onto a narrow road that led towards the distant streetlight and a glow that must be Battambang. She struck out towards it.

B.J. bloody McCallum could just damned well keep up, because she was going to do this—find her father one last time. But this was it. The last time. Because if her father got some harebrained scheme again, she was personally going to tie him up and keep him prisoner in her basement. At least that way she'd know he was safe.

Another sarong-clad man stepped out of the darkness, guarding the entrance to the yard around his stilted house. He yelled at Kaitlin, and she held up her hands and was easing past when B.J. intervened again.

He got into an argument with the man until Kaitlin turned on him.

"Would you just stop?! I don't need you to defend me or help me. I'm perfectly capable of finding my own way past these people. They don't seem to think I'm a danger, but you with your height and your bulk—you put them on the defensive, just like you do everyone else."

And me, perhaps?

She shook herself of that thought and kept on toward the light and the blessed line of cars and trucks.

"Kaitlin, wait. Slow down. Those men could be waiting for us. We need to be careful."

Like B.J. McCallum had ever been careful about anything. Like he could keep her safe. In fact, he'd done nothing but drag her farther into trouble ever since she stumbled into him, and that was just sooo like her father. No wonder he drove her to distraction, and that just couldn't be true because she loved her father.

Then why'd you kiss him Kaitlin?

Because she was stupid and had a weak moment and hadn't updated her 'do and don't do' list, but it wouldn't happen again. She was clear. She focused on the beacon of light ahead. When she got there, she really would take care of herself.

§

The night air was blessedly cool, and solid ground a nice change from floating around in some dinghy, but chasing after Kaitlin Blackwood was *not* what B.J. had pictured coming after. The long narrow road ran on straight ahead, not much more than a worn path between two rows of stilted houses that stood on higher ground above flooded fields. Along the roadway, rickety fences of wood and wire and cactus protected courtyards from the road and animals left loose to graze. And at the moment, these fence lines were guarded by a row of suspicious men waving farm implements and some particularly wicked looking curved machete-type knives.

Not what a man wants to run into back o' Bourke.

"Kaitlin, wait up."

The damn woman didn't slow. If anything, her stride increased, erasing the sweet sway of her backside.

The rough ground made her stumble, and the way she flinched he knew her arm was a problem, but she didn't make a sound. Just kept walking as if getting away from him was the only thing that mattered.

Damn it, he wasn't some mongrel who deserved bad treatment. He didn't deserve this at all from the bloody woman. Spewin' mad she was. Stomping off through the darkness as if she didn't have a care in the world except getting as far away from one B.J. McCallum as possible.

As if he were the problem.

It was one little kiss. He hadn't gone all pash on her—although maybe he should have. Might have done something for her disposition.

Who was he kidding?

A little roll in the hay would have made his day.

"Kaitlin, hold up." He lengthened his stride to come up beside her, ignoring the silent men who stood guard along the way. They'd given up arguing with him and seemed content with seeing them on their way.

He caught her good arm. "Would you at least talk to me? What burr's got up your butt?"

She just pulled loose and kept walking.

"All right. All right. The kiss was ill-considered. Not the right thing to do, but I wasn't solely to blame, luv."

He said it softly, like a peace offering, and wondered where he got the patience. The woman managed to push all his buttons. Unfortunately, they included the ones to take care of her. Kaitlin might be tall and she might be strong willed, but there was a vulnerability about her that, now that he thought about it, always made him crazy with worry.

"It was stupid of me," she said.

She kept walking, but maybe a mite slower.

"It's the situation. Puts us together in close quarters. You were hurt. It wasn't unexpected."

She stopped dead in her tracks. "What does that mean? Like it's inevitable that I'll succumb to your charms? Like I can't help myself?"

Not exactly what he'd been going for. The streetlight caught the mad in her gaze. Definitely not what he'd been going for.

"I meant that us getting closer wasn't a surprise. We've got a history." Even now he wanted to touch her.

She rolled her eyes. "Well, you shoulda sent me the memo, because I sure as hell *was* surprised, even though I did the kissing, and I'm nipping it in the bud right now. Don't touch me again, buster."

She strode past him again.

And he wouldn't, either. Not if she was the last woman on earth. Time to do what needed to be done. Given how Kaitlin was feeling, she might even agree to it.

He caught up to her again. "Your arm's giving you trouble."

"Hurts like hell." But she shook her head as if she wanted to deny it.

"You need a doctor. Someone who can clean it properly and stitch up your hand and give you some antibiotic."

She glanced up at him then, the streetlight making her blue eyes pale. The eastern sky was lightening. The swift, tropical dawn couldn't be far away.

"I thought catching up to the kids was everything. What've you got in mind?"

Bite the bullet, mate. This is it.

"I think we should split the sheets. I'll get you to a doctor, but then I'll head out on my own. Get a ride to Pailin. After you've seen the doctor, you can get on with finding yer dad however you want."

It came out in a rush, too much like a confession. He held his breath, waiting for her reaction.

Chapter 30

The incessant night insects buzzed around Kaitlin's face and she waved them away. But it didn't stop the buzzing in her ears. Cool night air, the scent of lake water and mud and a hint of garbage, the throbbing pain of her arm and hand, all got in the way of her focusing on what B.J. had said.

Leave her here. He was getting a little of his own back after she walked out on him before. She should be used to it, given her dad, but it still caused that little old curl of hurt and resentment in her gut.

Well, it was for the better. There wouldn't be anymore temptation for either of them and she'd be rid of this bossy, infuriating man. She was sure he'd be happier for it, too.

Still a flipping good-looking man, unfortunately. Finally she nodded. "Good idea. We were always better off on our own."

Then why did she feel so sad again? Like after she'd left him six years ago.

She started walking again, trying to hide her confusion, and reached the single streetlight ahead of him. Aside from the darned dogs still barking behind her, the night was silent along the pitted, paved road.

The light placed an eerie orange glow over a group of moto-taxis and pedicabs parked scattershot in the grass at the side of the road and the sleeping driver in, or under, each one. At least she hoped they were sleeping. In the weird light, *Night of the Living Dead* came to mind.

She felt B.J. come up behind her and prayed he didn't touch her. Or look too closely at her, either. It was taking all her strength to hide the pain in her arm and hand, and frankly she didn't know how much farther she could go on without getting it tended to.

"So. We can part ways here." At least her voice was strong. "You tell one to take me to a hospital and you can go wherever you want."

"Too right. All those dogs barking—I'm surprised the police haven't come."

But B.J. looked at her perhaps a little too closely. He opened his mouth as if to say something, but then seemed to catch himself. He stepped past to a pedicab and shook the contraption.

The driver bolted upright and rubbed his eyes as he took in the darkness and the distant dawn, his sleeping brethren, and the two westerners in front of him. Rubbed his eyes again, as if he couldn't believe them.

Not that she blamed him. Prior to coming to Cambodia, *she* wouldn't have believed she would be doing this, either.

He said something in Khmer in a voice loud enough that the other drivers stirred. B.J. said something and it sounded like he started to barter when, from far down the road towards what she figured must be Battambang, the sound of a car engine announced a set of headlights.

Fear spiked through her. And the darn car looked like it was coming at speed.

"B.J.?"

He waved her away a moment, and the vehicle came on. Fast. Yes, faster than any sane driver would be driving on this pitted pavement. She grabbed his arm.

"B.J., we've got a problem."

That caught his attention. When he wasn't focusing on bartering with the driver, he followed her gaze. "Bloody hell!"

He caught her hand and yanked her around. Kaitlin almost screamed at the knife-edged pain that ran through her as he dragged her away from the streetlight. Not back the way they had come.

"You're hurting me."

He released her. She hesitated, but followed as he plunged across the street away from the light and the water.

"The boat. We could get to the boat."

"We wouldn't get away this time, luv. They'd be waiting for us."

He led them into darkness, down a narrow, uneven path that led between trees. A dog started barking and a whole chorus followed. Must be more houses.

Behind she heard the squeal of tires, car doors slamming, and angry voices. She increased her speed, fighting to keep up with B.J. Dammed man was in better shape than she'd thought for a dissolute drinker. But then she shouldn't be surprised, given the hard body that had stretched beside her on the boat.

He was pulling away, fading into the darkness in front of her. She increased her speed, but each footfall sent pain searing through her. Her arm felt like a knife was impaled there and it twisted in her flesh every time she moved.

She chanced a look behind her. Silhouetted figures gave chase. Four.

She increased her speed, ignoring the pain.

"Kaitlin! Bloody hell, woman, come on!" B.J. slowed.

"Go on! I'll catch up."

She tried to increase her speed, but her legs felt like she was battling deep water, as if the darkness had suddenly become molasses.

And behind, the angry voices said the men were getting closer. Dammit! She was better than this. Faster. She'd run marathons.

B.J. darted back for her and grabbed her uninjured hand to drag her, staggering, after him.

She looked behind again. Only two men.

"They're too close."

"Shut up and run. There'll be another road ahead."

She did, praying he was right.

Darkness.

Moths and mosquitoes in her face.

Insect hum.

The stink of raw sewage.

The perfume of lilies.

Fleeting impressions; the only thing constant was her sobbing breath and pounding heartbeat. And B.J.'s warm hand, dragging her on.

How another road was going to help them, she didn't know, but she followed, the pain making it hard to think, hard to know if this was the right thing to do. Just obey. Just get away.

A set of headlights suddenly cut the night, blinding them. B.J. slid to a stop and used his arm to shield his eyes.

"Fuck."

He dove to the side, dragging her with him, but she stumbled and fell. Would have gone right down if he hadn't had her hand. She scrambled up again. Staggered after him, past a house, down a steep slope that didn't bode well, and then she was in water up over her shoes, her ankles, running, and the water was a silent, shimmering sheet in the coming dawn.

Dammit the darkness was fading, leaving them vulnerable and exposed as they dodged barking dogs, as a group of armed men appeared in front of them from between a stilted house and a straw-thatched shed.

B.J. slid to a halt. He turned around. Two armed men ran up behind them.

B.J. shoved her behind him, knee-deep in the water, and her shoes sank ankle-deep into mud and murk. He yelled in Khmer, but whatever he said, it didn't make any difference. The armed men converged and B.J. backed them further out so the water came almost to her waist.

"Do ya think you could swim, luv." He squeezed her hand, strength and determination incarnate.

She looked at the expanse of water and swallowed back pain and fatigue. Apricot dawn shimmered on the horizon and in the smooth surface that stretched a least a mile to what looked like more flooded forest. She'd give it a try, but....

"To where?"

He cast a glance back, and at her, and all the certainty seemed to ebb away in the face of the new risen sun.

"Bloody hell," he muttered.

He released her and turned back to the men with the guns.

Chapter 31

Everything had gone to the crapper, and B.J. couldn't see his way out of it.

In the bright light of the new sun, six men faced them, their long shadows trailing like gigantic reinforcements behind them. Two held modern pistols and the others held rifles that looked about twenty years out of date. Not quite AK 47s. M1, by the exposed muzzle and the position of the sights. Bloody things had been used during the Vietnamese invasion against the Khmer Rouge and still held on. Too good at killing things, too.

And here he was, weaponless, and ass-deep in tepid water. Not the way it should be. Not anything the Nasho taught you to deal with.

Taking a chance and diving into the water seemed like the best hope of escape, but Kaitlin's pallor and the way she cradled her arm said she was about done in.

And it was his fault she was here.

"You should have let me leave you in Siem Reap, luv. Look where it's got ya."

"I'd probably be sitting in some cell right now."

"A tad more comfortable than freezing our balls standing here."

"Your balls, maybe. It's not that cold." She started to step up beside him, but he held her back.

"You should let the woman go," he said in Khmer. "She has nothing to do with this."

"Come out of the water and we will find out," said a pistol-wielding man with a scar on his face.

"Your choice, luv. Swim for it or give in." He glanced at her, tall, fine boned, and strong, but today the clear gaze that had always reminded him of a Valkyrie had gone muzzy at the edges. Pain lines and dark circles rimmed her eyes. The arm was worse than she was letting on.

And he hadn't noticed. Bloody hell, again.

All his mad at her disappeared when he thought of what she'd done with that injured arm. Valkyrie was right, but a wounded one.

"Follow my lead, and hopefully we'll get out of this alive."

He took a slow step forward.

"Stop where you are and raise your hands," scar-face ordered in Khmer.

"You going to leave us standing here all day? Or maybe you want to come and get us?"

A jerk of the pistol and an order to his men, and all the weapons rose in unison, aimed at B.J. and Kaitlin.

"Ah, what's going on B.J.? It doesn't look like you're helping things."

Just like her to question him. He bit back a response and slowly raised his hands. Idiot. Fool. Wanker. He was all of them, and his first fool's act had been even being civil to Kaitlin.

"Just follow my lead," said through clenched teeth.

"I can't raise my hands. At least not this arm." Pain thickened her voice.

He stepped back beside her and lowered one arm around her shoulders.

"She's hurt," he explained as he led her forward, praying the explanation was good enough.

When the water only reached B.J.'s knees, four of the men waded in and grabbed them. A rifle stock slammed into his gut.

He doubled over. Kaitlin was torn away and he lunged for her, but the next blow came for his head.

He barely got his left arm up. The rifle caught his forearm and sent a bolt of pain up through his shoulder. His arm went numb.

But Kaitlin. They had her on the shore. She was fighting as best she could, with her injured arm.

B.J. slammed his right fist into a man's face and lunged through the water after her, praying the mess of fighting figures would stop anyone from shooting him. So much for getting in amongst them and picking them off on his own when the time was right.

He tackled the two men assaulting her. Pulled them down on top of him. "Run!"

She just stood there.

The others had splashed out of the water.

"Run, damn you! You don't have to bloody well think about it, do you?"

She backed up a step. Turned.

Too late. Two other men grabbed her, wrenched her arms behind her so she screamed.

B.J. fought to regain his feet, but the scarred man came up and shoved a gun in his face. He froze.

Then a rifle stock found the back of his head. He went down in the mud, to Kaitlin's protests, and the world reduced to rifles blows and kicks and a blood-scented darkness that came on too fast. And Kaitlin's screams.

§

"B.J.? B.J., can you hear me?"

Diesel exhaust fumes caught in his throat and the world vibrated around him.

He'd blacked out again, it seemed.

Not hard to do, when the world was a sea of pain whenever he woke. But Kaitlin's voice reminded him he needed to be awake. *Not good for the concussion, old man,* he could almost hear old Nick saying.

He opened his eyes onto a torn canvas ceiling that leaked a steady stream of light and rain down onto his face.

"Damn it." He rolled over onto his side; not easy to do with your hands tied behind your back and tethered as he was to a stanchion in the back of a lumbering lorry. Muddy road spun past sickeningly fast below the spaces between the floorboards.

He struggled to sit up against the wooden crate beside him, and the lurch and whirl of the world nearly made him liquid laugh down his front. He swallowed back bitter bile and closed his eyes, waiting for the world to quit moving.

Unfortunately, the lorry hit another pothole and he hadn't braced himself in time. He slammed back against the rusted floor of the lorry bed, every bruised muscle in his body protesting the new abuse.

"Fuck me!"

"That's a reasonable assessment of the situation."

The wry humor wasn't what he expected from Kaitlin. He opened one eye at her.

After their captors had tired of kicking the crap out of their Aussie friend, and after he'd regained his ability to string two thoughts together, they'd marched them back to the road, where they separated Kaitlin from him, stuffing her protesting into the car. Him, marched—make that staggered—down the road, one tall, bloodied westerner escorted by four armed men. Until the police van drove up and they all crowded in.

That ride had ended somewhere outside of Battambang—he thought. The way consciousness seemed to fade in and out, he couldn't be sure of much. Except Kaitlin was there, crammed in beside the packing crates.

Which was both the worst and the best situation.

And now, however many hellish hours later, she sat looking disheveled and in pain, but, backlit as she was by the view of jungle-covered mountains out the rear of the truck, she was still Kaitlin-the-Valkyrie, determined to get through whatever came.

He coughed, tasted blood, and spat. "How long?"

"In the truck? At least two hours. Hard to be sure with my watch behind me." She shook her head, but the shake, rattle, roll of the truck made her wince. "How bad are you hurt?"

"A few mozzie bites. Piece of piss." Another crash and fall into a pothole and it was his turn to wince. At least he didn't black out this time.

"Seriously, B.J. If we're going to get out of this, we need to know each other's abilities."

Her blonde hair had pulled loose of her pony tail and lashed around her wide blue eyes. Pain and fear were etched there, carefully contained, but she had to be paying a hell of a price with her arms twisted behind her like that.

Well, two could play at that game. "I'm awake. I'm bruised. I've probably got concussion. Other than that, I'm fine."

Well, maybe that was a lie. The grating in his side felt like a rib was probably broken and his right hand felt like the punch he'd thrown just might have dislocated a finger. All told, not a bad collection of wounds, considering the beating they'd laid on him. "And you, luv? How's the arm?"

"I don't feel it much anymore. Except when we hit a bad bump."

"So in other words, it's killing you, right?"

"To quote an Aussie I know, 'too right'."

Another slow smile, and he soooo wished it was coming at him in some other situation.

"And your hand?"

"I lost the bandage in the fight with those guys when they separated us."

Which meant the wound was probably filthy and breeding infection like crazy. He *had* to get her to a doctor. Actually, he had to get her out of this whole mess, preferably in as good a shape as she came into it.

Not going to happen, mate.

"B.J., I've been thinking."

Never a good sign. Thinking about things too long just stopped them from getting done at all. He'd learned that in the military and watching the justice system try to bring down the snakeheads. Nope, sometimes it was better to just leap in with both feet.

"Yee-ah?"

"Well, they could have killed us outright, couldn't they?"

"Yee-ah. But that would have left a couple of bodies in the middle of the tourist circuit. Not good for business or for the government."

She nodded. "That might be it. But it seems weird that they let me keep my daypack. They just checked it—for weapons, I think—but then they gave it back."

She nodded at the canvas bag next to her. In her shadow, and shoved in between her and a crate as it was, he hadn't noticed it.

She closed her eyes and leaned back against the lorry stanchion she was tethered to. Behind them, the road stretched in a muddy river, threading the remains of deforested jungle down the long incline of mountain foothills. The Cardamom Mountains—or close to it. The lorry driver ground through another gear and the vehicle lurched and slowed as it ground up the steeper hill. All the wooden crates shifted and B.J.'s space expanded slightly. Enough shifts and the cargo could shift right out the back of the truck.

And kill Kaitlin in the process, if the blue exhaust fumes flooding back didn't do it first. They doubled her over, coughing.

"We need a plan to get out of here, B.J.," she said when she came up for air.

He closed his eyes. Here it came again. Trying to plan everything.

"Planning's your thing, luv. Me? I prefer to fly by the seat o' me DAKS."

"Not exactly the way to fill me with confidence."

"And just what *do* you feel confident about, because that we can plan for."

He met her gaze, like he was holding a shield up. Maybe he was, because she'd gotten entirely too far under his guard as it was, with those clear blue eyes of hers and the circles of worry under them. And then there was the way her hair kept catching at the edge of her mouth.

God, she was strong and yet so vulnerable, and he hated seeing her like that and in pain.

She dropped her gaze, her sigh raising her shoulders.

"When we know something, we'll plan," he said. "Until then, we're sort of forced to deal with what comes. On the fly."

"I hate this." She shook her head.

"Would that be being tied in the back of a truck not knowing if you're going to live?"

"No." She looked at him crossly. "Not having a plan."

Then she smiled and shook her head. "God, I'm pathetic."

"Now I wouldn't exactly say that, luv. More infuriating and frustrating and entirely too anal retentive, but you're still a charmer for all that."

"Nope." She shook her head again. "I can't seem to move without planning things out. Fat lot of good it's done me. It just slowed us down and made me do stupid things like phoning the police." She looked pointedly at their surroundings.

Which was true. Of course, the fact she'd been with him might have had something to do with it. But this wasn't the time to be reminding her of that little detail.

"So maybe next time you can follow my lead without asking questions?"

His question hung there a moment as the truck geared down again and then took a ninety degree turn. B.J. straightened. He knew where they were. Phnom Yat, the small hill south of Pailin had a turn like that near a mobile phone transmitter and a small stupa.

Soon his suspicions were confirmed as the truck picked up speed and, about a kilometer away, entered a roundabout.

"Better answer me, luv, because we're coming into Pailin.

Chapter 32

Out the rear of the truck, the landscape flattened out except for distant blue mountains and, closer by, the bulk of a low hill topped by a grey-white spire—one of the solid white Buddhist temple spires called a stupa—and a hideous telecommunications tower.

If she only had a phone that would work here, but that wasn't in the inventory of items left in her bag. She'd been trying to remember what was in there ever since she was put in the truck.

Shadow puppet.

Tall trees grew lushly on the sides of the hill, whereas the flat area was cleared and cultivated here and there with grain and corn.

Letter from her father.

Neat, stilted-wood houses stood in the fields, but were replaced here and there by grey, official-looking, stucco structures.

Camera.

Wallet.

They had money to pay for whatever they needed. If they could get....

"What's Pailin like? Can we get help here?"

B.J.'s chuckle cut through her considerations.

"You're doing it again, luv—trying to plan our way out of this mess."

Damn him. Damn her. She just couldn't stop... "I just thought maybe there'd be someone to help us. Maybe we could pay them. There're some decent looking buildings here."

The truck slowed and more exhaust streamed into the canvas bed, and a paroxysm of coughing cut off all breath.

When the blue smoke cleared, a fine spray of red mud rose through the canvass flaps and settled on everything. Terrific. Just flipping terrific. The way it coated her skin, she'd look like a statue with blue eyes in a few minutes.

"Kaitlin, believe me. Pailin is a frontier town. Any official worth his salt has been bribed far beyond any money we could come up with. Best that could happen is they'd take our money and *then* hand us back to whoever these guys are."

She looked back at him, tethered between the crates near the cab. He was so swathed in shadows and mud that only occasionally could she make out his face. What she saw wasn't pretty. A cut somewhere in his hair had caked one side of his handsome head with blood. His shirt hadn't fared any better, and had enough blood on it she'd have been writing about him as seriously injured with head wounds.

Not good, even if he managed to keep his voice strong and confident enough he could still get under her skin. Not good because she'd begun to realize that B.J. might be the only one who could get the kids, her father, and herself out of this mess alive.

That, and the fact that she didn't like to see anyone in pain, were why she had to help him. Wash away the blood and treat the wounds underneath.

He'd done it for her, after all.

And a fat lot of good it had done.

She was using the planning to keep her mind off the pain that could turn her into a gibbering idiot if she let it. The only good thing was they'd tied her so tight her hands and arms had mostly gone numb over the course of the journey. They'd probably be no better than flippers if she did try to help him.

And then B.J. would probably just laugh at her and tell her she didn't have what it takes. Too tied up in planning and not enough fly by the seat of the pants.

She ground her teeth.

What else was in her purse? Tissues. There were tissues and an address book that she had no business bringing on a trip like this given it contained all her local contacts in Seattle. Another proof she was a bit of a dolt when it came to travel.

"What's the building on the hill? A monastery?"

"Phnom Yat. The story goes that a Burmese couple was drawn here for the gem mining at the end of the nineteenth century. After they'd worked the mines for years, they received a message from the jungle spirits saying that there was too much hunting and tearing down of the forest. The spirits said that if the gem hunters stopped hunting the animals and made offerings to the spirits, there would always be gems to be found. So the couple built the stupa on Phnom Yat as a place to make offerings. Not that it's done any good. The hunters still come and the forest is cut down and the gems stopped being found. People around here still recall the days of the Khmer Rouge as the good old days, because those were the days when mining made the area rich and there were hospitals and schools and building going on."

What else was in her purse? Camera, but she'd said that.

"So people are hungry for money to keep the good ol' days."

"Strewth. And they're not going to fuck it up by helping some stranger."

Guide book.

Something to think about. "Would monks help us? Are there any NGOs who might help us?"

He didn't answer.

"You didn't think of that option, did you?"

Migraine pills and anti-malarials.

"Nooo. I didn't, to be honest, and that might be an option. Except it seems these guys just might be desperate enough to move against an NGO group. Do we want to take a chance on bringing hell down on some innocents?"

Notepad and pencil. Fat lot of good they'd done her.

She shook her head and didn't bother protesting that he and her father seemed to have no trouble at all raining trouble down on *her*.

"So all we can do is wait?"

"That's about it, luv. And take advantage of anything that comes our way."

Nail file.

Her arm throbbed. Every part of her ached from the long, bumping journey and her stomach thought her throat had been cut it was so long since she'd eaten.

Nail file? Really? Hadn't they taken everything that could be a weapon?

But she actually had three nail files, all packaged together in a little plastic carrying case. Two were the large, soft emery boards, but the third was a small metal file, perfect for dealing with the worst pesky nail chips and stored neatly between the two emery boards so it wouldn't be easily spotted.

"B.J., I think I might have come up with something to take advantage of."

There was an audible groan from the front of the truck and she could just see him rolling his eyes. "What?"

With that kind of attitude, hell would freeze over before she'd tell him. "Never mind. It was stupid."

Stupid enough she was going to prove him wrong.

She struggled sideways, ignoring the knife-in-the-arm pain of the wound from the boat and screwing herself around until she could snag her pack with numb fingers. It was like working with sausages. Make that frozen sausages. At the end of tongs. And each time she shifted, the nylon cord they'd used on her wrists cut deeper into the grooves two hours of struggle had worn in her flesh.

But finally she got the pack behind her and opened. It was like those guessing games you did at a child's party—the child blindfolded and having to identify the things they found in a bag. The trouble was, her numb hands kept dropping things, and even though she knew what was in her purse, everything felt weird and unknowable. Thin metal cylinder. Heavy.

Flashlight.

She'd forgotten her maglight. She could have used it last night.

Shadow puppet. She wished she could see it, maybe figure out where her father was leading her, because Pailin didn't exactly seem like the kind of place that would draw him if all the jewel mines had run out. Of course, from what B.J. said, there had been that ruby.

Every twist of her wrists sent pain screaming up her arms. Every pain-averse part of her told her stop, but the self-preservation part of her was stronger. A warm trickle across the back of her hands said she was bleeding again. Flipping hell. Had they found the file when they confiscated her jackknife?

Her fingers closed around a distinctive, rigid plastic holder with a rough edge at the end from too frequent use. Two plastic emery boards protruded from the broken end.

She had to sit for a moment and calm herself, for fear she'd drop it back into the bag and have to go through the agony of finding it again.

The fact it was still in her pack meant they might not have found the file. She could hope. Pray, more like.

She fumbled the emery boards out of the case and knew there was no way she could get them back in place. Once she had the file, she was committed, because there'd be no hiding it again as long as she was tied.

And she'd have to be doubly careful, because if she dropped the file, it was doubtful she'd find it again in the bouncing, shifting vehicle. A sudden jar could send the file skittering across the floorboards. Or through them.

Carefully, hands still in the daypack, she separated the two emery boards and found the narrow metal shaft she sought. Pointed like a weapon. Rough and serrated along its half inch wide sides. And thin enough it might just be able to saw through something if applied with enough force.

Sausage fingers fisted around it and, carefully, removed her treasure from the pack.

She looked back at B.J.; his head bounced limply on his shoulders, so the concussion had taken him from her again. Which meant it was more important than ever that she take the lead.

She got the file turned around so the point faced her wrists and started picking at the yellow rope. Not easy to do when she couldn't see. Harder to do when she kept jabbing the point into the raw flesh underneath the rope.

But finally she jabbed the point into the rope and it held. She worked it through what felt like a couple of plastic strands and started sawing.

The motion was about the worst thing she could have to do. Her wrists bled. The pain was intense—beaten out only by the wound in her palm that was taking the brunt of the work and, by the feel of it, was bleeding again, too.

Get over it, Kaitlin. Do what needs to be done. You've done it often enough when getting your father out of jams.

But it had never been like this. And it had never been physical or threatening to her personal safety. Mostly.

There had been that time in Dubai when an Arab merchant had accused her Dad of theft. She'd barely got him out of there before the merchant and his men took matters into their own hands and cut her father's hand off.

But that had been more a matter of getting his travel documents in order and bribing one of the merchant's men to get her dad out of there.

The sawing action worked; a few of the rope's cords broke.

The truck geared down and turned onto a street lined with concrete buildings and walled courtyards.

Dammit, she didn't have much time.

Kaitlin jabbed the point into the rope, missed and got her flesh. Yelped and almost dropped the file. She looked at B.J.

Nothing. Guy was definitely hurt more than he let on.

She tried again, sausage fingers making her slow and inaccurate.

Got it and sawed frantically.

Another few cords parts. She repeated the action, watching out the rear of the truck as they left the area of neat concrete and headed into the countryside again. Southward, by the look of the sunlight through the rainclouds. And by the look of them, there was more rain to come.

Flipping hell, she should have remembered the nail file sooner. She should have been working on this miles ago, not trying to get it done when they were almost arrived in town.

The truck jumped and bounced over the pot holes, making any sort of aim almost impossible. Her purse spilled open and her notepad went skittering across the floorboards and slipped through them. Lost. She froze for a second, but the darn pad wasn't going to do anything to help her. She started back with her ropes. Another stab into her wrist and the blood was flowing into her hands, making the file even harder to hold. If she kept on like this she was liable to slash her own wrist, and wouldn't that be just ducky.

She tried the edge of the file against the rope and sawed. More of the wound threads parted. The rope had only been a quarter inch. She had to be making headway. And if she could get them free, she and B.J. could leap off and get away.

A sharp pins-and-needles pain in her fingers suggested her circulation was improving, but that wasn't going to help her at all if she didn't get the damned rope cut.

The truck geared down again and slowed. Brakes squealed under them and B.J. groaned. Still not awake, though, which was bad for both of them.

The truck stopped and she heard one of the truck cab doors open and close and the sound of chains. A gate, maybe?

Saw, woman! Saw!

She kept at it and felt a few more threads give. The truck rumbled forward and into a courtyard, and then a gate was behind her and the man ran to close it. No escape, then.

The truck stopped and the engine died. In the sudden silence, all she could hear was her own rough breathing. The man at the gate was coming towards the rear of the truck. She had to finish now or hide the file somehow.

She yanked at her bindings, but they still held. Dammit, what was she going to do? There was no way she could get the file back hidden in her purse. On her person?

It was her only hope. She fiddled the darned file with tingling fingers into the back of her trousers and into her underwear. Nestled there, it wasn't going to go anywhere.

She hoped.

Then she yanked the pack closed and slid it beside her, just as the man leapt up into the truck. He grinned down at her with betel-stained teeth and said something she was sure she wouldn't like if she understood.

She just stared up at him and tried to control her shaking. Sweat poured down between her breasts and down her back, and it wasn't from the heat.

He walked over to B.J. and kicked him in the leg and B.J. erupted, kicking the man in the stomach and sending him flying across the truck to land with a thud half on Kaitlin and half against a crate.

He scrambled up making noises she knew had to be oaths. Then he was on B.J., still tied down helplessly. Kicks to the head, the torso, sent B.J. rolling into a ball, trying to protect himself.

In vain.

Kaitlin realized she was screaming, fighting her bonds, when another man tore the rear canvas tarp back. He yelled an order at the man inside, whose last kick missed B.J. and thumped one of the crates aside, but B.J. still lay limp on the floorboards.

Blood flowed from his nose and ran down the crates beside him.

And all Kaitlin could do was fight to breathe, because the man beside her smiled.

And exposed blackened teeth.

Chapter 33

"Y ou!"

The memory flooded back. His hand on her arm. The monsoon rains of a century ago in Phnom Penh and feeling lost.

But she wasn't lost anymore. She knew exactly where she was: a prisoner in the back of a truck in some godforsaken muddy Cambodian town not too far from the Thai border. With a nail file in the crack of her butt, no less. It might have been funny if B.J. hadn't been in need of serious medical attention.

The man smiled with one of those damned inscrutable expressions, but he had to be gloating. After all this time, he had her just where he'd wanted her to begin with.

"Miss Blackwood. Daughter of Jeremy Blackwood."

"So you knew all along who I was."

He bowed his head in a half-nod. "Of course."

And his English was better, too. Not so heavily accented, or rather, more accented with French.

Her head felt too full, trying to put all the facts together.

"B.J. needs medical attention."

"Mr. McCallum should learn to mind his own business."

"So? What? Your man beats him to within an inch of his life and that's supposed to be a lesson?"

He shrugged. He, flipping hell, shrugged and turned to speak to someone else in the courtyard. Two men in loose-fitting, blue uniforms jumped into the truck. One pushed her aside and grabbed her hands. She froze, praying he wouldn't notice whatever damage she'd done to the rope.

He only untied the cord that tethered her hands to the metal stanchion and hauled her up. They didn't even check her wrists.

Probably didn't suspect she was capable of anything. Just another westerner who didn't know how things worked. But she was learning, wasn't she? And one thing her mentor had always said when she was a cub reporter: she might make mistakes, but she never made the same one twice.

The guy who had untied her shoved her out of the truck, and down into mud that almost covered her shoes. The nail file grated uncomfortably against her skin.

The compound wasn't large. Sunlight leaked around threatening clouds and illuminated concrete block walls that were topped with glittering, jagged half-bottles. The compound itself was large enough to hold their truck and one other, but the churned-up mud suggested that many feet and tires had passed through here.

Kaitlin swallowed back fear, focusing on how all the facts were coming together. There was a story here, if she'd just wait for the information.

At the rear of the compound stood a large, almost windowless, concrete block building. Not exactly inviting. More like a cell-block, come to think of it, and the last thing she needed was another barrier to freedom.

Black-tooth motioned her towards the building, but she resisted. "I'm not leaving B.J. And I want my pack."

"What you want is of no consequence." Black-tooth's icy voice could steal the strength right out of her legs, but she'd be damned if she'd give him that satisfaction.

"Listen," she bristled. "I don't have the faintest idea why you're doing this, but if you want anything from me, you'll give me my pack and you'll keep B.J. and me together."

She drew herself up to her full height and glared down at him, and then realized she might have made an error if he was one of those guys with a small-man complex.

He met her gaze with more of the flipping inscrutable gaze. Then he smiled again and she didn't know which was worse. "If it is so important. It won't change anything."

An order in indecipherable Khmer and they dragged B.J. towards the back of the truck. He came to with a groan just before they dumped him out and managed to get his feet under him instead of landing on his face in the muck.

He stood wavering, his face bloody and swollen so one eye was partially closed and she wanted to go to him. His quick scan settled on her like she was his whole reason for being. "Hey, luv. Nice day. You all right?"

The grin he managed spoke of more strength than she'd thought possible.

"You look like hell."

"I feel like I've been run over by a lorry, instead of riding in one."

His gaze shifted from her to the Cambodian man before them and B.J. worked his shoulders and straightened. "Who the hell are you, then?"

And she wanted to scream "Shut up, you stupid, proud Aussie idiot," but the damage was already done.

"The man in charge. You may call me Duck." A name that really didn't suit him, so she must have gotten it wrong.

B.J.'s eyes widened and he staggered back a step before he caught himself. "Well goodday to ya, Mr. Duck. Name's B.J. McCallum. I'd offer my hand, but it seems that's a little impossible."

What the hell was he doing? Talking like an ignorant Aussie good ol' boy wasn't going to help anything.

Duck, or whatever his name was, jerked his head for them to be taken away.

"My pack." She reminded.

Duck looked from her to the pack with interest. It sat in a heap of blue canvas where she'd shoved it. He retrieved it and it hung from his fist like a precious hope. All she had of her father. "Perhaps I will hold onto this. Such a precious thing should not be lost."

Kaitlin had to bite her tongue when Duck slung the pack over his shoulder.

Everything. Every last thing she had was there, including the precious puppet. But he turned away, and three armed men shoved them across the compound toward the block building and a low, black-stained, wood door.

§

It took everything B.J. had to stay upright, and even then he swore as he staggered like a bloody, drunken, two-pot screamer. But he made it to the door. Inside, a narrow hallway bisected this part of the building, with narrow steel doors leading off of it. A whiff of piss—and fear—puffed into his face and everything went on high alert.

Stained concrete formed the walls and floor. Somewhere water drip-drip-dripped, and he got the sense of death and dying from the dark marks calligraphied on the walls.

He slowed. Too much like a prison. The windowless walls made him think of other prisons he'd seen. King County lockup after they picked him up for falsification of evidence. Toul Sleng Genocide Museum, the old Khmer Rouge prison and torture center in Phnom Penh. He didn't want to go in, but a shove between the shoulders sent him staggering forward into Kaitlin.

She almost went down, but her guard grabbed her. She yanked away and turned to B.J.

"Stay strong," he said. "I'll get us out of here."

She opened her mouth as if to say something, but the guard ripped her away. Their footsteps grated and echoed down the dimly-lit hallway, but there were other sounds, too. Small creeping, screeching sounds, like fingers on metal. Or moans. Either would fit this bloody place.

The guard in front opened a door into a dark, windowless cell. He shoved Kaitlin inside and she barely had time to turn back to them before the door slammed shut. The image of her face in the last narrow bit of light, fear winning through her strength before the door slammed shut, was burned into his brain.

"You hurt her and I'll kill you," he said in Khmer.

Both men laughed and shoved him to the next door. The door opened into darkness, and the stink of old urine and something viler assaulted his nose. Like blood had been allowed to coagulate and begin to rot.

They shoved him inside and the door slammed shut, leaving him blinded except for a dim crack of light under the door. Given what he'd seen of the muck on the floor and the stink, he settled down on his heels close to the light, his tied arms behind him, but his legs buckled and he ended up leaning against the door. At least they couldn't get in without alerting him.

He should get up. He should put up a fight. But his body wouldn't move and he hated himself for it. He should be getting out, rescuing Kaitlin.

Instead he could barely keep his eyes open. Couldn't keep them open, and her face was blazoned on the insides of his eyelids.

Kaitlin. Sure, she was a bloody pain in the ass, but she was good people. And she was just doing what any proper tyke would do to help her father.

And then I go and get her involved in chasing down a child-trafficking ring. Shit. Sure, her clues to her father's whereabouts suggested Pailin, and the ruby might be a link to him, but that didn't mean he was in any way involved with the snakehead, child-trafficking scene. So just why had he allowed Kaitlin to come with him? He could have pushed her out of the moto-taxi in Siem Reap. He could have avoided driving with her to Jorani's. So many points where he could have averted this situation.

But instead he'd dragged her into the middle of it. The best, most upright, ethical, and obsessively fastidious researcher he'd ever known, and he'd leapt to the conclusion that there was a link between her father and the children's abduction and had dragged her along with him—to this.

It wasn't a good feeling. As a matter of fact, it left him a little sick to his stomach and aching to undo what he'd done—if that was even possible, given the man outside.

Duch.

Every part of him wanted to panic. Duch was a name to strike fear into the hearts of anyone who knew Cambodian recent history. Kang Kech Eav, also known as Duch, had been a school teacher, but became the most notorious prison administrator in Cambodia. He organized and oversaw the meticulous imprisonment and torture of men, women, and children. He left behind him the horrific photo-records of prisoners at intake and of their emaciated, mutilated bodies just before or after death. He went so far as to set aside specific days of the week for particular killings: the day for the wives of my enemies. The day for the children.

They were the darkest days of Cambodian history, as millions of people were killed or starved or worked to death.

And this man, who could not be the real Duch, because the real Duch was dead, chose that name. No one but a crazy person would choose such a name.

How the hell did you deal with someone that crazy?

He thought of Maly and the other children. They didn't stand a chance. It was up to him. He might be bloodied and beaten, but he could do something.

He had to.

The sound of footsteps came through the door and he fought to get his legs under him and upright, but they didn't stop by his door. A click, a clang, and voices.

Kaitlin. She didn't understand what they were dealing with.

He kicked his door, terrified at his helplessness.

"Kaitlin!"

"B.J.?!"

He heard more voices. Angry this time.

"Kaitlin! Don't do anything stupid. Give them whatever they want!"

Only the sharp smack of fist against flesh answered him. Silence, voices, and the sound of dragging.

"Fuck me! Kaitlin! Kaitlin answer me! What have you bastards done to her?"

A door clanged and silence fell as thick as the darkness. He couldn't help her.

The sound of dripping filled his head. It could be water. It might be blood.

Chapter 34

Bindings that still cut into her wrists. Grit under her cheek and dirt in her mouth. Those were the first things Kaitlin was aware of. But there was light through her eyelids, so she wasn't in that horrible cell. Not trapped in darkness and too much fear.

Not the cell, then… B.J.! She remembered his yell, remembered struggling to get free to go to him, and then—nothing.

So that had worked out well. And now she had no idea where she was. Fear rippled through her and clenched her stomach.

The acrid scent of Chinese cigarettes stung her nostrils and made her want to cough. No voices, no sound, but the sense of movement. Like someone waved the smoke towards her. Or maybe there was a sound.

Breathing. Hers. And someone else's. The soft, sucking, inhalation of the smoker, the gentle puff of the smoke, and then it was in her face again. Breathing someone else's used air.

It was like the final defilement and she shuddered and rolled over on her back and opened her eyes.

Concrete bricks for the roof and four walls, but at least she could see them. Those few minutes in the dark cell alone had done more to break her will than anything she'd ever experienced. She didn't like the way it had shut down her logic and ability to plan. It was like light was necessary to feed her brain. *Child of the Enlightenment* came to mind.

Stupid thought. Her life was reporting from the dark.

Correction: the edges of the dark. She had never really stepped over the edge before.

Now she had. Fallen. Tumbling. Freefall.

Another soft sucking sound and a trail of smoke blew over her head. She followed it back to the mouth that released it.

The edge of a wooden desk blocked her view. She sat up and got her legs underneath her. Struggled to standing and found herself facing the man who would forever be Black-tooth.

"You have no right to treat me like this. I'm an American citizen. My Embassy knows I'm in the country and will be looking for me." But her voice wavered unconscionably. He'd know it was a lie.

He just looked at her with this weird, vacant gaze that brought to mind 'psychopath,' and he took another puff of his cigarette. Darn thing trailed at least an inch of ash, but it didn't fall. An ashtray near his hand overflowed with ash and butts smoked right down to the filter.

"I know who you are, Ms. Blackwood. And I know what is the truth. I have had you followed since you arrived in Cambodia."

A chill ran up her spine. The only way he could have known to have her followed was if he had spoken to her father. He could be locked in another one of those horrible cells.

Then she realized that spread around Black-tooth's ashtray was everything from inside her pack, the puppet, and her father's letter open before him.

"Where's my father? What have you done to him?"

Was that a slight rise of his brows? A query? The sign he was surprised?

God, she wanted her notepad—now lost on the road. Wanted the time to decide how to respond, because either (a) this man didn't have her father, or (b) he was prepared to string her along to get something from her, and she wasn't sure what it was he wanted.

Of course, there was a (c) option, as well. Black-tooth could just be a sadistic bastard who was playing with her before he killed her or had her killed.

She swallowed back the sour taste of fear. Not a good thought to have.

Focus, Blackwood. Focus. Plan.

Black-tooth simply looked at her, then scanned the items spread on his desk. He picked up the letter.

"Your father writes of his dealings with the government. What was he doing, Ms. Blackwood?"

"If I knew, I wouldn't tell you anything."

"And yet you are here, where he was not so many months ago."

Her heart leapt. So she had interpreted the clues correctly. Or B.J. had. She doubted that she'd have discovered the map in the puppet on her own as quickly.

So he didn't have her father. Or he was stringing her along to see what he could get from her. She wished she'd had a chance to prepare for this. Always, before an interview, she had planned out the possible questions she'd ask.

Act like she knew something or not? One could get her tortured and the other could get her killed. What was it going to be? She could almost hear B.J.'s voice in her head.

Door number 1 or door number 2. B.J. would have already made the decision and damn the torpedoes, while she stood here with sweat running down her forehead and stinging her eyes.

"How the hell should I know where my father is?" It came out more bitter than she'd expected. She met Black-tooth's obsidian gaze. "He runs off and I run after and pick up the pieces."

Like this guy would understand.

"Where do you run to?"

God, his eyes were like mirrors. Nothing showed through. What was he after? What did he want? "Here. Pailin. After him and the kids you abducted."

"And how did you know how to get here?"

She met his gaze and swallowed. Didn't look at the puppet that he was fingering. Suddenly it was more important than ever that this man didn't know about her father's puppet. There had to be something more to it than just a map to get her to Pailin. Her father wouldn't go to all that trouble just to point her here. She thought of the puppet and of the tangled web of branches and vines in the carving. Could there be something more there?

"Jorani. Before she died, she said Pailin. B.J. was coming after the children and I didn't have any other leads. I came with him."

"And what led you to Jorani?"

"He had said something to the girl at the hotel in Phnom Penh about a donation to the orphanage. I went to Siem Reap hoping I'd find him there."

Black-tooth looked at her a moment as if assessing what she said. Then he shouted and a man came to the door. Black-tooth ordered something and the man retreated again.

"We will see if such a thing is true."

"What? You're going to…."

Oh, God, Champei. Kaitlin had sent them after the lovely hotel clerk.

She had to do something. Tears of frustration threatened. She was no good at this kind of subterfuge. Not without planning. She'd talked herself into a trap, just like she knew she would if she couldn't plan. That was the whole reason for planning—you didn't do anything wrong. You didn't hurt other people.

If she gave up the shadow puppet, she could stop this. But if she did, they might find her father.

She realized she was looking at the carved leather. When they came for Champei, she would tell them about the envelope and what it contained. Black-tooth would know everything then, anyway. And she would have hurt Champei in the process, and the woman didn't deserve that.

Better to use what meager advantage she had. "I'm not telling you anything until I see B.J. and the children released."

A slow smile coiled across his face and she felt like she faced a serpent about to swallow her whole.

"You play a dangerous game, Ms. Blackwood. Why wouldn't I just torture your information out of you?"

Please, God, let her look stronger than she felt. "Because torture takes time, and that's something you don't have. And you can't be sure I'd talk."

Her last words were just bravado and they both knew it, but his mask of inscrutability kept her from knowing whether she'd guessed rightly. He looked down at the desk, directly at the puppet, and shoved it aside like it meant nothing. Her father had done a good job of disguising his map, she had to give him that. An able adversary for Black-tooth.

"Who is to say whether I even have these children of yours—these orphans."

Kaitlin could have shouted the halleluiah chorus. She'd hooked him! He was considering it!

Which meant the value of her information must be huge to him. Which meant her father was in more trouble than even she'd realized.

"You do. They were seen leaving in a truck like the one in your compound. You haven't had enough time to clean them up and move them." She hoped. She prayed. Based on what she knew of the child smuggling business, they usually brought them through the border in small groups with snakehead women posing as their parents. She stood brazen and casual—at least as much as anyone could, with her hands tied and a nail file stuck down the crack of her butt.

She just wanted B.J. free with his children.

Black-tooth shouted and his man reappeared at the door. Another order and the man disappeared again.

Black-tooth steepled his hands. "We will see what you have for me."

She channeled B.J.'s bravado and shrugged. She wouldn't say more until she knew B.J. was safe and he had seen to the kids' safety.

If he was capable of it. A little tendril of fear undermined what little plan she had.

Last she'd seen, he'd barely been able to stand.

Chapter 35

The darkness seemed to amplify every sound. A skittering across the floor. A squeak that seemed to echo in the small space. His breathing, rough and uneven. But not the sound B.J. wanted.

The rough wood door was unyielding under his cheek as he listened for the sound of Kaitlin returning. He just prayed they *would* bring her back. Too many had disappeared in this country of mass graves in desolate places.

"Not Kaitlin. Not bloody Kaitlin."

But his words only dropped into the dark and disappeared with about as much impact as he was having on Kaitlin's safety.

"Bloody hell, I was supposed to protect her!" He slammed his shoulder against the door, ignoring the bruising that was already there and the pain in his arms from where they twisted behind him. When they'd taken her away, he'd hauled himself up and thrown himself futilely at the door long after all sound disappeared from the world beyond the cell.

Well maybe not all. A muffled sound came from beyond the door. Crying? A moan? Or the wind in the eaves and a monsoon rain? The clouds *had* been coming.

Damn it. This time he kicked the door, then turned to pace around the room. He had to move. He had to do something. He would not succumb to the helplessness that oozed into him like the darkness.

"Damn it, no!" He drove his shoulder into the door again and felt it give against the hinges. And then hold. Why the hell couldn't they have built this place with the same crappy craftsmanship he often saw in Cambodian government buildings?

He stood there, panting, and too many memories crawled across the dark like a negative of Kaitlin's shadow puppet. A night-bound street. A man. A fifteen-year-old girl.

He squeezed his eyes shut against the memory, but the darkness was there, too. He had been eighteen. Cora, his blonde-haired younger sister, caught in a crystal-meth daze, standing gaunt and wounded in micro-mini and provocatively torn shirt.

"Cora, come home," he'd begged. "We'll get you help again. We'll get you clean."

She took a hesitant step towards him, but a man materialized out of the dark, beach-boy blonde and big, in silk and too many gold chains, like some dark spirit. Or a devil hooking her back. Strong fingers caught her shoulder.

"Sweetheart, why you want to go with him? He's only promising pain, but I got what you need to keep the pain away."

"Cora, listen to me." A much younger B.J. begged. "He's a fraud. He's an Aussie pimp is all, not anyone who loves you. Come home. Come with me. You can stay with me, if you want to, until you're clean."

And rob him blind like she had before, but it didn't matter. Nothing mattered but saving her.

Cora blinked like a roo on a highway. "B.J.?"

She reached for him. He reached for her, but the Shark in show-pony clothing knocked his hand away. "Get lost, man. She's my property now. Come on, sweetheart."

"Like hell."

The Shark held up his hand. "Mate, I've got no problem with ya. Let me just have a word with my woman and we'll sort this all out."

B.J. hesitated; the night was all around him and he really wanted this to work out, for Cora to be able to just walk away. He nodded.

And the Shark cold-cocked him with a fist the size of a sledgehammer to the side of his head. B.J. went down, the darkness gone brilliant with blinding stars.

And when he could see, there was only darkness and he was alone.

Like now. He'd let Cora go and she'd never come back. Three months later, the police had shown up with news that her body had been found, beaten to a pulp. He was *never* going to allow that to happen again.

"But ya did, ya bloody wanker. You let those assholes shove you in here and drag Kaitlin off."

Just like Cora. Just like the kids, for that matter.

Maybe Kaitlin was right—he was just a screw-up who went off half-cocked and didn't think things through. If he'd listened to the welfare worker and gone with one of them to find Cora… but he'd known better. If he'd listened to Kaitlin and maybe tried the authorities first, she wouldn't be in this predicament. Maybe she wouldn't be here at all.

He'd prided himself on being a man of action, but maybe that was just an excuse. Maybe he was just an idiot without a plan about anything at all.

"Bloody useless," he muttered, but a sound ended his pacing. A line of light leaked under the door.

"Kaitlin!" he roared. "Kaitlin, answer me!"

There were only footsteps. If they'd hurt her, he'd kill the bastards. He would.

Then came the clank and creak of another door and a silence. Muffled order: "Out."

A rushing sound followed. What the hell was going on? And then came the clang of a bolt sliding and his door yanked open so he nearly fell out into the blinding light of the hall. He caught himself.

Blinked. Surely to God it wasn't true. He wasn't seeing this.

But a sea of small faces blinked up at him from beyond the three armed guards. Faces he knew. Faces that sparked with hope when they saw him.

"B.J.!" The piping voice he knew so well. Maly with her long, ebony hair and crooked jokester smile.

And then the sea of faces surrounded him and pressed their warmth and life into him and he went to his knees. Maly threw her arms around him and filled his face with the warm scent of little girl. He couldn't help huimself: he cried.

Until the guard ripped her away. Until they knocked the others back with the butts of their weapons. Twenty-five children huddled in the hallway, and there was nothing he could do. The images of the prison that had become Toul Sleng Museum filled his head. Children tortured, just like their parents. The helplessness had gotten into his bones. Stolen his strength.

No! He wouldn't let it. He struggled against his bonds, the helpless rage almost strangling him. He wouldn't let it. Couldn't let the kids see how frightened he was for them. And Kaitlin. What had happened to her?

"It's going to be all right," he said in Khmer and saw the wavering hope steady and hold. Good.

He stumbled to his feet and straightened against the pain, because he couldn't afford for the kids to see just what shape he was in. Couldn't afford to be weak and injured at all.

"So? What do you want?" he demanded of the guards.

The guard just shoved him ahead of the children and all of them out the door.

Torrential rain greeted him like a wall and drenched them as they waded through three inches of mud. Both trucks still stood there. At least he thought they were the same trucks. The wooden crates had disappeared, though, and there was no sign of Kaitlin. Hopefully, that was good.

Maybe—maybe they had released her. *Don't be a fool.* That wasn't something they'd do.

They shoved him to the other end of the concrete bunker and inside another door. The children crowded in behind him and the air stank of sodden cloth and fear and the heavy tang of Chinese cigarettes. Maly had wormed her way forward and snuck a small hand into his tied one. He looked around and managed a smile for her. Keep her hoping. But she didn't smile back.

The darned kid was too bright for that. She'd taken all the bad news, about her fainting spells and all the things she couldn't do, with wisdom much older than her age. She'd been here before.

The guards jabbed a gun barrel at B.J. to stop him in front of a scarred, wooden door. A single knock and a word from inside and they pushed him in. Maly and the others came with him.

The scent of rainwater and roses met his nose before he registered Kaitlin's presence. She stood with her back to the wall away from the man and the desk in front of him, but her face was defiant.

"Kaitlin…?"

"I'm fine." Her voice was clipped, but knowing her so well, he heard the strain underneath. "I've made a deal on our behalf."

She didn't even bloody well look at him and he followed her gaze. Duch sat watching them from behind his desk like an Eastern Brown snake. On his desk were spread what must be the contents of Kaitlin's pack, with the letter from her father front and center. To one side, almost ignored, lay the shadow puppet.

When B.J. met his gaze, Duch smiled. B.J. stepped in front of the children.

"The annoying Mr. McCallum. Are you in better condition to partake of a conversation?"

"No thanks to you and your bloody guards."

"And who is this sweet young thing?" Duch motioned at Maly, who peeked from behind B.J. with huge black eyes.

"You leave her out of this."

Duch smiled his black-toothed smile. "So this one is important to you." He crooked a finger at Maly and ordered her forward in Khmer.

The little girl whimpered and held to B.J.'s leg.

"Leave her alone," B.J. protested.

"Come here!" Duch ordered.

Maly looked up at B.J., but what could he do? She shook her head and stepped forward.

"Stop it! Stop it right now!"

Kaitlin left her place at the wall. She blocked Maly from Duch and stood there, defiant. Not a good thing to do in the face of a man who fashioned himself after the chief torturer of the Killing Fields. A bloody good way to get yourself dead.

But there she went, doing something he never thought he'd live to see. Kaitlin Blackwood doing something unthinkingly stupid—and working without a list.

"We made a deal. You'll release them. Now. Or I'm not telling you anything."

"What the bloody hell are you talking about?" B.J. thrust himself between Kaitlin and the desk.

"Would you just shut up, for once?" She stepped around him. "I know what I'm doing."

But she didn't. She couldn't. You never deal with the devil, because the devil always wins. But she glared so magnificently down at Duch, she might as well be a different Kaitlin.

"Well? Do we have a deal or what?"

"How do I know you have any information? I could release these ones and get nothing in return."

Release? A thrill of fear ran through B.J., because a release of the children would cost her dearly "Kaitlin, maybe you should rethink this?"

"I'm getting you and the kids out of here. That's what you wanted, right?" She turned, her eyes pleading with him—for help? To understand? To just go along with her madness?

To trust that she had a plan with no list?

None of them worked. He shook his head. "He's a bloody liar and a cheat, Kaitlin. And worse. Far worse. Do you know who Duch is? Was?"

She sighed and shook her head, looking beautiful and brave and far too vulnerable. "The man I have to deal with. Now just let me do this."

"Well?" she asked Duch.

The black-toothed man's smile had broadened, but finally he nodded. Why he would agree to anything when he could get the information another way—by torture if necessary—didn't make any sense.

Something was wrong. Very wrong, and Kaitlin couldn't be aware of what she was walking into.

"Kaitlin, he's styled himself after a murderer. A torturer. What makes you think he'll do what he says?"

"Because he's desperate," she said with her gaze fixed on Duch. "Because he wants what I have."

She narrowed her gaze. "I'll tell you one thing. My father left me a map, and that's how I got here."

Had the bloody woman gone mad? She was bartering a map she didn't have. Duch would kill her for sure when he found out she'd lied.

But Duch finally nodded.

He yelled for the guards to take him and the children, and they hustled into the office and grabbed B.J., and shoved him towards the door.

"Kaitlin. Rethink this. You don't know what he'll do."

She looked at him and finally nodded. So maybe she was coming to her senses. Maybe she understood his warning.

"I want them taken to a local NGO. Unicef or Save the Children or Care or something like that."

Duch frowned, obviously not happy with the way things were going. "You think you can order me? I need more than your word there is a map. I need to see this thing."

"Kaitlin, no. Don't."

Fighting through pain, he tried to get back to her, but Duch's men wrestled him to the door. And Kaitlin only glared at him. She was like a missile on a wild trajectory with no way to stop her.

"Do you think I'm stupid?"

B.J. wasn't sure whether she was talking to him or to Duch.

"I show you the map and you kill us all. I want to see B.J. and the children safely at an NGO. Then I'll show you."

Duch's face had gone so tight, his lips were no more than a seam that split when he amended his order to his men. He stood up, came around the desk, and grabbed Kaitlin's arm. He leaned in. "If you lie, your death will be most painful."

And bloody hell, he meant it and would rain pain on Kaitlin like the monsoons poured. But Kaitlin wrenched away from him and stood her ground like the last tiger. "I want my things, too."

Duch swore and nodded at one of his men. The guard dragged everything off the desk and into the pack, then gave it to Duch.

Then they were marched out to the courtyard, Kaitlin treading on B.J.'s heels through the downpour. B.J. dropped back beside her, the children flooding around them like leaves knocked free by the rain. Until the guards bellowed and threatened. Then they became a tight little group huddled around B.J. and Kaitlin.

"Just what the bloody hell are you doing?" he hissed at her.

"Getting you and the children out of this. You see, we had this all wrong. The kids were never the central thing. My father was. It was about him and the rubies. He must have given one to Jorani for helping with the puppet, but something went wrong. You never should have been involved."

"What the hell are you talking about?" It couldn't be true, could it? Jeremy Blackwood was a nice enough bloke, even if he gave his daughter fits.

But she jerked a nod and then they were forced into the back of a lorry to sit at gunpoint as Duch and a driver climbed in front.

But the guards kept them separated. Maly was forced to sit beside Kaitlin, who bent down to smile at the little girl.

Maly threw B.J. a questioning look and B.J. nodded. Kaitlin was good. Safe. Maly slid a little closer to Kaitlin and B.J. closed his eyes against the flooding sense of panic. Something was going to go horribly wrong. He could feel it, and over the years he'd learned to listen to his gut. The one time he hadn't was when he'd produced the fateful photos in the snakehead case.

He had to protect them—protect Kaitlin from herself—and he was fucking helpless.

The lorry's engine roared and rumbled and sent a rich flood of carbon monoxide into the truck that sent them all coughing. The vehicle jerked and bounced out of the courtyard. The gates swung shut behind them and it would have been a relief if the situation hadn't taken them from the frying pan into the bloody fire.

He held Kaitlin with his gaze, willing her to look at him, to understand what a mistake she was making. She had her head bent near Maly's in an earnest conversation. Most of the other kids had more or less learned the language as well, because Jorani had seen English as the hope for these kids being able to earn a living as adults. What would happen to them, now, was another thing altogether.

But he couldn't think about that now. Kaitlin glanced up at him and met his gaze. She glanced back at Maly and smiled. "Nice kid," she mouthed.

He wanted to yell. Scream at her for what she was considering doing, and she must have read it on his face, for she simply closed her eyes and shook her head. Her lips moved again. "My decision."

Always so sure of herself, only this time it was going to get her killed, sure as a pint leads to a piss.

The truck bounced over potholes as it picked up speed, and the children sat strangely silent around them, as if they knew the gravity of their situation. But then they did, didn't they? They'd been there before, in the days before Jorani rescued them. All the little figures huddled, round-shouldered beside him when they should be children. Should be laughing, playing, like at Jorani's.

Damn it, he'd make this work somehow. He'd work with Kaitlin in whatever unworkable plan she'd come up with and try to make things work.

Try harder than you did to make your relationship work?

Water a long time under the bridge. He'd been an idiot to do what he'd done, but the situation had been dire enough to call for desperate measures. Unfortunately it had led to a hell of a lot of unintended consequences, because he hadn't exactly wanted to end his relationship with Kaitlin.

Being with her the past few infuriating days had reminded him of that too sweetly.

Beyond the truck's canvas sides, the town appeared through the sheets of rain that stained its cream-colored buildings grey. Light traffic buzzed around them: motorcycles, loaded lorries making the trip between Cambodia and Thailand, most probably carrying the cheap clothing made in Cambodian sweat shops to sell to foreign tourists in Bangkok and at beach resorts. No one cared that men, women, and children were virtually slaves. No one cared enough to stop the trafficking in children, either, except for a few NGOs.

The truck slowed and turned onto a side street with a few small, colonial-style houses set back in amongst rain-blackened trees and mud-filled yards. Signs for Doctors without Borders and one or two Cambodian charities bloomed out of the rain.

Could she do this? Was she getting them out of this? Or was this just some cruel joke of Duch's to show them what they couldn't have. He wouldn't put it past the bastard.

The truck slowed further and then ground to a stop. The rain thundered overhead as the engine roar changed to idle. Duch came around the rear of the truck.

"Out. All of you." Repeated in English and Khmer, and B.J. prepared to throw himself at whichever guard threatened Kaitlin.

The children helped each other off the truck and stood in the rain. Kaitlin leapt down and the rain slicked her t-shirt to her body, her fair hair to her head. She looked weary and right at the edge of her strength, but determined to see through whatever it was she'd set in motion.

B.J. came to the edge of the truck bed. Try to take out Duch or some of the guards?

His hesitation gained him a rifle butt in the back from one of Duch's guards and he fell out of the truck again, landing on his injured side. All air whomfed out of him and he lay there a moment catching his breath through the pain.

"B.J.!" Kaitlin tried to get to his side, but the guards stopped her.

He staggered up and grinned at Kaitlin through the rain and mud.

"Note to self: stop doing that."

But she didn't smile back, only looked at Duch.

"Where are we?"

"Your CARE office in Pailin. I think they drill wells or some such helpful thing. Or perhaps they teach reforestation." His tone said he didn't see the point.

"I wanted an NGO that specializes in child welfare," Kaitlin said.

Duch just looked at her. "There was no such specificity in your request. I have done what you asked."

Impasse—and Kaitlin got that look she got when she was calculating something. At least the house looked like someone was there. Figures moved beyond the windows. There was a soccer ball abandoned beside the door.

She nodded. "Kids, head to that house." She nodded in the direction of the house. Maly looked to B.J. and he nodded. If this was her gambit, then he'd try to make it work. The children scurried across the yard and someone met them at the door. Stopped them. Came outside.

"Untie B.J. and me," she ordered.

Duch virtually snarled at her, but then his face became a mask again. He muttered a half-heard order and one of his men produced a knife and went behind B.J. Then the point found its way between his shoulder blades and he knew it cut his shirt and the flesh over his spine. A warm stream of blood joined the cool of the rain.

B.J. froze at the wash of new pain.

More pressure and he would never walk again.

Chapter 36

When Black-tooth's man went behind B.J., B.J. went so still, Kaitlin knew something was wrong. The rain poured down, drenching everything, including the file between her butt cheeks. The darn thing was going to rust there at this rate. But the rain made it hard to see anything clearly. Except Black-tooth's smile, and that was enough to reinforce that her gut was right.

She'd screwed up somehow.

"B.J.? What's wrong?"

"A little matter of a knife in the back, luv. I don't think he's cutting anything but me."

"Hey! What's going on?" An American voice from the house.

"No one move," Duch said, ignoring the NGO staff. "I release no one else until the map is produced."

She wasn't sure what to do. She'd worked on the fly, and look where it had gotten her. She had worked from the premise she could bargain them to safety, not that she'd have to save B.J. from quadriplegia or worse. That was the problem with not planning. Things took a wrong turn and look where it got you. One instant decision demanding another, like droplets of water. Eventually the water would wear everything away. All the normal, sensible, safe places in the world.

"My pack." She ignored B.J.'s warning look. They were in no position to bargain—much.

Black-tooth swung her bag off his shoulder and opened it up, waiting.

"Have your man take the knife out of B.J.'s back."

"I think, Ms. Blackwood, you are in no position to bargain."

The man on the porch of the house had stepped down and gathered the children behind him. He was striding towards them, and she was going to get someone killed if she didn't hurry up.

"The puppet. Pull it out and I'll show you."

Black-tooth looked dubious, but he fished in the bag and brought out the puppet, ripped loose of its plastic when her things were searched. Rain quickly stained the leather black.

"Look at it. Turn it sideways slightly. It's not a tree, like it looks like. It's Cambodia. See the large flower on the left rim? That's Pailin. That's why I'm here. And the mess of vines below the blossom is a map to my father."

She said it in a rush and prayed Black-tooth couldn't tell what was false or the truth. She watched his face as he turned the map this way and that, and then his features went flat, controlled, and she'd learned that meant he'd made a decision.

"Free us. You've got what you wanted."

"What the hell is going on?" The man from the NGO, a tall, thin man of about forty, pushed his way past the guards.

Duch ignored him, jerked his head at the man holding B.J., and grabbed Kaitlin's arm. The guard shoved B.J. into the NGO's man's arms and the guards leapt up into the truck.

"No," Kaitlin protested and tried to pull loose, but like in Phnom Penh, Black-tooth's grip wasn't to be denied. She twisted and kicked, but he was prepared this time. He slammed a fist into her solar plexus and she doubled over. Pain everywhere. No breath.

She couldn't breathe. Tears blinded her and he dragged her forward. With no air, she was weak. With no air, she couldn't make her body do what she wanted.

Then she was lifted into the cigarette-reek of the truck cab and Black-tooth leapt up behind. She found strength to kick and caught him in the chest. He fell back into the mud and rain, but was back before she could scoot her way out to the street.

Then the door behind her opened and the driver grabbed her shoulders. Between them they wrestled her into the cab, slammed the doors, and got the engine going. The engine clunked into gear and the truck started rolling.

B.J., still bound, appeared by the cab and threw himself at the door. Kaitlin started to fight, but Black-tooth produced a gun.

"Fight and I kill him."

She froze. Not having the infuriating Aussie in the world would be a very bad thing.

Out the window, B.J. threw himself at the truck again. Swore. Shouted, but she couldn't hear what he said. She could only look at him and his desperation in the side mirror as the truck picked up speed. And her past—all her past—was left behind.

She looked down at the gun now pressed into her side.

She didn't like her chances at a future.

§

"No! Kaitlin!" B.J. kicked at the truck's wheel as it sped past him and felt like the blow had landed in his gut. Kaitlin gone, her blue eyes huge and defiant as she'd met his gaze.

But there was fear there, too. And—bloody hell—relief, and he knew she'd done this whole thing to get him and kids free. And that was far too much the type of thing Kaitlin would do. After all, she'd been giving up her life for years for her father just because he loved her.

But fabricating a story about the tangle of vines on the puppet being a map—that was something new for her. Sure, they'd talked about the possibility, but the tangle had really looked like just that.

"What the hell's going on?"

The prissy-assed American grabbed his shoulder and B.J. swung around.

"What the bloody hell does it look like? They just kidnapped my girl." He would have hit the bloke, if his hands weren't still tied.

"Who are they?"

B.J. swung back to look at the truck's disappearing back end. "Don't rightly know, but the bastard in charge calls himself Duch, if that means anything to ya."

The man's face paled a little. "Khmer…"

"…Rouge," B.J. finished. "So you do know your history. And they've got Kaitlin and that can't be good. Now would ya bloody well untie me so I can go after her?"

The man nodded and fumbled at the ropes. "No good. We need a knife."

He led B.J. through the rain and mud to the house. "Who're all the kids?"

"Orphans Duch had planned to sell. They'd been rescued once from the snakeheads. Apparently that makes them fair game to take again. Duch's men burned down the orphanage and killed the woman who ran it."

"Fuck me," the American said.

"Too right."

The man herded the children into the house along with B.J. Three other people were there, two men and a woman. One of the men went into the kitchen and returned with a sharp knife they used on B.J.'s bonds. The woman picked up a phone and dialed the police. Fat load of luck with that one, mate.

"Bill Walters." The first American stuck out his hand while B.J. rubbed circulation into his wrists and dealt with the pain. Outside, the rain obliterated any sign that Kaitlin or the truck had ever been there. If he got going now, he could catch them—barely.

Kaitlin.

His heart hammered a little harder. No way he wasn't going to find her. He accepted Walters' hand with pins and needles in his fingers.

"B.J. McCallum. Any of you blokes got a car?"

"You're going after her, aren't you?"

"What'd'you expect?"

"But you're bleeding," the woman said, frowning at the blood.

"Flesh wounds. And I got no time to worry about the others." Like the way his ribs grated when he moved. Medical attention would come after Kaitlin was safe. "So, that car?"

Walters shook his head. "Company car's in the shop as we speak."

"You can have my bike," the woman offered. "Motorcycle. I brought it in from Thailand. Works pretty good on the back roads."

Just what he needed, some girlie bike, but beggars couldn't be choosers.

"You got any weapons? A pistol maybe?"

Walters and the others looked at each other. "After what we just saw, I'm not sure we should give up what we have."

B.J. looked at Maly and the other kids. "You keep the kids safe and you'd be doing me a favor. But I've gotta move if I'm going to catch her."

He went to his knees in the midst of the children and caught Maly in his arms. Hers came around him and the other kids crowded in, in a warm mass of affection that caught in his chest. He buried his face in Maly's sweet-scented hair and lost himself for a moment in the warmth of her childhood. Safe. For the moment, anyway.

"You stay here with these people. They'll keep you safe. Understand?"

She nodded into him and pulled back to smile. "You will find pretty lady, right?"

"Too right."

"Then you come back?"

"I'll try."

She nodded sagely and the others echoed her. "You come back. We be waiting for you."

He stood up before things got mushy and pulled out his wallet. Handed it to Walter. "Take whatever I've got. Just feed them and get them some place safe if I can't do it."

He glanced down at Maly, hoping she hadn't caught what he'd said, but her little face was grave and she had hold of his hand like a vise.

But Walter waved off his offer. "You just get back here. We'll do everything we can, from this end. Anyone we should call?"

B.J. thought a moment. "Call the *Seattle Post Intelligencer*. Call a man named James McKillup and tell him Kaitlin Blackwood is in trouble and that I've gone after her. Tell him we need protection for these kids. Bloke'll know what to do or he'll figure it out quick."

The woman jingled a single key and B.J. accepted it gratefully and followed her outside, the children following him like a bloody train, Maly still clutching his hand.

He had to pry her fingers off his, and when a single slow tear ran down her cheek, it broke his heart.

"Don't go, B.J."

He picked her up in his arms. "Now didn't I tell you I'd be right back, luv?"

She nodded and hung her head. "You said you'd try. I love you, B.J. I don't want you to leave."

Damned kid was too quick on the exact meaning of words. He swallowed and had to close his eyes. When was the last time anyone had said that to him? "I know, luv. I love you, too. That's why I'll be back."

"Maly go, too?"

"Impossible, sweetheart." He gave her a squeeze. Separating her from him was like tearing out part of his heart. He couldn't look at her as he handed her off to the woman and turned to where she'd pulled a tarp off the bike.

Thankfully, not a woman's toy. A rugged, dual-purpose Yamaha. He looked at the woman with new respect. "Nice bike."

"I thought so. Good for the roads around here. Take care of her, though. She's new."

"I'll do what I can."

He threw his leg over, wincing at the pain in his ribs. Thankfully he'd borrowed bikes often enough in Siem Reap, he felt comfortable settling into the seat. Keyed it on and the engine roared, then fell back to a purr.

He set it in motion and rode it across the yard, pushing water like a prow wave.

And then he was on the street and headed the way the truck had gone. Following a bloody map carved in leather.

Just how long did Kaitlin think she could string Duch along?

Chapter 37

If she could just quit shaking she might be able to think, but the gun in her side, the vibration of the truck, and the stink of Chinese cigarettes and garlic, all threatened to make her sick.

And thinking of the pistol when it had pointed at B.J. He'd been an instant from death and he didn't know it. She closed her eyes as the truck geared down for the latest corner, and pressed herself back, her bound arms trapped between her and the seat so she didn't slide any closer to either the driver or Black-tooth.

It was bad enough being crammed into the cab like this. At least in the back there'd be fresh air and the chance—slim, but a chance—that she might finish cutting the ropes. She might have been able to leap free of the truck and escape.

But from here there was no such chance, and the damned file was working its way down in her underwear and becoming increasingly uncomfortable in the rough-riding cab.

The truck came to a crossroads with a cluster of rain-sodden, thatched huts, and Black-tooth muttered. The truck stopped and Black-tooth held the puppet out for her. Outside, faces appeared at the doors to the structures. People lived there, but there was no way they could help her. They were just more victims-in-waiting for the likes of Black-tooth.

"You tell me this is a map. We are now out of Pailin to the south. Where do we go now?"

His eyes carried only the promise of a hard death if she didn't produce, but how could she possibly produce when the whole thing was a lie?

She looked down at the puppet. In for a penny, in for a pound. Might as well use the puppet-map ruse to keep them going until she had a chance to escape. It was all she could do, and it was the most difficult thing she'd ever done to just go with what was happening and make decisions on the fly.

"It'd be easier if you untied me."

He just shoved the puppet at her again.

"Can't blame a girl for trying." But she studied the puppet.

From the large blossom they'd determined was Pailin, a series of vines and flowers twisted and coiled around each other. They could be a map, she supposed. One of the vines even had veining in it. And if she followed that vine back, it was actually joined to the Pailin blossom.

"Are there other roads south out of Pailin?"

"Only one main road south."

Okay, so she might swing this. At the mass of vines, three tendrils met at a blossom, but the veined one coiled straight onward into the mess of vines.

"We keep going straight," she said. Into a mess of lies. A coil of snakes. How long she could keep this straight she didn't know, and how the heck she was going to get out of this and find her father and her way back was beyond her right now. Just keep the story going as long as she could.

§

The rain and the flooded streets made driving the motorcycle at speed almost impossible. Six inches of water made the potholes impossible to see. He'd put the bike on its side once—thankfully when he was slowed for a corner—and had the road rash from the gravel to prove it. Still, he pushed the speedometer up past sixty kilometers an hour and took his chances.

The downpour filled his face. He kept his head down and peered out of the tops of his eyes. Rain and wind slicked his muddy clothes to his chest. Each pothole he hit sent a jolt of pain through his chest, but it didn't matter.

Kaitlin was what mattered.

He'd managed to find the main southbound road, but it had petered out to not much more than a rural backwater between villages. Still, the fact there had been only one road gave him some confidence. That and the fact that when he crossed the Sangker River, a bullock cart driver had confirmed that a truck had come this way.

Ahead, through the rain, loomed the darkness of the Cardamom Mountains and some of the least traveled parts of Cambodia. It was also the homeland of illicit logging and poaching, though the bloody government had promised, under threat of international sanctions, to stop it. The whole bloody country was up for sale.

But that was a likely route south as well. *If* Kaitlin had figured out that the knot of vines on the puppet really was a map, and *if* her father were somehow involved with the monk's gemstone, then Kaitlin and Duch were traveling in the right direction, because over the western spur of those mountains sat Trat, the Thai gem center, with all its mining activities on the Thai side of the border.

A crossroads loomed ahead and B.J. slowed, sending a wash of water to the gravel edge of the road and back at him. It washed up over his boot tops. At the rate he was going, he was going to get jungle rot for sure. And there sure as hell wasn't any sign pointing the direction to where the lorry had gone.

He pulled to a stop where the three roads met. A group of thatched huts stood around the road. B.J. stood up and the world swung around him. He slumped back in the saddle.

He knew the slightly panicked feeling in his body. It wasn't just the need to rescue Kaitlin, it was the fact he hadn't eaten in—what?—almost forty-eight hours. He had to find something or he'd be no use to her when he found her. He parked the bike and went to one of the huts. The doorway remained dark.

"Hello! Anyone home?" he called in Khmer.

A thin male face came to the door and behind him, in the shadows, gleamed the eyes of a woman and children like joeys in headlights.

"What you want?"

The Khmer was thickly accented and B.J. frowned, not sure he could even make himself understood. Right. Many of the people in this area came from Burmese hill tribes who immigrated here for the jewel mining. They'd become a subculture unto themselves around Pailin.

"Can I pay for some food? Rice? Fish? Anything?"

The man shook his head and went to disappear inside. B.J. leapt forward. "Please! I need help. Did a lorry pass by here? A truck," he amended.

The man slowly turned. "Truck? There are many trucks. How should I know?"

Couldn't the guy just talk straight? B.J. ground his fists into his sides. "It was a large truck with canvas sides and it would have come past here just recently."

The man just looked at him.

B.J. scrambled for his wallet and hauled out an American ten dollar bill, which might as well be the official currency because the Cambodian Riel notes were rarely used. At least in the cities and in the areas expats frequented.

The man didn't move, just added a layer of suspicion to his already unfriendly gaze. But the bill did its job on someone in the house. A voice murmured and someone shoved the man forward until he turned and yelled in some non-Khmer language.

B.J. stepped right up to the door. "Please," he yelled in Khmer. "That truck holds a woman prisoner. They may kill her." The man still just looked at him and B.J. wanted to throttle him, shake him into understanding. They had Kaitlin and Kaitlin was—well—just what was Kaitlin to him?

"Please. At least tell me which way the truck went."

The man stepped to the door and pointed down one of the side roads.

"You're sure."

A wordless nod and B.J. shoved the bill at him and scrambled for the bike. He climbed aboard and kicked the engine into gear, when a woman came from the house carrying something. With her long dark hair now coiled low on her neck and her fine bones and large eyes, she must have been a beauty once. Now she just looked gaunt and tired. Behind, in the doorway, five little faces looked out like chicks from a henhouse. The man was nowhere to be seen.

She held out a plastic bag. In it was a handful of rice and a crescent of sun-dried fish. She half bowed as she gave it to him. Smiled. "Thang. Hoo."

"Thank you." He grabbed the bag, wolfed down the rice and stuck the rock hard fish in his pocket. Then he handed her back the bag. "Good. Thanks." He gunned the engine.

"No." She shook her head and looked behind her at the house. "Truck go." She pointed straight ahead. South. Toward the Cardamom Mountains and he knew in his gut she was right.

He grabbed her hand. Kissed it and eased the bike around her and was gone. Thank God for at least one honest person in the world.

Kaitlin was in front of him. The woman who infuriated and confused him. The woman who he'd betrayed and who would never trust him again. The woman who had just bargained herself away to free him and the children. The woman who made him feel panicked and unsteady whenever he thought of something happening to her.

Chapter 38

How long Kaitlin had jounced along pressed between the unpleasant heat of Black-tooth and his driver, she didn't know. Long enough that her hands had lost all feeling, crushed as they were behind her. Long enough that her stomach thought her throat had been cut, and long enough that the road had become an unending stretch of red mud. It wound through rain-soaked green forest or stretches of logged-out devastation, where small huts had sprung up and people tried to eke out an existence in the ruined landscape between the stumps.

For the past few hours as the last light fell, the road had been winding upwards following a small river swollen by the rains. It seethed white in their headlights and in places had run over the road, but the lumbering truck had just ground a gear downward and gone through and on, following the map's directions.

Yes, a map. She looked down at the leather, softened a little from her handling and the heat and humidity in the truck cab. The driver was forced to keep wiping off the inside of the windshield. The side windows were totally fogged and she was stuck in this miasma of fuggy, cigarette-smoke laden air, trying to stay strong and hide her fear and also hide her growing realization that the puppet she had used as a ruse did indeed seem to be a map.

The question was how long she could continue to direct Black-tooth and his man along it.

As long as you want to stay alive.

But her father had hidden this map so there was something he wanted to hide. Her father was probably at the end of that map and sure-as-shooting (one of her father's favorite expressions) Black-tooth wasn't going to do anything good when he got wherever the map was taking them.

Which meant her only hope was to get away before they arrived wherever they were going.

The truck's wipers swiped futilely across the glass. Nothing could wipe away the thundering rain, or slow the maelstrom of water across the road that suddenly gleamed in the headlights.

The driver slammed on the brakes, sending Kaitlin face first into the dash and the puppet to the floor.

She lay there waiting for her vision to clear and listening to the thunder of the rain on the shell of the truck. A warm trickle down her cheek told her the pain probably equated to a gash on her forehead. Behind her, Black-tooth and the driver argued. Finally a pounding on Black-tooth's cab door interrupted them. Kaitlin tried to move and the movement sent a sharp pain through her breast bone. Involuntarily, she groaned. She'd slammed her chest and shoulders pretty good. Not going to help her escape efforts if the chance ever came.

She stayed still, putting off testing the pain to see what was going to happen.

Black-tooth opened the door to a soaked guard from the rear of the truck and let in a blessed gust of rain-laden cool air that shocked and revived her like water thrown in her face.

On the other side of her, the driver opened the door and climbed down to appear in the headlights, inspecting the road. He came around to Black-tooth and shook his head.

Of course they argued. She lifted her head. Black-tooth ordered everyone around, but this time the driver kept shaking his head. From what she could see at the edge of the headlights, she was glad the driver stood his ground. Muddy water that was too much for a culvert inundated the road with a mass of churning water and stone. Even a vehicle the size of the truck could get in trouble in a torrent like that.

Finally Black-tooth shook his head in disgust and climbed down from the cab himself. Kaitlin took that opportunity to right herself and sat forward, waiting for the pins and needles in her hands to pass. At least the ropes were loosened enough that she had circulation.

Cigarette butts and food wrappers filled the passenger-side wheel well. The map lay on top, but she couldn't rescue it with her hands tied like this.

From outside, voices rose above the pounding of rain on the roof and she shoved herself back to see what was happening. Black-tooth and the driver still argued, the driver waving his arms at the raging torrent in front of them. It was surprising the man even argued, given Black-tooth's authority, but she was glad he did. She didn't want to even think what would happen if the truck got stuck trying to cross the river.

As she watched, a broad tree drove down the river, slammed into the road, and lodged there, broad branches further blocking the road.

Not, apparently, what Black-tooth wanted to see. He yelled. He walked away, towards the guards who had ridden in the rear of the truck. Then he turned and produced a pistol and shot the driver in the face.

The man went down and Kaitlin sat there trying to understand what she'd seen. Impossible, but the driver was a grey lump in the mud. An execution.

It was a flipping execution.

Black-tooth kicked him, once. Twice. Then he said something to the guards and they rolled the driver over and tossed his body in the river.

Kaitlin finally remembered to breathe. She inhaled a ragged, cigarette-stink laden breath and held it. *Enjoy it while you can, girl. You don't figure a way out of here and your future probably holds a similar end.*

Black-tooth glanced up at her and then disappeared towards the rear of the truck. One of the guards came around and opened the cab door, but he didn't climb in, just grinned up at her, did a few not-so-friendly little pelvic thrusts, and then reached in to cut the lights.

The sudden darkness left her blind and she waited for the attack to come. But the guard just slammed the door and left her in the dark. Then the vehicle swayed under her as someone or someones leapt up into the back.

Black-tooth must think she was cowed enough he didn't have to worry about her trying anything. She'd tried to give him that impression. It hadn't been that hard. But now might be one of the few chances she had to do something about her predicament.

Plan, Blackwood. Figure it out. But it was hard to see through all the steps of what could happen. There were just too many permutations.

First thing, though, was to get rid of her bindings. She dug her fingers into the back of her waistband. She'd work it out as she sawed.

§

The monsoon rain had only gotten worse the further B.J. came into the mountains. In the rain, the steep, winding roads were an almost impassible mess, even for his borrowed motorcycle, but each time he'd thought the bike was going to lose it, the heavy tread of the tires had churned in the soil, caught, and held him upright, until finally he was here.

Darkness except for the single beam of his headlight. Water everywhere and mud covering everything. On one side, what must be a stand of tall, virgin forest that had somehow escaped the international logging companies, loomed over him and the road. On the other side, his headlight disappeared into nothingness as the land fell in a steep slope towards a raging river. Not anything he bloody well wanted to take a header off.

He felt small; an insignificant spot of light in the darkness, and yet he had to do the most important thing in his life. Find Kaitlin and get her out.

Four hours he'd been following a hope and a prayer that she was in front of him. At first he was able to stop and ask people if a truck had passed by, though often it required a bribe to loosen a tongue. Which suggested these people had had the fear of God put in them, or maybe they remembered the Khmer Rouge heydays, or the Khmer Rouge who held out in these hills until 1996.

Or longer, if Duch's name meant anything.

Maybe the fear and the Khmer Rouge were one and the same.

Which just about made him sick with fear for Kaitlin.

But for the past hour or so he'd been riding roads where there were no people, or at least no people he could see, though he'd had this sense of being watched. It had kept him traveling too fast for the conditions.

The next curve came up fast, sloping down and to the right and studded with rocks. He hit the brakes. The bike wobbled under him and the back end started to slide sideways. He fought to right it, fighting the front end as it tried to aim for the sky as his back end tried to overtake the front.

No bloody good. The bike toppled.

Down in the mud. Leg caught under the weight of the bike. Sliding down the road towards the curve.

Mud in his eyes, his mouth. He grabbed for the ground, grabbed for anything to stop himself. The road curved and he didn't. Momentum carried him too fast towards the edge of everything.

The bike's rear end slammed into a rock and cranked the front end left, throwing B.J. around ahead of the bike to where the headlight illuminated—nothing.

The edge.

He was going over. There'd be no rescue for Kaitlin, and the stupidest thing he'd ever done in his life was to wreck his relationship with her. He realized that now. Infuriatingly stubborn and principled as a Sunday school teacher, but Kaitlin was special. At least special to him.

The high-pitched screech of metal jarred him and the bike shuddered to a stop against an outcropping at the edge of the cliff, leaving him hanging head and shoulders over nothingness.

Chapter 39

The combination of frantic sawing with the nail file and vigilance against Black-tooth's return demanded all of Kaitlin's attention even while she knew she should be planning. The rain still thundered on the roof. Darkness masked everything except the cigarette and diesel stink and the roar. It was like she sat in a drum, or inside a thunderstorm, and the migraine that she had thought had died came snarling back with the constant percussion.

The crushing pain ate most of her brain—or at least that was what it felt like. She could work the file, but even that vibration up her arms was enough to make her cry.

Damn it, she *was* crying. Thick tears running down her face while a plan wouldn't come.

She back-handed them off her face with her injured hand and almost stabbed herself with the file.

Looked at her hands, barely seen in the darkness. They opened and closed like flowers. Or sea urchins.

Stupid thought.

But she had done it. She had freed her hands!

And all she wanted to do was curl up in a ball and cry at the pain.

Of course, after the pins-and-needles pain came the throbbing of the wound in her palm, bloody and raw, now, because of her efforts with the file.

She closed her hand into a fist. It would have to do.

The pounding in her head made it almost impossible to see, but she leaned over to cautiously look outside. Rain sheeted the night-blackened, passenger-side window and rearview mirror. Only streaked darkness to see.

She pulled back and leaned over to check out the driver side window and got more of the same.

Now was her chance. If she could get away, she could hide in the jungle as she made her way back to civilization. Then she could get help and come back for her dad. Maybe B.J. and the people at the NGO would help.

No. Not B.J. She'd dragged him through enough and he had the kids to care for.

But it had hurt to leave him behind even more than the last time. He'd be happier for it, though. And what else could she expect?

Not much of a plan, but it was the best she could do. She stuck the file in her pocket, then reconsidered and shoved it back in her pants. If they found her, she didn't want her weapon found. Let them think she'd cut the ropes with something left in the truck. Then she fumbled and found the puppet. No matter what happened, she was going to find her father.

Easing up the door handle with her good hand was the hardest thing she'd done in a long time. Would it make a noise? Would an overhead light go on? She couldn't remember if one had come on when Black-tooth opened the door. Would her shift in position be registered by the men in the back? Was there a guard outside?

Rain and cold air smacked her face as she took a chance and shoved the door slightly open. She licked the blessed water off her lips. It had been a long time since she'd eaten or drunk anything. She reached back into the truck. Black-tooth and the driver had bought evil-looking Chinese snacks at a village far back along the road to Pailin. She fumbled around and came up with a half-eaten bag of what looked like dried green peas. Not much, but it must be edible. She stuck them in her pocket.

There had been no response from the rear of the truck, but she had to move quickly, silently, smoothly. Black-tooth wasn't going to leave her unattended forever. He just thought she was cowed and injured.

And not the most bloody infuriating woman going, as B.J. had dubbed her long ago.

She pushed the door open far enough she could slip outside and the deluge soaked her in an instant and slicked the truck metal under her feet.

She held on tight to the rearview mirror for fear of falling and any sudden shift of the truck alerting Black-tooth. At least she was tall—she didn't need to leap down from the cab. Ignoring the piercing pain in her wounded hand, she held on and slowly slid down the cab to the ground and then slowly released the mirror, biting back an oath at the slow slide of metal over her wound.

Whether her efforts did any good, she didn't know, but no one responded from the rear of the truck, which gave her a chance.

Her feet sank into ankle-deep mud and running water. The churning maelstrom of the stream around the fallen tree was a thundering barrier ahead. The rain fell in sheets around her and made it even harder to see through the darkness as she tried to get her bearings. Tall trees and jungle hugged the road sides offering greater darkness.

The hiding place for her.

Yes. Get into the jungle and then follow the edge of the road back the way she'd come. When she got far enough away from the truck, she could even walk on the road. It was the only and the best plan she could come up with. Retreat until she could bring reinforcement, and pray that Black-tooth wouldn't go on without her and the map.

He had studied the puppet over her shoulder. If Black-tooth found her father, it wouldn't go well for one Jeremy Blackwood, that was for sure. She blinked back her headache pain.

Maybe there was something she could do.

She crept to the truck's front tire and felt blindly around it for the air stem. Rain drummed on her head to add to her pain as she fished the file out of the back of her trousers and awkwardly stabbed it with her injured hand into the end of the stem.

The hiss of escaping air answered her actions, so she'd accomplished something. A slow leak wouldn't alert them.

She straightened and returned the file to her back, hating the grate against her tender skin and turned to go.

Stopped. A wave uneasiness washed over her. She'd never held much stock on the notion that you could tell when someone was watching you, but this was a crawling feeling up her back. She was as certain someone was watching as she had been that B.J. had enjoyed the view of her rear as she climbed into a moto-taxi in front of him.

Her body flushed cold and she peered through the rain at the back of the truck, expecting to see someone.

No one.

It had to be her imagination. The product of her migraine, maybe.

So get away, Blackwood. Or are you just going to stand around until they catch you again?

She crept away from the truck to the side of the road. Broad, elephant-ear shaped leaves released reservoirs of muddy water when she tried to push through. The first one smacked her in her face and her lips tasted of clay, but as she moved farther back from the road, the water grew cleaner. And then she was standing in the shadow of the giant trees, the main monsoon blocked by their broad branches. It was a relief to her poor head and her rebelling brain. She rubbed her face and swallowed back the pain, tried to eat some of the Chinese pea-snacks, but the crunch hurt too much. She sucked them instead and started moving parallel to the road, or at least she hoped she was.

The jungle floor was alive with dripping water and the sound of insects and—frogs. At least she hoped it was frogs.

Something scurried away from her through the underbrush and she jumped sideways.

Ahead of her, something made one of the platter-like leaves release its water and she stopped, all of her injured senses reaching. No one was there, right. Black-tooth hadn't raised the alarm at her escape. She'd hear the shouting this close to the truck, wouldn't she?

Even with her migraine.

She was letting her imagination get the better of her. She'd been as tough as B.J. the rest of the trip, and she sure as heck wasn't going to turn into a weakling when he wasn't there. She hadn't needed him in Seattle and she didn't need him here.

She didn't.

Clutching the puppet against her injured side, she kept going, shoving through the vines and thick foliage and praying she didn't run into anything or anyone. Like B.J.'s spiders.

Gradually the roar of the river fell behind her. The rain began to decrease—or at least it seemed like it, under the jungle cover. The music of the rain on leaves was replaced by the constant fall of water drops off the leaves like a light rain.

She relaxed a little. She was going to do this. She was going to get away and rescue her father, just like she'd rescued B.J. and the children.

Which suggested maybe you *could* do things without having a complete plan all mapped out. Surprising, actually. Maybe it was possible to have success without worrying over all the options and having all the contingencies in place.

In front of her a tall figure suddenly materialized out of the darkness and she stopped in her tracks. She leapt sideways and found herself facing someone else. Leapt again and slammed into another figure and fell back. Backed up toward the road, but another unseen person stopped her.

Surrounded, she shoved the puppet in her waistband and fumbled for the nail-file, but it was too little, too late. They had her arms twisted behind her before she could reach it and invasive hands ran over her. She caught the flash of leering white eyes in a face that leaned in too close, but they didn't find it. Was that a whiff of—aftershave—up her nose?

Then someone grabbed her shoulder and shoved her forward through the rain-soaked jungle. Uphill. Away from the road and her route to safety.

All without a word being spoken.

All so *not* according to plan.

§

Too much air between B.J. and the unseen river far below him. He could hear it even through the roar of the rain. The bike was a leaden weight over his left leg and he wasn't sure he could move either the bike or his trapped limb.

Godstrewth, it was a good thing, because he'd be landing and drowning about now, otherwise.

His broken ribs stabbed pain through his side as he tried to sit up and bring his upper body back to solid ground. The bike was in the way. There was no place for him to lie. And grabbing hold of the bike only shifted it and him a little closer to the edge.

He scrabbled for something—rock, bush, anything, to hold onto. Bloody hell, there was nothing, but he wasn't—couldn't just hang here. Who knew how long it would be before someone came along who could help him.

Or not help him, as was probably the case.

Which—along with the fact Kaitlin was getting farther and farther from him every moment he hung here—meant he better get his ass in gear.

The darkness made it hard to see anything that might help him. His abs screamed at the effort to hold himself straight and not sag like a rag down the cliff. The raging pain in his side made it hard to think or move, but he bloody well had to.

He twisted his torso downward and felt bone shift unnaturally in his side. He gritted his teeth and panted through the pain, but his face hung close to the cliff wall. He started to examine it.

There. Vines of some kind, or maybe roots like the thick Fromages trees produced at Angkor, growing from the rock. One thick strand became a branching mess of the stuff, and when he yanked at them, they didn't come loose. Maybe they could hold his weight if he could pull his leg loose.

Maybe. About as much happy chance o' that as of Outback rain.

He hauled himself up and steeled himself to the pain. It was only going to get worse.

Something moved beyond the bike.

He peered through the rain, but there were only shades of darkness. The mass of trees on the uphill side of the road, the huge trunks standing like darker sentinels between the lighter masses of foliage, and—against that patch of foliage—was that the figure of a man?

B.J. froze. "Hey, mate, I could use a hand here."

Nothing moved except the rain streaking across his face and slicking his hands, plastering his hair on his head like a mass of pot-scrubbing bristle.

"Come on, mate. Don't leave me hanging."

Still no movement. A figment of a desperate mind, probably, and he was wasting his strength talking to no one.

Get on with it, McCallum, ya wanker. Get loose or fall, but hanging here is just gonna kill ya.

He folded against the cliff again, grabbed hold of the vine-roots, and sent a little prayer to whatever power there was. This time he made sure he held on solid. Then he braced his free leg against the bike and—pushed.

Metal grated against stone. Something caught on his DAKS leg and tore the cloth before digging into his leg.

He stopped, panting against the pain in side and leg. Something on the bike dug into his calf muscle and held. To pull any more was just going to tear right through his flesh.

He swallowed and used his shoulders to press upwards. Maybe he could find a resting place on the road now. Maybe he could slide his leg farther under the bike and at least be on solid ground.

It hurt to move. Bones ground in his side as he tried to shove himself backwards up the cliff face and shimmy his butt down to the sodden bike seat.

When he was done, only his shoulders and head still hung over the cliff. He lay there a moment, just breathing in relief, and then sat up.

The bike was a bastard for weight, far heavier than he'd figured, but he managed to wrestle it up until he could pull his leg free. Miraculously, except for the sting of road rash under the mud and the torn pant leg, he didn't seem any worse off than he had been before.

He closed his eyes in thanks and heard a sound he hadn't heard in a long walk of years. F88 assault rifle being cocked and readied. In another lifetime, one had been an extension of his arms and eyes and he could smell the gun oil, knew even through the darkness a barrel was aimed at his head.

"What'd'ya want, mate? Ya going to kill me now that the road didn't?"

No sound, but something hard jabbed him in the back of his neck. Universal signal that he was either a dead man, or to get up.

Positive thinking said he'd already be dead if it was the former. He got his legs under him and stood, letting the rain sluice the mud off of him. Bloody left leg hadn't gotten off as good as he'd thought. Putting weight on it sent pain spiking up his calf.

He turned slowly, holding his hands up, but the weapon stopped him before he could see his captor. But he got a sense of height. Taller than any Khmer.

Then the rifle barrel stabbed him in the back and sent him stumbling forward. Another figure materialized out of the darkness and he heard someone grunt, and then there came a distant crash. He spun around, only to be clubbed back in his direction, but he'd seen what they'd done.

The bike was gone. Thrown over the cliff edge. Anyone finding it would think he'd gone over with it.

The rifle in his back sent him slip-sliding across the road and into the jungle.

Chapter 40

The constant dripping from the jungle beat on Kaitlin's temples and down the part of her hair in counterpoint to the migraine that now pounded in her head. It left her vision filled with red streaks and explosions of light that blinded her to the brush and massive trees. The stink of torn foliage and mud made her stomach flip-flop, and every step and squelch and cry from the forest seemed to reverberate like she existed inside a timpani drum.

For the third time she walked into a sharp branch that cut next to her eye. She staggered back with an involuntary yelp.

Someone caught her shoulder and shoved her forward again. She held her arms like a blind man and staggered forward. Until someone grabbed her shoulder again and steered her past something. Her outstretched hand struck tree trunk.

"Thank you," she said.

Was that a grunt behind her? Maybe her captors understood English. She'd caught that whiff of aftershave a time or two more on the seemingly endless struggle through jungle.

"Where are you taking me?" Try to make contact, make herself human. That was what all the research into kidnapping said. It was harder to hurt someone you thought of as a person. "My name's Kaitlin—Kaitlin Blackwood. I'm an American. I don't belong here. People will come looking for me. They know where I was going."

A sniff from behind her as if her captor were laughing.

"Please. I mean you no harm. I…."

The rifle barrel jabbed her back in a clear message to keep going and shut up. She staggered on.

The track they pushed her on was hard, slippery mud and thick brush and uphill slopes where her street-hikers were as useless as if she wore high heels. As a matter of fact, high heels might have been better because they at least might grip the sliding hillside with the spikes of their heels.

As it was, she spent half her time on hands and knees or sprawled in the mud. The most her silent captors did was haul her roughly to her feet.

And the worst of it was, she had no idea where she was. She'd fallen once too many times when they were crossing gullies. The result of her tumbles had left her with little sense of what direction they traveled. Beneath the trees like this, there wasn't even a wind to suggest direction. It was an unending staggering hike, made up of too many stumbling downhills, but she could tell they were higher. The air had gotten slightly cooler. Or maybe it was just the later hour or the imagination of an exhausted mind.

She slammed into another tree and her legs gave. When she tried to get up, her legs didn't seem to work. How long had it been since she rested? Since she'd eaten? The unseen rifle barrel found her cheek through the darkness.

She tried to stand, but her legs gave again and the pain in her head left her unable to concentrate.

"I'm sorry. I can't get up." She shook her head and instantly regretted the movement. Walking, she'd been able treat her wounded head like a carton of eggs. Movement side to side was not a good thing. Just the scent of the torn leaves and damp earth sent her stomach churning.

The rifle jabbed her again and she looked up blindly at the darkness.

"I'm sorry. I haven't eaten anything in a couple of days. I haven't slept in about as long, and I have a migraine that's just about taken off the top of my head." She rubbed at the pain in her temples. *Fat lot of good that's going to do, Kaitlin. They probably don't understand English.*

The rifle disappeared from her cheek for a moment. Something else materialized in front of her face. She flinched away and the migraine stabbed into grey matter and exploded. White light filled her vision and she moaned involuntarily.

When her vision cleared enough to see bits of the darkness, the thing in front of her was still there. Silver. Crinkly. Her poor brain came up with an interpretation of what she was seeing. Emergency rations. She'd seen them in her early days of reporting, doing a fluff piece on women in the military. The story had grown into a hard-hitting piece of journalism looking at the 'Don't Ask-Don't Tell' policy about gays and her first recognition as a true journalist.

She accepted the ration bar and tore it open, then stuffed her mouth even though she knew she should eat slower. Her migraine made her stomach clench at the sweet-stickiness of the bar and she almost threw up what she was chewing.

But food was imperative because she needed strength. She needed strength because she had to be able to walk, because if she couldn't walk, who knew what these men would do to her? Kill her right here, probably.

She forced herself to eat slower. Managed to swallow small bits against her gag reflex and the sting of bile in her throat.

The last of the bar was a tough swallow without water, but she managed. The surge of energy was almost immediate. She crumpled the paper and stuck it in her pocket and then stumbled to her feet to stand, weaving.

Okay, so she *felt* stronger, but that didn't mean she was quick on her feet.

The return of the rifle barrel to her side forced her around and started her going. The ground sloped downwards again, passing between half-seen giant trees. But this time there was a difference in the air. It ran cooler against her face as if she weren't just crossing a gulley, and there were more trees that stopped any movement of air. This felt like she had entered a larger valley. Above, she just made out the shapes of the canopy branches.

Dawn was coming. She'd walked all night.

Around her the jungle turned grey, then green as a new day began. Her second in captivity.

Life stirred around her, birds cried and twittered and darted through the trees. The huge elephant-eared leaves sagged, heavy with water caught in their centers. Something small darted across her path in a rustle of leaves, and thick spider webs hung between branches of some smaller trees.

As the light grew, she became aware of the four men who traveled with her. Clad in black, and with their features masked with bootblack. They were tall and built like men who made a living from their bodies and they moved silently through the underbrush like this was nothing new to them. They held weapons ready across their chests and looked like they were prepared to use them. They didn't look or act like friends. Not exactly like she could cut and run. If she had any place to run to.

But she'd been right. As the light increased, placing a pink pall across a pale, blue sky streaked with thin clouds, she could see that the ground fell steeply in front of her and the daylight and wind came through tree branches beyond which she glimpsed another green ridge about a half mile distant. So it was a larger valley.

The wind sent cascades of droplets from last night's rain thundering onto the leaves around her as she and her captors descended silently and finally joined a trail. A real trail.

If she hadn't been almost ready to cry with fatigue, she could have shouted for joy. No more tripping over twining roots and vines. No more shoving through branches and God only knew how many spider webs that caught on her skin and in her hair until she did a mad dance and shiver to remove any unwanted riders.

The joy was short-lived as her silent escort pulled in closer around her and shoved her off the path again to a narrow side trail. But in this light she could study her captors.

Tall, she'd already noticed—and the aftershave had sort of suggested it—but these weren't Khmer or Thai or anyone from Asia. At least not the orient, she amended.

Pale skinned under the bootblack, and massive. Muscles bulged through black t-shirts and fatigues like something you'd see in an old *Rambo* movie. One had a moustache and another, the man who kept jabbing her with his rifle, had brilliant blue eyes in a bullet-shaped head. They all wore black skull caps pulled low over their ears.

Westerners. So maybe they did know English.

"Where are you taking me?" she tried again.

Her escort remained as quiet as ever, only shoving her faster. She fought to keep up, but her weary legs and the pounding migraine did her in.

She stumbled and started falling sideways through the foliage between her path and the trail.

Mr. Bullet-head grabbed for her, but wasn't fast enough. She fell, face first, half onto the trail, and started to push herself up, but Bullet-head grabbed her before she could, dragged her back with branches and underbrush slapping her face, before yanking her upright. She hung in his massive grip like a kitten in its mother's grip.

But this wasn't any mother. Well, maybe a mother *&^%*.

God, mind, would you quit being stupid?

"Ya little dickhead." He hissed. "Ya want to blow yer ass off?"

Accent. Australian or South African, but her money was on Aussie. He shook her and tossed her away. She glared back at him.

"Landmines? You've put in landmines? Are you nuts? Don't you know there's treaties banning the damned things?"

There was only a slight roll of his eyes and then he jabbed the rifle at her. The universal sign for shut up and move.

She did. Stumbling through the jungle and more afraid than she'd ever been, meeting with gangbangers. Anyone who would put in landmines had an utter disregard for human life and the long-term toll those instruments of war took on a people. Landmines were the 'gift' that kept on giving—atrocities mostly.

God, she needed to think. To figure out what to do, because the landmines proved beyond a doubt that these weren't good people. The mines were either to keep people out or keep people in, and she really didn't want to find out which.

From somewhere ahead came the scent of cooking fires and the sound of a river and the horrendous racket of machinery that sounded like a drill. The clank of machinery and the roar of an engine cut through the jungle-quiet directly to her brain. She stumbled, almost fell, and grabbed hold of a tree trunk to hold herself upright. The wall of jungle ended abruptly in a clearing and the man in front of her pushed through the last of the trees.

Blinking past pain, she followed him, but her brain was churning apart. In the bright sunlight her vision sparked like the Fourth of July skyline and made it impossible to see—or stand.

A river ran on one side of the clearing, its surface a too-brilliant foam-white and thundering with the heavy rain run-off. Enough to turn her stomach.

A metal Quonset hut flashed daggers-in-the-sun from the far end of the clearing. Between stood a ramshackle assortment of wood and thatch huts, like a hurriedly constructed village complete with loose chickens, and a deep ditch that, at the moment, under the watchful guard of more armed men, had an array of what looked like Khmer cutting into clay-colored soil with the drill of a high-pressure hose.

Drilled her brain as well, or might as well have.

The assault doubled her over. She covered her ears, but it didn't stop the pounding. Her knees gave. She fell and retched up the remains of the ration bar. Collapsed onto her side in the mud with her hands over her head.

"Stop." She begged through bile and tears. "Stop. Please."

Bullet-head only picked her up by the back of her shirt and dragged her across the clearing, past a black car with a dented fender she knew she'd seen before.

Angkor. Two men. And B.J.'s rescue. She hoped he and the kids were safe and well.

Between the Quonset and a heap of metal spare parts stood another, smaller, metal-sided structure with a barred door and dented sides. Someone yelled and dented the sides from the inside as she watched.

Then one of her escort had the door open and bullet-head simply lifted her up and tossed her inside. The door slammed shut and there was only darkness and breathing and the thumping of the drill through the walls and the ground.

Chapter 41

In the darkness of the Quonset hut, she knew someone was there. She scrambled up from where she'd fallen and struck out to fend off whoever was there.

"Kaitlin? Are you all right?"

The words came through garbled by the pounding that came up through the ground, and that shimmered in the air like rainbow colored daggers clashing blades against her skull. She couldn't exactly make sense of them.

At least at first.

But she couldn't find the strength to answer, just pulled her arms in over her head and ears because even the soft words were like cut glass in a wound. Worse than her hand, for certain.

Someone touched her shoulder and she moaned and pulled away. Her skin hurt from her clothes. From the pressure of the earth under her. A touch was a blow.

At her moan, the touch disappeared.

"Jeezus Murphy, what the bloody hell's going on?"

The voice. She knew that voice, that tone. She swallowed back the urge to vomit again and focused on the voice. Keep talking. Keep talking and she might be able to put herself together again.

If the flipping pounding would only stop. If her brain would stop consuming itself like one of those darned far-eastern dragons that ate its tail. Or a demon churning her brain.

The pounding suddenly stopped and through the metal walls came the sound of yelling, but she exhaled as if she'd been holding her breath. Could inhale and exhale again without that simple act causing her pain.

She blinked and darkness was a good thing. Just the barest line under the door and small spots of light where the rivets were, so she lay in not-quite dark. More like a brilliantly starred night.

"B.J.? Is that you?" It was the barest whisper and it still felt like finger nails across the inside of her head.

"Kaitlin! Are you all right?" he had her in his arms so fast she hadn't time to protest or to caution him she might be sick again. His mouth was on her tortured face, his hand stroking her hair until she thought she would scream.

"Stop! Please." He released her like she had burned him and she huddled on the dirt floor. As her eyes adjusted to the man-made starlight, she could make out the way his face and body had gone rigid. He crossed his arms.

She shoved her hair back from her face.

"It's a migraine, B.J. They've gotten worse since we split up."

His expression softened a little. "I could say it serves ya right, but I won't."

She managed to raise a brow at him and hoped it was a sign she was going to live through this. "My, you're magnanimous."

B.J. shrugged. "You do what you got to, luv." A beat. "If I remember it rightly, what you need is sleep."

Which was true. At least at home a dark room and silence and a bed were her best friends—along with a Percocet.

"Then get some shut-eye. I figure it'll be a bit before they start the drill up again. At least that's what happens at most mining operations: they drill to loosen the soil and then use a manual sluice to clean and check out the rock."

She felt him like a comforting bulk beside her in the darkness. She reached out and caught his hand and his fingers twined around hers and held on tight. It was a good feeling, a right feeling. She held onto it as she slid into uneasy darkness.

§

Kaitlin's hand felt so small in his. And limp. Far too limp for the vibrant woman she was.

"Kaitlin," he whispered and squeezed her hand, trying to keep his voice soft and irritate her headache as little as possible. She had lain like this for three hours, according to his watch.

No response. In the dim light through the roof of the hut they'd penned them in, she lay curled in on herself like a cowering cat, blonde hair covering her face. He stroked it away and she twitched and moaned. He pulled his hand away, remembering her sensitivity when in the throes of a migraine. Asleep? Unconscious?

Either way, it was an escape from the bloody hell he'd dragged her into with a little help from her father.

But unlike her previous migraines, iron-scented heat radiated off her like a flame; and a fever suggested something other than a her usual headache. With a fever like this, she needed water and to be kept cool, neither of which he was able to do as the sun heated the small Quonset. Already the metal walls were hot and the air inside with them. The only good thing was the still-damp earth that made up the floor. That might help cool her.

Then again, it might make the whole place a bloody sauna.

Kaitlin stirred and groaned.

"Kaitlin?"

She winced at his voice.

"B.J." Her lips curved in a small smile. "Trust you to be here, too."

Didn't she remember they'd already spoken? That boded ill for her mind.

"Not exactly what I planned to be doing with my time."

"I bargained you free."

"And you expect me to just leave you a prisoner? Come on, girl, I don't hate you that much." Not at all, as a matter of fact.

Her blue eyes slitted opened, but her gaze said she was afraid to move. "How'd you get here?"

He told her, ending with the bike getting tossed over the cliff. He shrugged. "Another debt to pay. And then they marched me back o' Bourke to here."

"Who are they?"

He had to smile. "Now, there's my girl. Reporter to the end."

He looked to the locked door, because by the sound of it, they were getting ready to start the drill again.

He leaned down to her. Inhaling her muted roses and rainwater and the too-bright fever tang of iron. "I don't know, luv. Not from these parts. Didn't speak the whole time they dragged my sorry ass through the outback," he said softly, hoping it didn't hurt her too much.

"One of them's Australian."

The feel of her hair and her scent filled him with a tenderness he hadn't felt since they split up—except with Maly.

"Well, Aussies have been known to sell their services."

He touched her arm. "Can ya move? Sounds like that drills going to be starting again. I want to save you from the worst of it."

She nodded, like the trooper she was, and struggled up to sitting where she closed her eyes and swayed.

"You're talking mercenaries, then."

"That'd be my guess." Bloody hell, just what was he going to do to help her?

He pulled off his shirt and caught how her glance strayed to his chest and stuck there.

"What? Ya worried? I don't take advantage of sick women." He held out his shirt. "Thought you could wrap this around your head. Maybe stuff it in your ears. Might help keep out the sound a little better."

Kaitlin met his gaze. "You sure you don't just want to show off your pecs?"

Before he could respond, the drill's engine roared to life and Kaitlin doubled over, grabbing her head.

B.J. hurriedly twisted his shirt into a band and tied it around her head and she covered her ears with her hands. Then he pulled her into his chest, placing his hands over hers.

She trembled in his grasp, every muscle tense, her breath hot little puffs on his bare skin. Gradually she relaxed and allowed herself to be pulled in, pressed one ear to his chest and let him help cover the other with his hand over hers. It was little enough, but all he could do. He kissed her sweat-damp hair.

Aside from the boat, it was the most intimate he had been with a woman in a very long time. Yes, he'd had sex. A western man in Cambodia could have a girl pretty much when he wanted, but that wasn't his style. He'd mainly fallen into arrangements with tourists passing through, which meant a lot less entanglements. A good thing, when you're still somehow tied up over a woman.

Seeing Kaitlin, and experiencing all her exasperating ways, had made him realize that.

He stroked her hair with his free hand. Kissed her sweat-damp forehead and felt her shiver against him. At his touch, or at the fever, he wasn't sure.

Kissed her hair again and she shifted against him. Her blue gaze met his and he read the acknowledgement. Acceptance, even. There *was* something between them. Neither of them could deny it anymore.

He dipped his head and knew he was taking a chance in more ways than one. Lips found hers, and this time she responded. Small eager touches of lips became something greater, longer, like something in his chest was about to explode. His heart?

Then she pulled back and he held his breath. Was this rejection, again? He didn't know if he could take it. Her eyes were closed as if she were caught in a breathless moment, but then her eyes opened with such wonder in them even through the cloud of pain that he could have done a whole host of halleluiahs. She smiled and caught his hands, placed them over her ears again and then leaned into him as if taking comfort in their closeness.

He laid them both down on the still-cool earth.

She lay still for a moment, and he could feel her shudders. Small ones, as if she were trying to hide them from him, but then she pushed herself up to look down at him.

The mock starlight through the roof dappled her face as she met his gaze with telepathic intensity. She ran a fiery palm down his cheek.

"I'm glad I found you again," she said.

And that was a miracle in itself, because Kaitlin Blackwood was never one to make herself vulnerable. He gently pulled her down beside him.

"I love you, too," he said, so softly he doubted she could hear him.

Chapter 42

B.J.'s touch was like feathers on her too-tender skin. His breath like warm winds when cold seemed to eat through her. The hard-packed earth radiated chill and damp deep into her bones and she shivered.

Make that shivered and moaned and wasn't sure if it was the cold and the pain or the emotion that caught in her chest like an incipient dagger. He could hurt her so much if he rejected her. More than any migraine would, because a migraine would pass. A broken heart, she wasn't sure would. Just why she'd admitted feelings to him, she wasn't sure. Except she was still alive and so was B.J. Except she wanted to feel alive for however long she still had.

Except the pounding in her head felt like she was dying and she still hadn't really confessed to him, had she? Not the full extent of her feelings. Not the fear for him that had led her to bargain her life to Black-tooth for his safety.

But she still held back didn't she? Kaitlin-idiot-Blackwood, always holding something back because she hadn't planned this. Certainly hadn't planned on finding emotions like this in the jungles of Cambodia. The painful feeling caught in her brain and her chest.

She rolled away from B.J. and clawed at her head, trying to push her brains back in place and stop the pain. Stop everything. Stop breathing. Stop the fear that she was opening herself to more pain. She curled in on herself. Surely if she made herself small enough the pain would reduce, too. She might be alone, but she knew how to be alone. Had learned that after her mother died and B.J. was gone.

Just like he'd probably leave her again.

Stupid thought. She'd walked out on him last time.

"Jeezus. Jeezus, Kaitlin." She felt him sitting above her. "Jeezus man, yer a righteous dickhead going along with this."

Touch on her shoulder that surely shattered her freezing flesh. Then she was hauled up off the ice-cold floor and arms—strong—came around her and pulled her into a warm chest again. She clung there, trying for heat. Praying for the pounding outside and inside to stop. At least slow its jackhammer on her skull so she might stand a chance of sorting out these painful feelings. What was she afraid of? That B.J. was too much like her father? Too full of life and too ready to embrace it, face to the wind and dangers be damned?

The jarring roar of the drill suddenly stopped and there was only the pound of her blood in her bones. And a slow steady beat under her ear. That sound she could stand. It seemed to grab hold of the wild pounding in her head and slow it.

Heart. B.J.'s heartbeat.

Yes, that was it. B.J. His arms around her and she was pressed up against a half-naked man and flipping hell, she'd been a fool to have ever left him.

If she could only get warm. Flipping Cambodia, and she was freezing to death. Who knew?

Those warm arms around her and maybe they cut through the cold a little. The warm-male B.J. scent filled her nose and wasn't unpleasant. In fact it *was* pleasant. Seemed to help slow her pulse and the pain.

At least a little. She leaned into him and felt his pulse through his chest, the slow, steady breathing, his cheek resting against her head, a kiss on her hair.

"I'm so sorry, luv. I should have known better than to have let you come with me. Bloody Wanker."

A kiss between each phrase. He rocked her against him, apologizing.

"Stop," she managed. "It was my fault."

She clenched her eyes shut against the pain the words had brought.

"You're with me, then."

Another kiss on her hair, another well-intended, too-tight squeeze of her bruised flesh. Didn't he know he was hurting her?

She pulled away again, choosing the cold over more flayed flesh.

"Kaitlin, you're shivering. You've got one helluva fever."

An arm tried to come around her and she shook him off.

"No." She didn't dare shake her head.

"Shh."

And the almost-silence was a relief.

"Someone's coming."

She heard movement but still didn't open her eyes, because with all this pressure in her head she might be blind. Something rough against her skin reminded her of the puppet still under her clothes.

Then came a screeching sound that sent her curling into herself with a moan.

Then came the blaze of daylight against her eyelids and she knew everything was coming to an end.

§

After the dim light of the Quonset, the daylight blinded B.J. He sheltered his eyes with his hand and tried to see who stood there. Two silhouettes were all he could make out, and the rumble of machinery. But along with the scent of sun-heated water, at least cooler air flooded around him after the furnace of the Quonset hut. Not that that helped Kaitlin.

She was bloody well burning up and quaking like a leaf in a South Pacific storm, where she cringed at the back of the bloody hut.

"What do you wankers want, then?"

"I want—I want to shhee my daughter." B.J. blinked against the brilliance again and one of the shapes took a form he recognized. Jeremy Blackwood. The man he remembered was tall and straight and a tad too good-looking for his own good. It helped him talk himself into places he never should have gone in the first place. Sometimes it even helped him talk himself back out again. Or charmed his way back into Kaitlin's good grace.

Tall, like his daughter, with the same blonde hair. But his eyes were dark brown instead of the cornflower blue Kaitlin had gotten from her mother—as if Kaitlin could keep a secret or be dishonest to save her life. Her father, however...

But right now the man looked shrunken, shoulders slumped, and bones too bloody prominent, as if a skin tarp were pulled over a pile of derelict machinery like that piled beside the larger Quonset. His thinning hair was a tangled, sweating mass around his ears and forehead. His usual carefree, piece-o-piss attitude had disappeared and the man wobbled where he stood.

Drunk. The man had a bloody gutful of piss. Maybe that helped deal with the blackened bruises on his face.

"So there she is, ya drunken sod. There's yer precious daughter," said Jeremy Blackwood's companion.

The bloke holding Jeremy Blackwood's arm was built like the bruisers who'd escorted him through the jungle. Big. Taller than Kaitlin's father, though he wasn't much younger—mid-forties maybe—and he was of a height with B.J. He was bald and armed with a pistol at his belt and an assault rifle slung over his shoulder. He also had the massive chest, arms, and thighs of the confirmed steroid user.

Not good. Those types of blokes had tempers and the strength to do serious damage. In the military they'd always been good for a fight at the drop of hat, coin, or anything else that set them off.

B.J. eased himself up off the ground and out the door to shield Kaitlin. "She's ill. She has a bloody big fever. Jeremy, she needs a doctor."

A strange, floating sense of déjà vu settled over B.J. Something about how the guy held Kaitlin's father like a limp rag. Something about the shape of his head and the pale, pale gaze that settled on B.J. as if he were an annoying beetle to be crushed underfoot.

"Dad?" Kaitlin blinked like a bloody wombat caught in a searchlight. "Dad!" She struggled to get up, but her legs just gave.

"Kaitlin, girlie, are you all right?" Jeremy tried to go to her, but the strangely familiar wanker held him back with no effort at all.

B.J. offered her a hand and she crawled out of the hut to stand swaying beside him.

"Dad, what's going on? Who are these people?" She cowered at the sunlight, even though her eyes were squeezed shut.

"Thieves. A whole lotta thieves—paid for by a friggin' Thai business," Jeremy mumbled.

Kaitlin started to go to him, but B.J. restrained her. Something about this guy and women. He almost had it.

"The ruby." He said and felt all eyes turn to him.

Jeremy's bleary gaze widened. "Nah. Couldn't'a come to you, B.J., ol' man, ol' pal. I sent it to a friend in Siem Reap with a message for help."

"Well, it never made it. It landed in my lap in Angkor. The monk you sent it with died and the note never turned up. This guy, or one of his men, did it." A guess, but a good one by the way the guy's gaze zeroed in on B.J.

"Something else to be responsible for, Jeremy, old man," said the wanker. "Just like your daughter's presence, I'll wager. So just how'd you do it, sweetheart? Your Da send you a map or something?"

Sweetheart.

B.J. froze.

How many times over the years had he winced at the use of the word because of the memories it evoked? But this was worse. This was having the devil reborn in front of you. This was surfing off Bonzai and having a great white appear under yer feet, because he recognized the voice, and it went with the shape of the head and the size.

Chapter 43

Standing outside the smaller of the two Quonset huts, to Kaitlin the two men were only two black, corona'd figures like dual eclipsed suns, but her hearing seemed unnaturally clear and distinct. With the migraine, the sudden sunlight glare sent dual daggers right into Kaitlin's brain. She swallowed back the bile that soured the back of her throat as she faced her captor and the man who sounded—unbelievably—like her father.

Her father's voice, with an alcoholic slur. Not like him. Not at this time of day.

The cold, cold voice of the man with him. Mercenary, someone had said, and that made sense.

"Dad? Why are you drinking?"

"Tryin' t' get me drunk. Thinks I'll lead 'em to the jewels, then, but I won't. Don' say nothin', Kaitlin. Nothin' at all."

Jewels?

The twin eclipses blurred into one and she heard a thud, a groan.

Someone got hit.

She swayed forward to intervene, but B.J. pulled her back with a growled warning.

Danger. Ruby.

"Ya can quit thinking yer so smart, old man. Ya might not answer me, but ya might want ta change yer mind when I spend a little time with your daughter." A pause. "And what's this one to ya, then, other than a pain in the arse who takes photos of monks? My men brought 'im in last night off the road on the off chance anyone coming this far might be a partner to ya, Jeremy. They got orders to bring everyone in or else get rid of them."

Her father said nothing and Kaitlin clung to B.J.'s arm.

"Yer daughter seems to like 'im, but maybe I should just get rid of the problem."

"No." Still blind, she tried to step in front of B.J., but he stopped her. If she could only see, only think. But the world was a haze of black and white, almost like the shadows of the darned puppet under her shirt, and she couldn't understand the pattern it made.

She blinked. Blinked again and felt like an owl—an ignorant one—because each thought seemed disconnected from every other.

"Don't you dare touch him," she said.

A low laugh. "That's what I like, a fighter. Should be fun, Jeremy. Or maybe the boyfriend'll tell me where the jewels are. How 'bout it, big guy?"

Kaitlin swallowed back the pain and squinted her eyes open. "What's he talking about, Dad?"

"Brian's lookin' for the jewel field, girlie. An' I won't give it to him."

Map, again. Darn it, her mind was moving so slow, nothing was making any sense. A jewel field. Some Australian mercenary type had her dad.

The puppet was a map. Damn, her mind was moving too slow for the situation and the heat was burning her up.

B.J. stirred beside her like a waking beast.

"I know you, you bastard. You're the Shark."

She turned to B.J., her own tangled thoughts run out of her head. *Ruby.* "He's my dad."

"Not him." B.J. seemed to have grown six inches in height. If it was possible, everything about him seemed to have gotten larger, like a bristling cat, and he rocked slightly on the balls of his feet, his chin jutted out like a fighter. Anger radiated off him like iron-forged heat.

He shoved her back a step, his gaze locked on the man with her father.

The second corona'd figure. Squinting, she could almost make out features. Pale eyes. Frightening. Bullet-head. Yes. That man.

"You're not coming anywhere near Kaitlin, mate."

A low rumble that must be a laugh. "And who's going t' stop me?"

"I've grown up a mite since you killed my sister."

"What?" Kaitlin spun towards him, but went down in a heap when her legs got tangled. Cold ground. Cold. So cold. She wrapped her arms around herself and wondered if she'd ever get warm again.

The bullet-headed figure went still.

"I'm talking about seventeen years ago. I was a wet-behind-the-ears kid trying to save his sister from the bloody street and this is the bastard that cold-cocked me and dragged her back into that life. Or death, as it turned out. I never bloody-well saw her again."

The words didn't make sense. "You never told me you had a sister."

"Simple. Cause I don't. Not anymore. But Cora was my little sister and a beauty, just like you."

The earth seemed to move as she struggled up. B.J. was going to do something stupid again. It was written all over his face. Like attack Bullet-head unarmed, and the mercenary must outweigh B.J. by a good fifty pounds of all-muscle, not to mention the weapons he carried.

It would get him killed. It would get them all killed. That certainty, at least, came through the sparks and blazing light and pain.

She couldn't let him do that.

She leapt. At bullet-head, and caught him in the gut with her shoulder. It was like running into a wall and her arm went numb. She almost went down, but grabbed his shirt. Tried to get her legs under her to kick him where it counted.

His backhand caught her across the side of her face and sent her crashing back against the metal Quonset. More stars and the corona's figures had become three. Two men grappled while one came towards her.

"Kaitlin! Girlie!"

She staggered up. Her head hadn't exploded off her shoulders like it felt. She could still move. "I'm okay, Dad."

B.J. needed her.

She stumbled to the two struggling men.

B.J. glanced up from where he and Bullet-head wrestled. A shout, and armed men started to run towards them from the mud pit. More flooded out of the large Quonset hut. No way they could fight them all. Gunfire and a bullet ricocheted off of the Quonset hut behind her.

"Run, damn you. Run!" B.J. yelled.

No way in hell.

She kicked bullet-head and someone else took a shot. The ground beside her exploded. Another, and a hole bloomed in the side of the Quonset. More shots.

A bullet burred past her head and she went blind again. More shots.

The man rolling on the ground with B.J. was screaming for the shooting to stop.

"Kaitlin, get down!" Her dad yanked her down and tried to cover her.

She covered her ears as each shot drilled her brain. Her father's alcohol-soaked breath filled her face. Her stomach turned. She blinked back tears and managed to see again. Why were they shooting at them? Did they want to take a chance on shooting her father with his unique knowledge, or her who provided the leverage they needed? It didn't make sense.

Bullet-head and B.J. grappled on the ground. Bullet-head's men had taken cover. Someone was shooting at them.

Gunfire thundered into her brain leaving her flatline for thought-logic-plan. The two wrestlers fought for Bullet-head's fallen pistol. His rifle still was slung across his back.

"Who the hell'd be shooting at us?" Her father's muffled words as he shoved her back towards the Quonset.

There was only one possibility. "Black-tooth. Or the man I call that. B.J. says he calls himself Duck or something."

Her father's bleary eyes suddenly cleared. "What the hell did I drag you into?"

"This, apparently."

"Worse than this if the Khmer Rouge are involved."

Something she didn't have time to worry about.

A hail of gunfire slammed into the mineworkers. Those that survived the first barrage ran screaming towards the jungle. Bullet-head slammed a fist into B.J.'s face and straddled him, pounding him with those massive fists.

Jeezus, he was going to kill B.J.

Answering fire from Bullet-head's men made the jungle shiver around them. More screams imprinted indelibly on her brain, but it left the air suddenly quiet above them.

She was on her feet without thinking. Her palm found a metal bar from the pile of equipment next to the Quonset hut beside her and her vision tunneled onto the man on B.J.

A bullet cut through the air by her head and blew her sideways as she darted forward. She lunged and brought the metal down on the back of bullet-head's head.

The man collapsed like a cement sack beside B.J. and she didn't know what to do. She let the metal pole drop.

B.J. scrabbled for the man's lost pistol and stood above him. Aimed the weapon.

"No! You can't just kill him." If she hadn't already done it when she hit him.

"Bastard's doesn't deserve to live."

"B.J., don't. You'd be just like him."

He looked at her, and for a moment the mayhem went away and it was just the two of them. He sighed and put the weapon away, but kicked Bullet-head once more in the side. Then he grabbed her arm.

"Come on. Jeremy, you, too. Keep your heads down." B.J. led her, stumbling, towards the rear of the large Quonset.

His hand was too tight on her forearm. The wind and the glare off the Quonset siding were too harsh on her skin, and the gunfire, even though it was aimed away, seemed to have lit her brain afire so the pain came in red waves that blinded her again. She wanted to lie down and sleep forever. Or die. Yeah, death would be better than this pain cracking her head open like some darned creature from *Aliens*.

"Kaitlin!" A shake. "Kaitlin, luv, stay with me."

She hadn't realized her eyes were closed until she was pressed into something rough like a tree and warm hands sleeked down her face, held her chin.

"Kaitlin. Look at me. We've got to move fast, because we won't have long. Out friend back there will come to and be after us. So will Duch."

She thought she opened her eyes. At least suddenly more glare drilled into her head and she gasped and doubled over retching.

"What's wrong?" her father asked.

"Migraine, I hope, but the bloody fever's suggestin' something worse." Someone smoothed the cloth still wrapped around her head.

"Migraine."

"Ye-ah. You'd know she gets them sometimes—if you were ever around for her."

She hauled herself up using B.J. for balance, but didn't dare open her eyes. "I'm fine," she lied. "I just can't see."

Or barely stand.

Their pause clearly spelled out their disbelief—and frankly she wasn't too sure herself, given the frigid cold that froze her skin. Not right when sweat was pouring into her eyes.

Those warm hands glided up and down her arms, giving warmth, but not enough. Maybe if his arms were around her. Maybe if she was pressed to his chest.

She pulled back, not wanting protection. "Just get us out of here."

They started through the jungle, B.J. leading them on a cautious, circuitous route from behind the Quonset into the trees. It was strangely quiet.

"Black-tooth's men should be here," she whispered.

"Not behind the Quonset. No view of the camp, or that's what I'm hoping. Now quiet."

Crouched down, he led her through mud up to her ankles, the thick foliage slithering over her skin. Her father's alcohol-soaked, heavy-breathing came behind her.

Flipping hell, she kept stumbling and making more noise than she meant to. The swirl of sound and reek of mud-and-torn-foliage sent her retching again.

So much for quiet.

"I'm sorry," she said as she wiped away the worst of it. B.J. must think she was a weakling and trouble.

"Nothing to be sorry for, luv." It was him that held her hair back. Him who rubbed her comfortingly between her shoulder blades. "Can ya go on?"

She managed a nod and went to stand, wobbled, until her father awkwardly caught her arm over his shoulder.

"You lead. I've got Kaitlin."

"You were never there for me Dad."

His alcohol-soaked breath was too much in her nose. She tried to pull away, but almost fell. Finally she accepted his help, but turned her face away to avoid being sick down his front.

"I only ever wanted to make things good for you and your mother. I wanted to make life easy for all of us."

"You wanted to make life easy for you." She realized it now. Even though she loved him, he'd hurt over the years. "None of the day-to-day to deal with. Just one adventure after another."

"I wanted to make it big for you."

"Well you made it big, all right. A big pain in the butt."

"I was trying to get you and your mother what you needed."

"What we needed was *you!*" It hurt her heart.

He went silent, creeping beside her, uphill, through the unseen trees and the humming-buzzing-rustling life they carried, even though the blaze of gunfire behind them was a pall over everything. She'd never realized how much noise there was in a forest. Rustling and cracking and creaking branches and leaves squeaking against each other. And all of them filling her head too loudly.

She stumbled and her father steadied her with an arm around her waist. It was getting harder to move. The pain in her head radiated fire down her back and out into her arms and legs. Just lifting one foot in front of the other took every bit of concentration.

Blind, she tripped over a tree root and went down into a muddy pool between the roots. Pain firestormed through her and her brain crisped. She floundered there, trying to stand, but couldn't find the strength to move. Couldn't recall why she had to. Just curl up and cry. Just curl up and die to get rid of the pain.

She felt B.J. come up beside her and hunker down. "Bloody hell. Look at her."

"Why'sh she shaking?" The voice of a man who'd never been there when she was sick. Who had never held her hand when she scraped her knee.

"Her fever's worse, what'd'ya think?"

He caught her hand and the sharp pain of the touch stole her strength, stole her brain and her breath. The earth moved under her and everything telescoped into the dark.

§

"Bloody-fucking-hell. Oh dammitalltohell. Your hand. Your poor hand."

He knelt in the mud, the gunfire still too bloody close behind, a wave of helplessness inundating him.

Her slim palm was almost shapeless with swelling, the lifeline and the fate lines were both pulled tight and smooth as if awaiting rewriting. Or her life was bloody over, which could be the case with an infection like this. The slice in her palm was pulled tight and glossy, the lips pulled apart and oozing puss like a whore's mouth.

"Shit. Shit. Shit."

Something like this could go right into the bloodstream. Or so he seemed to recall from his military first aid training. An infection like this could do more than weaken the patient. It could get into the brain. Meningitis, if he remembered rightly.

Not a migraine. Or maybe partly both, but either way, this was one terribly ill woman he had to save. *Like you're so successful at your attempts to save anything.*

"She needs a fucking doctor," Not some Aussie wanker.

"Medical kit. I gotch one," Jeremy Blackwood slurred. He huddled on the other side of her. The man seemed to have collapsed in on himself since his few terse words with his daughter.

"On you?"

"Nah." A drunk's shit-eating grin. "Got one stashed at th' camp."

"Camp. You've got one stashed back at the Shark's camp?"

"Ya think I'm stupid? At *my* camp. The one Brian's damned well tryin' t'get me t' take him too." Another shit-eating grin. "Got him buffaloed, I do."

B.J. stood up, hauling Kaitlin's too-limp body with him. "You want to help her, get us there. Hopefully we can help her enough until we can reach a doctor."

"Someone's coming," she whispered.

B.J. almost dropped her. "I thought you were passed out."

A small smile crossed her lips. "Surprise! I couldn't leave all this fun."

She winced as if just speaking hurt her. And her voice was so faint he could barely hear her, and with a weird humor that was soooo not Kaitlin. Her throat worked as she swallowed with effort.

"Someone's coming. I feel it. The earth moves."

Delirium. Had to be. Which couldn't be good. He stuck the pistol in the back of his waistband and scooped her up. She moaned a protest and plucked at his shirt with limp fingers. He nodded to Jeremy. "Which way?"

Jeremy Blackwood scanned the hillside as if orienting himself—as if he had any certainty of finding his way anywhere in his state. But he pointed uphill and across the slope—away from the direction B.J. would have headed. B.J. nodded, praying it was the right decision, and started off. "Stay close."

As if the man ever had, but this time it was a matter of life or death. Maybe this time he'd be there for Kaitlin, because B.J. sure as hell was.

Her deadweight threw him off-balance while he tried to keep her safe from the worst of the foliage. He stepped as softly as the mud allowed, easing through the forest as silently as possible. Old military training came through, it seemed.

'Course, Jeremy Blackwood muttered and hummed and crashed through the platter sized leaves when he wasn't picking himself up after falling. Bloody man couldn't have been quiet to save his life. But each time B.J. paused, Jeremy reoriented their direction as if he knew what he was doing.

Ankle-deep mud sucked each step down and slowed them, but he was going to get them out of here. The uphill slope reversed into a steep gulley with a rushing stream at the bottom. They'd have to wade across if they were to get to wherever Jeremy Blackwood was leading them. Then it'd be uphill again.

Uphill, both ways, more like. If he didn't just lose them in the jungle. B.J. started down the gulley slope.

"Stop right there, mate."

B.J. froze in his tracks, his stomach leaden as the huge mercenary stepped out of the brush beside him.

"I should just fucking shoot you all, right here."

"And I should've just bloody well shot you when I had the chance." B.J. hugged Kaitlin into him, and backed a step down the gulley. Kaitlin radiated iron-tinged roses and rainwater.

"You're not going to shoot us. You need us for what we know." B.J. glanced down to make sure Kaitlin's shirt still covered the puppet, then up at Jeremy, swaying at the ravine edge. From far off still came the rat-a-tat-tat of exchanged weapons' fire, but its rhythm had changed. Instead of a steady barrage of fire, there were single shots followed by wild volleys. "Besides, I think you've other problems to deal with than us. By the sound of it, your men are pinned down and they're not taking sniper fire too well. Not used to being on the bloody receiving end, I'll wager."

"Drop your weapon."

"Weapon?"

"My fucking pistol, ya wanker. Now drop it."

Fuck. He'd hoped to keep that advantage. "I can't get at it, now can I? My arms are a bit full."

He hefted Kaitlin and she groaned.

"Shh, it's all right, luv. It'll be good." He kissed her hair.

His adversary turned a shark gaze on Jeremy and jerked his head. "You. Get his gun."

Jeremy gave a bleary nod, took a step to obey and slipped in the mud. He grabbed for a branch, missed, and went down—hard. Started to slip and dug in his heels.

The mud seemed to shift under him. The ravine-side, sodden from the rain, gave way.

Liquid soil grabbed B.J.'s ankles and he staggered. Then Jeremy Blackstone slammed into his knees and took his legs out from under him.

He twisted and fell. Better this than the mercenary's gunfire. He pulled Kaitlin in closer and rode the momentum down the gulley.

A shout from above. A cry. A shot. He could only hope the Shark had gone down, too. He surfed-sat the seething wave of mud, clinging to Kaitlin as trees rushed towards him, as the leaves and branches whipped him.

He plunged, feet first, into the wall of foaming water. Cold ripped his breath away. The force kept him from breathing. Water tumbled him sideways and ripped at Kaitlin. He clung to her. It left him with nothing to fend off the stream's rocks. Nothing to swim with.

He smashed into something more solid than he was. Came up gasping for air. Had to choose between grabbing hold of rock or Kaitlin. The water swept him away and under again. Had she breathed? Was she drowning?

He had to get them to shore. Kicked. Kicked again and came up for air again. Brought Kaitlin's head up, but he didn't see her breathe. He clung to her with one arm and tried to swim towards the shore. Luckily the ravine wasn't wide, but the river was far deeper than he'd thought. A flash of khaki in the water and Jeremy struck him in his free arm, before the water ripped him past.

Bloody man floundered like he'd never seen water. Let him go? Get Kaitlin to shore.

There was no question. Kaitlin had to be his choice. He kicked towards the shore. The water slammed him into another boulder and this time he threw his arm over it and hung on, hugging Kaitlin into the solid surface as muddy water tore at him.

He snugged Kaitlin between himself and the rock, then started edging his way to the shore. The murky river foamed around them, ripped at Kaitlin's hair, her pale face, but he was *not* letting her go. Never letting her go again.

His feet touched bottom.

A few more inches and he was able to grab Kaitlin again and, holding onto the boulder, wade in to shore.

There, he collapsed into the mud under a huge elephant ear plant that still dripped from last night's rain. He pulled Kaitlin into him and buried his face in her sodden hair. Roses and rainwater.

Chapter 44

B.J. came to with the river rushing past him and the wind through the heavy jungle canopy. The heavy, moist air and the stink of mud filled his nose. And the scent of roses and rainwater. Fever-glazed, blue eyes looked up at him.

"Kaitlin." His chest clenched. He ran his fingers down her cheek, uncertain whether this was real or a dream.

In answer, her lips curved in the most beautiful smile he'd ever seen. He could almost forget their dire situation.

He kissed her. So soft lips, and he wanted more. Wanted the full weight of her body on his, her hair like a pale rain shower around his face, but she was too hot. Too weak, and the high points of color on her cheeks said she was very, very sick.

He pulled back. "I was worried you'd drowned."

A slight denying movement of her head, but she grimaced in pain. "You were sleeping." A whisper. "I slept, too."

Passed out, more likely. But maybe the river dousing had brought her fever down a little. That was good, wasn't it? He gently caught her injured hand. So swollen.

"We need to get help for you."

She frowned. "I'm better now—at least a little."

"Not enough. The bloody infection is eating you up. We need t'get you to a doc."

"Not too many of those in the middle of a jungle."

That reminded him of her father. "We lost your Dad in the river."

She tried to sit up and made it with his help. She wavered a little and looked confused. So unlike Kaitlin. "What happened?"

"Yer Dad was leading us to his camp—the one the Shark was trying to get yer Dad to lead him to. Yer father says he's got a medical kit there and that it might have what you need. But the gulley hillside let go and sent us into the river. Not good, but better than the alternative. The bloody Shark caught up with us." He shook his head. "Ya shoulda let me kill him."

Her fever-ridden gaze met his. "Why didn't you ever tell me about your sister? It helps me understand what happened in Seattle." She ran her good hand over his face. "I'm so sorry, B.J."

He caught her hand and kissed her hair. "It was a long time ago. We need to take care of your needs now."

She grimaced and closed her eyes for a moment. "What I need is about a million years of sleep, but I've got to find Dad."

"Well, he went past us in the river. I couldn't stop him. He could be in the Mekong by now."

Her expression turned Kaitlin-stubborn.

"Listen, luv. Looking for one man in this forest would be a fool's game. We need to get out of here while it's daylight and while you're still feelin' well enough."

"Optimist, now, are you?"

"How so?"

"Assuming we'll get out of here."

Which was right. They were truly back of Bourke, and after following Jeremy Blackstone's directions and the tumble in the river, he didn't really have a clue where they were or where they should be going.

"We need to get back to the road," he said. If he had things figured right, it was downstream and then east, up over the ridge.

"I thought we were headed for my Dad's camp."

"A good idea when we had yer old man to guide us. Drunk as hell, but he seemed to know the way."

"But Dad thinks that's where we're going. He'll go there and wait." The stubborn expression deepened and he knew what that meant: go with it or duke it out.

Or simply pick her up and carry her, which might be possible in the condition she was in, but he didn't want to think of the aftermath of such a choice.

"We've got no idea where your father's camp is. He's got to know that." *If* he made it out of the river. *If* he could find his way to his camp.

And *if* he was in any shape to get there under his own steam without running into the bloody Shark and company.

Not too good odds, but Kaitlin was already shaking her head. She pulled up her shirt and exposed the puppet—wet now and running red-brown dye into her skin. "We've got the next best thing to dad."

She pulled it out and flattened it on the wet soil in front of them, then looked up at him. "See? It is a map. More than we thought. I figured I'd string Black-tooth—sorry—Duck—along. I told him the puppet was a map. I figured I'd get him lost enough in the mountains to give you and the kids time to get away." She shook her head and gave him a reproachful look. "As usual, you didn't do what you should have. But I led them a merry chase into the mountains using the marks on the map to make decisions about which track to take. After a while, I got the sense we really were traveling in the right direction, because each turn led to another logical turn. I was starting to think I *was* going to lead him somewhere when an opportunity came for me to escape." She smiled again. "And so I found you and here we are, but I think we could probably use the puppet to get where he was taking us."

He looked down at the piece of carved leather. Little enough to pin their hopes on. "You're not on the road, now, luv. How're you going to orient yourself? You need reference points to follow a map."

She clambered off his lap and it was like losing one of his senses. Or maybe more. Her scent. The heat of her. The brush of her drying hair on his chin.

"Listen to me. The more I used the map, the more I realized just what an artist Jorani was." She pulled the puppet up and set it on her knees. "See here?"

She pointed to the mass of carved vines, and her finger traced the fine veining in them. "The veins are the roads, it's true. But there are ridges and valleys shown through the texture of the leather."

She caught his hand and ran his fingertips over the leather.

"Feel it?"

He had to admit, there might be something to it. There was an unevenness to the surface. More than the cutouts for the shadows made by the puppet. And why bother working the leather like that if all you were concerned with was shadows and light?

"All right." He held up his hands in defeat. "But we still don't know where we are in this mess of vine valleys. You orient us and I'll consider following your lead."

She tried to stand, but it took B.J.'s assistance to get her upright. She was failing again; there were color spikes in her cheeks. The river dousing had taken her temperature down, but it was temporary at best. "I need to see."

He helped her hobble out of the trees to the river's edge. The water level had lessened some since he'd hauled them both free, but the sun had also started to fall.

They'd slept a long time.

Too long. Long enough whoever won the deadly battle at the camp could be searching for them.

Kaitlin was searching the slopes above them. Finally she looked at the river. "You know, this river looks about the same size as the one that blocked Black-tooth's truck last night. If they got through this morning when the water had lessened a little, and if this is that river, then we must be about here."

Her finger stabbed the map, but there was no way she could be right. "There's no way to be sure. There are too many rivers in the Cardamom Mountains."

"Would you just listen and quit fighting me? The river was—here." Her finger found another spot on the leather. "Last night we went up and over a couple of ridges before we came to the camp. Those mercenaries must be mining that area in hopes of finding something in case Dad never reveals his secret. At least that way they can keep their Thai backers convinced that they're looking. But that would put us about here." She indicated another spot. "So if we left camp like we did and headed uphill, then that would have put us about here to cross the river. And we did."

She looked at him, like she was pleased with her logic, but B.J. still wasn't convinced. "This isn't the time t' run off willy-nilly, Kaitlin. We need to get ya help, and bloody soon."

"Well, you give me a better option. You'd have us follow a river to God knows where in this jungle."

"If your map reading's right, it'll take us back to the road. Then we can get you to a doctor. That's most important."

"And the road would likely lead right back to being captured. No. If dad's been able to keep his camp hidden this long, that's where he'll go and that's where I'm going, whether you like it or not."

She turned away and started walking up the river bank, following it back the way they'd come.

"Bloody, fucking hell," he muttered. And followed her. Just bloody perfect. The one time the woman had to do something spontaneously, she had to do it now.

§

The steepening slope strained the muscles in her thighs, and the thick foliage along the river ripped at her face and sometimes forced Kaitlin to step precariously into the edge of the river, but it was better than standing still and trying to decide what to do. One foot in front of the other. Pushing away the leaves and branches, picking herself out of the mud when she fell. Trying to make out what was in front of her as the sun fell and the shadows lengthened. That she could do.

It didn't hurt her brain.

Or at least it was what she could do for now. Her darned knees shook with each step and the flipping shivers were coming hard and fast enough she tried to stay away from B.J. so he wouldn't see.

But they'd made progress, following the river upstream, fording thankfully smaller tributaries until finally the top of the ridge was in sight—angled sunlight through tree canopy.

She dug deep and closed her eyes, then lengthened her stride. Just a few more feet. She could last a few more feet. Just focus on that.

She grabbed a branch to haul herself up over a fallen tree and found herself in a natural clearing filled with platter-leaved plants and a mass of vines that had covered the stricken giant.

Late afternoon sun blazed towards her from the far end of another valley that ran east-west through the mountains, but high enough that the river they had veered away from the past few hours still flowed down its length. Southward there seemed to be a break in the ridge she stood on where the river must flow through. Dark green forest filled the valley floor, but a bare patch to the side spoke of the deforestation that she'd read about happening in Southeast Asia.

B.J. came up behind her and settled warm arms around her shivering shoulders.

"Nice view, luv, but I don't think that's quite going t' do it. How's that map of yours working fer us?"

She stepped away and fumbled the map out of her clothes. It was hard to focus without the full sunlight. Harder to focus with the shivering blasting through her.

She ran her fingers over the puppet. Over her time in the truck and her time traveling in the jungle, its ridges and grooves had become familiar—but now her quaking made it hard to distinguish the slight changes she's been following.

She closed her eyes for relief from the sunset and tried to read the map's ridges like Braille. There was the ridge she hoped they were standing on, but her wavering fingertips couldn't distinguish the grooves in the hardened leather.

She fisted her fingers and tried again. No better, rough leather that made her stomach turn.

B.J.'s presence loomed over her and she opened her eyes. "I think we go down," she said unsteadily, hoping it was true. Downhill she just might be able to do. Another climb like the last one just wasn't going to happen.

His hands came to rest on her shoulders, two points of heat in the ravaging cold.

"Bloody hell, Kaitlin, you're burning up."

"I'm fine," she tried.

"Not bloody likely, luv. Look at me."

She opened her eyes and peered up at him. Swallowed at the worry in his gaze. Was she really that bad?

"I'm fine. I'm upright and walking. That's all I need to be."

But his expression only deepened as if he'd rather she was limp in his arms. "Where too, then?"

She glanced out toward the sunset and away. Too bright, and it only blinded her. "Hold the puppet steady so I can read it."

His intense gaze pulled hers up to him.

"I can do this. Really."

And suddenly his arms were around her. His lips on her hair. "Jeezus, I hope so luv. I don't know where you're finding the strength for this, but I love ya for it."

Love? No way, no how. B.J. only thought of himself, not her.

But there were twenty-five orphans and a mad dash across Cambodia that spoke otherwise.

Selfishness was not part of him anymore, it seemed. She eased herself back.

"You don't love me. It's just this situation." But his words sent a chord strumming inside her. It had been a long time since she'd felt it and—if she were honest with herself—the last time had been with B.J.

Not with James. Not even a little, and that was strange. And sad. The last few years she'd been fooling herself.

Her relationship with James McKillup had been—convenient—for both of them, but not love. For love, there was only one man, and he was standing right here before her.

"We should get going. Hold the puppet steady for me."

He did, and she ran her fingers over the swirl of vines and flowers, hoping her shaking wasn't too obvious.

There was the ridge again. There might be a slight indentation and the fine feeling of the thread of the road. And there might be a deeper incision of river. The rough spot might just be a flower bud somewhere in the midst of ridges.

Or she might be wrong and she could just be leading them farther into jungle where she would die. *Like her father?*

She bit her lip. Took a plunge.

"We go down to the river and follow it again. The camp is a ways along."

She thought. She hoped.

She started down the steep ridge into the valley. Tangled undergrowth grew thicker here in a profusion of vines and orchids and fluttering blue butterflies that caught the last rays of sunlight.

But the last glitter of light caught like shards in her brain. She had to avert her gaze, but the pain came in waves again. She blinked back weary tears, but they still flooded her eyes, making the world a runny mass of colors.

She felt it first—the earth slipping away. Then came the groan of stone moving and suddenly her legs were torn out from under her. She slammed down on her side, saw B.J.'s terrified face up above. Heard his yell, and then he was gone as she tumbled over with mud-tree-brush all around her, as the jungle rushed her into the valley.

Chapter 45

B.J. swore and plunged after her. This bloody-well couldn't be happening. Not this. Not again. Not after all that they'd been through and not after he'd sworn to protect her.

The mud trapped his feet. The roar of the mud slide made it hard to think and the stink of torn foliage made him heart-sick. Below him the roar of the mud slide died and a plume of mud and debris rose up through the trees.

Bloody hell. Bloody, blooming hell. The way the slide had taken her, she'd had no chance. No chance at all to ride the damn thing down.

She could be buried.

She could be broken, and he hadn't been there for her.

He ignored the risk of the slide area and leapt straight down it in huge bounding strides that set off trickles of more mud around him. The whole bloody hillside could come loose, but Kaitlin needed him—and now. There were only a few short minutes she could live without air if the mud had buried her.

Down. The trees to either side of the slide area hid the sky.

Down. And the light disappeared so he could barely see until he suddenly stood among the huge tangle of mud and broken foliage.

"Kaitlin!" In the dim light it was impossible to see. The mud covered everything. "Kaitlin, talk to me."

He wallowed through deep mud and found himself at the edge of the slide debris, where white wood thrust like bones out of the mud.

"Kaitlin?" Fear made his voice tremble.

Something moved.

Something white and low down. A hand. A fucking hand.

Please God. Please.

He was on his knees, digging in the slick mud, following the hand down. A forearm. An elbow. A shoulder. The back of a head, hunkered down. Another hand covered her face, and then he cleared the mud away and Kaitlin stared blue-eyed up at him, and then closed her eyes as he dug the mud away from her face and shoulders, her torso.

He grabbed her and pulled, but the mud wanted her, too. Like a living thing, it wouldn't let go. He was forced to release her and dig more, down over her hips, her thighs.

This time when he staggered up and pulled her, she moved. The earth gave with a horrible sucking sound and he staggered back with Kaitlin in his arms, mud-slicked as an eel and shoeless. He sat down hard and something clicked. Safety coming off.

Something hard jabbed him in his back and the pistol was pulled free of his waistband.

"Nice work, mate. Now get her on her feet, and let's cut the crap. Yer taking us to the camp or else this one is deader than she looks now."

The march through the jungle was a bloody nightmare. B.J. had tried to get Kaitlin up, but the fall had sapped the last of her strength. She had sagged in his arms like the dead weight the Shark had named her.

And so he had carried her, hauling her up in his arms and praying she was all right as he led them through the thick foliage deeper into the jungle. The river was a distant beckoning thread of hope. Make it there and he could follow it. Find a way to either get them away or take the Shark down.

But the chance of taking his nemesis down was slim and none with Kaitlin in his arms and the elephant-ear and vine foliage so thick he could barely shove his way through it while avoiding the horrible tangle of the bloody spider webs that seemed to grow more thickly in this part of the jungle. He needed her well enough to fend for herself.

"Kaitlin, luv?" He half buried his words in her mud-tangled hair.

Overhead, the canopy hung night-blackened against an indigo sky, and all the greens in the depth of the jungle had turned indistinguishable shades of grey. The noises around them changed from bird cry and the rustle of monkey in the canopy to the incessant buzz of night insects and the bright cries of gecko and small animal.

He felt what he hoped was a small nod against his chest. He could be mistaken. It could be wishful thinking. Aware of the spiders, he slowed to cautiously push through another mass of leaves. Ahead, the unseen river roared.

The assault rifle jabbed him in his back. "Move it. We ain't got all night."

Which was probably right. If they weren't free of the Shark by daybreak, it was highly unlikely he'd let them live. Of course if they found Jeremy's camp, all bets were off, too. Death seemed likely either way—unless he could get them away.

Another wall of leaves and he shouldered his way through and almost staggered and fell when he stepped out onto a sodden river bank. Here, the run-off had receded and left high banks covered in slick mud and debris.

He slipped. Slipped and again and went down to his knees, losing Kaitlin's legs so she slumped and fell. Her feet caught in the water and it ripped her away. He lunged, barely caught her, and yanked her back. Sat there panting and rallying strength.

A boot in his side sent him sprawling. "Get the fuck up, asshole. Get going."

Silently swearing revenge, he staggered up, hauled Kaitlin with him, and cradled her against him. She was burning up again, her roses and rainwater scent burned away with copper.

"Stay with me, luv. Stay with me."

A heated hand caught his and squeezed, giving new hope through his exhaustion.

He kissed her hair in answer. "Please, stay with me. Get well. Did I ever tell you I was a fool?" He shook his head and followed the river, a dark thread through an even darker waking dream. The assault rifle jabbed him every time he slowed.

"I was an idiot to fake those photos. I was a total wanker for letting you leave. Did you know that?" He whispered to her. If they didn't make it, he wanted her to know. Wanted her to understand. "I never got over you, but I knew I'd done something you'd never forgive. I was an idiot. I should have come back. I should have proved I was made of better stuff than your father."

There was no movement. It had all been his imagination and he was losing her again. This time forever.

Another jab of the rifle and he almost snarled at the demon behind him. The bloody man had taken everything from him. His sister and now Kaitlin.

No! He wasn't going to let it happen again. He'd find a way to undo this situation.

He clenched Kaitlin to his chest and looked at the water. Another dousing? They might stand a chance if the water could rip them away fast enough, but in the rising moonlight, the long tail of light only rippled on the water. Not fast enough.

He shoved between trees that grew down to the river and almost fell into a pathway of hard-packed earth. He looked left and right. A trail that showed more use than a game trail. It followed the river.

The Shark shoved him forward and seemed to recognize what they'd found. "This it, then? The way to the camp?"

"Does it matter if it is? It's bloody going in our direction." B.J. started forward. At least the trail meant it was easier to walk and easier to protect Kaitlin from the branches and bloody spiders.

The moon placed distorted shadows across the path: deep pools of darkness that disguised long threads spun across the open space. This was the kind of space the spiders liked to build—under heavy canopy in open spaces. The ones in Angkor built where logging had taken down most of the largest trees.

Spider silk caught across his face and he couldn't brush it away. Caught in his hair and he wanted to dance and duck and run away. But Kaitlin stopped him. Kaitlin he had to protect, and to do that he'd face spiders, or Sharks, or anything else.

The trail cut an almost smooth path through the jungle, following the river's edge and then gradually cutting away from the water.

Suddenly, the trees fell away to either side and he stepped out at the edge of what must be a natural sink hole. Forest giants circled away to left and right, long vines trailing grey-black growth down the sides of the hole. Smaller trees placed an impenetrable roof over whatever lay below. Except—something silver-grey gleamed in the moonlight, like a great fin sticking out of the tree canopy. He recognized the shape.

Not a natural sinkhole, he amended.

Crash site. By the shape of the wing, a Vietnam-era bomber, he'd bet. Probably exploded on impact, but the wing and fuselage had been impaled into the destroyed forest floor like a jungle god.

And the jungle had grown back to worship it like the jungle had grown back around Angkor's temples.

"This is it?" The Shark came up beside him, his bald head gleaming in the moonlight like it would off a surfacing great white.

B.J. said nothing.

The trail spiraled down the side of the crater in a narrow, crumbling path. He followed it, edging sideways to carry Kaitlin. Earth crumbled under his feet. This path was never meant for the weight of two people.

Gradually the trees gathered above him and cut off the moonlight and the sound of the jungle above, so he traveled in darkness and eerie silence and the shudderingly light touch of gossamer threads across his skin. Spiders.

Too many of them. The trees seemed full of their movement— scuttling, shifting, waves of them. He pressed back against the crater wall and pulled Kaitlin in tighter. He didn't want to move. To breathe, or open his eyes. But the jab of the rifle kept him moving. Down and circling around the edge of the crater, like he was in a slow motion swirl into an antipodal toilet.

Flushed.

And then he touched bottom, the tree canopy above him, and he opened his eyes on another world.

Chapter 46

A ghostly glow filled the underside of the trees. Iridescent white growths grew on the trunks of the trees, creating white columns against the overwhelming gloom. Huge, white moths fluttered between them, and distantly, beyond the glowing tree trunks and the massive, burned-out remains of the plane, a glowing block of light suggested a standing structure.

His arms burning from the strain of carrying Kaitlin for so long, B.J. shuffled forward under the Shark's urging. The earth was dark under his feet, hard to see the snaking roots and the impact ripples that tripped him up, but he kept going. Had no choice, given the rifle in his back.

There was something strange about the place aside from the glowing. Something he couldn't quite put his finger on. Something to do with the glowing white trunks and the barren floor.

He wound through the trees towards the structure. If this was Jeremy's camp, then that would be where the medical pack was. It was also the place the Shark would kill them once he had proof this was the place that he sought. And there was nothing on the ground he might make into a weapon.

Bloody hell.

Moonlight placed weird shadows across the hard-pack, and the shifting leaves made it look like the shadows moved on their own.

Small creatures in some greater shadow play, and he and Kaitlin were exactly that.

If he could only get them out of here—but there was no way he was simply reacting this time. This time he had to be sure he took the Shark down for good.

Walking through the grove was like walking through a strange acropolis that had sunk into the earth and become one with it. Except, to either side at shoulder height, the field of columns was knit together by fine gossamer threads.

Webs.

B.J. stopped dead. Webs, and in the stillness of the crater the ghostly veils moved under the weight of too many distended bodies, like dark buttons on his mother's old tufted sofa.

The whole bloody crater was full of the things. Even along this straight path through the trees, above his head the columns were thick with webs and evil-looking packages of wrapped victims. Birds, possibly. And there a dangling tail that could be a monkey.

But the webs stopped a good seven feet from the ground. No, from the earth crawled a fine mist that shifted and coiled around his ankles like a living thing.

His skin crawled and he was certain something had dropped down the back of his shirt. He shivered and stopped again where the tree-glow backlit a spider that must be a good four centimeters across. The legs added another eight inches.

"Not exactly the kind of thing you want to run into in the middle of the night," he said.

"Fucking bugs."

Shark swung the barrel of his assault rifle and tore the whole web down. The spider fell and scuttled away into the darkness and mist that had risen up to B.J.'s shins, making the ground and the spider hard to see.

Definitely not something he wanted to run into. But maybe the Shark's aversion was like his own. Maybe it was something he could use.

He cleared the columns and found himself in a small clearing against the crater wall that drifted with waist-high tendrils of the thickening mist, with a distant view of the sky. The moon's light barely reached them, but a mass of stars filled his slice of the heavens. The Southern Cross hung there, and a reviving breeze lifted a strand of Kaitlin's hair against his hand, but the breeze bore the scent of more rain. Near the wall of the crater stood a small, metal-sided building that had to be Jeremy Blackwood's camp.

He would get them out of here, but first get Kaitlin the help she needed.

"I'm going to see if there's a medical kit inside," He said.

When the Shark didn't answer, B.J. glanced around.

The Shark had moved off to the crater wall, where a mass of vines and roots had been hacked away leaving a blackened scar amongst the glowing vegetation. The uncovered earth showed the scars of picks and shovels and a debris pile at its base where something glittered.

Shark toed the debris pile and a glittering stone clattered free and rolled across the ground and into a pool of weak starlight. Gleamed.

Like another stone had done at Angkor, though this pebble wasn't as big.

"Ruby," B.J. said.

"Damn straight, mate. Some of the best seen in these parts in a host of years. The Thai mines at Trat are getting by on seconds. There hasn't been a good find of gems in Cambodia in years. But what friend Jeremy produced at the assay office has got a lotta people excited."

"So you had spies at the government offices."

"Not me, no. But the people I work for do. Friends in high places, if you must know."

"And where do friend Duch and his pals fit in?" Keep the Shark busy, because while busy he wasn't killing someone.

The Shark hawked with vehemence. "With the Vietnamese, of course. They own this government. They're selling off Cambodia to their corporations and the Chinese. What they aren't bartering off to the Khmer Rouge hold-outs. Fucking communists. My friends have other plans—like closer associations with Thailand."

He smiled and raised his weapon.

A coup. He was talking about a bloody coup, and undoing the hardscrabble peace Cambodia had obtained after all of the Khmer Rouge years. Every part of B.J. wanted to attack. Wanted to seize the Shark by the neck, because another war was about the last thing Cambodia needed. They were barely clinging to their culture as it was. And there were too many orphans already.

But if he attacked he left Kaitlin defenseless, and it was highly unlikely he'd get both Kaitlin and himself free.

He headed for the hut, hoping for a weapon and hoping the Shark would forget him. No such luck. The man abandoned the ruby field for the moment and shoved B.J. aside. Pushed inside the shed, scanned it, and hauled out a shovel and plastic kit emblazoned with a white cross and dumped them at B.J.'s feet.

"You've got five minutes, mate. Then you've got work to do."

He strode back to the gash in the crater wall and started stuffing his pockets with stones picked out of the debris pile. God knew how rich the find must be, if so many stones were just left in the debris. Then the Shark hauled out a penlight and ran it over the gash of earth. The light caught and glittered in too many blood-red stars. A few stones from there and the orphanage could be set. A few weeks of stones and he could quit work forever.

It had to be Jeremy's strike, what had made him say those things in Kaitlin's letter.

He laid her gently on the mist-covered ground and she moaned and curled into herself like a bloody prawn. Heat radiated off her like a copper cloud and the mist seemed to cling to her skin as if she were disappearing from him. Something blocked the moonlight and the clearing went dark. Only the eerie glow of the foliage remained. He opened the watertight medipack.

Jeremy might be a rounder and have abandoned his family in all ways that counted, but he did know how to pack a medical kit. Neat rows of bandages sat in precise compartments. A bundle of syringes and needles were held in one corner, and in amongst ointments and antiseptic creams sat foam indentations that held precious glass vials.

Fumbling the delicate vials out of the foam, B.J. checked for anything he might recognize. Chlorpromazine for infection might help, but he didn't find it amongst the selection. What to use. Five minutes and surely to God they were almost up. He grabbed a vial, didn't recognize the name, but there had seemed to be some order to the way Jeremy had packed the kit, with drugs for infection grouped together in one corner, spider and snake antivenin in another section. A good idea if you were alone and possibly not in good shape when you were trying to help yourself.

He ripped open needle and syringe packets, filled a syringe.

"Sorry, luv." He rolled her onto her side and hiked her t-shirt up and her waistband down to expose a smooth hip and buttock. Half-closed his eyes and stabbed the needle in.

She flinched, big time. Moaned.

He tidied her clothes and pulled her to him. "I'm sorry, luv. Had to be done." A few pats of rain found her face and glowed in the phosphorescence. Overhead, the stars had disappeared along with the moon.

"Five minutes are over. Get moving." A boot found B.J.'s back and almost toppled him over.

He settled Kaitlin by the equipment shed Jeremy must have hauled in piece by piece on his back and smoothed her hair off her face. Then he turned to the Shark.

He was going to finish this, and it looked like his bloody nemesis was going to give him the weapon to do it.

Shark motioned to the shovel and B.J. tried to hide his satisfaction as he picked it up. Hefted it for balance.

Not bad—it would do in a pinch, and this definitely was one. He looked back at the Shark.

"Dig."

"Dig where?"

"Do you think I give a flyin' fuck? Dig. Deep enough for two. Wherever you want. Don't want no bodies lying around when we set up camp here."

How about back in Seattle, mate. Or in Sydney about twenty years back.

B.J. dug the point of the shovel into the hard pack. Hard was right. Not the best place, and under the trees there'd be roots to deal with.

"It's gonna take awhile."

"Dig."

B.J. did. Used his anger to ram the shovel into the soil, to pry up small shovels full, while keeping an eye on the Shark or whatever Jeremy called him. The man would always be the Shark to him.

The rain increased as he shoveled, running into the small hole he'd made, so each mist-laden thrust of the shovel caused a small tidal wave that slopped over his boots. Rivulets of water ran across the ground and collected into pools, but the mists concealed that fact unless you were paying attention.

He was. He hoped the Shark wasn't.

And suddenly the lack of spiders at ground level made sense.

B.J. glanced back at the shed and Kaitlin. She leaned against its side—a side that glowed white almost to roof height, as if the mold or whatever it was that coated the structure and plants only grew that high. As high as the spider webs.

The rain splashed around him and the Shark took cover in the shed's doorway, leaving Kaitlin in the rain. She stirred and swiped at the rain on her face. A good sign. Maybe the antibiotics were working. He could hope.

Pooling water covered the ground and the mist increased, sending thick threads through the trees. He kept digging, jabbing the shovel into the earth, tossing sodden spades' full towards the debris pile. The idiot thing was the grit under his shovel was full of irregular stones he was sure were more than rubble. The bloody bomber had crashed right in the middle of one of the richest ruby deposits he could imagine.

But that only meant that forces would spare nothing to claim this place. Which meant he would die here if he didn't do something quickly.

"Ya know, having me dig our graves isn't exactly original, but then you never were an original thinker."

The Shark just straightened in the doorway and shifted his rifle. The pistol was stuck into his waistband. A place a man could wrestle it from, if he could get close enough.

"You even remember my sister?" he asked.

The Shark ignored him.

"She was fifteen. Three years younger than me, and you'd pretended to be her boyfriend. Then you hooked her on drugs—meth. And then you told her she had to pay you back for them. She was so ashamed she wouldn't come to her family. So you put her to work on her back."

The bloody Shark didn't move.

B.J. ground his teeth. "She was blonde—a lot like Kaitlin—but small-boned and fragile looking, with large brown eyes and a way of smiling that could light up a day. She liked to sing and was good at it. When she was little, she used to sing in a church choir. And she loved horses. It was my mum's one regret—that they could never afford it. When Cora died, my mum used to blame herself: if she'd only gotten Cora a horse, maybe she wouldn't have fallen in with the likes of you."

The Shark stepped out of the shed's cover. "Would you shut the fuck up? Believe me when I tell ya, they all look the same when they're on their backs begging for it."

The violence B.J. held in check almost boiled over. He dug his nails into the shovel handle and drove the blade into the earth. Water splashed over his feet and into his boots. The level was rising faster than he'd expected. This soil—mostly clay by the look of it—must form an almost perfect container for the water. And it was rising faster as the rain increased. Time to act on his plan.

He shook his head and wiped his brow of water and sweat. Drove the shove into the soil again, but held back. Acted like the shove hit rock and let his shoulder sag to feign defeat. The clouds opened above and torrential rain filled the crater so it was hard to see or hear.

"You better see this," he yelled. "No way in hell am I going to get any deeper."

The water was almost up to his knees. The hole he'd dug was almost impossible to see and the sides of the crater had become one continuous waterfall that was growing in volume with every minute the rain fell. The crater must be the lowest spot—next to the river. The whole thing was going to be under water soon and the bloody Shark still hadn't figured it out.

"Dig, asshole. And quit the drivel about your sister. Bitch ain't here. She is." He pointed the rifle at Kaitlin, who now lay in water up to her waist. Thank God he'd leaned her against the shed.

"Whatever you say, mate. I can dig till the cows come home if you want me to wreck this. Maybe a good smack'll shatter it."

He raised the shovel as if to drive it into the hole.

"Wait."

He paused as the Shark ducked out from his cover and crossed to him. B.J. tensed.

"What's the fucking problem?"

The assault rifle jabbed in B.J.'s direction.

"There's a bloody big stone right there."

"I don't see anything."

"There." B.J. pointed at nothing, but the Shark didn't oblige by moving closer.

"What the fuck are you talking about? There's nothing there."

B.J. sent a prayer skyward, because if his next step didn't work, he'd be a sitting duck for that rifle.

"You're blind, mate. I'll show you." He stepped down into the hole he'd dug, hip deep in water and rising as the rain poured down. He immersed his arm in water, pointing. "See there? Or are ya blind?"

The Shark stepped closer. One step. Another. Leaned over and B.J. brought the shovel up like a battering ram into the Shark's face.

The Shark saw it and leapt sideways at the last minute. Brought the stock of the rifle down at B.J.'s head.

B.J. lunged up through the water, so the blow deflected off his shoulder. He grabbed for the pistol at the bigger man's waist. Almost had it.

The bloody wood and metal slipped in his grip. He tried for the trigger, but the bloody safety was on. Shark's rifle stock found his face. Again. Again. Like running into a battering ram.

Dazed, he collapsed back, neck deep on his knees in the water, the deadly end of the rifle dead-aimed at his face.

"Get up. I should shoot you right now, but I like the thought of letting you die slow, watching her die first." He jerked the weapon towards Kaitlin.

The rising water had reached her chest and she seemed to almost float. He needed to get her and get the hell out of this drowning pool.

"Get up." The Shark jabbed the rifle barrel in B.J.'s back, shoving him towards the trees. "Move."

B.J. did, disgusted at himself. How the hell had he let things go that wrong? He'd had a plan. Isn't that what he'd always known Kaitlin wanted of him? A solid plan?

Yer plan just didn't work, ya wanker. Yer no good at it.

He was right. Kaitlin's body bobbed in the water, the deluge of rain flooding her face. She was going to drown even if she didn't sink.

"I need to get her to higher ground and shelter. She's sick."

"Too bad. Ya both should have thought of that when I asked ya nicely about the location."

He forced B.J. in among the trees. Shoved him face first against one B.J. could just clasp hands around and fished a set of plastic handcuffs from his pocket. Twisted and snapped them closed around B.J.'s wrists so he stood frustrated and helpless as the Shark splashed over to Kaitlin and shoved her through the roaring water into the way of the rushing waterfall flowing over the crater edge.

The falling water pressed her under the surface and she came up choking and struggling weakly. The Shark shoved her back under the flow.

"No! Leave her. Ya don't need to do this."

The Shark turned back to him. "So this one's yours, too? Didn't ya learn with the last one that I can do anything I want—including get rid o' them?"

B.J. froze. "You remember Cora."

The big old Shark smiled with all his teeth. "Sure. I remember all my girls. And the idiot kid who tried to save her. As if ya stood a chance. She was mine, a yabbo. Just like yer ass is mine, now."

Kaitlin struggled weakly against the hold that kept her face under the water. Then the Shark dragged her over to the debris pile and wedged her between it and the wall, directly under the waterfall.

B.J. fought his bonds, but it was no good. Too tight to let him slip loose. The guy knew his business.

Then the Shark splashed across to B.J. "Have a nice life. A short one."

Laughing, he splashed away through the glimmering columned trees. Overhead, in the darkness, the spider webs glistened and streamed with water, the heavy-bodied spiders clung to the tree trunks, and the broad teak leaves thundered with rain.

B.J. looked up into the rain. The canopy broke the worst of the fall into his face, but the luminescent spiders scuttled above and must have felt his struggle through the tree trunk. The bloody b-jeezus spiders came lower.

§

The Seattle rain fell the heaviest Kaitlin had ever known. It filled night-bound Market Street with ankle-deep water. No, knee deep. No, waist deep, and the people were leaving. People pressed through the dark water and floating, abandoned cars like small tugs leaving wakes as they passed through the light of Kaitlin's doorway, where she pressed her face against the glass. Clung to it like a moored ship.

If she ventured out, she knew the cold water would take her. If she stayed here, she might be safe, but alone, locked in her island behind the glass.

Maybe.

She watched as last stragglers pressed past her house. A man—tall, blonde, with wiry hair—shepherded a group of children through the flowing water, lifting first one and then another onto his shoulders, into his arms, others clinging to him lest they be swept away.

She knew him. B.J.

He reached a Coast Guard cutter that sailed down the street rescuing people and began to hand the children up one at a time to safety. They made it and clung there, but before B.J. could catch the safety line, an abandoned car slammed into his side.

He went down and under. Came up and she heard his yell. He went down again.

"No! B.J.!"

She slammed her palm against the glass and it cracked.

Go or stay? Take a chance and save him, or stay safe and dry?

He didn't deserve to die. Not when he'd saved the children.

Unthinking, she punched the glass, punched through and slashed her arm so blood ran thick down her shirt and pain coursed through her system like a drug. Rain pounded on her head and set off a series of explosions that pixilated the dark like newspaper photos. The roaring water took her. Swept her away and under, through the canyon of streets.

She fought up for air and rain—no, a waterfall—filled her face and she was drowning. Pounded down. Her head pounded in so she was hollow and there was only the echoing pain.

She fought up, fought free, and peered through the pounding rain and the shattering sledgehammer in her head. B.J.—where was B.J.?

She saw him. Someone had tied him to a pier along the water. The ferry pier glowing through fog.

No, a Greek column.

No, a tree. Water poured all around her, slammed down on her head and shoved her under again.

Seattle streets.

No, a jungle. Jungle—Cambodia. Monsoon rains.

She floundered up and half-swam, half crawled towards him.

"Kaitlin! Kaitlin, are you all right, luv?"

She blinked and tried to figure out where they were. Rising water, certainly. It was like they stood in a filling basin. *Toilet bowl, more like.*

Dad's camp. That was it.

Tried to stand, but her legs wouldn't obey her. "I'm coming, B.J. I'll save you."

She floundered through the water towards him. She was gasping when she reached him. The world spun slowly, then picked up speed as she clung to him.

"We have to get you loose."

A voice. She thought it was hers.

"Can ya undo the cuffs? Maybe go to the hut and look for a knife."

She followed his look. Far away through the mist and the darkness and water glowed a structure, but she knew she couldn't make it that far. A long journey was beyond her.

She shook her head. "I can't. But I have this." She fumbled her nail file out of her underwear and slid around the tree, shivering from the loss of his heat, from the pounding in her head.

Shaking hands that she couldn't still jabbed the point of the file into the plastic.

When she tore it loose, she dropped it.

"Noooo." She fell to her knees, the water up to her nose. Fumbled through the water and—found it. Her fingers closed around the metal, but when she tried to stand, it was beyond her. She reached up, but her strength wouldn't lift her arms higher than her shoulders. She clung to the smooth-barked tree as the water rose around her chin. Damn it, she had to do something, but her breath came in sobs and the water splashed into her mouth and choked her.

"Just a little higher, luv. Just a little."

She tried again, but the knife blade behind her eyes made it hard to move. She was shaking so hard she could barely hold onto the file.

She struggled to get her feet under her, dug her fingers into the slimy mold on the tree trunk, and had to rest for a minute. Laid her head against the slimy tree, closed her eyes, and inhaled the scent of life and her growing fear.

Seattle drowned.

No, she drowned. She came up coughing. She must have passed out and slumped into the water. Or else the water had risen.

Was still rising.

But she still held the file. "B.J.?"

"Kaitlin! Thank God. I've been calling you. Bloody cuffs wouldn't let me slide around to you."

"I'm going to try to get you the file. I—I don't think I can break the cuffs myself."

She couldn't feel her legs. Her hands faded from her in the cold. Shivers coursed through her, making it impossible to think.

Don't think. Just do. Wasn't that from a movie?

She shoved off the ground and managed to reach his hands. He caught them—her.

His warm touch. So warm with life. His hands would feel wonderful on her skin. He clung to her fingers.

"No," she whispered. "You have to get free." The world narrowed to a single column of light and everything else was darkness and shadow. "This." She shoved the file between his fingers and knew she probably stabbed him, but he had the file. It was all she could do.

The light column faded as she slipped back into the water.

Back into drowned Seattle.

Chapter 47

Kaitlin's fevered fingers slipped free and left him with only a thin strip of metal and the welling blood she'd drawn in his palm. A soft splash followed, barely heard in the roar of the rain.

"Kaitlin?"

"Kaitlin?"

He craned his head around the tree's curve, but the rain and the darkness half-blinded him. There in the eerie glow, blonde hair trailed in the water. A pale face came into view, water pooling in the hollows of her eyes.

"Fuck me. Kaitlin, no! Wake up!"

He yanked back against the cuffs, but that didn't do a sod of good. *Think, ya wanker. Fer once in yer life, think about what yer doing and do it—slow and steady.*

He fumbled the file backwards in his hands so the pointy end met the plastic cuff. He copied Kaitlin's move of stabbing the plastic, but he twisted, yanked.

The bloody file bent in his grip.

Fucking thing. He'd throw it across the bloody crater if he was free.

But that wasn't anything he could do now, because he wasn't free.

Kaitlin's body floated loose of the tree and farther away from him as if there were a current in the forming lake. Fuck. If he didn't get free in a hurry no telling where she'd be.

So think, man. Take a deep breath.

He did. Inhaled raggedly as sweat and rainwater stung his eyes.

By fucking Braille he aimed the file point at the edge of the plastic and gouged a small piece away. He repeated the action. Hard to do when his fucking hands shook with the need to get away and get Kaitlin. *Well, the longer ya take doin' this the bigger chance she'll drown, mate.*

Another deep breath and he jabbed the point. Worked it around to widen the hole in the plastic and then ran the file through and began to saw.

The tension on his wrists loosened. It was working. The bonzer woman was brilliant coming up with the file.

One side of the plastic gave and broke and he was able to twist and yank free. He staggered back from the tree and fell into the water. Sputtered up, water streaming off him and the file still clutched in his fist.

Useful little instrument was about the only weapon he had. He shoved it in his pocket and cast about for Kaitlin. No sign of her.

Fuck.

Chest deep in water, he plunged amongst the trees. He carried his own glow with him, because the front of his clothes and his arms were covered in the glowing mold from the tree. At least the canopy lessened the pounding rain, but he looked up at the spiders. Tattered wisps of webs had left the tree branches and the higher reaches of the trunks seething with the beggars. If Kaitlin snagged on one of the trees, would they come for her?

He avoided the glowing trunks and shoved faster, like a ship heading for open water from Sydney Harbor.

Still no sign of Kaitlin. Jeezus, where was she?

The current. Remember the current. He stopped and watched the way debris flowed across the rising water. Shoulder height now. If he didn't get out of here soon, he'd be swimming.

He followed the debris and soon found himself near the crater wall. Debris of leaves and sticks was pummeled by the water falling down the wall. There. Kaitlin, leaves half-covering her body. He plunged through the Sargasso Sea of leaf matter and then froze. Lifting itself out of the water was a three inch wide spider. Obviously knocked off its tree, it had floated for a while and now took cover on the raft of Kaitlin's body.

B.J. closed his eyes and fought the irrational fear that would have him run in the other direction. The spider just hunkered down on her chest and fucking looked at him with its fucking bug eyes.

Move, B.J. What's the plan?

Plan? Hell, his hands were shaking so hard he could barely think and his balls were like shriveled prunes between his legs.

Back into the water for the spider. Maybe right into the pounding waterfall that would surely drown it.

He grabbed Kaitlin's head and shoulders and started to edge her towards the fall, but the spider scuttled towards his hand and he fell back in the water.

No good. No good. He forced himself back beside her. Grabbed her and shoved her under.

The spider bobbed up in his face.

He splashed it away like a kid in a water fight, grabbed Kaitlin, and plunged back towards the trees. Hugged her to him. Warm. Burning up, really. But if she was burning, she was still alive, right?

"Kaitlin, luv. Oh, God." He kissed her hair, her cheeks, her lips.

"B.J.?" So soft it was more just a sigh against his skin, barely heard over the roar of rain. But her arms came around his shoulders and held on like it was life or death.

The best feeling he'd ever had, even if their situation was dire.

"Let's get you out of here, luv." He kissed her again. God, if they got out of here, he'd never let her go again.

The water had risen up to his chin. He had to carry her high on his shoulder like a child as he following the gushing edge of the crater around. Finally he found the spot where the water cascaded in steps over the path down the wall. Far above him a dark figure was just reaching the crater edge.

Something white moved through the gloom.

A shout, and then suddenly the Shark plunged backwards through the air and into the crater. The splash inundated B.J. and sent him sprawling back against a tree. Something scuttled above him and he grabbed Kaitlin and shoved away.

The Shark came up swearing, rifle up and ready, but he was faced to the crater wall, looking up the water-covered pathway. He brought the rifle up and a blaze of bullets tore through the foliage above.

Two choices, B.J.: haul Kaitlin back into the trees and pray he doesn't see you. Or do something about this asshole.

He released Kaitlin with a kiss on her forehead and prayed she'd be safe in the water. He was taking one hell of a chance, given he had no idea who the Shark was shooting at. Had Black-tooth's men tracked them into the forest? But there was no way they could stay in the crater and live. If the Shark won the battle, there'd be no one to save her. No question, then. He had to win.

But this was the Shark. The man who had near enough killed Cora. And who would kill other girls, too, given half a chance.

This was a machine who lived only for killing and meeting his own needs.

The Shark had finished strafing the jungle at the top of the crater and headed for the path again. He still hadn't noticed B.J., where he stood at the edge of the trees.

Wrapped the file in his fist, pointy end stabbing ready, B.J. shoved silently through the water, the roaring rain for once to his advantage.

The Shark was at the base of the cliff, shoving through the spumes of water onto the lowest reach of path. When he turned, there'd be no missing B.J.

B.J. lunged. Brought the file up and plunged it down towards the back of the man's neck.

The Shark must have seen him at the last moment. He twisted away so the file tore through the Shark's scalp and temple and down into his cheek in a huge bloody mess that only enraged him.

B.J. leapt back, or tried to, but the water slowed him. The Shark brought his rifle around.

Back away and he'd be shot, or...

B.J. closed in, the rifle between them. The file filled his fist and he slashed at Shark's face—a stupid weapon against the killing power of the rifle.

Shark yanked the rifle free and tried to bring the muzzle up. B.J. couldn't let him. He threw himself at the man, knocking them both onto the cascading path.

Shark stumbled and slammed into the wall.

Slashing with the file, B.J. went after him, fending off the rifle with the other fist.

Shark reversed his weapon and drove the stock towards B.J.'s face. He twisted and the blow struck his shoulder and went through him, numbing his arm.

The Shark struck again hitting his side. Bones cracked and B.J. staggered, breath whoomfed out of him. He was better off in close where the rifle couldn't come to bear.

He lunged at Shark and the rifle stock smashed towards his face. B.J. ducked under the blow and stabbed with the file. It caught Shark in the chest. He yanked it free and stabbed again.

Blood bloomed in a dark stain, but the rain washed it away. B.J. threw himself at his enemy and forced the man up a step against the crater wall. Water poured down over his head. Shark yowled and fought. Grappled with B.J. and dropped the rifle when the weapon caught between them. His fists pounded B.J.'s ears, his thumbs tried for B.J.'s eyes.

Then he stopped. He was trying for his pistol. B.J. grabbed the Shark's wrist and twisted. An explosion in the water said he'd caught the weapon just in time.

The water poured over them both and blinded B.J. as he tried to force the pistol away and bring the file up. Not to be. The gun was everything. He was dead if Shark got it free. He stabbed the file into Shark's hand. The man yowled.

Stabbed again at whatever he could and the Shark shoved him away. B.J. clung to the pistol. Stabbed again and the pistol suddenly disappeared in the water.

"Fuck!" the Shark yelled. "I am so going to enjoy killing you."

A fist found his injured side and almost doubled him over. The Shark came for him, diving through the water. B.J. stumbled back, trying to find breath when the knifing pain made it hard to move.

He backed again, floundering. The water was deep enough he was forced onto tiptoes. Forced back towards the trees. The water took his feet out from under him and he was swimming backwards as Shark caught his legs.

He went down into dark water. B.J. inhaled a lungful. Slammed the file upwards and caught the Shark's chest. The Shark's hands found his neck and held him down.

His chest spasmed. He couldn't last much longer. The edges of awareness had turned velvety black with nothing.

Think, ya wanker. Think. What would Kaitlin do? He thrashed and stabbed again, but the hold on his neck didn't weaken.

Aim for the vulnerable areas. He slashed low, aiming for the groin, but the Shark's combat trousers blocked his blow.

Higher then.

The head and neck.

He swept out his arm and stabbed. Metal found meat and hair, but slipped off bone. He stabbed again. The Shark had two choices, let him go or let him do this.

Either way he had a chance.

The hands tightened. He had run out of time. His hand was a leaden weight at the end of his arm and he didn't know if he held the file anymore.

Once more. Once more and then you can die.

He slammed the file upwards once more and it hit home and suddenly the hands weren't there anymore. B.J. floundered up.

Gasped for air in the darkness and the glow of the tree.

The Shark. Where was he?

A dark form bobbed upright under the leaves of the trees, and silhouetted by the glowing trunks and tattered webs. The Shark plucked the file out of the side of his neck.

The file. B.J. felt naked without it. And the Shark had locked that pale gaze of his on B.J.

He could run for it, but he had to get Kaitlin. *Nothing ya can do now, Beej, ol' boy. Stand and fight.*

Or?

He kicked and slid through the water a little closer, the wisps of a plan forming. The trick would be to do it, without getting himself killed first.

Right. You do that, mate.

The Shark roared and lunged, but B.J. was prepared. Years of water polo in high school and his military training came back to him.

He lunged left through the water, so Shark missed. He splashed closer to the trees, with the Shark in pursuit. If the Shark caught him, he was a dead man.

But maybe the wounds had slowed his enemy, because B.J. avoided his grasp. He waited until the Shark was close, and then turned and slammed the heel of his hand into the man's face, even as the file found his side and ripped upwards.

Pain. Explosions of it skyrocketed through him and stole his breath.

But he couldn't afford to feel it. He slammed his fist into the Shark's face again. Ignored the yank of the weapon pulled free. The explosion as another pain-flower bloomed.

There.

He avoided a slash that could have taken out his eyes and slammed his fist into the Shark's face. Blood all around, copper in the water. He shoved the Shark against a tree trunk and grabbed for his file hand, praying he was right.

Tattered webs fluttered in the rain. A slight movement at the edge of

B.J.'s vision and then three spiders plunked onto Shark's hair.

B.J. dove under the water and grabbed the Shark's waist. Lifted him up, while he held the man's hands.

The Shark kicked and his screams carried under the water. The bloody spiders might not kill you, but enough venom could paralyze you. He hoped.

It didn't take long and the Shark's struggles weakened. B.J. released him and plunged away from the trees. When he came up for air, all he could see was the Shark floating next to the trees and plucking weakly at an unending stream of spiders that ran down the trunk and dropped into the water. The seething mass covered him.

He thought he might be sick, except he had to find Kaitlin. The water had taken her again; he retraced his steps and found her halfway back to the Sargasso of leaves.

He pulled her into him and kissed her sodden hair. She still burned with fever. He had to get her out of here or she was dead. They both were. As lightheaded as he was, he had to have lost a lot of blood and was losing more every minute.

"Come on, ya can do this, one more time."

He pushed, dragged, hugged Kaitlin back to the path up the crater wall. Now came the hard part. He stepped up on the immersed lower path and slipped back into the water. Tried again and then wrestled Kaitlin's limp form into his arms.

Cascading water poured over him and ate away the path he trod. When he finally stepped free of the lake the crater had become, there was still thirty feet of crater to climb, with water gushing across his feet and cutting the path.

By the time he reached the top, he could barely move. He staggered up over the top and caught movement out of the corner of his eye.

No. Not after all this. Not after they'd won free.

He whirled to face the new danger.

A blood-covered Jeremy Blackwood stood there.

Chapter 48

My daughter? Is she…?"

Jeremy's face was a white moon in the darkness above the bloody remains of his cream-colored suit. Around them the rain sluiced down, but the normal forest was a peeping, squeaking, crying source of life. Not like the evil silence of the crater. Or the roaring of the deluging water. No, here the rain actually came with a wind, and in the south, down the valley, were stars.

Real stars. The Southern Cross included.

It was like he could breathe again.

He went to his knees. "She's alive, but very, very ill. I found your medical kit in the crater and gave her something I didn't recognize when you didn't have chlorpromazine. For all the good it's done."

He stroked the rain and her matted hair off her face. "She needs a doctor, not some idiot messing with her back o' Bourke."

Jeremy limped to them, cradling his left arm.

"What happened to you?" B.J. asked.

"Not much. A stray bullet when Brian cut loose with his gun." He shook his shaggy head and looked not so much like himself as a mangy, half-drowned cat. "Caught me in the bicep. Arm's not working so well now."

"Walking wounded both of us—but we gotta get her outta here."

Jeremy nodded, touched Kaitlin's pale face, and frowned in the darkness. "I've never seen her like this—at least not since she was a little girl. She's always been so strong. So competent."

"She's had to be." B.J. said and staggered up with her in his arms one more time. He almost dropped her from the stabbing pain in his side, but he managed to get her up, get her arms around his neck. Then he faced Jeremy, who seemed to weave in and out of focus.

"You think she had to compensate for a father like me."

The night noises made it hard to think or see. "Listen, mate. I'm not thinking anything at all, except we need to get to wherever we're going before I fucking lose it, okay?"

The wavering figure paused and B.J. closed his eyes. He needed to get on with it because he didn't know how long he could stay upright at this rate.

"The camp's just around the lip of the crater. The shed down there's just for equipment."

He led off, through the gloom and the rain, stepping carefully through a screen of elephant ear leaves to a faint trail that wound through the trees. Almost like a game trail. Something that most trackers would overlook if they were looking for a mining operation.

The old fool was better than B.J. had thought.

Overhead, the south wind ran through the canopy and stirred the leaves so he couldn't tell whether it still rained or not, but the heavens lightened and finally a thin stream of moonlight ran through the leaves.

The heavy rain stopped, but the elephant ears released refreshing pools of cool water over him whenever they were touched. Black-winged moths flitted through the gloom and overhead, a band of monkeys swooped through the tree limbs, disturbed by something.

Then the trees parted around a small clearing, where a low lump of a wood hut hunkered amid low palms and tall grasses against the eaves of the forest. The air smelled of wet foliage and old fires.

"You've lived here for awhile, haven't ya?"

"Too long. I was here too long, this time. I should've gone home to Kaitlin and her mother." Jeremy shook his head. "It just always seemed like a good idea to delay a little longer. Dig a little more, stockpile a little more. I've done it my whole life, and so I missed Kaitlin growing up."

B.J. heard the regret in the older man's voice and knew what that was all about. "You'd be better tellin' her that, than me."

"If she'll listen."

"She'll listen." At least he hoped so. Prayed she'd make it through. "So you got anymore magic up your sleeve—say, a doctor?"

Jeremy cast a look over his shoulder. "I'll do you one better. I've learned what this jungle is like. You have to keep spares of everything."

He nodded towards the jungle beyond and led B.J. along another short path and surprised him by bringing him to an overgrown road and a heap of camouflage. When Jeremy cleared it away, a used US Army surplus jeep stood there, loaded with wooden crates.

"Bloody hell," B.J. marveled. "Does she drive?"

Jeremy shrugged. "Did last time I was here. Now why don't you get Kaitlin settled while I get the old girl started?"

B.J. clambered up into the seat, the rear taken up with crates and burlap bags, and settled with Kaitlin on his lap. No way was he taking a chance on losing her again.

When Jeremy joined him, the jeep roared into life and he eased the clutch into gear and the jeep out onto the road.

"Don't you worry someone'll find it?"

"The jeep? Nah. No one comes this way. No one even knows the road is there. Just wait, you'll see. I was careful."

He pushed the jeep probably faster than he should, the vehicle slewing around each curve and tearing up swaths of foliage so, in the moonlight, the air seemed filled with a fine mist of plant matter. B.J. braced himself against the floor and dash and held onto Kaitlin's limp form with one arm.

"Just hold on, luv. Just hold on a little longer."

Jeremy slowed the jeep and came to a stop. "Here's what I was talking about." He winked and climbed down, then walked ahead to where the road disappeared into a wall of trees.

He was gone a few minutes and then suddenly a wall of jungle swung towards them and then Jeremy came jogging smugly back.

"Like it? It's based on the spring gates you see on ranches in the states. I've just improved the model to include a platform for plants."

He chuckled and thunked the jeep in gear to drive forward, clear of the gate onto what looked like an old logging road. Then he leapt out again and closed the gate behind them. The road disappeared into a wall of jungle.

"Fucking amazing." B.J. looked down at Kaitlin. "You should be seeing this. Now I know where you get it from."

She only moaned and stirred in his arms as the jeep bounced into the ruts of the road and started northeast towards Pailin.

The jeep roared down the road, chasing the edge of the rainclouds northwards, jungle whipped past in the darkness, but gradually the darkness lightened and the brilliant stars faded away as they wound through the hills.

He leaned over to Jeremy. "We should be careful we don't run into the Shark's men."

Jeremy shook his head as he watched the road. The old man was good, driving fast and navigating the rain-rutted road. "In another direction. I took them down a side road and they set up their mine there."

"They're dispersed in the jungle now. And if they aren't, Duch's men are."

Jeremy nodded, but only pushed the jeep faster. They fishtailed up a grade and at the top looked down over a river valley. The road wound down towards a river and beetle-backed truck B.J. recognized parked in the middle of the road that ran next to the river.

"Duch. Bloody hell."

Kaitlin stirred in his arms and blinked up at him. "B.J.?"

His heart just about stopped in his chest, and then he had her in his arms.

"Kaitlin. My God, luv." He pulled her into him, buried his face in her now-dry hair, and inhaled her scent of rain and roses—and iron.

"Hold on, buster. You're hurting." She pushed away a little and he looked at her.

High points of unhealthy color bloomed on her cheeks and sweat still beaded the edge of her mess of hair. But she was awake and apparently lucid, which was bloody well better than she'd been in the crater. He rubbed his thumbs along the edge of her lips.

"Would you believe it's good to see you?" Good? He hadn't realized how afraid he was he'd lost her, and by the look of her, she still wasn't out of the woods.

Wind whipped her hair into her eyes. "Where are we?"

"Cambodia."

An impatient nod.

"Cardamom Mountains."

A moment of thought and another nod.

"Your father's jeep."

"My father?" She struggled to sit up. "He's alive?"

"Right here, luv. Beside ya. Driving like a madman."

She twisted to see, and her father grinned at her and turned his attention back to the road. The fact she sank back against B.J.'s chest was the most wonderful experience he'd had in far too long a time. Except for the kids. The kids were good for feeling like he had a purpose in his life, too.

Jeremy drove them towards the truck, but slowed as they neared it.

"What's the matter?" Kaitlin asked.

"We got Duch's truck up ahead."

She twisted to look forward around the twists in the road, catching a glimpse of it whenever the jeep came perilously close to the edge of the river.

"If that's the truck I came on, it's not going to follow. I flattened two of the tires. They only had one spare."

"You noticed that? You sure?"

She looked up at him, her gaze catching on his features as if still assessing, and he knew he might have gotten her out of the crater, but she didn't know that. She didn't feel the lightheadedness that had him praying he didn't have to get up again. His clothes might be dry, but a sticky warmth down his side said the bleeding continued. *How long can a man leak like a sieve and live?*

"I'm not sure about a lot of things, B.J., but that's one I am sure of. I used the nail file."

He grinned and shook his head. She was a piece of work, his woman. It just made her more precious. "Handy little things, those. Gonna have to get me one."

As the sky turned dawn-grey, they neared the truck that hunkered on the road like a great toad beyond tree trunks that had crashed down the ravine of a smaller tributary.

"What the hell do we do now?"

Jeremy just shook his head and twisted the wheel. The jeep plunged off the road and down into the rushing river that was still swollen from the night's rain.

Water flowed from the gunnels. Water ran in across the floorboards. The old engine complained, but the ancient jeep just rammed its blunt nose through the water. They came even with the trees and two of Duch's men scrambled out of the rear of the truck, where two tires lay on the ground.

"Looks like you mighta been wrong, luv." He nodded at the two tires. "They're ready to roll, by the look of them."

"But aimed in the wrong direction, and Brother Duch isn't here. Maybe Brian's men killed him," Jeremy said. He turned back to the river and the jeep, edging the vehicle back up to the road just beyond the truck and Duch's men.

A shout came from behind them. B.J. craned around. Four figures had shoved out of the jungle and one he recognized. Duch.

"Bloody hell! Hit the gas, mate."

Bullets slammed into the rear of the jeep. The vehicle bucked and kept going. B.J. yanked Kaitlin down into the wheel well and Jeremy scrunched down until he had to strain to see the road in front of them. Streamers of sunlight arced through the sky like spotlights and cast shadows across the road.

More bullets hit the wood crates Jeremy had stacked in the rear of the jeep and slivers of wood showered them. The jeep slewed around a twist of road and kept going. B.J. pushed upright. "You can bet your ass they'll have that truck turned and be after us."

Jeremy nodded and guided the jeep one-handed. His other cradled in his lap as tree shadows bloomed black and white across the road and his face.

"You're hurt, Dad."

He glanced in her direction. "So are you. And so, I suspect, is B.J. Just look at him."

Kaitlin did, and a concern that warmed him filled her face. But she needed to focus on herself.

"I'm fine. Right as rain, luv."

She frowned like she didn't believe him, which was fine. Right now he was the stronger of the two of them.

As the sun rose over the valley wall, the roar of another engine whined behind them. Jeremy went faster, careening around the twists and turns, increasing their lead on uphill grades, but the truck seemed to gain on them every time they hit a downhill. It was going to be close. It was going to be damn close, and that meant they needed a plan for when they hit Pailin.

They careened through the crossroads where B.J. had bought food and directions, the jeep building distance abtween them and the lumbering truck.

Ahead, the landscape lay open, the Cardamom Mountains left to the south and rolling hills towards the sprawling jumble of Pailin. Northward, beyond another range of hills, lay the highway eastward back to Siem Reap and Angkor, or west to Thailand.

The border.

If they could cross the border, they'd be safe. But if he crossed the border, he might never get back—and then what would happen to Maly and the other kids? With Jorani dead and with him gone, there'd be no orphanage and certainly no money to operate it.

He looked down at Kaitlin and tightened his arms. One last time. At least he knew what he'd had and lost, but she needed her chance to be happy. If that meant with James McKillup, then so be it.

"Aim for the border. It's pretty loose here."

Jeremy gave a nod. "Shoulda done that as soon as the paperwork was filed. Had a ticket, but one last night in Phnom Penh to celebrate seemed like a good idea at the time." He glanced at Kaitlin. "Guess it's time an old man gave up on good ideas."

She blinked at him, then looked up at B.J. "Do I say I've heard it before, or do I be thankful he's even thinking it?"

"I'd say be thankful."

She gave him the most wonderful smile. "It must be the fever—I agree with you." She reached over and caught her father's arm. "I'm glad I found you, Dad. I'm glad you're coming home, even if you haven't made your fortune."

"Who said anything about no fortune?" He winked at her. "What'd'you think's in back? I decided to think like my daughter and planned for emergencies like this."

Kaitlin blinked and looked back at B.J. confusion on her face. "He planned? My father had a plan?"

"Looks like, luv. And so do I."

Behind came a gunshot and a bullet pinged off the rear of the jeep.

"Just drive, mate. Just get us to the bloody border."

Chapter 49

B.J.'s arms tensed around Kaitlin as the jeep slewed around a corner on two wheels. The cinder-and-concrete block buildings of Pailin had sprung up around them. The engine roared and her father had his fist permanently stuck to the blaring horn. Bicyclists and motorcycles scattered. Pedestrians leapt for the sides of the road as the jeep blasted down the road, the truck in pursuit. In the closer quarters of the town, the jeep's advantage of speed was lost. Her father took corners at speed, probably hoping maneuverability would be on their side.

She'd never seen her father like this. The man who played the ponies and gambled away the grocery money in hopes of making it rich had his jaw set, two hands white-knuckled on the wheel, even though one arm oozed blood. It was a forceful determination she'd never thought him capable of. Her father was a will-o-the-wisp and about as forceful.

Not this man.

And yet he was.

It was like she was delirious, still caught in the fever dreams that had her cold and sweating both at the same time. She shivered.

She was weak enough, maybe she was out of her mind. That would explain the way she thought B.J. looked at her and the way her eyes kept wanting to close. The way she wanted to lean into B.J.'s chest and rest. If she could sleep, then she could wake up refreshed and her mind would be clear again.

But she didn't dare sleep in a situation like this.

B.J. pulled her upright and shifted so the two of them were almost seated side by side.

"What are you doing?"

He grinned that charming, mocking grin of his. "What, luv? Ya actually enjoyed sitting on my knee?"

What was she supposed to say to that?

The grinding gears as her father downshifted left her retort unsaid. Ahead lay the dusty, white-walled, corrugated-roofed buildings of the border. Armed soldiers walked their perimeter and patrolled the road.

"Slow down," B.J. ordered.

Her father did as he bid. B.J. caught her hand. Kissed her palm and grinned. "Did I ever tell ya I love ya?"

And then he was gone—had shoved the jeep door open and rolled out onto the ground yelling and screaming at the top of his lungs so that every soldier turned towards him.

Kaitlin almost threw herself after him, but the energy wasn't there. Only the fever and cold. "B.J.! No!"

She was up on her knees on the seat, watching as the Cambodian soldiers converged and effectively blocked the road in front of the truck long enough her father slid the jeep into the no-man's land between Cambodia and Thailand.

A guard came trotting up to the jeep and motioned them out of the vehicle.

"You got your passport, Kaitlin?"

It was the one thing she did still have, that and the puppet. She pulled the puppet out of her trousers and her passport from the still-damp cloth wallet around her neck. The blue passport was a waterlogged mess, but still held together. She looked from puppet to passport and wasn't sure which was which.

The shivers were worse and sweat stung her eyes.

"I don't think I can walk."

Her father spoke to the guard in halting Cambodian, but the man shook his head.

"Sorry, girlie. Looks like we've got to do this."

He came around to her, but she barely noticed. She was watching back the way they'd come. B.J. was fighting with the soldiers. The truck was hung up in a growing crowd. He'd end up in jail for this for sure.

She kept watching as her father helped her out of the jeep and the shaking worsened.

Her legs gave and she hated herself. B.J. was strong enough to do what he was doing to get her and her dad through the border, and she couldn't even do this? She grabbed onto the jeep to steady herself and the cold almost blew her off her feet again.

She accepted her father's uninjured arm. Couldn't help herself, and leaned heavily on him to drag herself across to the passport hut.

She handed in her passport, but a gun report spun her around and her legs twisted under her. B.J. It had to be.

And the world spun.

§

Three long months, and only now was she back in Cambodia. Traveling along the Poipet-Siem Reap highway on an air-conditioned bus amid camera-toting tourists who restlessly awaited the wonders of Angkor Wat. Outside the window, the rice fields and the low jungle she remembered from her trip to Jorani's orphanage spread as far as the eye could see.

She should have come sooner—as soon as she was out of the hospital, but her father and James, who had flown into Thailand, hadn't allowed it as weak as she was. The two of them and the embassy staff had forced her on a plane and back to the States to get the best medical care. James had made sure of it.

And she had spent three months looking at a shadow puppet—the same one, worn soft, that she smoothed on her knee right now.

"Excuse me, isn't that a Chinese shadow puppet?" asked the talcum-powder-scented older woman seated next to her.

Kaitlin smiled. "A shadow puppet, yes. But this is Cambodian."

"They were invented in China, you know," the woman insisted. She was dressed in neat chino trousers with crisp pleats, and a khaki colored blouse right out of an adventure catalogue.

Kaitlin smiled. She'd looked like that less than six months ago.

"Well, don't say that too loudly in Cambodia. Here they say they were created at Angkor, when a functionary noticed how the light shone through holes in the buffalo hide they used as carpet."

"Really?

"Really." She opened her Khmer language book and studied another lesson. This time she was prepared. Or as prepared as three months and changing priorities could make her.

The bus slowed and turned into the dusty depot. The tourists piled off and climbed onto another air-conditioned bus to be whisked away to whatever four-star hotel their tour had put them on. Kaitlin gathered her one small bag and walked away without looking back.

Her father had told her she was being foolish. James had said she was taking too big a chance, but all she knew was this was the right thing to do—the fly-by-the-seat-of-your-pants thing to do—the time to take a chance.

She hailed a moto-taxi and climbed aboard with instructions she'd had prepared for her by a Cambodian couple she'd found in Seattle. The driver knew where she wanted to go and took her—out into the countryside.

The fields blushed the new green of transplanted young rice. Palm trees and mango trees and pink dragon fruit cactus grew among the stilted houses. Eventually the pavement disappeared and the taxi rattled over gravel. She craned forward, wondering what she'd find. Three months, and who knew what would have happened? At least she knew from the woman at the Care Office in Pailin that the children had been allowed to return home to Siem Reap. The embassy had informed her that someone had rebuilt the orphanage.

The woman in Pailin had even found out that B.J. had been released. Of course, she didn't know where he'd gone. He could have left the country, but Kaitlin bet otherwise.

A scent of new-sawed wood reached her as they came around a corner. Ahead a long, stilted building rose in a clearing, its unpainted sides the color of amber. Beyond it, a simple Cambodian house stood on stilts, its sides also the color of new wood. Between the buildings and the road, a group of youngsters played a rousing game of soccer.

"Stop. Stop now."

The driver did and Kaitlin climbed out and paid him double what he'd asked, then took a chance and sent him on his way.

She stood at the side of the road for a long time. Long enough her unfamiliar presence stopped the soccer game and long enough a tall, familiar figure stepped out from under the traditional stilted house. Her chest closed up. Stupid tears started to run down her cheeks. B.J. It was so good to see him. Wonderful to see the man she loved. She started towards him.

Then a slight Cambodian woman stepped out beside him and she stopped in her tracks.

Maybe she'd been wrong. Maybe she'd been stupid to send the moto-taxi away. She looked after him, but he was long gone, the red dust of his passing settling back onto the road.

Well, there was nothing to do but finish her plan, such as it was. If it didn't go well, then that was a lesson for her, wasn't it? *Stick with the plan, girl.* Wasn't that what James had said, when he'd asked her to marry him after her return to Seattle?

She walked through the children, and recognized Maly about the same time the little girl recognized her. The child barreled over and threw her arms around Kaitlin's waist.

"You came! I told him you would." She glanced in B.J.'s direction. "You come see my room?"

Kaitlin knelt down to her and returned her hug. "I will, honey. But first I need to see B.J., okay?"

Maly leaned into her. "He has been very sad, okay. You be nice."

Another squeeze of that sweet-scented, little-girl body, and Kaitlin stood. "I will, sweetie. I will."

She started towards him and he left the woman behind him.

It was like time stopped, or maybe she just stopped breathing, but she felt breathless when she faced him and looked up at his face. That infuriating, wonderful, etched-in-her-mind face.

"So." She planted her feet to face him.

"Hello, luv."

He had his hands in his pockets, just like always, and flipping hell, couldn't he at least give her a hug?

"You rebuilt. I figured you would." She made a show of scanning the buildings to try to get a handle on what she was doing and what she was going to say. Her gaze came to rest on the woman. She looked vaguely familiar, somehow. "It looks good. It all does."

She turned back to him. "You look happy."

Too happy, and this woman—this too-familiar woman—was part of that happiness.

"I am. For the most part. Just a few things missing."

He grinned and her heart faltered. She'd dreamt of him for three months now—of putting all the bad stuff behind them. Of trying things again—on his terms this time.

So. "I figured I had to come back if I was ever going to find out if you lived or died and how you fared with Black-tooth." She shrugged. "Enquiring minds and all that."

He shrugged. "Duch couldn't kill me 'cause they took me into custody when all the shooting started. Then the folks at the NGO made a stink and maybe there was a little help from abroad, but Duch suddenly found himself behind bars, too. I'm sure he'd be out by now, but the bastard tried to have me knifed and a kid I met inside who'd had his sister sold by Duch took matters into his own hands. Funny how things worked out. Last I saw, he was still in the infirmary and it was questionable whether he'd get out. About that time they let me come back here and said all charges would be dropped if I'd give them the location of the rubies." Another shrug. "Figured it wasn't exactly a place I wanted to go back to, so I did."

He must have seen something in her face, for he cocked his head, his hair falling forward into his too-blue, laughing eyes that never seemed to take her seriousness seriously.

"That all that's brought you all the way to Siem Reap? Your father missing again?" His voice was cautious.

"No. Dad's back home, trying to make up for things. I left him holding the fort with Mac. Dad's still trying to atone for not being there for Mom."

His brows rose. "I heard you recovered okay and that Mac was hovering over you like an obsessed mother roo. Figured you'd be married and pregnant by now or something."

She couldn't meet his intense gaze and say this. "He was. He wanted to. He didn't want me to come here. But the thing with Mom and Dad got me thinking. It made me think maybe there are reasons to ask for second chances." It came out in a rush. She looked up at him and met his gaze. Was that a smile trying to creep onto his lips?

She swallowed when he didn't say anything. "So I thought I'd take one. A chance, that is. I quit my job."

"What? What bloody stupid thing brought that on?"

His disbelief charmed her, but then he always could.

"Actually, you did." She glanced past him at the woman again. *Take a chance, Kaitlin. Worst that can happen is you end up looking like a fool with all your emotions hanging in the breeze.* "I don't remember much of that trip through the jungle, but what I do remember is what you said at the border."

A slow smile dawned on his face and he hauled his hands out of his pockets.

"You told me that you loved me and it took three months for me to realize that I believed you and had to do something about it. So I quit my job and came."

"And what about James? He's a good man."

His eyes had gone more intensely blue, and he took a step forward so she had to tilt her head up to meet his gaze.

"Yeah, he is. But he's not you."

There. She'd said it. She didn't know if she could spell it out any clearer.

B.J.'s hands settled on her shoulders, then ran down her arms and sent shivers through her.

"You cold?"

She shook her head and held back, when she only wanted to throw her arms around him. "Only wondering who she is. What other commitments have you taken on, Beej? It *has* been three months."

"What? And I'm a man and only follow where my prick leads?"

She grimaced. "Something like that. Sorry."

"One apology when a whole chorus is needed, luv. This's Veata from Sovanna Phum. I asked her if she'd be willing to come up and continue Jorani's work teaching the children. She comes up from the city twice a month for lessons."

"She does?"

He nodded and she stopped him before he said anything else. Faced him and caught his shirt lapels in her fists. "So what you're telling me is you're available."

"For the right person, maybe."

She frowned. "You are enjoying this far too much."

"You know me—always taking pleasure in the moment."

She screwed up her face and dragged him down to her. "Damn you, McCallum. I'm offering myself to you. Now can you quit pleasuring yourself a moment and think of me?"

And then he kissed her and she realized taking a chance could be a good thing.

Read on for the exciting first chapters of *Shades of Moonlight*.

About the Author

Author of the unique Cartographer Universe series, Karen L. Abrahamson writes poetry, short fiction, and fantasy and mystery novels, as well as non-fiction for newspapers and magazines. As Karen L. McKee she pens romance novels. In her words, "a bad day of writing is still better than the best day working for a living."

A born wanderer, she currently lives in the Metro Vancouver area of Canada with two Bengal cats who channel James Dean's attitude. When she isn't writing she can be found with a camera and backpack in fabulous locations around the world.

To learn more about her, visit her website at www.karenlabrahamson.com

To find more of her writing, visit www.twistedrootpublishing.com.

Books By the Author

Romance
Ashes and Light
Shades of Moonlight
Judas Kiss
Second Spring
A Different Nightmusic
Mutable Things
Shadow Play
Coming Down Christmas
Surviving Safe Harbor

Fantasy
The Cartographer Universe (in chronological order)
The Cartographer's Daughter

The American Geological Survey Series:
Afterburn
Aftershock
Aftermath

Terra Incognita
Terra Infirma
Terra Nueva

To read the preview of another romantic adventure, turn the page to
try
Shades of Moonlight

Chapter 1 – Spirit Light

Pagan, ancient capital of Burma
Central Myanmar, Modern day

Kalla plunged through tall grass and thorn brush, the ornate wooden puppet clutched to her breast. Spirit light glinted like fool's gold in the stone underfoot. It shimmered pale blue from empty, parched fields and set beacon candles of azure and indigo from the tops of the huge step-pyramid temples that loomed out of the darkness. The rising wind scoured her chilled skin with dust, and the air smelled of ozone and lung-clinging jasmine.

And her fevered fear.

She had to get there. She had to protect.

She stumbled across a dirt road. Through a hedge of cactus, she ripped the red longyi that wrapped her legs and half-fell into a fallow field. Spirit light glinted on her skin.

"No." It came out as a whimper, but too loud in the night as she tried to wipe the shimmering dust away. Already too late. It glowed on her skin—seemed to run *into* her damp flesh. Flickering blue light flashed up her arm, even as she lurched up and kept on. Even as the spirit light seemed to stab into her brain.

And then there was the laughter.

She whirled, her midnight hair sweeping around her shoulders and the puppet. No. Her imagination. They couldn't know where she was. Keep going. Keep going.

The longyi's fabric restricted her panicked stride as she staggered on. The spirit light flashed tingling sparks across her skin, across the puppet, as her palm smoothed the antique figure's fine hair and protected the delicate Votaress' features, from the scour of the wind.

The puppet moved in her grasp.

Insanity, the scientist part of her said. Madness to be out here. Madness to be running like this, into the night and the darkness.

It was darkness that had killed her before.

She squeezed her eyes shut and almost fell across a heap of bricks. Small, collapsed temple. Her breath rang in her ears as she picked her way through, remembering how it had been before, whose temple this had been and the fine teak house that had stood here. A memory of pickled tea and garlic, but the air now smelled of sage and slow-moving river water. From the road came the sound of a jeep.

Military?

Cold sweat in her eyes, but ahead the spirit light shone bright blue flame from Dhammayangyi temple. A mountain with eyes, a yawning mouth. A mountain that would devour her; a mountain that was part of her.

Panting, she stopped, listening to the dying leaves chatter in the rising wind and the bats whoosh through the sky. Towering clouds blocked the moon.

She shivered with need, but the fear held her in place. Her mouth tasted of copper and bile.

To go in that place would mean—*ending? Beginning?* Insanity. She was going mad. The fever raged her thoughts into a whirlwind, impossible to comprehend. But she knew what waited. What had to be done. And that others would try to stop her.

But no one could follow her to the place she would go.

She staggered through the gate, the wind skirling wild Burmese music through the crumbling stone. Darkness, a void waited, but she swallowed her fear.

Do this thing.

And she would save them.

Do this thing.

The night seemed to hold its breath.

Do this thing.

The scent of musk and incense reached her on a fresh gust of wind and she froze, knowing the rough breathing she heard was not her own.

If she moved they would see her, but she had to get past. Get free.

A cautious step.

Then heated hands found her shoulders. Spirit fire swept through her and she knew she was lost.

Chapter 2 - Meet the Darkness

Ten days earlier
Somewhere in central Myanmar:
4 a.m.

Who knew three hundred miles would take over twelve hours and just about every ounce of strength Kalla Jervis had and *still* leave her in the middle of nowhere?

The pitted road lifted under the bucking jeep as she peered ahead through the darkness. The air through her window carried the welcome scents of moisture and life after hours of acrid scrub desert. Cook fires and curry. The strange smells of animal dung and incense. But a whiff of jasmine spurred Kalla's headache to life big time.

She fought the sick feeling as the mutinous jeep slewed around a corner. Damn. She was driving too fast given she had no headlights, but she didn't dare stop for fear this bucket of bolts would never start again.

She tapped the brakes as buildings materialized out of the darkness. A cream-colored bullock too solid to be a ghost lifted its head to stare at her with luminous eyes. Black-stained bougainvillea draped across low wooden buildings, spindly papaya trees, and thick foliage of jack fruit trees and teak. To the northeast, a deeper darkness showed where a lone mountain blocked part of the sky that might, just might, show a hope of fading into dawn.

Kyaukpadaung. Or else she was hopelessly lost. It had to be, by the map she'd studied the last time she'd had light. It meant she was getting close to Pagan and the archaeological project.

She breathed a sigh of relief—the first one since Alex and the others had failed to meet her delayed flight into Yangon.

Soon she could rest and refocus on what she knew—not navigate the problems at home or a desolate country that had far too few street lights and far too many miles of rough roads that had just added insult to her already aching head.

Relaxing, she steered the jeep around a curve that brought her into the centre of town.

Sudden headlights flared into her eyes. Blind, she slammed on the brakes, shielded her sight. The jeep careened to a stop, stalled when she forgot the clutch.

Lights all around—headlights and half-seen figures running and voices yelling—at her.

She fumbled the keys, cranked the protesting engine to get the hell out of there. Her door was yanked open. A hand dragged her out.

"Hey!"

The lights kept her blind. Male voices set off earthquakes in her head. Rice and curry and sweat stung her nose. Hands on her shoulders, her arms.

"Let me go, dammit!" Years of Seattle self-defense classes kicked in and she slammed her heel down on the foot of whoever held her. Jabbed her elbow into his gut. She yanked loose and turned in a fighter's stance as her vision cleared, ready to defend against wild men and bandits.

Not bandits.

Men in tattered green fatigues.

Soldiers, her mind registered. Myanmar soldiers. All with rifles aimed directly at her.

All the heat suddenly left her.

She straightened. Slowly.

Raised her hands. Slowly.

Damnitalltohell, she should have assessed the situation before she reacted. She was always in control, wasn't she?

Unbidden laughter bubbled up to catch in her throat. The whole damn tableau was ridiculous–like a clichéd drawing for a fairy tale or folk story—damsel in distress surrounded by a band of demons. All the picture needed was the handsome prince coming over the rise of the next hill.

Alex would do. Flare of trumpets, please.

At this particular moment she wouldn't mind Alex striding out of the darkness to her rescue. It would be a little proof that she was doing the right thing joining him and the linguist, Simon Renault, on the project.

One of the soldiers barked an order she didn't understand.

"Listen, I'm sorry, okay? You surprised me. I was blinded by your headlights. I didn't realize you were military."

She tried lowering open hands, but the jerk of the soldiers' rifles was pretty international.

So much gun-metal grey, all pointed in her direction. Did they have the safeties on? Heck, did they even *have* safeties?

She could die here and no one would ever know. No one would even come looking for her. No—Dad would look–if he lived long enough. He'd probably get his psychics right on it. Right. Like that'd work.

The strangled feeling too close to hysteria swelled in her throat.

And Alex might look, too, if he knew she'd actually arrived.

The leader of the soldiers nattered at her again. Two men stepped into the circle of weapons and grabbed her arms. They hauled her, resisting, from the safety of the jeep, while another soldier grabbed her keys.

Her stomach plummeted farther. This didn't look like they were going to let her go. What you going to do now, Kalla?

More men went to the jeep's rear and removed her extra-large black roller suitcase and the small trunk that contained her books and precious equipment.

"Hey! That's my stuff!" Because maybe they *were* bandits. The government couldn't be paying soldiers much, by the look of them. She'd heard soldiers on the coast had stolen supplies meant for the typhoon victims. These could be augmenting their wages by robbing unsuspecting travelers.

They unzipped her bag.

"Stop it, damn you!" She jerked in the men's hold. Tried to pull free, and a rifle butt jabbed into her belly.

Her knees gave. There was only pain and indignation. Come on, Kalla, you got to be the careful, methodical, cultural anthropologist you are if you're going to get through this with your skin intact. But....

How are all those fairy tales gonna get you out of this one? She could almost hear her sister's taunting voice.

She opened teary eyes, and the idiotic factoid that these soldiers wore tattered, green-canvas runners on their feet—not boots—struck her as overwhelmingly funny. She was friggin' Alice falling down that rabbit hole, and what nobody had told her was it was really a bottomless pit.

Biting back the hysteria, she struggled to her feet, the grips of the soldiers still too-hot, too-hard on her arms. Others hauled her belongings from her suitcase one by one.

Jeans. T-shirts. Oh god, her diaphragm, brought in anticipation of the reconciliation with Alex that her father had urged. They were holding it up, examining it with their flashlights. The fact they didn't seem to know what it was didn't stop her face from flaming.

"Perhaps, mademoiselle, I may be of some assistance?"

Well thank god, it was English. She twisted in her captors' grasp, but the not-quite French accent didn't prepare her for the man who coalesced out of the darkness.

She froze.

His blue-black hair fell across his forehead in a rough forelock that accentuated black eyes that seemed to drink in everything at once-and find a humor in her situation she just couldn't match. Darkness seemed to cling to him and set all her alarm bells klaxoning. He didn't look French. He was too tall, too athletic, and almost American in the confident way he moved. The fact his high, almost Asian cheekbones and full lips held her gaze just made it worse. This guy was a babe magnet and knew it, and she hated that kind.

The neatly pressed khakis he wore and the khaki shirt rolled up to expose the dark hair of his forearms just reinforced the mess she was: jeans with red earth soiling the knees, sweat-sodden t-shirt from the long drive, her long black hair falling out of its pony tail.

His predatory saunter across the square and sardonic smile set Kalla's teeth on edge. It didn't help that his gaze settled briefly on what the soldiers were examining. One look said this was a man who knew what they held.

His smirk deepened, but he didn't seem to even notice the weapons trained on him. He just waded into the scene with a graceful panther-stride, then stopped and spoke in a long string of fluid Burmese—or was that Myanmarese?-that made the soldiers lower their rifles.

Damn it, if she'd ever been good with languages she'd have dealt with the soldiers just as calmly. Wouldn't she? She shook her hair out of her face.

"I don't need your help." It was a stupid thing to say, but she didn't want to be in debt to this man.

"Pardon?" He said it the French way and motioned around her. "It seems you do, Mademoiselle…" He paused waiting for her to fill in her name, but she'd be damned if she wanted this guy—this Frenchman—helping her. She was dealing with things—or was going to. She tried to shrug loose from her captors, but no dice.

Nearby a car door thunked and she half-turned as a short, barrel-chested man approached. He wore a uniform and one of those over-large military hats that always seemed to go with despotic generals and too many medals on the chest, but....

He barked something and the soldiers released her arms. That was something, even if she didn't want to give the Frenchman credit. She rubbed her biceps, knowing there'd be bruises there later, but all her attention turned back to the too-handsome stranger.

His Burmese flowed like a river; natural. Was it as seductively accented as his English? How had he learned it? Burmese wasn't exactly the kind of thing they'd teach in school, even in France. *All a ridiculous number of questions about a man you're not remotely interested in, Kalla.*

The round-faced officer looked the Frenchman up and down and his frown deepened. He snapped a question, and then held out his hand.

The Frenchman fished in his pocket. Pulled out a packet of documents and handed them to the officer, all the time speaking another of those long strings of Burmese. There was a reason the language was written in its beautiful round script, because that was how it sounded. But this time she caught something. Western words she understood.

The worst kind of news, because they meant this stranger wasn't someone she could just kiss off. The recognition sent her headache jack-hammering harder and her vision dimmed, red and black at the edges.

"*You're* Simon Renault?"

Shades of Moonlight is availalble through your favorite bookstore or where e-books are sold.

Romance, Adventure and a Touch of Magic from Karen L. Abrahamson

If you enjoyed this book, you might enjoy other titles from Karen L. Abrahamson, available at your local bookstore or wherever e-books are sold.

www.karenlabrahamson.com